The Elusive Sun

ETHERYA'S EARTH, BOOK 2
By
REBECCA HEFNER

Copyright © 2019

RebeccaHefner.com

To those of us who refuse to give up on true love...even if it seems ever so elusive...

Table of Contents
Title Page and Copyright
Dedication
Map of Etherya's Earth
Prologue
Chapter 1
Chapter 2
Chapter 3
Chapter 4
Chapter 5
Chapter 6
Chapter 7
Chapter 8
Chapter 9
Chapter 10
Chapter 11
Chapter 12
Chapter 13
Chapter 14
Chapter 15
Chapter 16
Chapter 17
Chapter 18
Chapter 19
Chapter 20
Chapter 21
Chapter 22
Chapter 23
Chapter 24
Chapter 25
Chapter 26
Chapter 27
Chapter 28
Chapter 29
Chapter 30
Chapter 31
Chapter 32
Epilogue
Acknowledgements
About the Author

ETHERYA'S EARTH

The Passage

Paegus of Methesda

Cave of the Sacred Prophecy

Portal of Mithos

Strok Mountains

Deamon Caves

Valeria

Naria

Lynia

Astaria

The River Thayer

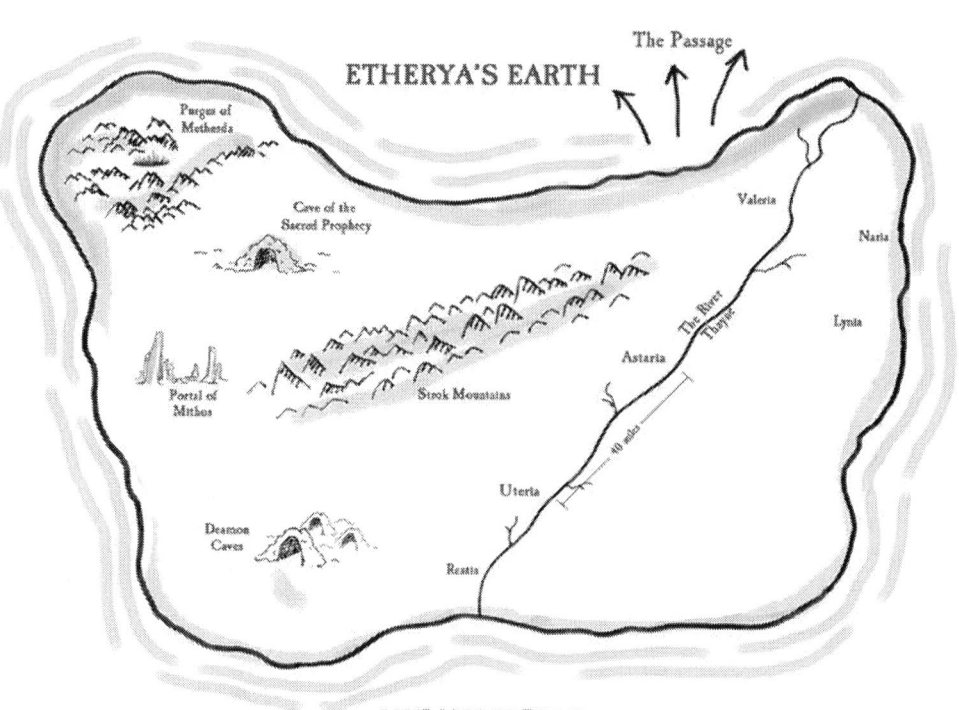

40 miles

Uteria

Rustia

HUMAN WORLD

Prologue

High-pitched squeals and laughter echoed off the moonlit trees as the children ran to the river. The first child came to a sudden stop on the grassy riverbank, her long blond curls bouncing with the abrupt movement. She looked down at the gurgling water, contemplating.

"Why did you stop?" the other child asked, coming to stand beside her and pierce her with his ice-blue gaze.

The girl wrinkled her nose. "I was getting tired." Tiny gasps of breath exited her lips.

The boy rolled his eyes. "Girls," he muttered, kicking the ground with his shoe. "So weak. I can't wait until I'm the leader of the army. I'll be the strongest Vampyre that ever lived." He proudly puffed his chest and straightened his shoulders.

"Except for your brother," she said softly.

Anger flashed across his pale face. "That's not true. Everyone thinks that Sathan is better than me because he's already king, even though he's only eleven. But I'll show them!" Tiny fists clenched at his sides. "A king is only powerful when he has a magnificent army. My brother will only be strong because of me."

The girl studied him in silence with her deep lavender gaze. "I don't think Sathan is better than you."

"Even though you're going to bond with him one day?"

She sighed and looked at the ground. "Yes," she said, lowering herself to sit on the spongy grass. "I like Sathan well enough but I wish I was betrothed to...someone else," she finished after a slight pause.

"Who?" he asked, sitting down beside her.

Small shoulders shrugged as her hands fidgeted together on her lap. "I don't know. Someone who I have more in common with I guess."

The boy tucked a strand of his shoulder-length, straight black hair behind his ear. "We have a lot in common. I think you're my best friend." He swallowed and looked away, embarrassed by his admission.

She reached over and grabbed his hand, her lavender irises filled with excitement. "You're definitely my best friend. Maybe I can bond with you instead of Sathan!"

The boy looked at their joined hands and then lifted his gaze to hers. "It won't ever happen." He shook his head. "You are to be queen. It was mandated by Etherya herself. We can't change it."

She huffed and pulled her hand back, crossing her arms across her chest. "Then, we can just run away. How can they force me to bond with someone?"

"I'm sorry, Lila," he said, touching her knee through her dress. "I would bond with you if I could."

She lifted her tear-filled eyes to his. "Run away with me, Lattie. Surely, we can find a breech in the wall that surrounds the compound."

Latimus' stubby fingers squeezed her knee. "You know that Etherya erected the protective wall herself. I won't know how to open it until I become commander of the army. It will be several years before I know the secret."

"Will you remember? When you become leader of the army and learn how to escape the compound, will you remember to run away with me? I need to know that you won't forget me. I love you." Her chin quivered.

The boy nodded. "I'll remember. I promise. In a few decades, if you still don't want to bond with Sathan, I'll help you escape."

"Oh, thank you!" Lila threw her arms around him and clutched tight, rocking back and forth.

Pulling back, he smiled at her. Their gazes locked, eyes widening as they held each other. She bit her lip, studying him. Their faces were only inches apart.

"We should go back inside," he whispered.

"Yes."

But neither moved; both held immobile by an unseen force. Slowly, she inched toward him, not stopping until she touched her tiny pink lips to his slightly larger red ones.

Their hearts beat furiously in their eight-chambered chests as they experienced the rush that can only come with a first-ever kiss.

"Lila!" a voice shrilled behind them. "How dare you!"

The children pulled away with a gasp, each standing up and brushing off their clothes, their eyes downcast.

"You are the betrothed of the Vampyre king, not his brother," the woman spat, looking at Latimus. "He isn't fit to tie your shoes, much less touch you!" She grabbed the girl's arm, pulling her away from the riverbank.

"I'm sorry, Aunt," Lila said breathlessly, unable to meet Latimus' gaze. "We were just playing."

"I've already forbidden you to play with him!" The woman turned to Latimus, shaking her finger at him. "If you ever approach my niece again, I will have you banished. You are not good enough to touch her! You will never be your brother! Do you understand me?"

"I'm sorry, Ananda," the boy said, lifting his chin and facing her with strength. "I take full responsibility. I won't seek her out again. I didn't know you had forbidden her to see me." His icy gaze flashed with an anger that seemed too intense for a nine-year-old.

The woman shook her head and roughly pulled her niece's arm. "Come, Lila. You are late for your classes."

The girl trailed behind her aunt, her blond curls bouncing furiously. She turned, gazing at the boy with watery eyes, and mouthed, *"I'm sorry."*

He stood firm, his arms crossed, watching her being dragged away. His heart was pounding in his chest, as if the organ knew that it would never be whole again. In that moment, Latimus decided that he would never give himself to another person freely. What was the point, when you were always second-class; second-best?

Kicking the ground with the toe of his shoe, he turned to stare at the river...and said a silent goodbye to his best friend Lila, the girl who was promised to his brother.

Chapter 1

The Vampyre compound of Astaria, 1000 years later...

"Thank you all for coming. We've got a bit of an announcement."

Lila smiled expectantly at her queen, Miranda, as she addressed them. Standing at the head of the long conference table, she was dwarfed by her bonded husband, who stood at her side. Lila sat in the chair to their right and was surrounded by the rest of their family.

Arderin, sister to King Sathan, sat to her right. Heden, Sathan's youngest brother and Darkrip, the queen's half-brother, filled out the rest of the seats on her side of the table. Latimus, Sathan's younger brother by less than two years, and Kenden, Miranda's beloved cousin, sat across from her.

"Let's get on with it," Latimus muttered, his ever-present scowl marring his handsome face. Lila had always thought him so attractive, with his angular features, ice-blue eyes and shoulder-length, straight black hair. He'd secured it with a leather strap, showcasing his slight widow's peak. "We were in the middle of training the soldiers on the TEC."

"Don't interrupt my wife," Sathan said, glaring at Latimus.

"Your wife can speak for herself," Miranda said, tilting her head back and giving him an impertinent look.

Sathan scrunched his face at her, his affection for her obvious in the playful gesture.

"But seriously, don't interrupt me," she said to Latimus.

He sighed and crossed his arms over his massive chest. Lila noticed the bulging muscles on his biceps and forearms. As the commander of the powerful Vampyre army, he was the largest man she had ever seen. The raw strength he possessed almost made her shiver as she glanced at him.

"It's still too early for us to tell the people, but since you're all family, we wanted you to know." Grabbing her husband's hand, Miranda broke into a huge smile. "We're pregnant. I'm about twelve weeks along."

Arderin shrieked beside her and jumped from her seat. Running to Miranda, she enveloped her in a huge hug, running her hand over Miranda's raven-colored, silky bob. "I knew it," she said, looking down at the queen. "I saw you puking, like, a hundred times over the past few weeks, and I just knew you were preggers!"

Miranda laughed and nodded. "You're too smart for your own good. I thought you knew." They embraced again, and Lila's heart warmed.

Miranda and Arderin had met under peculiar circumstances, but over the past year, they had formed a solid bond. They were also the two women who challenged Sathan the most, and their shared playful antagonism of him was a source of common ground. Arderin was her most beloved friend, and she had grown to love Miranda as well. Their connection was wonderful to behold.

Standing with the others, Lila rushed to give Miranda a hug, smiling into her magnificent olive-green eyes. "I'm so happy for you."

"You're next," Miranda whispered, surreptitiously glancing behind her toward Latimus.

Lila breathed a laugh. "My eternal optimist. I love that about you."

Turning, she lifted her arms to embrace Sathan, the man she had been betrothed to for a thousand years. The goddess Etherya had decreed her his betrothed when she was a baby. Being that she was descended from aristocracy, her blood almost as pure as his, Etherya had thought her a worthy future queen and mother for Sathan's heirs. Until Miranda came along and swept Sathan under her spell.

"You're finally going to have your heir," she said, staring into Sathan's dark irises. "I'm thrilled for you both."

Sathan pulled her into his chest, squeezing firmly. "Thank you," he said, placing a gentle kiss on her blond head. "Not so long ago, it would've been us making this announcement." Pulling back, he smiled. "Until you decided you'd rather be a diplomat than bond with me."

Lila laughed, shaking her head at his teasing. In truth, they had never loved each other passionately. Although she had always loved and honored him as her king, her heart had secretly longed for another. When he'd fallen for Miranda, she had gladly ended their betrothal, wishing him genuine happiness.

"I didn't stand a chance against Miranda. She's amazing."

"So are you," he said, hugging her close once more. Whispering in her ear, he said, "Give my brother time. He'll come around. It's obvious he cares for you."

Lila detached herself from his embrace, doubting his words. Latimus' distaste for her was much more obvious than any feelings of affection. Choosing not to dwell on it, she observed her family.

That's what they had become to her, although she shared no blood with anyone in the room. Yet, Sathan had incorporated her into their unit as if she was one of them. Arderin and Heden were her most precious confidants, and she had grown very fond of Kenden. Darkrip was mysterious and brooding, but he had never bothered her, so she let him be.

Latimus...well, he was an entirely different matter altogether. If she was honest, she had probably loved him since they were children. Memories of them playing together along the riverbank, all those centuries ago, swarmed her as she watched him embrace Miranda. He and the queen were close, and his smile for her was genuine. Lila's heartbeat quickened at his hulking form, his palm cupping the Slayer's cheek. When he wasn't scowling, he was absolutely gorgeous.

"Oh, my god," Arderin said, pulling her from her musings. "How exciting is this? We have to throw her a shower!" She clutched her wrists, and Lila grinned at the intense squeeze.

"Of course. We'll do it together."

"I'll be the DJ," Heden announced to the room.

"No!" was the unified response, and they all chuckled. Heden, the carefree youngest royal sibling, was known to be the partyer of the group. He always extended their banquets several hours by taking over the DJ duties, which had become a source of amusement for them all.

"We don't exactly know when the baby will come," Miranda said. "Slayer babies have a nine-month gestation period, but Vampyre babies gestate for fifteen months. Since this is the first Slayer-Vampyre hybrid ever, we're winging it. We'll need your help along the way. Sadie and Nolan are aware and will monitor everything," she said, referencing the physicians for each main compound. "My body isn't used to having a Vampyre inside it, and Sadie has warned me that my morning sickness is going to be severe. If I blow chunks on you, don't blame me. You can blame my blood-sucking husband."

"Hey," Sathan said, pulling her into his side with his beefy arm.

Miranda bit her lip and winked up at him, love for him swimming in her olive-green eyes. "Unless Latimus is being a dick. Then, I'm probably barfing because he's pissing me off."

Latimus rolled his eyes, shaking his head at her joke. "Well, there went the mood. I'm heading back to the troops. You coming?" he asked, addressing Kenden.

"In a minute," the chestnut-haired Slayer said. "I want to talk to Miranda and then I'll be down."

"Fine." Nodding to Miranda and Sathan, he stalked out.

Lila observed everyone embracing once more. Love and happiness filled the room. It was a beautiful moment. As she stood, something flitted in her chest. Perhaps it was longing. Perhaps it was loneliness. Whatever it was, it left her slightly unsettled.

Bidding good night to them, she quietly left the conference room for the privacy of her chambers.

* * * *

Latimus stood on the hill under the light of the slitted moon, watching the troops train. They sparred with each other, Vampyre amongst Slayer, and he was pleased. For a thousand years, he had commanded the Vampyre army. Since the night of the

Awakening, when the Slayer King Valktor murdered his parents, King Markdor and Queen Calla, his people had been forced to raid the Slayers for their blood.

Sathan had always struggled with the raids, his need to feed his subjects battling with the knowledge that so many Slayer lives would be lost to his powerful army. Latimus had never shared his brother's internal conflict. He was born to be the commander, strength and fortitude emanating from his every pore. Although war and death were tragic, he saw them as necessary—a means to an end; a way of keeping his people alive. Granting his people's safety and security would be his greatest legacy.

Kenden came to stand beside him, his six-foot, two-inch frame dwarfed by Latimus' own six-foot, nine-inch build. There was a firm, calm strength that emanated from the Slayer. As the commander of the Slayer army, he had been Latimus' greatest foe for centuries. After the Awakening, no one had expected the Slayers, smaller and weaker, to build a competent army. Kenden had defied them all and assembled a magnificent military, shrewd and adept.

Kenden's mind was quick. The Slayer was calm when challenged, agile when threatened and cunning when faced with an underestimated foe. Latimus' strength and combat skills, combined with Kenden's calculating mind and cleverness, had now led them here. They possessed the most powerful combined army on Etherya's Earth.

"The troops seem to be adept at using the TEC," Kenden said, observing the men spar.

Latimus nodded. "They've got it. We need to plan the attack to get the Blade back."

"Agreed. I'm thinking the next full moon."

"Yep," Latimus said, thoughtfully chewing the gum he'd thrown in his mouth. "Two hundred troops? A hundred Vampyres and a hundred Slayers?"

"That should do it," Kenden said.

Latimus continued to chomp his gum as they silently assessed their men.

"I can't believe Miranda is pregnant," Kenden said finally. "My little cousin is having a baby. It's amazing."

"Sathan's been consumed with fucking her since they first met. It was only a matter of time."

"Um, yeah," Kenden said, rubbing the back of his neck. "Don't really want to discuss my cousin's sex life or frequency thereof."

Latimus breathed a laugh. "Sorry."

"And what of you? Do you have plans to bond with anyone?"

Latimus shrugged. "Never really interested me. I was born to be the commander. It's all I've ever wanted to be."

Kenden nodded. "I hear ya. Being an army commander never afforded me the opportunity to settle down. But seeing them so happy is nice. It makes me think there might be other things to consider once we defeat the Deamons."

Latimus remained silent, struggling to push the image of Lila's breathtaking face from his mind.

Frustratingly, it remained, haunting him as it always did. She was the most gorgeous creature he'd ever seen. Long, wavy blond hair, austere features, cheekbones that human models would kill for—but it was her eyes that entranced him. They were a vibrant violet color that he had never seen on another. It was if her irises had been formed from the leaves of the wet lavender flowers that grew by the riverbank. They were stunning.

He had closed his heart to her long ago since she was promised to Sathan. Never begrudging his brother for their betrothal, he accepted that Sathan was the better man who could give her the precious children she craved. Lila was extremely traditional, and he often heard her speak about how she wanted many offspring. As the army commander, he often wondered if he possessed the skills to parent effectively. Intense combat training had taught him that emotion was weak; compassion wasted.

Unable to squelch his love for her, he'd been terrible to her for centuries. Self-hate coursed through him as he remembered all the times he'd said something nasty to her or made her cry. It was a defense mechanism, built around his blackened heart to push her away. He'd hoped that by being terrible to her, she would leave him the hell alone.

And yet, she had always remained friendly to him. Cordial and welcoming and kind. By the goddess, he was some kind of ass. He had no idea how she had the patience. If he was her, he'd have plunged a knife into his soulless heart by now.

He'd supposed for all their lives that she loved Sathan. Only recently did he come to understand that she had never cared for him in that way. When Sathan fell for Miranda, it was Lila who'd broken the betrothal, mentioning that she had feelings for another. When his brother had informed him of their discussion, he made clear that he felt she was speaking of Latimus.

Incapable of believing that she could care for a black-hearted bastard who had treated her so badly, Latimus began to surreptitiously observe her. Against all odds, he realized that Sathan was right. The woman he loved with all his heart seemed to want him back.

Sadly, it was too late. If he'd known there was even the slightest possibility that she wouldn't bond with Sathan, he would've lived so differently. But the past had been forged. His murderous actions on the battlefield, combined with the terrible way he'd treated her, meant that he didn't deserve to touch one hair on her gorgeous head. Much less, let himself even consider tethering her to him for eternity. She deserved much better than the war-torn brute he'd become.

All these centuries, she'd remained a virgin, as the goddess decreed the king's betrothed should do, and hadn't ever been touched by a man. What a waste. Someone with her beauty should be loved, passionately and frequently, by a good man who could appreciate her.

He knew that many suspected his true feelings for her. He didn't give a crap. Fuck them. Regardless of how things turned out for Sathan and Miranda, he didn't believe in sappy fairy tales. The best he could do for her was to push her into the arms of a noble man. A husband who would care for her and love her in the ways he couldn't. Someone who would be a good father to her children and cherish her with soulful words. After all the centuries of being a bastard to her, he could love her enough to let a better man have her. She deserved no less.

"Let's have a strategy session in the morning," Kenden said, dragging him from his thoughts.

"Dawn," Latimus said.

"I'll tell Sathan and Miranda. I'm going to head down and close out the training."

"Thanks," Latimus said. "See you in a few hours."

As Kenden trotted down the hill, he rubbed his chest, right above his heart. Looking at the darkened moon, he contemplated Lila for one more moment. He was doing the right thing by pushing her toward another man. Even though he ached to have her himself, that just wasn't an option.

He loathed self-doubt and was annoyed that this woman brought it out in him. Firm in his choice, he headed inside to clean his rifles.

Chapter 2

Lila sat beside Heden in the tech room as he pulled up the itinerary on the screen. "This is the final one," he said, pointing to the monitor. "Three compounds in six days. You're our own little world traveler."

Smiling, she stood and stretched. "Thank the goddess. I feel like we've waited forever to get here, although the tunnel construction only took a year. I can't believe the men finished it so quickly. What?" she asked, noticing that he was staring up at her, his mouth agape.

"You need to do that stretching thing in front of my brother. Good lord, woman. You're smokin' hot."

Lila laughed, embarrassment heating her cheeks. He was always giving her compliments like that, warming her heart. Besides Arderin, he was her best friend. Always the perpetual joker, and so charming with his thick black hair, blue eyes and goatee, she had wished on more than one occasion that she'd fallen in love with him instead of Latimus. Sadly, her heart had not complied.

"I think I heard you say the same thing to the pretty woman whose ear you were licking at Arderin's birthday party last week. Maybe it's time to come up with a new line?"

Chuckling, he nodded. "Busted. She was definitely smokin' too."

Lila smiled, charmed by what an incredible flirt he was. "Well, thanks for firming up the itinerary. I'm excited to complete my first official mission as Kingdom Secretary Diplomat."

It was the title her father had held, centuries ago, before he and her mother had perished. The Vampyres had recently completed an underground high-speed rail system that could reach each compound in less than thirty minutes. Since the Vampyres weren't very adept at adopting new technology, it was her job to ride the train to each of the three satellite compounds and introduce it to their people. She would meet with the governors of each compound and do press to ensure quick adoption.

Once that mission was complete, she would eventually travel with Kenden to the two Slayer compounds, whose underground trains were in the final stages of completion. The War of the Species had lasted a thousand years; Vampyre and Slayer locked in an endless slaughter. Finally, peace was at hand. It was magnificent to behold, and she was excited to have her tiny place in history to cement harmony between the species.

"You'll travel to Valeria first, then Naria and end up at Lynia. Two nights at each compound. Sathan is going to assign a bodyguard and some troops to you. He said he'll know who by tomorrow."

"I told him I don't need all that," she said, waving her hand.

"Crimeous has the Blade, and we're not taking any chances. Let him protect you. I can't have anything happen to my buttercup."

She shook her head at his silly nickname for her. He was always quoting *The Princess Bride* and thought she favored the main character. "The trains are extremely secure, but if Sathan wishes to assign more men, that's his decision. I'll only be on the trains for thirty minutes at a time, so it seems pointless, but he's the boss."

White papers sputtered out of the printer, and he collected them and rose to hand them to her. "I emailed the itinerary to your phone, but here are a few hard copies so you can look everything over. You head out at the end of the week. I'm going to miss you."

"I'll miss you too," she said. "Anything else you need help with here?"

"Nah, I'm good. It's almost dawn. Think I'm gonna turn in. Wanna come with?" He waggled his eyebrows as he teased her.

"Stop it," she said, playfully slapping his chest. "I wouldn't know what to do anyway. Your lady lover from the other night is a much better choice."

"Is that why you're holding back from confronting Latimus? Because you're a virgin? Trust me, he won't give a damn."

Lila sighed, not wanting to discuss this topic. At all. "He's obviously not interested, and that's fine. I have no desire to confront him."

"Wow. You're a terrible liar. Good grief. I'm never telling you any secrets."

"Shut up," she said, laughing. "I'm an awesome liar." Heden rolled his eyes, and she swatted him again. "I just wouldn't even know where to start with him. He and I are complete opposites. Some things just aren't meant to be."

"Well, if you love someone, I think that trumps a few simple dissimilarities. And if you're worried about the sex thing, don't be. I think he'd cut off both of his balls and all of his limbs for one roll in the sack with you, virgin or not."

"Gross," she said, giving him a teasing scowl. "There's no need to be vulgar."

"So damn proper. That's why we all love you, Lila. You remind us that we're supposed to have manners."

"Yes, you are. But I've given up hope. Now, I'm going to bed before you say something that makes me call for the vapors."

He pulled her into a beefy embrace and gave her a loud smack on the cheek. "Sweet dreams of my brother. See you at dusk."

Pushing him away, she gave him a lighthearted glower and headed to her bedchamber. Once there, she prepared for bed, pulling on the silky tank and shorts that felt so good against her skin when she slept. As she brushed her teeth, she looked over the itinerary Heden had printed for her. Placing the papers on the dresser, she checked to ensure the blackout blinds were secure. Climbing beneath the sheets, she fell into sleep—and did, in fact, dream of Latimus.

* * * *

Two commanders and two rulers assembled around the table at dawn. Sitting at the head, Sathan spoke. "I'd like to discuss the train implementation as well as the attack on Crimeous to retrieve the Blade of Pestilence."

Latimus nodded, seated at his left. "We'd like to attack Crimeous during the next full moon. Kenden has mapped the Deamon caves extensively, and with Darkrip's help, we know where he's hiding the Blade. If you guys are good with that, we'll start training for the mission tonight."

A look passed between Miranda and Sathan, making Latimus feel uneasy. "Is there a problem with that?"

"We don't want to stage an attack so close to the train implementation. Lila will be traveling to all of the compounds, and we don't want her vulnerable," Sathan said.

"Yeah, and?" Latimus said, lifting his hands, a bit exasperated. "You're going to assign Bryan as her bodyguard and send along four Slayer soldiers to be their eyes and ears. We already discussed this."

"We've decided to make a change," Miranda said, her green eyes firm. "We want you to accompany her as her bodyguard instead of Bryan."

Latimus felt his mouth drop open as his gaze darted between her and his brother. After several moments, he let out a laugh. "Damn, Miranda. I know you like to joke, but that one isn't funny. Anyway, back to the attack on Crimeous—"

"I'm not joking," she said, interrupting him. "We think it's the best course. Crimeous is familiar with underground caves and can materialize anywhere. We don't want her protected by anyone but the best."

Fury bubbled in his chest as he regarded them. Turning to look at Kenden to his left, he asked, "Am I going crazy? Or did these two idiots just tell me that they've decided the most powerful war commander on Etherya's Earth should play bodyguard for a spoiled Vampyre aristocrat?"

Kenden, always neutral and undramatic, slowly lifted his hands, palms up. "I've got no dog in this hunt. Sorry."

Wooden legs scraped the floor as Latimus stood and addressed his brother. "After everything I did for you when you couldn't keep your dick in your pants around *her*,"—he gestured to Miranda—"you have the balls to relegate me to the position of bodyguard in some twisted matchmaking attempt? Are you serious right now?"

Sathan's nostrils flared. "I think it would be best if you two left us to discuss this in private."

"Fuck you!" Latimus said, causing Sathan to stand. The brothers glared at each other, their hulking bodies filled with rage. A muscle corded in his brother's neck, and Latimus imagined ripping out his throat with his bare hands.

"Guys, stop. Seriously." Miranda stood and placed an arm on Sathan's forearm. "Maybe we should discuss this more."

"Leave us," Sathan said. Latimus clenched his jaw, feeling his teeth grind together. "I would like to discuss this in private."

Miranda sighed. "Fucking idiots. C'mon, Ken." They both walked to the door and exited, but not before she turned and said, "I'll be right outside. Don't kill each other. I mean it."

The door closed with a soft click of finality.

Sathan lifted his arms, palms facing forward. "I don't want to fight with you about this, Latimus. We want Lila to be protected by the best. You're the best. I don't see why you're getting so upset."

"Because I'm the commander of the damn army, not a fucking bodyguard," he said, exasperated. "Who in the hell do you think you are to demand that I traipse around like a sap protecting her all day? Bryan is more than capable."

"Bryan is a strong soldier, but you are stronger. I'd also prefer that you test the security systems rather than one of our other soldiers. I don't know why you're getting so emotional. I seem to remember you telling me that I was a pansy because of Miranda. I'd rather be that than a coward. It's time you and Lila face your feelings for each other. If you're able to do that on this trip, then that's a bonus, but I want her protected. I've made my decision."

"I told you I'm not interested in encouraging any feelings she has for me. They're based on some ridiculous memory of what we had when we were kids. That was centuries ago. She deserves a man who can give her the life and the children she wants."

"You are perfectly capable of having children, Latimus," Sathan said, his tone sardonic.

Latimus gritted his teeth, infuriated. "I have never begrudged you anything, Sathan. I've been told my entire life that you're the better man. I've done my best to help you protect our people and fought tirelessly with our soldiers. And now, after all that, you have the audacity to pull this 'king' shit with me?" he asked, forming quotation marks in the air with his fingers. "Are you seriously going to go there?"

Sathan shook his head, his expression filled with sorrow. "I don't know who told you those lies but I know of no better man than you, brother. You have been my confidant and most trusted advisor my entire life. The fact you believe differently means that I've failed you somehow. I want to make that right."

Latimus groaned and pinched his upper nose with his thumb and index finger, closing his eyes in frustration. "I don't want any of the things you're trying to force on me." Opening his lids, he said, "I don't need children or a family or a bonded mate. Those are your dreams. I'm content with my army and with protecting our people. You think you're helping, but I just don't want what you want."

Sathan shrugged. "Then, that will make the trip easier. It should go by in a snap. Once you return, we'll plan the attack on Crimeous for the next month's full moon. You'll barely realize any time has passed at all."

Latimus crossed his arms over his chest. "And if I refuse?"

Sathan shook his head. "Don't go there. You won't like the consequences."

"Threats, is it? Against your own brother. What will it be? Sanction? Banishment?"

"If I must."

Latimus laughed bitterly. "My time should be focused on retrieving the Blade. This is absurd. I hope that your attempts at matchmaking are worth it if we fail."

Clenching his teeth in anger, he stalked toward the door. "Send me the itinerary. I'm done with this discussion." He slammed the door so hard he was sure it could be heard at the Slayer compound.

Miranda grabbed his forearm as he strode by her in the darkened hallway. "Latimus," she said softly.

"No, Miranda," he said, pulling away from her touch. "I need to concentrate on retrieving the Blade. You know this is absolutely ridiculous."

Her eyes glistened with wetness. "We just want you to be happy."

Rolling his eyes, he gave her his best look of disgust and walked away. He pounded down the stairs that led to his basement bedroom. Furious, he grabbed the scotch on top of his dresser and took a swig. Annoyance at two people he cared for immensely coursed through him. Frustrated, he sat on his bed to drown himself in the coppery liquid.

* * * *

An hour later, Miranda's head lay limp on the toilet, resting on her shaking arm. Inhaling another breath, she retched, dry-heaving into the bowl. Exasperated, she groaned and pounded her free hand on the porcelain.

Sathan entered the bathroom, and she waved him off. "Don't come any closer. I'm gonna blow chunks all over you."

"Fuck that," her husband said, sitting beside her and wrapping his huge legs and arms around her. Gently, he began to stroke her hair.

"So gross. You're comforting me as I hug the toilet. We've really gotta talk about your seduction tactics."

His full lips turned into a smile but it didn't reach his eyes. Hurt for her emanated from his handsome face. "I hate that you're so sick. I feel like an animal for doing this to you. I wish I could carry the babe for you."

"Um, yeah," she said, gazing up at him as he rubbed her hair, "that would be great. How can we make that happen?" Gasping, she stuck her head in the bowl and puked. "God, you'll never want to sleep with me again. Go away."

"No way," he said, clutching her tighter. "We're in this together. I'll hold you all day if I have to."

Her heart swelled with love for him. Gazing into his black irises, she let him soothe her as he caressed her hair. Finally, she said, "I think it's passed. I need to brush my teeth."

Placing a soft kiss on her forehead, he lifted her off the floor and carried her to the bathroom sink. Lowering her, he stood behind her as she reached for her toothbrush and paste and commenced brushing.

"Are you going to watch me while I brush my teeth?" she asked, her words garbled by the object in her mouth. "That's kinda creepy."

Laughing, he shook his head at her in the reflection. "I'm worried about you. You're trembling. I want to make sure that you're okay."

"I'm fine," she said, reaching up to pat his face, loving his scowl in the reflection as she placated him. "I'll be in bed in a sec. Promise."

"Stubborn minx," he muttered, placing a kiss on the top of her head. Turning, he headed into the bedchamber, and she heard him rifling through the drawers. Finishing, she rinsed with mouthwash and dried her face.

She pulled off her tank top and black pants, throwing them in the hamper, and donned one of his large black t-shirts that sat in the top drawer of the dresser. They were her favorite thing to sleep in because they smelled like him. She spent every other week at the Slayer compound of Uteria, and he wasn't always able to accompany her for the entire stay. Being surrounded by his scent helped her sleep when he wasn't holding her.

Climbing into bed, she snuggled into him and lay her head on his chest. He turned off the bedside light, plunging them into darkness. Worry ran through her as she played with the tiny black hairs on his chest.

"Latimus is really pissed at us."

"Yeah," he said, stroking her arm as she sprawled against him. "I've never seen him this angry at me."

"Did we make a mistake? Forcing them together on the trip?"

Sathan sighed, his huge chest expanding and contracting. "I don't know. He told me tonight he's always accepted that I was a better man than him. I didn't know he felt that way. He's always been so strong and stoic. It pisses me off that he won't let himself experience true happiness."

"Maybe he just wants to focus on the army. I don't want to push him into something he doesn't want."

"Maybe," he said, "but I've observed him around Lila. It's subtle, but I can see that he cares for her. She's not so good at concealing her feelings. It's obvious she cares for him. I wish they'd just confront each other and get it out in the open. I've never seen him so afraid. It's strange."

"Love makes people do weird things," she said, sliding to lie fully on top of him. "Look at us. I decided to marry a Vampyre. That's clearly a new level of insanity."

His chuckle vibrated through her as he pushed her lower on his body. The silky tip of his cock slid against the wetness of her core. "Damnit, Miranda. I promised myself I wouldn't fuck you tonight. You need to rest."

"Screw you," she said, pushing herself onto him, reveling in his deep groan. Needing him to soothe her worry, she slid up and down on his shaft, clutching him inside her deepest place. His broad hands grabbed her hips, helping her to move faster. As the pace became more frenzied, she leveraged her palms on his pecs, forcing him deep and hard inside her. Losing herself, she rode him, letting the pleasure take her.

Snarling, he rolled her to her back, his thick cock relentless in its pounding. With his beefy hand, he pulled the shirt off her quivering body. Burying his face in her neck, he licked the smooth skin over her vein. Lathered with his self-healing saliva, he plunged into her.

"Oh, god," she cried, throwing her head back as he drank from her.

Her gorgeous husband moaned, the sound vibrating against her as his hips jutted into hers.

Cursing, she came, feeling her walls contract around him. His low rumble ran through her as he jetted his seed into her, bucking wildly above her. Replete, she relaxed under his large body.

Shivering, she felt him lick her neck, closing her wound. Then, his dark irises pierced hers in the dimness.

"I know you're worried, sweetheart," he said. Wide fingers stroked her hair as she waited for her breath to return to normal. "I can feel the concern pulsing through your blood. I don't want you to work yourself up. We've made our decision and we need to stick to it."

Growing sleepy, she nuzzled her nose into his chest. "Should I talk to Latimus tomorrow? He seems to listen to me."

Rolling over, he pulled her to sprawl on top of him. "If you like. Although, I'm not sure if he'll listen to anyone right now. All we can do is what we think is right. In the end, he's going to have to find his own way."

"I know," she said, drifting off. "But I love him. I want him to be happy."

"Me too, sweetheart. Now, go to sleep. I need you to rest."

For once, she followed her husband's command without argument.

Chapter 3

Dusk arrived, and Lila set about the mundane task of starting her night. Once she was showered and dressed, she checked her phone.

Miranda: Sathan and I would like to discuss the trip with you. Can you come to the conference room?

Curious as to why both rulers needed to be present, she replied.

Lila: Sure. Be there in a few minutes.

Thoughtlessly, she rubbed her palms over her denim-clad thighs. She had only started wearing jeans recently, spurred on by Arderin and Miranda, and she found them very comfortable. For the past centuries, she had mostly worn gowns, long and flowing, the garb of the Vampyre aristocracy. Her two friends were much more progressive than she, and once they'd talked her into jeans, she'd found herself wearing them, along with slacks, much more often. It was quite freeing.

Giving herself one last look in the mirror, she studied her appearance. Almond-shaped, lavender-colored eyes stared back at her, surrounded by her completely normal features. Her blond hair fell to her waist. Smoothing her hand over it, she realized that she'd worn it as a shield for all these centuries. Lately, she had contemplated cutting it but hadn't had the courage yet. Not being able to hide behind her hair would leave her vulnerable, and that was something she was deathly afraid of. So much had changed for her in the last year, and she struggled with the gravity of her new reality.

Being born a blue-blooded aristocrat, she had been ingrained with the "duty first" motto since she could remember breathing. Duty to her king. Duty to her people. Duty to her station. Duty to produce heirs. It was all she'd ever known and all she'd ever expected of her life until Sathan had fallen for Miranda. Once she realized she wouldn't be queen, she'd begun to chart a new course for herself. It had been terrifying, but she also felt a tiny seed of something emerging inside her. Something fresh and raw and wonderful. It felt a lot like independence and it cautiously thrilled her as she navigated her new existence.

Still, her current circumstances felt strange and quite lonely. Miranda was now queen and pregnant with the kingdom's heir. Where did this leave Lila? Every single purpose for her life was now being met by someone else. She certainly didn't begrudge Miranda. The Slayer was a true friend, and she was so excited for the baby.

Never loving Sathan romantically, she was thrilled that he'd found a bonded mate who made him so happy.

But that left her at a crossroads. Where the heck would life take her now? She'd been at a juncture like this once before. Several centuries ago, her parents had died, after a fateful excursion to the human world. Being an only child, it had opened a huge gulf of loneliness deep within. The royal family had been so kind to her, taking her in since she was Sathan's betrothed. They'd given her a home at the castle and a life to lead until becoming queen.

But some days, at dawn, when she lay down to sleep in her darkened bedchamber, tears would well in her eyes as she pulled the covers close. A chasm of lonesomeness would open inside her eight-chambered heart, and she would do her best to push it away. Although Arderin and Heden were amazing at making her a priority in their lives, she sometimes felt so empty.

She'd always assumed that the loneliness would abate a bit after having a child. Now, she was more alone than ever. Stuck in love with a man who wanted nothing to do with her. The possibility of having children seemed further away than ever. It was quite abysmal and maddening if she took too much time to dwell on it.

Sighing at her reflection, she shook her head at her musings and headed downstairs. When she entered the conference room, she saw Sathan and Miranda staring out the window, his arm around her small shoulders.

"Hi," Lila said softly, not wanting to startle them.

"Hey," Miranda said, turning and giving her one of her bright smiles. "Sorry, we were daydreaming. I want so badly for Etherya to lift the curse. We were hoping she'd give us some sort of sign that Vampyres can walk in the sun again. So far, no such luck."

"As peace grows between the species, I'm sure it's only a matter of time," Lila said.

"Hope so." Miranda sat down and gestured for her to do the same. Sathan sat between them at the head of the table.

"Are you ready for your journey?" he asked. "We're all so excited for you. This is a huge step forward for our compounds."

"I'm ready. Have you decided who will accompany me as bodyguard?"

The two rulers looked at each other. Lifting her chin, Miranda said, "Latimus is going to accompany you. He's been briefed and will be ready to leave at dusk in three days' time."

Lila's heart slammed in her chest, a feeling of dread spreading through her. "I don't think that's a good idea. I thought you were leaning toward Bryan."

"We were, but we want you protected," Sathan said. "There's no one better to do that than Latimus. Crimeous' powers have grown exponentially, and we won't take any chances with your life."

Lila absently played with a strand of her long blond hair. It was a habit she had formed centuries ago and usually employed when nervous. "He'll think you're sending him with me to punish him. I can't believe he accepted the assignment."

Miranda pursed her lips, stealing a glance at her husband. "He wasn't thrilled," she said, returning her gaze to Lila's. "But he understands that we must ensure your safety at all costs. He's accepted and will be ready on Friday."

Lila inhaled, her finger twirling around a tawny curl. "I know what you both are trying to do. It will never work. No one can force Latimus to do or feel anything he doesn't want to."

"My brother is definitely a stubborn son of a bitch," Sathan said, "but he's also become so mired in his army that I'm afraid it's hindering him. Getting him off the compound and away from the soldiers for a few days will be good for him."

Lila looked back and forth between them, bringing her hands to fidget together on the table. "I don't like you meddling in my private life. I'm sure he's furious. I just don't think this is a good idea."

"No one hates their privacy invaded more than me, Lila," Miranda said. "But our first priority is your safety. That's the reason for this decision. Any other consequences are second-tier."

Lila breathed a humorless laugh. "I almost believe you, Miranda."

"Lila," Sathan said, placing his hand over hers on the table and squeezing. "We just want you to be safe and happy. Please, don't fight us on this."

"He's going to blame me for your decision. I can't see a scenario where he'll be amicable to me at all."

"I'll speak to him. I promise he'll be cordial to you. I'll make sure of it."

Chewing her bottom lip with one of her fangs, she regarded him. The man she'd been betrothed to for a thousand years. Fear wrenched her heart that Latimus would hate her even more than he already did.

"We love you," Miranda said, clutching her other hand. "We need you to be strong so that you can accomplish this roll-out effectively. Having Latimus with you will make you stronger."

"Okay," she said, giving a short nod. "If it's what you wish, then I'll comply, of course."

They both smiled at her, and she pulled her hands from theirs. Standing, she addressed them. "I just want you to understand that this is difficult for me. I'm worried that things might not go smoothly." Miranda started to speak, and she held up her hand, cutting her off. "I trust Latimus immensely but am quite uneasy around him at times. Regardless, I accept your decision and need to start packing. I'll see you both later, at Heden's party."

Frustrated, Lila left the room, unable to acknowledge their calls for her to stay. Needing a moment, she strode up the stairs to her bedchamber and closed the door behind her. Resting her back against it, she lifted her gaze to the ceiling, covering her beating heart with her palm.

A full week in close proximity with Latimus. It was terrifying. She'd always had the betrothal as a buffer between them. They'd never really had an excuse to constantly be in each other's presence for such a long period. It would leave her vulnerable, and she was afraid her true feelings would show. Knowing he would never allow himself to care for her, she felt a bubble of anxiety in her throat. Inhaling a deep breath, she told herself to remain calm. Only through a composed demeanor would she be able to endure their trip. Resolved to her fate, she wrung her hands at her sides, trying to eliminate the anxiety. Steeling herself, she headed to the tech room to make the final touches to her speeches.

* * * *

Several hours later, Latimus stood by the ballroom door, telling himself he wasn't waiting for Lila to arrive. His idiot younger brother had decided to throw himself a birthday party and was standing at the head of the room gyrating to some godawful music as he held headphones to one ear.

The room was filled with fifty to sixty Vampyres. Close friends of the aristocracy, some of his soldiers and family. Annoyed at all of them, he rested his back on the wall. He despised social gatherings. He'd only agreed to stop by for an hour or two because Arderin had begged him. As the sole light of his world, he was unable to say no to his charming little sister. Lifting his arm, he looked at his watch, hoping he'd met the minimum time requirement and could leave to find some peace.

"No way," his sister said, bouncing up to him and grabbing his arm. Pulling, she tried to coax him onto the dance floor. "Please? You never dance with me. Just one song. It'll be so fun."

Smiling in spite of himself, he grabbed her hand and twirled her around. "There, I danced with you. Now, go bother someone else. I saw Naran checking you out. He'd make a good bonded. Go dance with him."

"Seriously?" she asked, her expression droll. "He's the most *boring* man on the planet. Is that the best you think I can do? Good god."

Latimus studied her beautiful features. Ice-blue eyes, waist-length, curly raven-black hair. Skin as flawless as the day she was born. She was absolutely gorgeous, and he had a feeling she knew it. He hoped that one day she would find a man worthy of her. "You're passable. I'm sure you can find someone to dance with you."

White teeth flashed as she gave him one of her dazzling smiles. "You're hopeless," she said, swatting his chest. "Oh, here comes Lila. I'm out."

Gritting his teeth, he surreptitiously glanced toward her, watching her approach. Her scent surrounded him first. Lavender and rose, it haunted his dreams every night. As she neared him, he couldn't help but admire the flare of her hips in her tight jeans. She'd started wearing them recently, making Latimus wonder if she was secretly trying to kill him with a severe case of blue balls.

Lila was a curvaceous woman, her pear-shaped body the standard he held all other women to. While some women longed to be skin and bones, he loved her curves and her naturally large breasts. By the goddess, her breasts were amazing. The tops of the ivory globes flirted with the V-neck of her thin sweater as she approached, and he felt himself grow rock hard. Mother fucker.

"Hey," she said, her voice so soft against his brother's terrible music. "So, I guess we're traveling together to the compounds."

"Yeah," he said, commanding himself not to drown in those lavender eyes. "Guess so."

"I'm sorry" she said, shaking her head. "I don't know why they're forcing this on you. I feel terrible."

"Forcing it on us," he said, cursing his heart as it pounded in his chest. "Maybe they're trying to see how patient you really are. A week with me is torture."

She laughed, and his dick twitched in his pants at the sight of her white fangs. "I'm sure it won't be that bad. We'll just agree to be cordial to each other."

"Fine," he said, lifting his gaze to stare at the dance floor. He just couldn't look into those violet irises anymore. They enthralled him.

"Oh, Arderin's dancing with Naran. They make a cute couple."

"She just told me that she thinks he's boring. But maybe he'll win her over."

She chuckled as she stood beside him, both of them assessing the dance floor.

"Do you want to dance?" she asked, looking up at him from her six-foot, three-inch height. He was half a foot taller and outweighed her by over a hundred pounds, but in that moment, he felt like she had all the power. Locking his gaze with hers, he allowed himself for one second to imagine how it would feel, holding her in his arms and swaying to the music. She would curve that voluptuous body around him, his erection cradled by the juncture of her thighs.

He was about to burst in his pants. Fucking embarrassing.

"I don't dance. But thanks. Camron came down from Valeria. You should ask him to dance. He always seems taken with you." Latimus had noticed on more than one occasion how the governor of the Valeria compound watched Lila. It usually made him throb with jealousy, but since he had no claim on her, he always let it stew.

"Maybe I will," she said, staring absently at the dance floor. "He's one of my oldest friends. I've known him forever."

Latimus tilted his head to look at the crown of her golden hair. She'd known him longer than anyone. He was pissed that she didn't seem to remember that. Cursing himself a fool, he noticed Darkrip stalk into the room.

The Slayer-Deamon approached him, his footsteps purposeful. Latimus stood to attention, understanding something was wrong.

"My father is going to attack Uteria within the hour. I saw it in his mind. He's erected a barrier so that I can't read his thoughts, but sometimes, they break through."

Silently cursing Crimeous, Latimus gave a nod. Lifting his smartwatch, he spoke a text to Kenden.

Latimus: Meet me in the barracks in five minutes. Crimeous is attacking Uteria. We need to deploy two hundred troops. Radio Takel and Larkin so they're aware.

Kenden: Ten-four.

"Can I do anything to help?" Lila asked.

"Stay here and keep everyone calm. Thanks, Darkrip." The Slayer-Deamon nodded and skulked from the room.

Leaving Lila, he approached Sathan where he swayed with Miranda on the dance floor. Informing them of the attack, they headed to the barracks with him. As annoyed as he was at them, now was not the time to be divided. Battle was what he was born for, and he was ready.

Chapter 4

Latimus attached the TEC to the Deamon's head, clicking the button and watching the blade deploy into the fucker's forehead. He perished instantly. Savoring his victory, he stood and searched his surroundings.

The TEC, which stood for Third Eye Contraption, was a new weapon that Latimus, Kenden and Heden had developed to combat the Deamons. The species had a vestigial third eye that had never evolved, leaving a vulnerable patch of skin on their foreheads between the eyelids. The TEC could be latched to their heads and the click of a button would deploy a deadly blade into the spot. It was a huge advancement in their war against the evil species.

"They're all dead," Takel said, coming to stand beside him. "You got the last one."

He was one of Latimus' most trusted soldiers. They had both been children during the Awakening and had grown into strong warriors together. When Sathan had fallen for Miranda and decided to station Vampyre troops at Uteria, Latimus had thought of no one besides Takel to take command. He, along with the Slayer soldier Larkin, had done a fantastic job at protecting the more vulnerable Slayer compound.

The night was dark under the New Moon, and he patted his friend on the shoulder. "Great job. You guys really handled those assholes. You and Larkin are a great team."

"We are. He's pretty badass for a Slayer."

Latimus chuckled and turned to face his men. "Did we lose any?"

"No," Takel said, shaking his head. "A hundred Deamons dead with no casualties on our side."

"Good." Jerking his head, he heard moaning a few feet away, his keen Vampyre ear picking up the faint sound. Stalking over, he found two Deamons still alive on the grass.

"Bind them and load them in the Hummer. I'll bring them back to Astaria and question them. They might have intel."

Nodding, Takel set about following the orders.

Latimus rounded up the troops, congratulating the men on a job well done. The Astaria-based troops loaded into the large tanks and headed home. He gave a warm goodbye to Takel and then climbed in the Hummer, Kenden beside him in the front seat, the two Deamons unconscious and bound in the trunk.

"The men fought well tonight," Kenden said. "I think they're close to being self-sufficient. If Crimeous attacks again, we might want to wait a few yards from the wall and see if Takel and Larkin's soldiers can fight them off on their own."

"Agreed," Latimus said.

Nodding, Kenden grabbed the handle above the door and sat firm as Latimus drove them to Astaria.

Once back at the barracks, Latimus instilled four soldiers to help him ready the Deamons for interrogation. When they were tied securely to the chairs, he poured water over their faces, causing them to wake. As his men stood behind him, Latimus got to the unseemly business of torturing his captives for intel.

* * * *

Meanwhile, as the last moments of night bled into day, Lila was berating herself in the kitchen. Earlier, when she'd approached Latimus in the ballroom, she'd thought it an excellent idea. Why not go ahead and address their impending journey in the safety of a room filled with sixty people? She knew he would never yell at her in that setting and they could discuss it calmly.

What she hadn't expected was to become a bumbling idiot. Shaking her head as she searched the fridge for Slayer blood, she recalled asking him to dance. What the heck was wrong with her? As if the powerful Vampyre army commander would want to waste time dancing with her. Embarrassed at her idiocy, she drank the Slayer blood. Setting the empty container in the sink, she vowed to stop acting like a dolt. How could she expect to not be rejected by him when she set herself up like that?

Feeling restless, she wandered the darkened hallways, rubbing her upper arms. As she approached the door that led to the barracks garage, she wondered if he was back. Had their battle been successful? Of course, it must've been. Latimus was so powerful. She couldn't imagine a scenario where he would fail on the battlefield.

Slightly opening the door that led to the barracks, she observed the room through the slit. Feeling her eyes grow wide, she brought her fingers to rest on her lips.

Latimus stood before two Deamons, both tied to chairs, holding some sort of taser in his hand. Every so often, he would touch it to one of the creatures' chests and set it off, causing them to scream in pain. Their backs were to her, but she could see foam dripping from one's mouth as he turned to spit blood on the floor.

By the goddess, she had never seen something so gruesome. Was this what Latimus did to all the prisoners of war? Had he done this since he assumed the role of commander at only thirteen years old? Dirt marred his handsome features as he inflicted cruelty on the Deamons. This was what he knew; what he'd been trained for. No wonder he was so cold and nasty. War and death were his entire world.

"Why do you keep attacking Uteria?" he asked, grabbing one of the Deamons by the hair. "Crimeous must know he can't defeat us there. Why does he keep commanding you to do this?"

"He is determined to find a weakness that will harm you," the Deamon said, spitting a tooth out of his mouth. "He feels confident that he will find a flaw, and when he does, he will use it to exterminate you."

Latimus growled and backhanded the Deamon, sending his head flying sideways. Lila gasped.

Latimus' head snapped up, his gaze locking onto hers through the slit in the door. Unable to move, fingers still over her lips, she stood. Shaking his head, he threw the taser to the floor. "Kill them," he said.

Her heart slammed into overdrive as he stalked toward her. Stupidly, she closed the door, turning to run to her bedchamber. She made it about five feet before he grabbed her arm and rotated her around to face him.

"Goddamnit, Lila," he said, pushing her back against the wall. "What the hell are you doing?"

"I'm sorry," she said, shaking her head against the wall as she looked up into his ice-blue eyes. "I was restless and wandering around and opened the barracks door. I shouldn't have. I'm so sorry."

Angrily, he rubbed his forehead with the pads of his fingers. "I don't want you seeing any part of this war. Do you understand me? You're one of the only people left in this world who hasn't been marred by battle, and I don't want you anywhere near it."

Emotion choked her as she realized he wanted to protect her. "I wish you didn't have to be near it. I want so badly for you to be free from it." Unable to stop herself, she lifted her hand and cupped his cheek.

"No," he said, pulling her hand away. "Don't touch me. It's not happening, Lila. There will never be anything between us. I won't pull you into my fucked-up world. Now, go to bed like a good little aristocrat and leave the war to the soldiers. I'm done with you."

Fury shot through her, and before she could stop herself, she crashed her palm into his face. He barely flinched, his jaw clenching as he glared down at her. "Don't *ever* speak to me like that again."

"Fine," he said through his teeth. "Just leave me the hell alone." He all but threw her arm at her, backing away several steps. "I mean it." Scowling, he stalked back to the barracks.

Exhaling a huge breath, she sank into the wall. What an unmitigated ass! As she willed her heartbeat to settle down, she remembered his words. *I won't pull you into my fucked-up world.* Did he believe that he was protecting her by pushing her away? Did he feel she needed shielding from him?

Confused and shaken, she headed to her bedchamber. Unable to sleep, she ran a bath and submerged herself in the soapy water, trying to forget how good it felt when he'd held her against the wall, his hulking body so close to hers. By the goddess, she was so messed-up. Angry at herself, she sunk further into the water and willed herself to let the entire evening go.

* * * *

Self-revulsion coursed through Latimus' thick frame as he finished up with the soldiers. It was hours past dawn, so he had tasked some of the Slayer soldiers with disposing the bodies so that he didn't burn to death. Locking the thick garage door to the barracks, he headed inside.

Once in his basement room, he stripped off his dirty, blood-soaked clothes, grimacing at them as he threw them in the hamper. He had touched Lila while wearing them. The thought made him sick.

As he showered, he washed away the grime, unable to wash away his guilt at how he'd treated her. Although, she had given him a pretty nice slap across the face. Smiling to himself, he palmed his cheek, realizing it was probably the only time she'd touched him there. What a fucking sap he was, treasuring the touch of her blow. He'd really turned into a lovesick bastard.

Resigning himself to that fate, he leaned his palm against the wall and slid his other hand down to cup his shaft. Groaning her name, he began jerking his cock, imagining it was in between her pretty pink lips. Anger had flashed in her stunning lavender eyes tonight as he'd scolded her as well as a healthy dose of desire. Her scent had been laced with the smell of her arousal, and he gritted his teeth, knowing she wanted him. His hand moved at a frenzied pace, and he came, spurting onto the tile of the shower as the water sluiced over him. Panting, he lowered his head, hating that he couldn't have her just once.

As he dried himself and wrapped the towel around his waist, he scoffed. Once would never be enough. If he touched her, it would be over for him. Remembering his promise to push her into the arms of a better man, he decided he would encourage affection from Camron when they were at Valeria. Even though he'd most likely want to snap the man's neck for even considering touching her. What a clusterfuck.

Exhausted, he threw off his towel and climbed into bed. It was time for him to rest so that he could play bodyguard. Fucking great.

Chapter 5

Arderin clinched her teeth as she stood in front of her brother's mahogany desk. "You're being a jerk," she said, crossing her arms over her chest.

Sathan sighed, looking to the ceiling in frustration. "This mission is important. Not everything is about you, Arderin. You can ride the trains to the compounds once Lila completes the roll out and Latimus tests the security system.

"But Lila and Latimus both get to go!" She fisted her hands at her sides, knowing she was being a brat but unable to stop herself. "I could help them on the journey. I'm great at diplomacy. Please, don't make me stay here in this boring castle while they go. I'll literally die."

"I'm sure you'll survive," her brother said, his tone acerbic.

Anger bubbled up in her chest. "You're such an ass."

Shaking his head, he stood and walked around the desk. "Why do you fight me on everything?" he asked, clutching her wrists in his hands. "I only want to protect you. If you want so badly to help with diplomacy, you can help me with the fifty Slayers who are moving to Astaria this week. As Miranda and I unite the kingdoms, it's important that we have both species living on multiple compounds. You know I want you to help me here more. You're our kingdom's princess, and our people respect you. It would be great to have your help with their transition."

"I *want* to go to the human world and study medicine. That's how I can help our people. Now that Slayers will live on our compounds, you'll need more trained physicians than just Nolan and Sadie."

Sathan sighed. "We've talked about this, Arderin. The human world is too dangerous. Sadie and Nolan can train you here just fine."

"I'm not Mother," she said, yanking her arms from his grasp. "You're trying to protect me because you couldn't save her, but I'm my own woman. Can't you see, I'm shriveling and dying in this godforsaken kingdom? I can't even find anyone who wants to bond with me. At least I can become a doctor since I'm destined to die a withered old virgin."

Sathan's dark irises filled with compassion. "You're a beautiful and talented woman, sis. We all think so. I know you get frustrated with me, but it's hard for me too. You challenge me all the time. We should be united. It's what our parents would've wanted." Grabbing her hand, he pulled her closer and held it to his chest. "I love you, Arderin. Please, don't fight me on this."

Arderin felt her eyes well with tears. She loved him so much but was so angry that she didn't repeat the words.

"One day, I'm going to leave this kingdom and never come back."

His raven-black eyebrows drew together, pain flashing across his face. "Arderin—"

"No," she said, pulling from his grasp. "You've never understood me, Sathan. Neither has Heden. Latimus is the only one who recognizes what drives me. I feel a calling. I know that's hard for you to understand, but it's there, and I need to follow it."

"I don't want to deny you anything. You know that. But I can't let you go live in the human world. I'm sorry, Arderin. I want so badly for you to be happy."

Rolling her eyes, she straightened her spine and headed toward the door. Upon opening it, she pivoted to him. "One day, I might just go. It would be better to go with your blessing and traveling there without your help will be tough. But I'm running out of patience, Sathan. Think about it." With finality, she slammed the door.

Muttering to herself, Arderin stomped down the hallway and into the foyer, fisting her hands at her sides. Stopping under the brilliant diamond chandelier, she tilted her head back and cursed.

"I could transport you to the human world."

Gasping, she turned to see Darkrip standing in the shadows of the foyer. He leaned nonchalantly against the wall, his broad back against the centuries-old royal blue wallpaper. Arms crossed over his chest, one leg supported his weight while the other was bent, the sole of his black loafer on the wall.

She turned to face him fully. Several feet separated them, but she felt an invisible tug toward him. Such had been the case since she'd first met him. He'd shown up on the infirmary table, injured and bleeding, and she had stitched him up. Arderin had always been entranced by the study of medicine and had researched the subject extensively. Although Vampyres had self-healing properties, she could think of nothing nobler than helping others heal.

He had said awful words to her that day, showing her how evil he truly was. As the son of the Deamon King Crimeous, a serious malevolent streak comprised his nature. But he was also the son of Miranda's mother Rina, kidnapped by Crimeous and forced to bear him. His mother's blood was pure and benevolent, and Arderin wondered how he lived with the constant battle of good versus wicked within.

"I know," Arderin said, slowly inching toward him. "But what would it cost me?"

His broad shoulders shrugged. "We could work something out."

Disgust shot through her. "I'm not bargaining with you. I'd rather negotiate with a flesh-eating piranha."

Separating from the wall, Darkrip shook his head, making small *tsk, tsk, tsk* sounds from his mouth. His lips were wide, filling out the bottom half of his face, while his grass-green eyes bore into hers. She observed the Deamon tips of his ears under his dark buzz-cut and couldn't control the shiver that ran through her.

"When you get desperate enough, you will. I'm very patient. I lived with my father for almost a thousand years, mired in torture and death. Eventually, everyone has their price."

"You're an abomination! My brothers would kill you if they knew you were even speaking to me."

He rolled his eyes. "So dramatic. Miranda has your brother wrapped around her tiny little finger. I could use her to manipulate him against you."

Hating him, she gritted her teeth.

"But I won't," he continued, giving her a cruel smile. "I think that one day, your inquisitiveness will get the best of you, and you'll search me out. Remember how curious you were when you held my cock in your hand?" As she stood, her body frozen for some unfathomable reason, he stopped within inches of her, causing her to tilt her head back slightly to keep eye contact. He was a few inches taller than her six-foot frame.

"It felt so good," he said, brushing his body into hers.

Regaining her sanity, she shoved him away. "Leave me alone!"

He barely budged, his laugh sinister.

"God, you're so passionate. I've rarely met anyone more so. Be careful, or one day, I might not be so nice."

Revulsion ran through her. He was a child borne of evil and rape, and she'd do well to remember that. Inhaling a large breath, she stepped away from him. "You're not worth the dirt on the bottom of my shoe. Don't ever approach me again. Next time, I'll tell my brothers, and they'll murder you."

The deep chuckle surrounded her. "You're too interested and capricious to let that happen. Remember my offer. I'll transport you to the human world for a price. When you're ready, let me know." Closing his eyes and tilting his head back, he dematerialized.

Groaning in frustration, she lifted up the vase that sat on the table by the front door and threw it across the room, shattering it into tiny little pieces on the black and white tiled floor.

* * * *

The next evening, Lila struggled to pull her large suitcase onto the underground train platform from the stairs that ran from the main house's station. Gritting her teeth, she scolded herself for overpacking.

"Latimus can help you with that," Arderin said, pointing to him as he skulked off the train and onto the platform.

"Not a fucking bellhop," he said, breezing past them. He opened a small metal door that sat on the side of the dark rock wall and pounded on the lit buttons inside.

"The security system is online," Heden said, coming to stand beside Latimus. "I've got the mainframe controller here. Everything should be able to load into your smartwatch and tablet."

Nodding, Latimus closed the metal compartment and extended his hand to his brother. "Take care of Arderin. She might kill Sathan before I get back."

Chuckling, Heden shook his hand. "On it."

"I'm right here, assholes," Arderin said, rolling her eyes. Lila smiled, loving the interplay between the siblings.

"Quiet, imp," Latimus said, attempting to tickle her. She scooted away from him and stuck out her tongue.

"Are you guys all set?" Sathan said, walking down the steps. Four Slayer soldiers followed him and proceeded to enter the third car on the train.

"We are," Lila said with a nod.

"Miranda sends her love from Uteria. We're going to miss you." Approaching her, Sathan's beefy arms surrounded her. She squeezed him, wanting him to know that she was okay.

Whispering in her ear, he said, "I've warned my brother not to be a jerk to you. Make sure you give him hell."

Breathing out a laugh, she nodded into his chest. "Will do."

Latimus approached and shook Sathan's hand, although Lila noticed a chill between them. He must really be upset that he had to guard her. Great. Just what she needed on this trip. An angry, three-hundred-pound Vampyre. He hugged Arderin as she grabbed the handle of her suitcase, setting about dragging it along the ground.

Suddenly, it was whisked up by Latimus' large hand, and he deposited it on the luggage shelf of the train in the second car. Smiling discreetly, she reveled in his reluctant chivalry. Hugging the siblings on the platform, she stepped onto the train, waving at them as the engine started and propelled her into the dark tunnel.

"Thanks for helping with my bag," she said to Latimus, who was sitting on one of the seats across from her.

"I'm not your fucking servant, Lila. It won't happen again. You shouldn't have packed so much. We're only going for six days."

Smiling at his scowl, she sat across from him. The darkness of the underground tunnel blackened the window at his side, illuminated every few seconds by the lights that had been positioned on the stony wall. He really was a good man, even though he tried so hard to be an ass.

The conductor entered through the door that joined the cars together and proceeded to detail them on the journey to the compounds. After a few minutes, he walked through the connecting doors to the third car, briefing the soldiers there. When he walked back through the narrow aisle to the first engine car, Lila surreptitiously studied Latimus as he pounded the top of his tablet with his thick fingers.

He had some security setup for the trains housed there, and she figured he was testing it as they traveled. He'd pulled his hair into a small bun on the back of his head, making him look sexy. The profile of his long nose was perfect. How was that even possible? Hadn't he ever broken it in battle?

"Are you going to stare at me the whole ride?" he asked, not looking up from his ministrations.

Crap. Of course, the man who noticed everything on the compound would notice her staring. She scolded herself for being an idiot. Turning in her seat, she stretched her legs out, refusing to acknowledge him with an answer. After all, it was he who had spoken to her so callously the other night. He should be going out of his way to apologize to her.

Several minutes later, they arrived at Valeria. Lila noticed that Camron was waiting to greet them, as well as a reporter and a cameraman. Stepping off the train onto the platform, she embraced Camron in a warm hug. They had completed etiquette school together when she was a teenager, and she'd always been so fond of him. His kind brown eyes smiled down at her as his hand absently ran through her hair.

"You made it okay."

"It's such a nice, easy ride. Our people are going to love it."

"And I can come and visit you more often, which is a bonus," he said, his lips forming a smile.

"Absolutely." Turning, she introduced herself to the female reporter and male cameraman. The next few minutes were spent with her giving an interview about the train, the main objectives of connecting the compounds and answering the reporter's questions.

"As you can see, our great Commander Latimus also accompanied me," Lila said, pulling Latimus into the camera shot. He gave her a glare but smiled awkwardly at the lens. "The royal family and all of us in the aristocracy are committed to making sure that everyone has access to the trains. We are one people and want to encourage cross-compound intermingling."

While Astaria and Valeria were comprised of a majority of aristocrats and soldiers, Naria and Lynia were made up of mostly laborers and middle-class subjects. Sathan hoped to enlist his people to travel so that they could have a more unified kingdom. She wholeheartedly agreed and wanted to help him with her diplomacy.

"Commander Latimus, do you have anything you'd like to say about riding the train?" the reporter asked, shoving the microphone in his face.

"No," he said, crossing his arms over his chest.

"Okay, then," she said, turning to face the camera and speaking into the microphone. "Well, there you have it. Lila, our Kingdom Secretary Diplomat, and Commander Latimus have just completed the first train ride on the inter-compound underground railway. We'll bring you further updates as their journey continues."

The reporter and cameraman turned off their equipment and headed up the stairs.

"Latimus, thank you for coming. We're so glad that you're protecting our Lila on this trip." Camron extended his hand to him.

"Sure," Latimus said, shaking it.

"Now," Camron said to Lila. "Where's your luggage? I'll grab it for you. We saved you the best room in the castle."

Lila pointed toward her felt-covered suitcase, and he walked onto the train to grab it for her. She tried to hide her grin as Latimus scowled at his back. Letting Camron take her hand with his free one, she followed him up the stairs. She could've sworn she heard Latimus mutter a curse behind them.

Chapter 6

Latimus chewed on the ice from the drink in his hand as he surveyed the room. Of course, Camron had decided to throw a huge party to welcome Lila to the compound. He had no idea why Vampyres insisted on throwing themselves parties at least once a week. For a species that was created solely for war and protection, it seemed pointless to him. Swallowing a sip of his Jack and Coke, his gaze rested on Lila.

She was wearing one of her long, flowing gowns as she danced with Camron. White teeth flashed under the strobe lights as they moved to the rhythm of some human pop song. God, it was awful. He'd rather be thrown into battle with a thousand Deamons than stuck in this room.

As the song faded, a slow one began, and Lila smiled shyly as Camron pulled her into his arms. Blond hair flowed down his side, and she rested her cheek on his chest as Latimus had visions of snapping the man's head off and pulverizing it into a thousand pieces.

"Well, it looks like someone needs a dance partner," came a seductive voice beside him.

Looking down, he recognized the reporter from earlier. Rana? Or was it Raina? Who cared. Although, she was quite pretty with her light green eyes and dark, short hair. By the goddess, he hadn't gotten laid in so long he'd forgotten the last time. It wasn't like him to go for long droughts, but his thoughts had been consumed with a blond-haired temptress as of late. Rather annoying.

"I don't dance," he said.

She lifted a raven-black eyebrow, her expression mischievous. "Maybe not on the dance floor but maybe somewhere more private?"

Staring into her irises, he realized that he could have her naked under him in about sixty seconds flat. Fucking her would probably go a long way toward ridding his head of his insane desire for Lila. And then, he stopped himself. Who was he kidding? He'd been obsessed with her for ten centuries. He'd fucked countless women, all to no avail. He'd finally come to accept that no woman would ever rid her from his mind. Deciding that bedding this woman would create a problem he didn't need, he shook his head.

"I'm on a mission unfortunately. Gotta keep the head clear."

"Hmmm..." she said, licking her red lips. "Well, let me know if you change your mind, soldier. I'm happy to clear your head."

Winking at him, she sauntered off.

God, women really were insane. The one he wanted was off-limits, while others threw themselves at him. This wasn't the first time he'd been approached in the last year since Lila had ended her betrothal with Sathan. Continuing the abstinence regimen he was on was absolutely ridiculous. It was if he was waiting for her or something.

Sighing, he chugged the remainder of his drink. Needing some air, he stepped out onto the balcony under the moonlight to stew in his thoughts, making sure he could see Lila out of the corner of his eye as she danced with Camron.

* * * *

The next night, Lila threw on a long purple gown and set about introducing the people of Valeria to the train. The compound was the second largest in the Vampyre kingdom and housed many esteemed lineages of aristocrats.

She held a press conference from the second-floor pulpit of the compound castle. Although not as big as the forty-room castle at Astaria, it still housed over thirty rooms and was quite austere. As with her home, this compound exhibited a certain stiffness and frigidity, but there was also a magnificence and allure that permeated the air. Afterward, she sat with the subjects, answering many one-on-one questions. Latimus' presence always seemed to be near but not stifling. He was taking his assignment to guard her seriously, even if it was against his will.

After several hours, Camron led her to the large dining hall for a bountiful dinner of Slayer blood, delicious food and wine. Once finished, she found herself yawning as she stood up from the large dining table. It was filled with twenty or so aristocrats, all chatting amongst themselves as they finished their dessert.

Heading outside onto one of the balconies, she placed her hands on top of the stone railing, running her palms over the bumpy surface. She thought she saw Latimus follow her but didn't see him when she turned around to examine the shadows. The light of the moon blanketed her, and she inhaled a large breath, happy with her moment of solace.

"Such a beautiful night, only made more beautiful by your flawless face." Camron approached and stood beside her.

"Thank you," she said, grinning up at him. He was a handsome man, with his thick brown hair and warm brown eyes. Many of the girls she'd gone to school with had terrible crushes on him. Unfortunately, even then, she'd always loved another.

"Are you enjoying your trip so far?" he asked.

She nodded. "Your hospitality is amazing. I feel so welcome here."

"Good," he said, grabbing her hand as it hung over the rail. "I was hoping you'd say so." He laced his fingers through hers. "Lila, I don't want to scare you away, but I hope you know how much I treasure our friendship."

Squeezing his hand, she smiled. "I treasure our friendship too. I was just telling Latimus the other day that you're one of my oldest friends."

"Yes, we've known each other since we were babes, but you were always promised to the king. Now that you're free of your betrothal, surely, you'll want to bond with someone and have children."

Lila looked at the railing, hurt slicing through her. The only man that she desired to have children with detested her. It was really quite awful. "Of course, I want to have children. As many as I can. I've always dreamed of being a mother. And how about you? What are your plans for the future?"

Lifting his hand, he brought it to her cheek, ever so gently. "I want to have children as well. Many of them, with gorgeous blond hair and lavender eyes."

Her heart slammed in her chest as she processed his words. "Oh, Camron, you're so sweet. But I'm not sure—"

"Wow," he chuckled, removing his hand from her face. "I got the 'you're so sweet' line. That's torture."

"Sorry," she said, turning to face him fully. "I don't mean to hurt your feelings. You're a wonderful man and would make a great bonded and father."

"Then, why the brush off?"

Biting her lip, she contemplated him. "I'm just not ready yet. I was betrothed to Sathan for a thousand years. My life has changed so much recently, and I'm finding out what course I want to chart. I think that I can only do that on my own. This trip is a good first step for me, and I'm using it as an opportunity to explore my independence. I'm so excited to see Naria and Lynia. Did you know, I've never even been to either compound? I feel like I'm finally getting a chance to see a small bit of the world, and I want to seize it."

"Fair enough," he said, placing a soft kiss on her forehead. "But don't forget about me. I'll wait for eternity if I have to."

Lila sighed internally, embracing the romantic words. If only they'd been spoken to her by another. Enjoying his company, she remained on the balcony with him for an hour, laughing as they remembered stories of days long past. Finally, she tired, unable to hold her eyes open. Giving him a hug, she left the dimness of the balcony and headed to the bedchamber he'd prepared for her. Once under the covers, she imagined a dark-haired soldier saying those pretty words to her instead.

Chapter 7

Latimus scowled as he watched Lila give her last interview on the platform before leaving Valeria. The Slayer soldiers were already in the third car, and he was ready. The visit to Valeria had been filled with press, appearances and a healthy dose of his own indignation. After all, how was he supposed to feel upon hearing her conversation with Camron? The man was obviously in love with her. It should've made him happy that she had a worthy aristocrat who was willing to bond with her. Instead, it made him feel like shit. Every possessive bone in his body wanted to pull her to him and beg her to never speak to Camron again. Fucking A.

He'd known that he shouldn't eavesdrop from the shadows of the balcony, but he was charged with guarding her, and he hadn't been able to stop himself. Hearing her reaffirm how much she wanted a gaggle of children only confirmed what he already knew: he wasn't the right man for her. How could a man who'd killed as many as he even contemplate holding one of her sweet children? They would be so beautiful, with her pale ivory skin. His blood-soaked hands would ruin them. Of that, he was sure.

Watching her hug the reporter and the cameraman, she turned to him.

"Ready to go?"

"Yeah," he said, leaning down to grab her suitcase, hating that he was helping her but unable not to. He heard her saying goodbye to Camron, and she blazed through the door, sitting in one of the felt-covered seats.

"What a great trip," she said, stretching her long legs out on one of the rows of seats that sat perpendicular to her against the wall of the train. She fanned her hair out behind her, letting the waves come to rest over the back of the seat as she stared at the ceiling. And now, he was hard. Son of a bitch.

"Did you have fun?" she asked, turning her head to look at him as it rested on the top of the seat.

"Truckloads. Can't wait for Naria."

Suddenly, she burst out laughing, doubling over in her seat. Scowling, he thought of shutting her up by sticking his tongue inside her pretty mouth.

"By the goddess, you hate this, don't you? All of it. I'm so sorry. I know it's awful for you."

Against his will, he felt the corners of his lips turn up. She looked so gorgeous, her cheeks reddened from her laughter, her eyes glowing. "It's fine. Besides, it gives me a good opportunity to check out the security system." *Plus, I get to watch your ass as you walk up the stairs in those tight jeans.* He kept that to himself.

"Well, you're a trooper. Only two more compounds to go." Standing, she walked toward him, extending her hand. "Camron gave me an extra granola bar. Want it?"

"Thanks," he said, grabbing the wrapped bar from her. Suddenly, the train shifted, and she fell onto him, splaying over his large body.

"Whoa," she said, pushing her hair out of her face. "That was rough."

Desire swamped him, and he pushed her off him. "Something's wrong. Let me go check. We're not moving anymore."

Worry entered her eyes as they darted around the car. "Okay."

Standing, he pulled a knife from his belt. Turning the black hilt to her, he urged her to take it. "Hold onto this. I'm going to have you sit with two of the soldiers in the third car while we investigate."

Nodding, she clutched the handle. Grabbing her hand, he led her to the third car.

"I need two of you to come outside with me," he said to the Slayer soldiers.

"Yes, sir." The soldiers named Kyron and Lyle stood and accompanied him outside. Once in the darkened cave, he looked around, his keen Vampyre sight heightened in the darkness.

A shuffling off to the side, near the rocky wall, caught his attention. Jogging toward it, he realized it was a Deamon spy. With his thick hand, he grabbed the man by the neck, lifting him so that his feet hung off the ground. The Deamon gasped for air, his legs kicking beneath him.

"How did you get past our security system?" Latimus asked.

Crumpling on the ground, the Deamon held his hands to his throat as he struggled for air. "Crimeous can infiltrate any security system you implement. He is all-powerful, and it is futile for you to believe otherwise."

Snarling, Latimus pulled the spy up by his shirt collar. Placing his face within inches of the man's, he said, "Tell Crimeous that he can go fuck himself. Are there others with you?"

"No," the man said, coughing as he sputtered. "But if you kill me, he will only send more."

Latimus narrowed his eyes. "Will he? Let's see if that's a threat or a promise." Throwing the Deamon on the ground, he kicked him in his abdomen, causing him to double over with pain. Lifting one of the many knives from his belt, he proceeded to gut the evil creature from neck to abdomen, his intestines spilling onto the dirt floor. Blood gushed everywhere as Latimus stood over him, ensuring he took his last breath.

Once the Deamon was dead, he addressed the two Slayer soldiers. "Get this cleaned up and bury the body above ground. I'll send two four-wheelers from Naria to pick you both up afterward."

"Yes, sir," the soldiers responded.

Sparing one last glance at the crumpled Deamon, he pivoted to walk back to the train. And then, his heart slammed in his chest. Lila's stunning purple irises were watching him through the window of the train car. Locked onto him, she seemed to be communicating something to him. Was it revulsion? Disgust? Concern? He couldn't be sure. Hating that she'd now seen him torture Deamons on multiple occasions, bile rose in his throat. Thank the goddess that there were only four more days left on this journey. He didn't want her anywhere near the bloodshed that he'd become so accustomed to. Drowning in self-loathing, he stepped onto the third train car.

Informing the soldiers of the plan, he stalked to the engine car to instruct the conductor to continue on. Returning to the second car, he noticed that Lila was standing in the aisle between the seats.

"I thought you might want this back," she said, offering him the knife, held in both palms as she extended it toward him.

"Thanks," he said, grabbing it and stuffing it in his belt.

Those magnificent purple eyes darted over his face. "Thank you. That was very brave."

He studied her in silence, unable to read her. Finally, he said, "There's nothing brave about being a murderer, Lila. You'd do well to remember that."

"You're not a murderer," she said, her voice so sweet. "You protect our people so valiantly. Even if it's gruesome it's extremely noble."

"Don't make me someone I'm not. It's not fair to either of us." When she opened her mouth to argue, he held up a hand. "I need to continue testing the security system. We only have ten minutes left until we reach Naria."

"Okay," she whispered. Thankful that she let it go, he sat upon his seat, grabbed his tablet and tried not to notice how good she smelled as she sat across from him.

* * * *

The governor of Naria, Yemik, greeted them as they got off the train. Latimus tried his best to be cordial to him and the male reporter and cameraman who were with him. Lila went about completing her interviews. He made sure to stay far away from the camera, lest she drag him into the shot again. Being that he had to stay close enough to guard her, it took a bit of maneuvering.

He also made sure that the Slayer soldiers who'd disposed of the dead Deamon made it safely to the compound. Knowing that Crimeous' spy had been able to infiltrate the tunnel concerned him, and he made sure to dictate detailed notes for Heden so that they could improve the security system further.

Later that night, Lila gave her usual round of press and speeches, and he watched her from a safe yet secure distance. Being a diplomat came naturally to her, even though he knew her to be a bit shy. When they were children, he had always defended her when others made fun of her bashfulness. He'd felt such compassion when her pale skin turned red and the other kids taunted her. Wanting to help her, he would always jump in front of her antagonizers and defend her.

Latimus supposed she'd inherited her diplomatic skills from her father, the kingdom's first Secretary Diplomat. Both of her parents were deceased, and he wondered if she ever felt lonely not having any remaining blood relatives.

Naria was a pretty compound of ten thousand people, comprised of mostly middle and lower-class citizens, many of whom had enlisted in Latimus' army. He was thankful to have the soldiers from Naria and Lynia, as aristocrats were deemed too valuable to fight in their wars. To him, that was absurd. If one possessed the brawn and skill to defend their people and their families, he considered nothing more noble. It was one of the reasons he'd always hated aristocrats, thinking them haughty and selfish.

Naria had a protective stone wall, as did all the Vampyre and Slayer compounds. However, the wall at Astaria was the only one protected by Etherya's invisible shield. The goddess considered it necessary to protect the royal family after Markdor and Calla were murdered.

The visit to Naria flew by, and the night of their departure arrived. Of course, Yemik had to throw a party to send Lila off. Ensuring that Lila was dancing with Yemik, Latimus escaped to the second-floor balcony of the compound's main house, outside the great ballroom. He asked Lyle to watch her during the slow song so that he could steal five minutes of peace without her fragrant scent threatening to drown him. The castle wasn't as large as the ones in Astaria or Valeria, but it was still sizable, comprised of about fifteen rooms. The wide balcony gave him a much-needed level of privacy as he stood in the shadows, smoking a cigar that one of the compound's soldiers had given him.

The spicy scent of the cigar was no match for her lavender aroma. Steeling himself, he felt her approach and stand next to him.

"Goddess, I'm tired," Lila said, lifting her magnificent face to the sky, her eyes closed. "After tomorrow, we have one more compound to go."

He flicked a stray ash from his cigar over the balcony rail, silent.

"Arderin will be happy to see you. I'm sure you miss her," she said, opening those violet eyes to look up at him. "You love her so."

"I do," he said. Lifting the stogie to his lips, he took a long drag.

"Let me try," she said, reaching to grab it from his fingers.

"No way. These aren't for spoiled little aristocrats. You couldn't handle it."

Her pretty mouth formed a frown. "And what do you know of it? Maybe I'm tougher than you've ever imagined. After all, I've put up with you for the last thousand years."

Charmed by her in spite of himself, he chuckled. "True. But don't blame me if you cough your guts up." Handing the cigar to her, she took it and inhaled. Smoke exited her lungs as she began coughing loudly.

"Good god, woman," he said, patting her on the back. Taking the stogie, he threw it on the ground below them. Wanting to soothe her, he rubbed her back as she coughed against the balcony railing.

When her sputtering ceased, she tilted her head back, gazing up at him. His hand stilled on her back. "I think the party's over. I'm heading to bed," he said, feeling lame. He just couldn't handle those eyes.

"Why do always pull away from me?" she asked, turning toward him, aligning her front with his. He almost shuddered from the heat of her voluptuous body.

As his eyes roamed over her face, he realized she was a bit drunk. No wonder she felt emboldened enough to press into him. His cock jerked to attention, and he sighed. Grabbing her upper arms, he pushed her away.

"I'm going to say this one time, and one time only. We're no good for each other, Lila. You've made up some story in your head from centuries ago, when we were kids. It's bullshit. You deserve a bonded mate who can offer you the life you're entitled to and be a good father to your children. A warrior like me just isn't capable of those things. It's time you put this to bed. Camron is a good man and can make you happy. You need to bond with him and get on with your life."

Her blond eyebrows drew together as she shook her head. "That's not true. You're a good man—"

"No," he said, shaking her, needing her to understand that she deserved so much better. "Enough. Don't make me say something that will make you hate me forever. I've tried to push you away, but you still keep trying to force something that will never be. Let it go. Bond with Camron and live the life you were meant to live. There's no glory in being the mate of a war-torn soldier."

Sadness swamped him as her chin trembled slightly. Needing to let her go, he dropped his hands. Pivoting, he stalked back through the house to the room that Yemik had prepared for him, determined to push her out of his life.

* * * *

Lila stood on the balcony, the warmth from Latimus' broad hands still upon her upper arms. Willing away the wetness in her eyes, she looked to the crescent moon. It seemed to shine back at her, sending its light from so far away.

Sighing, she placed her hands on the stone balcony rail. Steeling herself, she finally accepted the truth: Latimus would never let himself love her.

As the realization coursed through her body, she felt sorrow and a hefty dose of anger. Yes, they were completely dissimilar people. Her, a high-born aristocrat, and he, a war commander. But underneath, were they truly so different? Both of them were guarded, and if she had to guess, she assumed he sometimes felt as lonely as she did. Would it be so terrible to comfort each other?

Fury swarmed her as she narrowed her eyes. Taking in the grass-covered field behind the main house, she clenched her fists on the railing. Deciding that he'd dismissed her for the last time, she inhaled a deep breath. He thought he had her pegged. Determined to prove him wrong, she contemplated the end of the trip. Chewing her bottom lip, she decided that she might have something else up her sleeve. How dare he assume he knew what man and what path was best for her? It was her life, and she was determined to show him and everyone else that she was ready to claim it. Firm in her resolve, she headed inside to rest.

* * * *

Early the next evening, they were set to depart, and Lila gave Yemik a warm embrace. Latimus watched her from the train. She'd been cold to him during the hour that led up to the departure. Maybe she'd finally realized that he would never allow himself to be with her in the way that she needed. Feeling extra grumpy, he scowled at her as she entered the train.

"I'm going to sit in the next car with the soldiers while we ride to Lynia," she said, her chin held high. By the goddess, she was so regal.

"Fine," he said, clenching his jaw as she breezed past him.

Minutes passed as he fidgeted on his tablet, missing her smell. She always seemed to use some flowery shampoo on her long hair, and it drove him wild. Finally, they arrived at Lynia, and she bounded from the train to meet the compound's governor, Breken.

After they embraced, she greeted the female reporter and cameraman, and Breken walked them from the platform up to the surface.

"As you know, we're not as formal here as the other compounds. Our main house only has six rooms and, unfortunately, we can't house you there. We've arranged for you both to stay in one of the cabins out by the wall. It's only a ten-minute walk from the town square, and we've installed a phone in each cottage that can contact the main house's servants at any time."

"That's perfectly fine," Lila said, smiling up at him. "We appreciate your hospitality."

The next several hours were consumed with her diplomatic activities at the main square until dawn was fast approaching.

They exchanged pleasantries with the townspeople and bid good night to Breken. Hopping in a four-wheeler, one of Latimus' Lynia-based Vampyre soldiers drove them to the cabins. The soldier deposited Lila's massive bag into her cabin, and she disappeared inside.

Settling into his own cottage, Latimus realized that he had finally succeeded in pushing her away. The thought should've been comforting. Instead, he felt empty.

After prepping for bed, he lay on the king-sized bed, reminding himself that he lived in a world of his own making. He was doing what was best for her.

During their time at Lynia, the hours had bled into each other as he guarded her, always in the shadows. She dazzled the men and women of the compound with her glowing smile and kind disposition. He longed for the trip to end, so he could forget the sway of her hips as she walked and the glistening of her fangs as she'd spoken to him in the moonlight at Naria. She'd been so cold and aloof with him since they left Naria, it unsettled something in him.

As he stood outside his cottage during their last night at Lynia, he heard the door of her nearby cabin close. Straining, he heard Lila talking on the phone.

"Thank you, Sathan. I think it's what's best for me right now. Although I miss everyone at Astaria terribly, I just need some space."

There was a pause, and then, "Absolutely. I'll let him know. I will. Talk soon."

Moments later, the click of her cabin door sounded, and he felt his eyebrows draw together. What was she discussing with his brother?

Restless, he entered his cabin to pour some Slayer blood into the metal goblet that sat on the little table beside his bed. Soft knocks sounded on his door, and he opened it, knowing he'd find her.

He was only wearing a pair of sweatpants and watched her eyes dart over his naked chest. Lifting her gaze, she said, "I need to speak to you."

Opening the door wider, he let her breeze past him.

"I'm not going to back to Astaria. At least, not tonight. I've already spoken with Sathan, and he's approved my stay here. I need a few weeks to clear my head after the trip. He asked that you leave two Slayer soldiers behind to guard me."

Latimus slowly sipped from his goblet, processing her words. "It's not safe for a lone female to stay behind in an unprotected cottage on our smallest compound."

"As I said, two soldiers will be stationed outside my cabin at all times. I'll be perfectly safe."

"I don't like it. Crimeous has many spies. I don't want you left vulnerable."

Her perfect nostrils flared, and twin splotches of anger appeared on her cheeks. "Well, it's not your choice. I've already spoken to Sathan. You and the other two Slayer soldiers are set to depart in three hours. I'm exhausted, so I'm heading to bed early. I just wanted you to know I wouldn't be with you."

She walked past him toward the door, and he grabbed her arm. "Lila—"

"Don't touch me," she said, shaking off his grip. Fury swam in her gorgeous eyes. "You've made it abundantly clear that you want nothing more than to be free of my company. Well, here's your chance. Safe travels home." Stalking toward the door, she shut it behind her.

Latimus looked to the ceiling, praying for patience, irritated by her regal haughtiness. Lifting his phone from the table beside his bed, he called his brother.

"Latimus. I trust Lila told you of her plan?"

"It's not wise to leave her here alone, Sathan. She'll be exposed. Especially as an aristocrat on a laborers' compound."

"I want you to leave two of the Slayer soldiers with her. They'll be able to protect her."

Latimus pinched the bridge of his nose with his thumb and index finger, annoyed. "I don't like it."

"Sorry to hear that, but it's her choice. I'll see you when you arrive at dawn. Arderin is excited to see you."

Sighing, he shook his head at his brother's stubbornness. "Fine. See you in a few hours."

Restless, he packed his things and cleaned the various weapons he'd brought with him. An hour before dawn, he knocked on Lila's cabin door. After a minute, she opened it, her eyes swollen with sleep. By the goddess, she was breathtaking, even upon waking up. How was that possible?

He pushed inside and lay several weapons on the wooden table that sat by the door. "This is a Glock, this is an AR-15 and this is a TEC," he said, pointing to the various objects. "I'm going to show you how to use them and leave them here with you."

"Latimus—"

"I need some additional peace of mind that you'll have protection. Don't fight me on this."

"Okay," she said, her throat bobbing up and down as she swallowed. Her thin arms were crossed over her silky white robe, thrusting her voluptuous breasts toward him. Reminding himself of his purpose, he set about showing her how to use the weapons.

Fifteen minutes later, it was time for him to depart for the train. He'd already informed the two Slayer soldiers that they were to stay outside her cabin and guard her at all times. Looking down at her, he was enveloped by a wave of sadness. Unable to lie to himself, he realized that he would miss her terribly.

"Be safe," he said.

"I will."

Left with no more words to say, he pivoted and stalked from her cabin. He and the two Slayer soldiers rode the four-wheeler to the platform and departed for Astaria. Sitting on the train, he rubbed his hand over his chest, cursing his heart. If he didn't know better, he would think it was broken.

Chapter 8

Lila sat in the tiny cabin, her back against the pillows on her bed, waiting for the sun to set. Absently playing with her hair as she stared at the wall, she contemplated her actions. A restlessness had consumed her as the trip wore on, and she'd found herself dreading returning home to Astaria. As much as she missed Arderin and Heden, she couldn't fathom returning to her life as usual.

During the last days of the trip, something had shifted in her. Like a sapling planted in the damp ground during the first days of spring, it slowly grew in her gut. She was still living life as if she was the king's betrothed. Still living in Sathan's house, his siblings her family, making sure that she put duty first.

But Sathan had moved on. He'd fallen in love with a magnificent woman, and she was truly happy for him. It was time for her to make a new life for herself, and as sad as it made her to distance herself from those she loved most, she needed to be open to something different.

She also finally accepted that Latimus was intent on pushing her away. She considered herself a caring and patient person, but one could only be rejected so long. Unable to squelch her love for him, she made a pact with herself to lock her feelings for him deep inside her heart. They would be a constant reminder that love didn't always equate to happy endings. In her life, she would have to be the one who loved herself. She would have to forge ahead and create her own purpose.

The thought was terrifying. For someone such as she, whose life had been dictated by everyone around her, independence was frightening. She greatly admired Miranda, who was so self-reliant and strong. By her own choice, she had started training to be a soldier when she was only a teenager. She had defied her father, assumed her throne and united two warring kingdoms. How did one naturally possess such confidence?

Lila didn't know the answer but she was pretty sure it didn't come by living a life that others chose for you. Although she was apprehensive, she'd informed Sathan she wanted to remain on Lynia for a few weeks, alone. After all, the best way to begin a new path was to start making your own damn choices. Giving herself a mental pep-talk, she rose and prepared to head to the main square of the compound.

The ten-minute walk was refreshing under the half-moon. Dressed in jeans, a thin sweater and cute sandals, she felt comfortable and told herself to relax. Lynia was a compound filled with warm, working-class laborers, many of whom she'd already met. Comprised of about five thousand Vampyres, it was the smallest of the compounds, giving it a certain charm.

When she got to the main square, she browsed the booths of the various vendors. Ice cream and cakes, jewelry and trinkets, clothing and pet supplies. All were on display. Smiling, she stopped in front of a booth where a man was painting a beautiful landscape portrait. Turning, his broad grin almost blinded her.

"Hello, beautiful lady. Are you interested in a painting?"

"Not tonight," she said, taken with his kind blue eyes and cap of white hair. He must have gone through his immortal change very late in life. "But your work is amazing. How long have you been painting?"

"Since before the Awakening," he said, his eyes sparkling. "I was only a young man of twenty-five during that terrible time, but I still remember the few years I saw the sun above the horizon. I haven't stopped painting it ever since."

Lila observed the gorgeous blue sky in his painting, longing to walk in the sun again. "It's very beautiful. You have a great memory."

"One always has space in their mind for memories of joy."

The images of her and Latimus playing by the river, all those centuries ago, when they were just children, flashed through her mind. "I think you're right."

"Oh, pretty lady, I've made you sad," the man said, standing and placing his brush and palette on the table inside his booth. "Perhaps you would like a free painting?"

"Oh, no," she said, taken with his kindness. "But you're very talented." She observed the various pieces of art he had showcased around the small booth. "I used to paint a bit too. Back in the seventh and eighth centuries."

"That's wonderful, bella," he said, clasping his hands together. "Why did you stop?"

It was a good question that she struggled to find an answer for. "I don't know. I just had other duties, and it kind of fell by the wayside."

"What a shame. A woman with your beauty must paint magnificent portraits. Here, I insist. You take these home with you tonight." He reached under his table and pulled out a small palette, two brushes and a small white, blank canvas. "You can start painting again."

"Oh, I couldn't—"

"Please, you would do me a great disservice if you decline. I feel it is my duty to spread good will around this sometimes horrid world. Please, my lady."

Fangs toyed with her bottom lip as she contemplated. "Okay, but let me pay you for them."

"Absolutely not," he said, stuffing the objects in a paper bag he pulled from underneath the table. "Once you finish, you come back and show me. I want to see. That will be your payment to me."

"You're really too kind, Mister..."

"Antonio."

"I'm Lila," she said, taking the bag he stuffed into her hands.

"Oh yes, I know. The pretty train lady. We were all so happy to see you here. We don't often see people from the main compound."

"Well, I'm happy to be here. I've decided to extend my stay a few weeks. Perhaps you can give me some recommendations on things to do?"

Thoroughly charmed, she spent the next half hour letting Antonio tell her about all the hot spots of Lynia. There was a wine bar that he insisted had the most amazing Rioja. A Brazilian restaurant where she could enjoy salsa dancing after having a dinner of Slayer blood and skirt steak. A museum filled with many ornaments and objects showcasing the history of Lynia. A coffee shop where he warned her to order the blond roast, as the dark roast was "too burnt."

He was overly animated in his speech, his hands waving as he spoke. Lila thought he might knock over the painting that sat upon the easel, but it stayed safely in place. Eventually, she gave him a warm smile and left his booth, promising to return often to see his new paintings. For several hours, she perused the main part of town, speaking to vendors and eating some of their tasty food. Finally, she decided to begin the ten-minute trek home.

About halfway, she heard a rustling behind her, causing her heartbeat to accelerate. Both of the Slayer soldiers that were guarding her cabin had offered to accompany her to town, but she felt safe on the compound and had vehemently refused. She'd also left the gun that Latimus had given her behind. Stupid, although she doubted she'd be able to use it effectively anyway. Steeling herself, she turned around.

"En garde! Don't go any further, or I'll be forced to take you prisoner!"

Laughter escaped her as she regarded her foe. A little boy of only eight or nine with a mop of red hair, brown eyes and freckles over his nose that were so pronounced she could see them clearly in the moonlight.

"I surrender," she said, lifting up her hands, still holding Antonio's supplies.

"That's no fun," he said, lowering the toy sword he held in his hands. "You're supposed to be scared and fight me."

"Oh. I'm sorry. But I don't know how to fight, so you'd beat me anyway."

"Girls. They never know how to fight. They always want to play with their dolls and braid their hair. Gross."

Smiling, she crouched down to his level. "Are you a warrior then?"

"Of course. One day, I will be strong and I'll fight in the wars like my father did."

Her heart squeezed at the fact he spoke in past tense. "Is your father a soldier?"

"He was the greatest soldier ever! He died the night that the queen fought Crimeous. He had to go live at Uteria for a while, and he never came back."

"I'm so sorry." Compassion for him rifled through her.

"Dying in battle is noble. My uncle says so all the time."

"And is that who you live with now?"

"No, I live with my mom, over there." He pointed with his sword to a clearing and a few tiny thatch-roofed houses. "But I go see my uncle a lot. He lives in one of the cabins by the wall."

"Oh, then he's my neighbor. I'm also staying in one of the cabins. I'm heading there now."

"He's nice. He got hurt in the Awakening but didn't die or anything. He and my dad were both strong soldiers. I will be too."

"Well, what would you say if I told you that I'm friends with Commander Latimus?"

The boy's eyes grew large as saucers. "Really?"

"Yep," she said, nodding. "If you like, I can put in a good word for you."

"Cool," the boy said. "Tell him I'm really brave."

Chuckling, she lifted from her crouch. "I sure will. What's your name?"

"Jack," he said, thrusting his small hand up at her.

"Well, hello, Jack. I'm Lila. It's an absolute pleasure to meet you." She shook the boy's hand.

"I was heading to my uncle's anyway. Can I walk with you? I can make sure I tell you all I know about being a soldier, so that when Commander Latimus asks, you can tell him. Okay?"

She was powerless to say no. Turning to walk to the cabin, he fell into step beside her, chatting endlessly. When she arrived at her cabin, he pointed to the third cottage down. "That's my uncle's place. If you ever need him or anything."

"Thank you, Jack. That's very kind."

"And I can protect you too, if you need. Just let me know." He swung his sword, slicing through the air multiple times. She tried to remember ever meeting a cuter child.

"I'll be sure to remember. Hopefully, I'll see you soon. Go on ahead to your uncle's house. I'll wait to see you get in the door."

He bounded off, knocking on the door of the cottage and entering. Grinning, she entered her own cabin and unloaded Antonio's bag. Her first night of independence had been truly wonderful. Feeling proud of herself, she collapsed on the bed and called Arderin to tell her about her day.

* * * *

Latimus' mood was serious as he sat with Kenden, Sathan, Miranda and Darkrip, planning the attack on Crimeous. The next full moon was less than two weeks away, and he was anxious to recover the Blade of Pestilence. The ancient prophecy stated that Crimeous' death would be at the hand of one of Valktor's descendants with the Blade. That couldn't happen as long as the bastard possessed the damn thing himself. Miranda had already tried to defeat him and lost. Darkrip was their next hope. If he wasn't the chosen one, then it could only be Evie. Rina had also borne her in the Deamon caves, but she was evil and lost to the world of humans. It was imperative that Darkrip succeed.

"So, we have the plan," Latimus said, his hand over the map of the Deamon caves that sat on the large conference table between them. "Darkrip will materialize here, where Crimeous is holding the Blade. We'll fight to retrieve it, and if Darkrip has a clean shot, he'll take it. If not, we'll retreat with the Blade and plan another attack to kill Crimeous once it's in our possession."

Heads nodded in approval.

"Okay, let's get to work. Kenden and I will alternate nights training the troops and make sure they're prepared. As Darkrip has confirmed, Crimeous can't dematerialize when he's being impacted by bullets, so the troops will be well armed. We know that he feeds off Darkrip's hate as well as our failures in battle, so let's remember to keep our heads clear."

"I wish I could fight with you all again," Miranda said. "I want to kick that bastard's ass. I have dreams of pulverizing his face, and our little warrior also wants to bash his head in." Leaning back, she rubbed her abdomen.

Latimus held his smile back, reminding himself that he was annoyed at her. Deep inside, he loved the stubborn little Slayer. She was a force to be reckoned with and had fought valiantly against Crimeous during their encounter.

"Remember last year's battle, Darkrip," Latimus said, his gaze shifting to the Deamon's green irises. "Your hate is warranted, but don't let him see it. It feeds his strength."

Darkrip rolled his eyes. "Thanks for the tip, Commander. I so enjoy being informed of things I already know by an arrogant Vampyre. Tell me more about the Deamon that I lived with for a thousand years and know better than you ever will. I'm hanging on every word."

"Okay, that's enough," Miranda said, shooting a glare at her half-brother. "I think we're set here. I'm excited to get the Blade back. Let's remember to work as a team."

They all stood, and Latimus folded up the map, handing it to Kenden for safe keeping. Not wanting to stay in the main house, he headed across the meadow to the cabin that he kept on the outskirts of the compound. Although he also kept a room in the basement of the main house, he sometimes found it stifling. The cabin allowed him a certain peace and calm that he couldn't find anywhere else on the compound.

Walking inside, he removed the weapons he kept on his belt, setting them on the chest of drawers near the door. Moving through the den, he entered the tiny kitchen, pulling some Slayer blood from the refrigerator. Straight from the bottle, he took a healthy swig. Deciding he wanted something a bit different, he grabbed the scotch from the counter.

Heading into the bedroom, he sat on his king-sized bed. Placing the scotch on the bedside table, he removed his clothes. Naked, he sat back against his pillows, going over the battle plans in his head, calculating. He absolutely didn't think of Lila. Or how beautiful she had looked in her virginal white robe when he'd left her.

Lifting his phone, he texted the Slayer soldiers at Lynia, making sure she was okay. Sighing, he threw the phone on the bed. He had seventy Vampyre soldiers stationed at Lynia as well as the two Slayer soldiers who guarded Lila. The Deamons had never attacked that compound, and he doubted they ever would. Being a compound of laborers, there weren't any riches or treasures there and the people lost would certainly not be aristocrats. Crimeous understood that hurting the aristocracy and killing off the oldest and purest bloodlines of the immortals was his way to true power. They were the ones who funded the wars and kept the military thriving financially. Latimus was convinced that this was why he attacked Uteria so often. The compound housed the most esteemed lineage of the Slayer species.

Having Lila there concerned him, but he trusted the Slayer soldiers to protect her. It wouldn't be a good use of Crimeous' resources to attack a compound just to kill one aristocrat, although having her there did send a chill down his spine. Worried for her, he stared at the ceiling, wishing he could think of anything else but her.

Glancing at his phone, he read the text that popped up. Lila was fine. Great. Grabbing the scotch, he drank from the bottle and accepted his inability to rid her from his mind.

Chapter 9

The next two weeks at Lynia were wonderful for Lila, and she was so thankful that she'd found the courage to stay. Some of the nights, she had dinner with Breken and his wife Lora, both of whom she found delightful. Other nights she spent at the main square, getting to know the people of the compound. Everyone was so welcoming and they treated her like royalty.

She found it silly that people would treat her with deference due to her bloodline, over which she had no control, and did her best to put them at ease. Many would discuss their views with her, and she listened to them all, understanding that these Vampyres had different hopes and fears than those at Astaria.

Many Lynians approved of Sathan's decree to end the War of the Species and align with the Slayers. Often, they spoke of their admiration for Miranda, whose valor in the battle with Crimeous had already risen to the status of epic. But they were also wary and cautious, knowing that Etherya had once loved the Slayers more than the Vampyres. The Slayers had been the first species she created from her womb, and that unsettled many. They feared that she would come to favor them again once peace was restored and forget the loyal Vampyres. They also questioned why the goddess hadn't lifted the curse that relegated them to never walk in the sun.

Lila listened to them all, assuring them that they must stay the course and that their sentiments must remain true. Peace amongst the species restored the balance of the world, and their desires would be met if their hearts remained loyal.

A few nights into her stay, Camron called her. Lying on the bed, she absently twirled her hair around her finger as she held her cell to her ear.

"It sounds like you're having a fantastic time, Lila. How strange that you chose to stay at a laborer's compound, but how diplomatic of you. Even though their bloodlines aren't as pure, they're still a part of this kingdom."

She wrinkled her nose at his snobbery. Such were the beliefs of many Vampyre aristocrats. There was an inherent classism that ran through her people. Her father had always instilled in her that all were equal, and he strived his whole life to get others to gravitate toward his way of thinking.

"The painter I was telling you about is older than both of us. He was twenty-five at the Awakening. You and I were only children. He has magnificent stories."

"I hope he hasn't stolen your heart. I might have to challenge him for you."

She chuckled. "No, my heart is still my own. It's enjoying being free at the moment."

"Well, that's good to hear. How long will you stay at Lynia?"

"Probably another few weeks. Eventually, I have to go home, but it's been nice getting a change of pace."

"I'm sure. I wanted to bring up our conversation on the balcony again," he said, his voice softening a bit. "As you know, it's time that I find a mate and bond. I've made it no secret that I want that woman to be you. Once you return to Astaria, perhaps you can ride the train to visit me at Valeria. I would like to court you properly, so that you'll find me irresistible and feel compelled to bond with me."

Lila sighed, wishing she could find it in her heart to love her handsome friend. He was a good man, and she wanted children so badly. Latimus had made it crystal clear that she had no future with him. What were her alternatives? It wasn't like there were a plethora of nice, handsome men like Camron hanging around to court her. Deciding that she should at least try to make a relationship work with him, she capitulated.

"I'd like that," she said. "How about I come up to Valeria the first night of the full moon after this next one?"

"I would be honored. I'll see that everything is prepared for you. I can't wait to see you."

"I feel the same."

After they ended the call, she held the phone to her chest, her mind churning. Camron was a good man whom she'd known for centuries and found quite pleasant and charming. She'd always wanted a large family, and he wanted the same. On paper, he was a perfect mate for her. Much more than a closed-off war commander who was determined to push her away.

She had been content to bond with Sathan, although she had never loved him romantically. If she had to, she could build a good life with Camron as well. A newfound confidence was growing inside her, and she was determined to build the life she wanted.

A few nights later, she finally decided to cut her hair. After a thousand years, she was going to cut away the shield she'd erected around her face. Terrified, she walked to town, self-doubt coursing through her.

When she arrived at the main square's hair salon, the stylist begged her not to do it.

"Oh, my lady, your hair is so beautiful. Please, don't make me cut it off. I can't be responsible for taking such beauty from the world."

Lila smiled at the woman, whose thick dark curls and ocean-blue eyes reminded her of the Italian humans she'd learned about in school.

"Your compliments humble me, but I'm determined to cut it. I do want to leave it a bit long, past my shoulders." She held her hand at the top of her back, showing her in the reflection of the mirror. "Can you do that?"

"If I must."

Trying to think of a way to ease the woman, she said, "What about keeping it and using it to help your stylists train? Could you make a wig out of it for them to practice on?"

"I'm sure they would be honored, having the beautiful hair of an aristocrat to learn on, but I don't want to disrespect you. You were betrothed to our king, and we want to honor you."

"Nonsense." Lila waved her hand. "It's my hair, and that's what I want you to do with it. Now, let's do it, before I lose my courage." She grabbed the woman's hand and squeezed.

The woman muttered something unintelligible and led her to the sink for a wash. Afterward, she directed her to sit in the chair by the mirror, and Lila closed her eyes as she got to work with the scissors. Then, she blew her shortened hair dry and styled it with a menagerie of hot curling tools.

Finally, after what seemed like an eternity, the woman turned her chair around so that she could see her reflection.

"I was stupid to think that your beauty would be dimmed by cutting your hair. It only made you more magnificent. What do you think, my dear?"

Lila studied her reflection, lifting her hand to touch the waves. Never had her hair possessed such fullness. Blond waves fell just past her shoulders, looking tousled and silky.

"I love it," she said, her smile wide in the reflection. "Wow. I've had long hair for centuries. I feel so free."

Chuckling, the woman took the smock from around her shoulders. "You look wonderful. I'm honored to have cut your hair."

"I'm honored to have you as my stylist. I'll make sure to ride the train and come to you next time I need a cut."

"Thank you, my dear."

Lila stood and reached into her pocket for the cash she held there.

"I won't accept your money," the woman said. "You can pay me on your next visit. The first one is always on the house."

Lila sighed. Why would the people of this compound never let her pay for anything? As the sole heir in her family, she had inherited her parents' massive wealth when they entered the Passage centuries ago. It was more than she'd ever be able to spend, and she wanted so badly to pay the woman who had helped her cut the shield she'd erected for herself.

"A tip for you then," she said, thrusting one of the more valuable bills at the woman. "I won't leave until you take it."

The woman smiled, patting Lila on the cheek. "Okay." Taking the bill, she stuffed it into her ample cleavage.

Feeling freer than she had in ages, Lila began the trek to her cabin. She stopped to chat with Antonio along the way.

"My darling, your new hairstyle is so beautiful," he said, the ever-present sparkle glowing in his eyes. "You must let me paint you one day."

"Thank you," she said, feeling herself blush.

"Have you finished your painting yet?" he asked.

"I'm close," she said, happy that he was encouraging her. She needed the push.

"I can't wait to see."

Lila bid him good night and began the leisurely stroll to her cabin. Jack showed up halfway, as he usually did when she walked home, and she let him chatter on about the other kids at school and the girls who ruined recess because they couldn't run as fast.

She made sure he entered his uncle's cabin and then donned her pajamas. As she'd done the past few nights, she pulled out the painting supplies that Antonio had given her, along with the paints she'd bought in town. She was using the small canvas he'd given her to paint the grassy riverbank at Astaria as it glowed under the moonlight. As she worked, she realized it wasn't half-bad. She used to paint quite regularly, and many of the aristocrats had lauded her work when she'd shown them during their visits to Astaria. Happy to be painting again, she finished the piece, excited to show Antonio.

Clothed in her silky pajamas, she lay down to sleep, her body humming with a new kind of happiness that she'd never felt.

* * * *

Latimus led the troops to the Deamon cave, silent and sure under the light of the full moon. Kenden was leading another battalion in from the opposite side, and he felt confident they would recover the Blade. Lifting his hand, the troops stilled behind him.

He attached the TNT to the ground. The lair where Crimeous was holding the Blade was only fifteen feet tall. Detonating the explosives, he blew a hole in the ground, creating a separate entrance. Ready to attack, he lifted his rifle and yelled, "Charge!"

Soldiers bounded through the opening, dropping several feet into the hole and heading toward the lair that housed the Blade. Sounds of Kenden's troops entering though the cave's natural opening flooded his ears, and he knew that they were attacking as well. Giving a loud war cry, he jumped through the opening in the ground.

Running with the other men, he approached the light that shone in the darkness of the tunnel. As he reached it, a lair came into view. It was sparsely furnished with a desk, chair and a bookshelf. The soldiers stopped as they realized there was no foe to face. The lair was empty.

Locating Darkrip, he approached the desk. Upon it sat the Blade of Pestilence. It seemed to sneer at them in the light of the torches that lined the cavern wall.

"Something isn't right," Latimus said to Darkrip, as Kenden came to stand beside them. "Where is your father? Why would he leave the Blade out?"

"I don't know," Darkrip said, reaching down to grab the Blade. Cautiously, he sheathed it in the holster he'd placed on his back in anticipation of recovering it. "It's possible he knew we were coming and left the Blade out to taunt us. He obviously isn't worried that I might kill him with it."

Latimus studied the half-Deamon. Was it possible that he could still be turned against them by Crimeous? Deciding to revisit that later, he shook his head. "Let's get to the surface. We've recovered the Blade, and I need to regain cell service to alert Sathan. I don't want our troops here any longer than needed."

Nodding, Darkrip dematerialized, and Kenden gave the order to retreat. As they exited the caves and watched the soldiers march back to the vehicles that transported them, he looked at Kenden. "Something is wrong. I can feel it."

"Agreed," the Slayer said, his expression wary.

Latimus' phone vibrated on his belt, alerting him of an incoming text. Palming his phone, he read it.

And then, he let out a loud curse.

Chapter 10

Lila awoke with a gasp. A feeling of dread swept over her, and she shot up in the large bed. Turning on the bedside lamp, she rubbed her arms, trying to ease the chill bumps that had arisen.

"Kyron? Lyle?" she called out to the Slayer soldiers stationed outside her cabin. Silence answered her.

Walking to the window, she tentatively lifted the blackout shades, hoping it was dark out. Thankfully, it was. Opening the shade, she looked out the window onto the grassy field, her eyes growing wide. Deamons swarmed the field, approaching the cabins.

Gathering her wits, she grabbed her phone and texted Latimus.

Lila: Deamons attacking Lynia.

Setting the phone on her bedside table with her shaking hands, she picked up the rifle and TEC that Latimus had left for her. As her heart pounded in her chest, she debated her choices: staying in her cabin and waiting for the bastards to attack her, or taking the offensive. A courage the likes of which she had never known coursed through her, and she gritted her teeth. Opening the cabin door, rifle and TEC in hand, she charged down the stairs to her cabin and onto the plushy grass.

She saw the two Slayer soldiers across the field, quick and efficient as they fought the Deamons. The Vampyre soldiers that were stationed at the wall fought valiantly as well. For the moment, they were holding them off.

A man came out of one of the nearby cabins, and she yelled to him, "Are you Jack's uncle?"

Nodding, he plodded toward her. She noticed a limp in his step, and he was missing one arm.

"There's a loaded gun on the table by the door of my cabin," she said, jerking her head toward the cottage.

The man walked in and grabbed the Glock, stepping back out to stand beside her. Two of the Deamons broke through the main group of fighters and approached the cabins.

"Start shooting," the man beside her said.

Adrenaline coursing through her, she tried to remember the tutorial Latimus had given her. Bullets sprayed from the barrel of her rifle, and the two Deamons fell. Two more were approaching behind them. Jack's uncle lifted the Glock with his sole hand and shot them both clean between the eyes, even though they were at least thirty yards away.

"Jack said you were a great soldier," she said, impressed.

"I used to be," he said, spitting on the ground. "They're not going to stop coming. Stay aware."

The two of them, the aristocrat and the wounded warrior, stood guard over the cabins, spraying bullets into the Deamons that got too close. Suddenly, the Dark Lord Crimeous materialized in front of them, only a few feet away. Sharp teeth, filed into points, sneered at her, and he seemed to float toward them in his long gray robe. His beady eyes traveled over her, clothed only in her pajama tank and shorts, and she wanted to retch. Jack's uncle stepped in front of her, shielding her, and her heart wept at his bravery.

"Well, well, the crippled soldier takes a stand," Crimeous said. "You must've been cut with one of my poison-steel blades so that your body wouldn't heal. How marvelous. Vampyres always heal too quickly in my opinion anyway."

The man lifted the Glock and proceeded to empty the round into the Deamon's chest. He barely flinched.

"Oh, boy, you're making me quite angry," Crimeous said. "Let's remedy that."

Extending his long, pasty arm, a knife appeared in his hand. With a yell, he stabbed it in Jack's uncle's side and violently pushed him to the ground. Terror filled Lila as the Deamon came closer. Quick as a snake, he grabbed her throat. Pulling her, he dragged her over the grass so that she sat fully under the waning moonlight in the open field.

"I've tried so hard to find a weakness in your army. Who knew that it was you? After all these centuries, all I had to do was attack the woman that the Vampyre commander secretly loved."

Lila gasped as he let go of her throat. Placing her palms on the grass, she let her head hang, sickened by the smell of his breath when he'd spoken.

He lifted the large knife, the blade gleaming under the full moon. "Your *boyfriend* was arrogant enough to raid my cave tonight. I left the Blade for him as a present. I've grown so strong that it matters naught if any of you have it."

Extending his arm, he grabbed her hair, forcing her to look at him. "It's made from the same steel as the Blade of Pestilence," he said, slowly rotating the weapon in front of her face. "If I cut you, you won't heal."

Lila remained silent, feeling her body begin to go into shock. Suddenly, she felt a breeze, and Darkrip and Latimus appeared several yards in front of her. Joy pulsed through her as she realized he must've gotten her text and had Darkrip transport him to Lynia.

"No!" Crimeous screamed, pulling her against his robe-clad legs. "Don't come any closer. I have read your feelings for this woman in your mind. I'll kill her."

She saw Darkrip lift his gun to shoot, and Latimus grabbed his arm to halt him. "I have a TEC, more weapons than you can count and seventy soldiers. Don't do it, Crimeous."

The Deamon threw his head back, releasing a cruel laugh. "Watch me."

Lila saw him begin to swing the knife toward her and she heard shots firing. His long, thin frame rocked with each impact, staving off his attempts to hurt her.

"I'm almost out!" Darkrip said.

Silence rang out, and Crimeous looked down at her. "I wanted so badly to rape you in front of him, but we'll save that for another time. For now, let's rob you of those children you crave." Out of the corner of her eye, she saw Latimus approaching, a TEC in his hand. Sadly, he was too late. The Deamon Lord stabbed her in her abdomen by her right hip and dragged the knife across until it met her left hip. Pain on a scale she had never imagined hammered through her body, and she struggled to breathe.

As if in a dream, she saw Latimus deploy the TEC on Crimeous' forehead. He screamed in pain but didn't perish. With a wail, he dematerialized.

Latimus dropped to his knees, his broad hands moving to her abdomen to assess the damage.

"Transport her to Nolan's infirmary immediately," she heard him say to Darkrip. She felt the Slayer-Deamon pull her into his embrace, and then she was flying...so far...so long. And then, there was only darkness.

Chapter 11

Lila gained consciousness, wheezing as she struggled to breathe. Darting her eyes around the room, she noticed that she was in a hospital bed, with tubes running into her arms.

"Whoa, there," a calm voice said from above her head. Nolan came into her line of vision as he stood by her bedside. "You're okay, Lila. It's Nolan. Do you know who I am?"

She nodded, her erratic heartbeat almost choking her. The kind human doctor smiled down at her warmly. Humans lived separately from immortals on Etherya's Earth, most of them oblivious that Vampyres and Slayers even existed. Nolan had come to live with them under peculiar circumstances, and she had always liked the kind physician.

"Okay, good. The tubes running into your arms are transfusing you with Slayer blood. I can take them out now if you relax." Watching him cautiously, she sank into the soft bed and let him remove the tubes.

"How do you feel?" he asked.

She licked her lips, struggling to remember the events that led to her being here. She had awoken to the Deamon attack, then Jack's uncle had fought with her and then Crimeous had stabbed her...

Lifting the sheet, she pulled away the hospital gown, baring her abdomen. An ugly red scar ran from hip to hip, a multitude of stitches holding it closed.

"He cut me," she said, still struggling to piece everything together.

Nolan nodded, his chestnut-brown eyes filled with compassion. "He used a blade fashioned from poisoned steel so that you wouldn't self-heal. I'm so sorry, Lila."

Warning bells went off at the pity she observed in his gaze. "What are you saying, Nolan?"

The doctor remained silent and contemplative.

And suddenly, she understood. The bastard had rendered her barren. Unable to control her emotions, she began to cry.

"Please, don't cry, dear," Nolan said, embracing her. "I heard you were so brave. The injured soldier that I treated said that you fought valiantly."

Lila pushed her face into his chest, her heart breaking as she realized that she would never be able to have children. In that moment, she wished Crimeous had murdered her. Being in the Passage would hurt less.

The caring doctor held her until her tears abated and she wanted to collapse from exhaustion. Overcome with emotion, she crumpled on the bed.

"I want you to rest before we discuss your prognosis. You need sleep, and your body needs to heal." She felt a prick of pain as he stuck a syringe in her upper arm and emptied the contents. "I don't normally inject my patients without telling them first, so please forgive me. But I need you to rest, and that will help you sleep. I promise you're going to be okay."

As Nolan stroked her cheek, her lids grew heavy, and she prayed for relief from her exhaustion. She probably should've been mad at him for injecting her without consent but she was just too tired to care. By the goddess, she was so tired...

* * * *

Latimus stalked down the stairs, through the darkness of the unused dungeon and into Nolan's infirmary. Seeing Lila so pale on the infirmary bed made him want to vomit.

"How is she?" he asked the doctor, whose back was to him as he furiously wrote in a chart.

Sighing, the doctor turned and leaned his back against the counter. "She woke a few minutes ago and realized the extent of the damage. She was understandably upset. I gave her a sedative so that she would sleep."

Latimus crossed his arms over his chest, unable to lift his gaze from her flawless face.

"Her greatest desire was to have children."

Nolan stayed silent for several moments and then spoke. "I would say that her greatest desire was for you to love her back. But what do I know? I've only observed the two of you for three centuries."

Latimus scowled, hating how calm and wise the human doctor was. It was extremely annoying.

"I thought she was in love with Sathan."

"For a great commander who sees everything, you've got a pretty large blind spot when it comes to her. And she broke the betrothal over a year ago. Surely, you've become aware of her feelings since then."

Latimus felt his eyes narrow. "I'm not worthy of her."

"I would argue that a person's worth is in the eye of the beholder."

Uncomfortable, Latimus rubbed the back of his neck with his hand. "I failed to save her and have been terrible to her for ten centuries. I don't know how she'll ever forgive me."

"Give it time," Nolan said, approaching him to pat him on the shoulder. "The wounds are raw now, both literally and figuratively. As you immortals know, time heals all wounds."

Latimus wasn't sure about that but he was too exhausted to argue. "Alert me when she wakes."

The physician nodded, and Latimus stalked from the infirmary. Once out of the dungeon, he headed to the tech room, compelled to speak to Heden. His brother was extremely close with Lila, and for once, he sought his advice.

He found him sitting in front of the several large screens that he used on a nightly basis. Closing the door to the tech room, Latimus ran his fingers over his straight, bound hair as he struggled with what to say.

"She's going to be fine, Latimus," Heden said, not turning from the screens.

"How long did you know of my feelings for her? The first time I realized you knew was when you mentioned it the night Miranda battled Crimeous." Lowering to sit on the large table behind the computers, he regarded his brother.

Sighing, Heden rotated in his chair and crossed his beefy arms over his chest. "I don't know. For several centuries at least. Why?"

Latimus studied his brother's ice-blue eyes, mirrors of his own. "Why didn't I fight for her? I'm a warrior for the goddess' sake. Why didn't I just fight for her and make her end her betrothal to Sathan?" Frustrated, he ran his hands over his face. "If I had, this might never have happened. Fuck."

"Don't do that," Heden said, standing and coming to sit next to him on the table. Resting his hand on Latimus' shoulder, he said, "You can't blame yourself. Things happen as they were meant to. It's hard for us to remember, but not so long ago, she seemed happy to be betrothed to Sathan, even if they weren't madly in love. Both of you were scared to follow your feelings. It was always strange to me. If I ever meet someone for whom I feel half the emotion that you two feel for each other, I'll never let her go. But we're different people, Latimus. You've been so regimented your whole life. You were taught that emotion was weakness. It's natural that you fought your feelings for her."

"I felt she deserved better. Sathan has always been a better man than me."

Heden shook his head. "Who told you that crap? I mean, yeah, you're an asshole about ninety-five percent of the time, but deep down, you're a really awesome person."

Latimus felt the corner of his mouth turn up. "I am a pretty big asshole."

"Yeah man. Like, seriously. It's becoming unbearable. You need to get laid."

Latimus scoffed and shook his head. "It's been a while. That's for damn sure."

"I understand why you pushed her away. I really do. You didn't want her drawn into your world of war and death, but she's been drawn into it anyway. Do you really want her to end up with another man? Shit, I've offered to bond with her myself about a thousand times. Unfortunately, she's so in love with you, I never stood a chance."

He felt himself scowl, imagining murdering his brother if he ever touched her.

"Geez, man, calm down. I'm kidding. I love her dearly but not in that way. Although, she's incredibly hot. I don't know how you keep it in your pants around her. She's freaking gorgeous. Inside and out."

"Okay, enough. I get it. She's a fucking angel, and I'm a heathen. What else is new?"

"Look, I don't know how she's going to handle the news that she's barren. It's devastating for someone who wants to have children as much as she does. But there are other ways to have kids besides bearing them yourself. She could still have a family. Knowing her, she'll find a way to make that happen. She's a lot stronger than she gives herself credit for. I've seen a change in her recently, and it's awesome. You shouldn't pity her. And you definitely shouldn't push her into the arms of someone you consider a better man. It's time you two let yourselves be happy."

"I don't even know what being happy is," Latimus said. "I can't remember the last time I felt that way."

"That's really sad, bro," Heden said, patting him on the back. "Seriously, it hurts me to hear you say that. You deserve so much better. You've protected us for a thousand years and saved countless members of our species. No one deserves happiness more than you."

Latimus contemplated his brother's words. Did he really deserve happiness? Someone like him, who had killed countless soldiers on the battlefield, reveling in their demise? A man who tortured without care and was almost incapable of feeling emotion? He just wasn't sure he fit the bill of someone who deserved joy.

"You always focus on the bad," his brother said. "Yes, you've had to do some fucked-up shit as commander. But you never focus on the good. On the wives and children of the soldiers that you send home safely because you trained them so well. Or the numerous Vampyres that sleep soundly at night knowing they're safe. Or the fact that you were instrumental in uniting the species again. It's pretty amazing."

Latimus shifted his legs, crossing one ankle over the other as they stretched out in front of him. "I have to sit down and really think about what it would mean to have a bonded mate as the commander. It's something I never anticipated wanting or happening, so I've just never thought about it. Could someone live that life with me? I touched her a few weeks ago after torturing two Deamon captives and I wanted to strangle myself. My hands and clothes were covered in their blood. How do I reconcile that with someone as pure and decent as Lila?"

"I don't know," Heden said, shrugging. "But I think that if you love someone, you just figure it out. I mean, look at Sathan and Miranda. It seemed impossible that they could end up together, and now, it's impossible to imagine them apart. They figured it out. If you want something badly enough, I think you just make it happen."

Latimus lifted his brows, acknowledging his brother's words. "When in the hell did you get so smart anyway?"

Heden laughed, giving him a huge smile. "I've always been the smartest brother. Everyone knows that." It was a joke they regularly shared, each of the three of them always proclaiming to be the smartest brother.

"Right. I'll remember that when I see you DJ'ing at the next party like a fucking idiot."

"Hey," his brother said, his expression filled with mock indignation. "That's too far, bro. Too far."

Latimus breathed a laugh and threw his arm around Heden's shoulders, drawing him close. "You're ridiculous."

"So, where are you at with Sathan and Miranda? Are you guys okay?"

Latimus crossed his arms over his chest, placing the heel of his army boot on the toe of the other. "I don't know. I'm extremely annoyed at them for meddling in my life. It's really none of their business."

"They love you and want you to be happy too. I've never seen people who want to better the lives of everyone around them more than those two. That includes you."

"I guess. I'll forgive them eventually."

"Poor Sathan. You and Arderin both hate him. I should use this to amend the articles of succession so that he chooses me to be the next king instead of you two."

Latimus rolled his eyes at his youngest sibling. "Fine with me. I wouldn't want to be king for all the riches in the world. He was born for it. You, on the other hand, would turn the kingdom into one big dance floor."

"Awesome idea," Heden said, lifting his index finger. "I'm making a mental note of that right now."

Shaking his head, Latimus stood. "You're one of the few people in the world that she considers family. I value your council on this. Please, don't say anything to anyone. I need to think."

"Okay," his brother said, rising to his full height. "You have my word."

Latimus gave him a nod and then headed through the door and down to his basement bedroom. Rage coursed through him again as he thought of Lila's injuries. As he showered, he contemplated all that Crimeous had taken from her. She was meant to be a mother, and his heart broke with the knowledge that she would never carry a babe. If he was honest, in the far reaches of his mind, he'd imagined her full with his child, although he'd never admitted it to himself until now.

Fury swamped him, and he punched the wall of the shower, reveling in the pain of his bleeding knuckles. He would avenge her if it was the last thing he did. It would become his life's mission. The Deamon Lord had made a grave mistake when he attacked his Lila.

Drying off, he tied the towel around his waist and rummaged around his room, restless. She was going to be devastated when she had time to fully grasp her new reality. How would she handle it? He knew her to be stubborn and stoic, eerily similar to his own way of handling difficult situations.

He'd questioned the man that fought by her side tonight. They had coptered him to the infirmary, and Nolan had treated his injuries before sending him home. He'd explained in detail how Lila had charged from her cabin, weapons in hand, prepared to fight the Deamons. It shocked him a bit. He had always known of her strength but also thought her a spoiled aristocrat at times. Learning of her bravery tonight had pushed him into understanding that there were layers to her he'd yet to uncover. Pride for her courage surged through him. He found himself wanting to discover more of her hidden secrets.

Sitting on the bed, he drank some Slayer blood from his goblet. It tasted bitter, and he ached for her as she lay unconscious in the infirmary. Needing to release his anger, he grabbed his gloves and headed for the punching bag in the gym beside the barracks.

Chapter 12

Lila lay in her bed, fidgeting with the royal blue comforter. It felt strange to be back in the room that she'd lived in for so many centuries. Although she'd only been gone from Astaria a few weeks, her life had changed so much in that short time.

Slipping her hand below the covers, she ran her fingertips over the scar at her abdomen. Nolan had informed her that he would take out the stitches in about a week. The laceration was long, but she didn't feel any pain. Just a pulling of her skin when she shifted. Her self-healing body had done its best to repair the wound.

Sighing, she ran her hand over her stomach. It would never grow full with a child. Her eight-chambered heart constricted as she silently mourned. She should've been angry. Of course, she was. But she also felt so numb. How did one who had been trained their whole life to be a bonded mate and mother resume that life knowing it would never come to fruition? The gravity of her new reality was almost incomprehensible.

A knock sounded on her door, and she called for whomever it was to enter. Arderin bounced into the room, her long, dark curls flowing behind her.

"How are you feeling?" she asked, her beautiful face filled with love and compassion.

"I'm fine," Lila said, motioning for her to sit on the bed beside her. When she did, she said, "Nolan says I should rest, but I'd really like to get up and walk. Lying around all day is quite boring."

Arderin smiled, and Lila felt the warmth from her hand as she reached up to soothe her cheek. "I missed you so much when you were at Lynia. I almost died. Like, seriously, Lila. You can't ever leave me again. Sathan is out of control."

Chuckling, she grasped her friend's hand at her cheek and pulled it to sit on her lap, clutching it tightly. "I missed you too, but you're too hard on him. He just wants to keep you safe. Look at what happened to me. I wish I'd listened to Latimus and protected myself better. I was foolish to think I was invincible at Lynia, and now, I can't change the past." Unable to control it, a tear slipped down her cheek.

"Oh, please don't cry," Arderin said, pulling her into a warm embrace. "No, you're going to make me cry too. Damnit." They rocked back and forth as they both shed tears for an unimaginable loss.

Pulling back, her dearest friend smoothed her hand over her face, wiping away the wetness. "I'm so sorry, Lila. I feel awful. I wish I could attack the bastard myself."

A garbled laugh escaped Lila's lips. "I don't think he'd stand a chance against you."

Arderin's full pink lips turned up into a smile. "You're going to be okay. I promise. Latimus never cared about having kids anyway. Maybe now, he'll finally stop being an ass and love you back."

Lila shook her head, looking down at the blue comforter. "I can't even think about that right now. I think I just need time to heal. I really enjoyed the time I spent at Lynia on my own. It was empowering in a strange way. I think I need to explore that before I make any plans for the future."

"How exciting." Her friend's ice-blue eyes sparkled. "I want so badly to live on my own, away from this stupid kingdom. Maybe I can come visit you wherever you settle."

"I would love that."

Arderin reached up to finger the ends of her blond tresses. "You cut your hair."

"Yes," she said, nodding. "I felt stifled by it after a while. It was so heavy and took me forever to style each day. Having it shorter feels nice."

"Well, you look amazing. It showcases your face in a way the long hair never did."

"Thanks," Lila said, squeezing Arderin's hand.

Another knock sounded on the door, and Lila craned her neck to see the Slayer doctor, Sadie, peeking her head inside.

"Is it okay if I come in?" she asked.

"Sadie!" Arderin jumped from the bed to give the tiny Slayer a hug. They had met when Miranda had held her captive, and against all odds, they'd formed a solid bond.

"Hi, Arderin," the burned Slayer said, hugging her tight. "How are you?"

"I'm okay," she said softly, turning to walk back to Lila's side.

"And how are you feeling, Lila?" the physician asked as she stood by the bed. She usually wore a baseball cap or hooded sweatshirt to hide her burns. Today, she was wearing a white lab coat and a red ball cap.

"I feel fine. There isn't any pain. Nolan said he can take my stitches out in a few nights' time."

Sadie nodded and sat on the bed. "Nolan flew me here so that I could talk to you. He thought you might feel more comfortable speaking with a female physician. Do you mind if we discuss your prognosis for a few minutes?"

Arderin made an excuse about needing to check her Instagram feed and left them to speak privately.

"I understand that I'm barren, Sadie. I'm sure Nolan did all he could. I don't blame anyone." *Except the bastard Deamon Lord*, she thought with a surge of anger.

"Nolan tried to save your uterus. It was badly damaged, but he operated on it for over six hours. Unfortunately, the damage was just too deep. He performed a hysterectomy so that your body would heal."

Lila played with her hands on the comforter. "I understand. I'll make sure I thank him when he removes my stitches."

The Slayer's kind eyes filled with compassion as she took one of her hands and squeezed. "You won't feel any lasting health effects from the removal of the organ. Your self-healing blood will continue to course hormones through your body as before. Vampyres are very lucky that way. Some human women suffer terribly from hot flashes and cold sweats when they have the procedure you had. Fortunately, you won't feel any of that."

Lila remained silent, not understanding how anything about her current situation could remotely be seen as fortunate.

"Your body will heal quickly, so if you want to resume sexual intercourse, you can do that once Nolan removes your stitches."

Lila had to laugh at that. "Sadly, there's nothing to resume. I'm still a virgin. It's quite embarrassing."

Sadie scrunched her face, the unburnt side showing her sympathy. "I'm still one too."

"Really?"

"Yeah," Sadie said, nodding. "I mean, I'm not exactly a contender for Miss Uteria or anything. I was burned when I was very young. After that, I accepted that no one would want to be with me. I mean, look at me. At least you're still so beautiful."

Lila clutched her hand. "I think you're very pretty, Sadie."

The Slayer smiled, showing her straight white teeth. "Now, you're just being nice. But that's okay. No one really compliments me on my looks. I'll take it." Standing, she pulled a paperback book from her lab coat. "I got this for you."

Lila took the book. It had a large picture of a rainbow and was entitled, *You Can Heal Your Life.*

"I found it the last time I was in the land of humans, completing a holistic healing course. The author, Louise Hay, was a victim of sexual and physical abuse as a child. Instead of letting that define her, she took control of her life and created wonderful things for herself. It's very inspiring, especially after a tragedy like what you've experienced. I found it helpful and hope you will too."

"Thank you, Sadie," she said, awed by the Slayer's kindness. "I will treasure it and make sure to read it right away."

Sadie grinned. "You're going to be okay, Lila. I know it doesn't seem like it now, but the people who love you will be there for you in your darkest days. Miranda was so amazing when I was burned all those centuries ago. I'm so glad I let her support me. Make sure you don't shut people out. You are so loved by everyone at Astaria, and I'm pretty sure by everyone at Lynia too. Miranda told me that several of the locals there have reached out, inquiring about your health."

Lila felt herself smile, humbled that the people whom she had met for such a brief time were worried about her. How wonderful.

"I'll make sure to come and check on you again before I leave for Uteria. I'll have Arderin text you my number. If you ever need anything, please don't hesitate to call me. I mean it, Lila." The Slayer gave her a nod and exited the room, closing the door behind her. Sitting back against the pillows, Lila opened the book and began to read.

* * * *

Two days later, Lila was up and about, trying to regain some sense of normalcy. She'd read over half of the book that Sadie had given her so far and found it immensely helpful and intriguing. Louise Hay had endured terrible things in her early life but had found the courage to forge her own path. Knowing the author gained the ability to do that was quite inspiring to Lila, and she was determined to do her best to follow that course.

Although, it didn't mean that it would be easy. Yesterday, she'd awoken an hour before dusk, tears streaming down her face. Clutching her abdomen, she had prayed to Etherya, begging her to restore her ability to have children. Sadly, the goddess had not appeared, and she had forced herself to rise, shower and get out of bed.

As she floated through her old life, she felt stuck in a haze, unable to regain proper footing. She met with Sathan, giving him all of the details about the train implementation that she hadn't already passed on. Their people were starting to ride the trains between compounds, and they were both pleased.

When they finished, Sathan stood and walked around the mahogany desk, pulling her into a warm embrace. Moisture welled in her eyes as the man whose children she'd almost borne comforted her.

"I'm so sorry, Lila. I don't know what to say. I wish I could fix this for you."

"I know," she said, pulling back and swiping a lone tear from her cheek. "Thank you, Sathan."

Dark irises, filled with concern, gazed down at her. "If there's anything Miranda or I can do for you, please, let me know. We're here for you."

Lila smiled, although she felt so cold inside. "I will."

She left him then, unable to withstand the sentiment in his eyes. Coming from an aristocratic family, she had always been very proud. She didn't want anyone's pity, even if it came from a good place. The looks that she'd gotten from her friends and the household staff over the past few days were driving her insane.

First, the lovely white-haired housekeeper, Glarys, had embraced her when she entered the large kitchen looking for Slayer blood. The woman had pulled Lila into her generous breasts, consoling her as she tried not to weep.

Then, Darkrip had passed her in the foyer. His olive-green eyes had been filled with empathy as he muttered how sorry he was and lamented his father a bastard. She'd smiled at him, asking him how he was faring at Astaria, desperately wanting to change the subject from her injury.

Heden had texted her, asking if he could see her, and she made up some excuse to avoid him. Hating to push him away, she just wasn't ready to see pity in his eyes as well. Instead, she told him she would come and find him in the tech room when she was ready. He texted her back that he was there for her and that he loved her. She missed his humor and was dismayed that her injury precluded him from joking with her over text as he usually did.

It was as if they all thought her a wounded bird, unable to ever fly again. By the goddess, it was absolutely dreadful.

Walking down the hallway that led to the entrance to the barracks, she saw Latimus approaching from the other side. Her heart slammed in her chest, and the coward in her wanted to run as fast as possible in the other direction. She hadn't seen him since the battle and she had no idea what to say.

He froze, his ice-blue eyes locking with hers. "Lila," he said, coming to stand in front of her. "How are you feeling? Arderin said that you were recovering well."

Worry filled his handsome features as she stared up at him. "I'm fine."

They stood so still, a foot apart, held immobile by emotion.

Blowing out a breath, he ran his hand over his black hair. "I don't know what to say. What he did to you was unforgivable—"

Lila held up her hand, cutting him off. "I can't do this. I just can't discuss this with you. Not yet and maybe not ever. I'm sorry."

His eyes roved over her face as he swallowed deeply. "Okay. I just need to know if there's anything I can do to help you. If it's within my power, I'll do it."

She glanced down at the floor. "Unless you can go back and change the past so that I murdered that bastard before he touched me, I think we're out of luck."

She felt her eyebrows pull together at his soft chuckle. "Are you laughing at me?"

"No," he said, giving her a warm smile. "It's just...I think that's the first time I've ever heard you use a curse word. I didn't know you had it in you."

The corners of her lips turned up. "I'm sure I've cursed before."

"Nope. Not in front of me anyway. Your Aunt Ananda would have a fit."

Now, she was truly smiling, thinking of her prim aunt's reaction. "She might force me to write it a hundred times on the blackboard."

"No doubt," he said, amusement swimming in his eyes. It was nice to see something besides sympathy or pity when someone looked at her. "Sadly, I can't change the past, but I can train you if you want. I'm an expert in that, if nothing else."

"Train me?"

He nodded. "I've overheard you telling Miranda how much you admire her skills with a weapon, and you just said you wished you'd killed the bastard. I can show you some techniques so that you're not left as vulnerable in the future."

Lila contemplated, biting her bottom lip absently. "I think I would like that."

"I'm heading out to train the troops, but you can meet me in the barracks gym at dawn if you want."

"Okay," she said, nodding. "Thank you. It's a very kind offer."

He arched one dark eyebrow. "Let's not get crazy. I'm still a huge asshole. I think you know that better than anyone."

A laugh escaped her throat. "You? Never." His broad smile made him look unbearably handsome, and she silently begged her heart to stop pounding.

"Meet me there at dawn. Wear something that you can move around in and sneakers."

"Okay," she said.

Pulling open the door, he stepped through, softly closing it behind him. Lila exhaled the huge breath she'd been holding, collapsing back against the wall. She'd dreaded seeing him after her injury and was thankful he'd been so cordial. Nervousness coursed through her at the thought of being in close proximity to him as he trained her, but she truly appreciated the offer. She'd relied on others' protection her entire life and it was high time she learned to defend herself. Excited for the lesson at dawn, she headed to the tech room to find Heden, feeling an extra bounce in her step.

Chapter 13

Latimus cursed himself an absolute fool the moment he'd offered to train her. It was the ultimate punishment, forcing himself to be near her, to touch her and not have her. And yet, how could he not? He wanted her well-protected, and this would be a positive step toward that goal. He also wanted to help her, and due to his station in life, fighting was one of the only things he could do well.

Lavender and rose surrounded him, and his dick stood to attention as Lila walked through the door to the gym located in the barracks. She wore a black t-shirt, the mounds of her breasts swelling through the V-neck, held up by a sports bra. Black yoga pants clung to her tiny waist and curvy hips, stopping mid-calf. Bright pink sneakers rounded out the ensemble.

She'd pulled her blond hair into a ponytail that bobbed behind her as she approached. He had noticed the new cut earlier this evening, and although he loved her long hair, he found her even more breathtaking with the shorter cut. Her beauty was immeasurable.

After his discussion with Heden the other night, he'd been unable to think of anything but her. For the first time in ten centuries, he felt a tiny hope that he might get over his fear of being unworthy and ask her to bond with him. And yet, he'd decided to hold back for a while, at least while she healed. What she had endured at the hands of the Dark Lord was terrible, and he didn't want to rush her into anything. Moreover, she was intensely proud, and he couldn't imagine that she would see any offer to court her or bond with her as anything other than pity, considering how badly he'd treated her over the ages.

And who was he to court anyone anyway? His idea of romance had consisted of fucking Slayer whores and jerking off to images of her in his mind for a thousand years. She deserved better than that, and unfortunately, he had no idea how to give it to her.

So, he would give her the one thing he could: the ability to protect herself. It was a small gift in his eyes, but hopefully one that would make her understand that he would do anything possible to help her heal. He wanted so badly for her to make a life for herself where she could be happy, even after the bastard had robbed her of so much.

"Hey," she said, those violet eyes causing his body to throb with wanting. "Am I dressed okay?"

His shaft pulsed inside his sweat pants, answering in the affirmative. He'd quickly showered after training the troops and had thrown on some gray sweatpants and a black tank along with his sneakers. "Yep. As long as you can move easily."

She stretched her arms up and rotated them down through the air. It took every ounce of his willpower not to lower his gaze to the globes of her breasts as they jutted up. "Sure can. So, where do we start?"

Telling himself not to be a horny prick, he got to work. Over the next hour, he taught her the basics of self-defense. He detailed the parts of the body where one can do the most damage: the eyes, nose, ears, neck, groin and knee. Palming her smaller hand in his, he showed her how to make a proper fist, but also how to use her hands in other ways. Striking with the heel of her hand, gouging, poking and scratching with her fingers. Afterward, he sparred with her—gently, since her stitches hadn't yet been removed.

After an hour, he felt he'd tortured himself enough. There was only so much a man could take when touching the woman of his dreams. "Those are the basics. You picked them up fast. You're a natural. I should've made you a soldier centuries ago."

Twin splotches of red appeared on her cheeks as she smiled. "I think you're exaggerating, but thank you. That was wonderful. Can I come back down and practice?"

"Sure. You're welcome to use the gym anytime. If you want to do some mat work once you get your stitches out, I'll be happy to do that with you. There are some techniques you can learn to escape attackers that have you pinned. They're pretty effective."

"Okay," she said, fangs displacing the plushy folds of her full bottom lip as she grinned, almost driving him over the edge. "Thank you. I'm sure you're tired. I really appreciate you helping me."

"Of course. I told you, I'll do anything in my power to help you, Lila. All you have to do is ask."

"Thanks," she said softly. Lifting her arms, she did some sort of stretching thing that forced him into action.

"I'll see you tomorrow night. Stay here as long as you want." Giving her a nod, he stalked through the door, into the barracks, through the main house, right down to his room. Throwing himself on the bed, he groaned in frustration. After tonight, he was designating himself both a saint and a fool. No other words could describe a man who could be in her presence, touching and smelling her, and not fuck her. Of that, he was convinced.

* * * *

Lila continued to use the gym over the next few days, practicing the techniques Latimus had taught her. Miranda, who loved to work out, also showed her how to use the treadmill and elliptical. Although she only traveled small distances according to the machines' electronic displays, she felt stronger somehow. Determined to take back control of her life, she focused on strengthening her muscles and healing her heart.

The book Sadie had given her was wonderful. The author was very inspiring, encouraging the reader not to be victims of their circumstances. She believed that even when terrible things happened to a person, they alone had the ability to control their reactions. Instead of being stuck in the atrocities of the past, she felt that one should let them go and chose to forgive their transgressors. Only then could they take back the power in their lives, becoming the victor instead of the victim. It was a powerful lesson to live in the moment, understanding that the past is over but everyone has the power to chart their future.

A few days later, after she'd had her stitches removed, she met Latimus again to go over the mat work he'd referenced in their first session. Using the large blue mat in the middle of the gym floor, he showed her how to escape various positions of captivity. Watching him contort over and around her, his huge arm muscles straining under his athletic tank, made pockets of saliva gather in her throat. He was absolutely gorgeous.

Toward the end of the session, he was showing her a move, and she felt the skin pull at her abdomen. He stiffened and fell awkwardly on top of her, making her expel a large, "*Oomph!*"

"Shit, Lila, are you okay?" he asked, his hulking body looming over her as he splayed half-over her body. "You grimaced."

"I'm fine," she said, noticing how breathy her voice sounded. "I just felt a pull at my scar."

His eyes searched her face, drenched with concern. "Do you need to go see Nolan?"

"No," she said, feeling the messy bun atop her crown shake along with her head. "It's fine."

She swore she felt his heart beating, although his chest wasn't touching hers as he loomed over her. Supported on his massive arms, he studied her. Blood pounded through her entire body, and her skin was burning with heat. His red tongue darted out to lick his full lips, and she thought he might kiss her.

Instead, he rolled off, grabbing her hand and pulling her to sit on the mat. "I should've waited longer to train you on this stuff. I'm sorry. I feel terrible."

And there it was. Pity lined his expression along with a healthy dose of compassion. By the goddess, he was the only one who hadn't pitied her yet. For some reason, it infuriated her. She wanted to live in a world where at least one person didn't find her helpless and broken. Hope died in her heart, and she lashed out.

"You don't have to look at me like I'm a leper," she said, standing and scowling down at him. "I know you all think he destroyed me. Poor little Lila. Well, it's annoying. I'm here, and I'm doing the best I can to recover gracefully. I won't take pity from you or anyone." Pivoting, she stalked out of the gym and into the dim barracks warehouse.

Halfway through the large room, his hand grabbed her lower arm, turning her to face him. "Hey," he said, hurt swimming in his blue eyes. "That's not fair. I don't pity you, Lila. It's really fucked-up for you to accuse me of that."

"Let go of me," she said, shaking off his arm. "What am I supposed to believe when you've spent your entire life mocking me for being a spoiled aristocrat? I'm sure you pity me more than anyone. Well, you can keep it. I'll be damned if I stand around and let any of you tell me how shattered my life is. While you all feel sorry for me, I'll get on with living it." Lifting her chin, she turned and walked back to her room.

Once there, she screamed in frustration, hollow at the loss of the one person who didn't look at her like a wounded animal. Observing the walls of her bedchamber, she felt trapped. Whether she liked it or not, this wasn't her life anymore. She had to get out of this house for her own sanity. Sitting down on her bed, she grabbed the journal she'd been keeping since her injury. It was suggested by Louise Hay that one keep a journal to help them set goals and intentions for building a better life. It also was a great way to write about her fears and sadness at being barren. Opening to a fresh page, she began writing intentions that would lead her away from the castle that she'd always called home.

Chapter 14

The next night, Lila was restless, so she wandered the great house. Ending up in the sitting room by the front foyer, she looked out the window into the darkness. She'd spent several hours writing in her journal yesterday, contemplating her future. One pathway that she could explore would be to visit Camron at Valeria, as they had originally planned. Although she wasn't able to give him biological children, he had claimed to care for her. Perhaps he would be open to adoption. There were many Vampyre children, orphaned by their long wars, who needed homes. In her eyes, nothing was more noble than giving a child a home and helping them build a full life.

But would Camron share her views on adoption? In the immortal world, bloodlines were very important. They were what distinguished aristocrat from laborer, wealth from middle and lower-class. Although she was still an aristocrat, she would never be able to give any man blooded heirs. Strange, since that had been her sole purpose in life for so long. What did that mean for her future? Did that devalue her in the eyes of the aristocracy or a future mate? Gnawing her bottom lip with her fangs, she contemplated.

Another option was to resume her life at Lynia. Although it had been the site of her greatest tragedy, she'd also felt her greatest freedom there. The compound had felt like a warm, new home for her, and she missed the people she had befriended there immensely. Especially Antonio and Jack. She smiled absently as she remembered the boy slicing his toy sword through the air, his cap of red hair swishing in the moonlight.

Her phone rang, and she pulled it from her back pocket.

"Hi, Camron. I was just thinking about you."

"Hi, sweetie," he said, his voice dripping with sympathy. Lila clenched her teeth, unable to tamp down the swell of anger at his placating tone. "How are you feeling?"

"I'm fine. We heal fast. Physically, I'm good as new." *Except, I'm missing my uterus.* Telling herself to stop the pity party, she asked, "How are you?"

"Very well. We were all so sorry to hear what that maniac did to you. Even though it's forbidden, I'm close to joining Latimus' army so that I can kill the bastard myself."

She almost laughed. Camron was a haughty aristocrat who wouldn't last five minutes in battle. "That's a very kind offer, but I'm determined not to let him beat me. I won't let him take my dignity and my pride away."

"Hear, hear," he said. "How brave you were to fight him, Lila. All of us here are so proud of you, and if there's anything we can do, please let us know."

Great. The entire compound must know that she was barren. At this point, the entire kingdom probably knew. She longed for the days when she was holed up in her bedchamber, her privacy her own.

"I was thinking that I'd still like to come up to Valeria at the next full moon, if you'll have me."

There was a long pause, and her heartbeat quickened. "Camron?"

He cleared his throat. "Of course, you can come. You know you're always welcome here. Melania will be here during the next full moon. You remember her from etiquette school, right? I think you both were good friends."

Realization sent a surge of rejection through her. "You're planning to court her."

Uncomfortable silence stretched through the phone. "I'm the last of my bloodline, Lila. I have to have an heir. It's my duty. If I had a choice, I would obviously bond with you, but I can't."

Her insides felt dead as he spoke. The man who had said such sweet words to her only weeks ago was now discarding her due to her maiming. The Vampyre bonding ceremony was filled with promises of "sickness and health" and "till death do us part." What if she'd bonded with him and then been attacked? Would he have thrown her away so carelessly then?

Understanding that most aristocratic men would share his views, she realized she had the answer to her previous musings. Her chances of finding a bonded mate now were so diminished, she might be alone forever. As someone who'd battled loneliness her entire life, her chest burned with the pain of that awareness. Hating the tears that welled in her eyes, she gritted her teeth.

Revulsion at Camron's disingenuousness ran through her. She wished she'd never even contemplated bonding with him. "I understand." Wanting to be done with the conversation, she recognized that she would be fine if she never spoke to him again.

"Lila, I don't want to hurt you—"

"We have a duty. It's been ingrained in us since childhood. I wish you the best. Goodbye."

Her thumb hit the red button on the phone. Good riddance. In that moment, as much as she hated that Crimeous had rendered her childless, she was thankful that it had led her to see Camron's true colors. An image of Latimus ran through her mind, and she scoffed that he had tried to push her into bonding with Camron because he was a better man. Latimus might be nasty and cold, but he was firm in his integrity, loyalty and honor. Camron wasn't one tenth the man Latimus was. Of course, he never saw himself that way, and that was one of the multitude of reasons why he wouldn't let himself love her.

And now, she was barren. If Latimus hadn't let himself love her before, he surely wouldn't now. Although he claimed to never want children, one day, the war with Crimeous would end, and Latimus would be free to build a life. The son of Markdor would need to bond with someone who could carry on his illustrious bloodline. Sadly, that woman would never be her.

Frustrated with men and bloodlines and society as a whole, she decided she didn't need any of them. She was tired of waiting to live her life until she was *chosen* by a male. How absurd. She was a strong woman who held a title bestowed upon her by the king. Making a firm decision, she headed to her bedroom to pack and begin her life on her own.

* * * *

Latimus stalked into the kitchen at dawn, starving after the night's training. Searching the fridge for Slayer blood, he poured some into a goblet. Noticing a notebook on the large marble counter of the island that sat behind him, he studied it as he sipped.

Heart pounding, he walked to the island and pulled it to him. Flipping through the journal, he observed Lila's pretty handwriting. Every single cell in his body screamed at him that it was so very wrong to read what she'd written, but he was unable to stop himself. Opening it to a page in the middle, he read.

I'm so afraid that I'm destined to be alone. How can anyone choose me now that I'm barren? The sole duty of a Vampyre aristocratic woman is to give their bonded mate heirs. Although Sathan bestowed the title of Kingdom Secretary Diplomat upon me, most aristocrats will still see me as a failure due to my barrenness.

Camron has always been so kind, and we've known each other forever. Could he overlook the fact that I can't give him biological heirs? I feel so adrift, drowning in pity as people look at me like I'm damaged goods. Thank the goddess for the book Sadie gave me. Without it, I'd be lost.

Latimus' head snapped up as he heard a sound from outside the kitchen. Lila breezed through the doorway, stopping short when she saw him reading her notebook.

A flash of pain contorted her stunning features. Then, the rage took over.

"How *dare* you?" she asked, walking into the kitchen and snapping the journal shut. Grabbing it with her pale hands, she held it to her ample breasts, covered by a pretty blue V-neck sweater. Those magnificent lavender irises bore into him, swamped with pain and betrayal. *Fuck.*

"I'm so sorry," he whispered, hating that he'd violated her privacy. "There's no excuse. I'm just so worried about you, Lila. I saw it there and I just...damn it...I shouldn't have."

"No, you shouldn't," she said, her voice as close to a yell as he'd ever heard. Lila was usually so proper and composed that her tone was always sweet and melodious. "Of all the people I thought would understand the need for privacy, I never imagined *you* would be the one to violate it."

He'd never felt more like a piece of shit. Not knowing what to say or how to make it better, he set the goblet on the counter and began slowly approaching her.

"Lila—"

"No!" she said, holding her palm up. "Don't ever come near me again! I don't know who you think you are—"

"I'm someone who cares about you," he said, grabbing her wrist, needing her to understand how much he wanted to help her recover from the Dark Lord's actions. "I'm so worried that you're not letting anyone in. I want to help you."

"By reading my journal? Screw you!"

He would've laughed at her use of the not-so-proper phrase if the situation hadn't been so tense. Wrenching her arm from his grasp, she took a step back.

"I'm so disappointed in you," she said. He thought he might drown in the tears that welled in her eyes. "I thought you were better than that. Leave me the hell alone." Pivoting, she all but ran from the room.

Looking to the ceiling, he sighed, trying not to choke on his self-revulsion. By the goddess, he was such an ass. Lowering his head, he noticed their white-haired housekeeper, Glarys, entering the kitchen.

"Well, well, my dear boy," she said, stopping in front of him and patting his cheek. "You went and messed up again, didn't you?"

"Yes," he said, scowling down at her. She'd been employed at the castle since before the Awakening and quite often served as a mother figure for him and his siblings. Latimus found her to be quite wise and thoroughly charming. "She left her journal on the counter, and I read some of it. I shouldn't have. I'm just so worried about her, Glarys. Damn it!"

"Now, you watch that potty mouth around me, young man," she scolded, shaking her head. "I've always told you I don't appreciate that language from you." The bottom of her dress swayed around her calves as she walked to the sink, beginning to wash his goblet. "And if you're so worried about her, why don't you do something about it? You two have been circling around each other too long in my opinion."

Latimus felt the corners of his lips turn up. "We have. Is it that obvious?"

Glarys gave a *harrumph*. "You should know by now that ol' Glarys sees everything."

"I'm trying to convince myself I'm worthy of her. How do I do that, Glarys? Especially when I keep fucking up all the time?"

Glarys set the cup in the drying rack and turned to him, studying him while she dried her hands with a striped towel. "That girl has loved you since before she could speak. It used to break my heart, seeing how she looked at you when she thought no one was watching. I know what others have told you over your life, son, and I know what you have to do protect our people. But you're a good man, and it's time you started believing it. How many chances do you need to get it right? Stop wasting time, Latimus. It's not serving anyone, least of all Lila."

Locked onto her light blue eyes, he could feel something coursing through his body, deep inside his blood. Son of a bitch, it felt like acceptance. Was he finally ready to push away his fear of being unworthy and ask Lila to bond with him? Struggling a bit to breathe, he leaned back on the island countertop.

"That's good," Glarys said with a nod. "You're gonna get there, son. Don't forget to save me a front-row seat at the bonding ceremony. Now, go on to bed. I've got to clean up in here."

Approaching her, he palmed her ruddy cheeks and smacked a huge kiss on her forehead. "You know I love you, right, Glarys?"

Her face turned ten shades of red, causing Latimus to chuckle. "Get out of here," she said, swatting him with the damp towel. "I don't have time for this."

Laughing, he pulled her into a warm embrace. Giving her one last peck on the cheek, he exited the kitchen.

Entering his room, he sat on the bed and contemplated what Lila had written. Did she really think that men would reject her because of her barrenness? How could that be remotely possible given how beautiful and kind she was? Any man would be lucky to have her on his arm as his mate for life.

Rubbing his hand over his chest, he breathed deeply, allowing himself to really *feel* what sat inside his heart for her. By the goddess, it was so strong and true. He'd never felt love as profound or genuine as he felt for Lila. Sitting there in the silence, his heart seemed to unlock itself, opening to all the possibilities they could have if they created a life together.

There, by the pale light from the lamp on his bedside table, he cemented the most amazing and important decision of his life: he was ready to bond with her.

Lying down on his bed, he thought of their future together. Every moment of his time would be spent giving her the life she deserved. Although he still felt extremely unworthy of her, no man was more determined than he. He might not be good enough for her, but he would fight until his dying breath to give her everything she desired. By the goddess, he wanted that so much for her.

Reveling in the thought of finally getting to hold her, he closed his eyes, unable to control the pounding in his eight-chambered heart.

Chapter 15

An hour before dusk, Latimus rose, ready for the night's training. He'd been instructing the troops with extra efficiency over the past few weeks so they were prepared to attack Crimeous. The next full moon was only a week away, and he was intent on ensuring their success.

As always, the rest of his time had been consumed with thoughts of Lila. After his realization last night, he was anxious to finish tonight's drills so that he could find her at dawn and discuss the decision he'd made. Worried that she would reject him, he told himself not to be a pussy. He'd faced countless Deamons in battle. Surely, he could talk a blond-haired temptress into bonding with him. Couldn't he? Good grief, he hoped so.

She'd been furious with him after their last training, reminding him of how often he'd chided her for being a spoiled aristocrat. Mentally kicking himself, he hated that he'd been such a damn fool. He'd been absolutely terrible to her for centuries. Even though she had feelings for him, would she reject him due to his cruelty? Praying to Etherya to open her heart to him even though he'd hurt her so badly, he stalked to the barracks door.

As he stepped onto to the plushy grass of the meadow behind the barracks, he saw Lila standing at the top of the stairs that led to the underground train platform. She held Arderin in a firm embrace, and Sathan, Miranda and Heden were looking at her with love and sadness in their eyes. Two suitcases sat at her feet.

"I'll miss you guys so much," Lila said. "Please, come visit."

"If Sathan ever lets me out of this godforsaken prison...I mean, compound...I promise I'll visit," Arderin grumbled.

Miranda shot his sister a scolding look. Lifting her gaze back to Lila, she said, "We'll come and visit you together once you're settled. Can't wait."

Arderin's eyes lit with pleasure as Sathan gazed at his wife.

"It would be great if we discussed these things first," he muttered.

"We'll be fine, dear," Miranda said, patting him on the cheek as he scowled at her. "Arderin and I make our own decisions, don't we?"

His sister rolled her eyes. "I wish."

Stepping toward them, Latimus couldn't stop himself from speaking. "You're leaving?" he asked.

They all turned, shooting each other looks filled with guilt. He was still annoyed at his brother and his wife for making him go on the train mission and hurt shot through him that they had kept Lila's departure from him.

"I made them promise not to tell you," Lila said, her chin held high in her always-regal way. "Please, don't be upset at them. It was my news to tell."

Latimus shot Sathan a look, furious at his older brother. All short or long-term relocations were supposed to be approved through him as the kingdom's commander, so that he could ensure safety. Being that Lila had been attacked recently, it was a huge breach of protocol.

"I think you guys should talk," Miranda said, squeezing Lila's hand. "We'll see you soon."

The four of them walked away, Miranda locking her guilt-ridden green gaze on his as she passed him. He had helped her immensely when Sathan thought she'd betrayed him before their bonding, and he was angry at her lack of loyalty. Deciding he'd deal with that later, he looked at Lila.

She looked so small, standing on the concrete above the stairs. Blond waves blew in the breeze, and she crossed her arms over her chest. Walking toward her, he stopped only inches from her. Two nights ago, as he'd passed through the foyer, he'd heard her speaking to Camron in the sitting room, telling him how much she'd like to visit. He'd been in a hurry, unable to hear the end of their conversation, and hadn't realized she'd committed to visiting him so soon. What a cluster, now that he'd finally decided to bond with her. Cursing himself an idiot, he glared at her.

"No goodbye? That's nice, Lila. Well, I hope you enjoy bonding with Camron and living whatever life you want for yourself. He always was a bit snobbish and formal for me, but hopefully, he'll be able to fuck you so that you'll enjoy it. Maybe he'll turn the lights off so you don't notice how inadequate he is." His words were inexcusable but he was just so enraged at her for leaving without telling him, further compounded by his family's betrayal, that he wanted to hurt her.

She gave an angry laugh and shook her head. "Well, it took you three weeks after my injury to start being terrible to me again. I'm sure it was extremely difficult for you. I applaud you that it lasted that long."

His nostrils flared, and he felt his teeth grind together. "Fuck you, Lila. All I've ever wanted is for you to have the life you deserved. I'm sorry it isn't filled with rainbows and butterflies. I'm not perfect but I've made hard choices that I thought were right."

"Yes, everyone seems to be so concerned with making choices for *my* life. Well, thanks, but I'm all set. I know you don't think very highly of me, but I'm a competent person and I'm done with letting you or any man tell me what life I need or deserve."

"Bonding with Camron won't make you happy."

Her mouth fell slightly open as she gave him an incredulous stare. "Says the man who pushed me into his arms for the past year. You need to get it together, Latimus. I think you've got some serious issues."

"Well, you're a coward. Running away at the first hardship you've faced in your life? It's bullshit. I thought you were stronger than that."

Throwing her head back, she laughed, the pale line of her throat gorgeous in the moonlight. "I've faced more hardship than you can fathom. Starting with the death of my parents centuries ago and compounded by the awful way you've treated me for ages."

"I thought you were in love with my *brother*!" he screamed, needing her to understand why he pushed her away. "You sat in your ice castle pining for him to bond with you. It was pathetic."

Shaking her head, she pressed her palm to her forehead, looking exasperated. "It's nice to reaffirm how you really see me. It makes me even more confident that I'm making the right decision to leave."

The reality of her departure set in, and he wanted to drop to his knees and beg her to stay. He wanted to promise her everything her heart craved and pull her into his arms so that she couldn't escape. Fear gripped him, knowing she would leave anyway. Terrified of her rejection, he gave in to his cowardice.

"You two deserve each other. Have a nice life looking down at those of us who are less than you from your ivory tower."

Lowering, she picked up her suitcases, one in each hand. "You don't know anything. You've always assumed you know everything about me. Everything I want. Well, you have no idea. I've loved you since we were children, but I'm done wasting my time on an angry person who can't get out of his own damn way. Have fun being miserable. I won't live my life that way anymore." Turning, she walked down the stairs, into the darkness.

His eight-chambered heart pounded as he dissected her words. If she truly loved him, then why was she going to Valeria to bond with Camron? Confusion coursed through him.

A voice in the back of his head screamed at him to follow her. To try one more time to convince her stay. Behind him, Kenden called his name.

"Yeah," he said, rubbing his forehead in frustration.

"Are you heading down to the sparring field?"

Sighing, he nodded and turned away from the platform. She'd already committed to visiting Camron anyway. There was no point in trying to change her mind.

Chapter 16

Lila arrived at Lynia, excitement fluttering in her stomach. She felt like she was coming home. Lifting her suitcases, she hurtled up the stairs to meet Breken. After a warm embrace, he led her to a four-wheeler with a Vampyre soldier sitting at the wheel.

"The cabin you used before was purchased," Breken said. "Since you were very clear you wanted to be in one of the cabins, we secured a different one for you. I found your artwork after you left, and it's been transferred there."

Lila smiled, remembering the painting she had finished the night of her attack. "Thank you, Breken. I'm so happy to be back."

"Of course. Lora and I are thrilled to have you here, and you're welcome at the main house anytime. If you need anything, please don't hesitate to call. Sathan now has two hundred troops guarding the compound, and although the heightened security is a bit stifling, we welcome it and feel that you'll be safe."

"I'm sure of it," she said, squeezing his hand.

He loaded her suitcases into the vehicle, and she set off with the Vampyre soldier. Upon arriving at her cabin, she realized she would be staying beside Jack's uncle's cabin. Excited to see the brave man again, she hopped from the four-wheeler. The soldier offered to carry her bags inside, but she thanked him and did it herself. Her days of needing a man to help her accomplish anything were behind her.

Once inside, she set about unpacking. She made the bed, lining it with her favorite blue comforter, determined to buy some pillows in town. She absolutely loved pretty pillows upon her bed. The cabin only had one main room, which housed the bed and a tiny kitchenette. A separate bathroom sat off to the side. Since she only needed Slayer blood for sustenance and had always had servants to cook any food she wanted for pleasure, the kitchenette would likely go unused.

As she set about unloading her toiletries in the small bathroom, she reflected upon her argument with Latimus. What a self-righteous ass he was. She had no idea why he'd assumed she was going to meet Camron, unless he'd been spying on her as she spoke to him the other night. Jerk. It served him right to let him think she was in the arms of someone else. Why would he care anyway?

A tiny bit of guilt ate at her gut as she remembered the look of hurt that had crossed his face when he realized she was leaving without telling him as well as his family keeping her secret. Even when he was nasty and vile to her, she hated to see him in pain. Sighing, she flipped off the bathroom light and opened her second suitcase to unpack it. Feeling her lips curve into a frown, she realized she'd forgotten the brushes and palette she'd meant to bring. Making a mental note to ask Arderin to ship them to her, she finished unloading the luggage.

Once complete, she pulled out her journal. Sitting on her bed, she looked at the intentions she'd set for herself. One of them said *Move to Lynia.* Check. Feeling proud of herself, she read some of the other intentions.

Finish five paintings in three months.
Sell one painting in the main square within six months.
Help Lynians rebuild after the Deamon attack.
Start an adult literacy group for Lynians and Narians.

Smiling, she assessed her goals. Some for her, some for others. The illiteracy rate on the two outlying compounds was high, and she wanted to help them learn so they could lead even better lives.

Tomorrow, she would head into town and get on with accomplishing her goals. She may never be a bonded mate or a mother, but she would make something of her life. Failure was not an option.

* * * *

A few days later, Latimus almost plowed down his brother in the hallway as he was heading to his room after the night's training.

"Whoa," Heden said, grabbing his upper arms. "Slow down, dude."

"Screw you, Heden," Latimus said. "I'm still pissed that you didn't tell me Lila was leaving."

Heden sighed and lifted his hands, palms facing the ceiling. "What do you want me do, bro? She made me promise not to say anything. I wanted to keep my word."

"Everyone in this house is determined to side with her instead of their own brother. It's disloyal and disgusting. You all are assholes."

"Wait," Heden said, grabbing his arm to prevent him from walking away. "There aren't any sides here. We love you, and we love her. All of us are just trying to do what we think is best. She suffered a traumatic and painful loss, Latimus. It's important you don't forget that."

"So, that means you all can fuck me over? Awesome. Glad to know where I stand. I hope she has a great life with Camron. They deserve each other."

His brother's features scrunched in confusion. "Camron? Why would she have a life with him?"

"Because she went to Valeria to be with him."

Heden looked perplexed. "Um...no, she didn't."

"What the hell do you mean?"

"She went to Lynia to try and resume the life she'd started to build there. She was happy there for a short time and wanted to see it through."

Latimus felt himself scowl. "I thought she was going to bond with Camron. I asked her, and she confirmed."

"Did you ask her, or did you yell at her and assume? Knowing you, probably the latter."

Latimus rubbed his fingers over his forehead. "Shit."

"Wow, man, you're some kind of asshole. No wonder she didn't correct you. She probably just wanted to get the hell away from you."

Fisting his hands at his sides, he growled in frustration. "I was terrible to her. The things I said were unforgivable. Fuck. Why do I always do this with her?" Furious at himself, he punched the wall.

"Okay, okay, let's not take our frustration out on the wall," Heden said, patting him on the shoulder. Latimus glared at him. "Or on your favorite brother. I like my face just the way it is, without any help from your fist."

Unable to stop himself, he scoffed at his brother's teasing. "You really find a way to turn everything into a joke. It's unbelievable."

"Compliment accepted," he said with a nod.

Latimus shook his head. "Ridiculous."

"So, what are you going to do now? You really blew it. How are you going to fix it?"

"I have no idea," he said, exhaling a large breath. "She hates me. I made sure of that."

"She loves you. I know this might be unorthodox, but maybe you should try being nice to her. It's a foreign concept for you, but it's widely known to accomplish the task of getting someone to like you back."

He felt his face crumple into a scowl. "I hate you."

Heden laughed. "Come on, bro. It's not that bad. How about actually making an effort to court her? She deserves no less than lavish gifts and pretty words."

"I don't know the first thing about courting a woman. I'm a soldier."

"Well, maybe it's time you learn. I'm pretty sure, with a little wooing, she's a sure thing. You just have to win her over. You're an expert at winning battles, so this challenge should be easy."

"Nothing with her is ever easy. I'm a huge fuckup when it comes to her. Maybe I should just leave her alone and let her get on with her life."

"You could, but I doubt that would ultimately make either of you happy."

"Fucking happiness. I'm so tired of everyone wanting me to be happy."

"Dude, you're weird. Everyone wants to be happy. Stop being afraid and go get it. You're such a coward when it comes to her. It's strange. You're so strong in every other aspect of your life."

Every other aspect of his life wasn't filled with a blond-haired temptress who drove him absolutely insane half the time. Running his hand over his hair, Latimus nodded. "I am. A huge fucking coward. It's embarrassing."

Pointing his finger in Heden's face, he warned, "And if you ever tell Sathan I said that, I'll deny it until my last breath."

"Not saying a word," he said. "Now, if you'll excuse me, I was on the way to my room to shower before I meet my, um, lady friend to usher in the day."

"You're heading there at dawn? Wow, there must only be one thing on the agenda."

"We're going to read Tolstoy together. It should be enlightening." He waggled his eyebrows up and down.

"Fine. Go get laid. One of us should."

"Go court Lila," Heden said, taking off down the hallway. "I'm sure she'll help you with that."

Right. Latimus was pretty sure that she never wanted anything to with him ever again. Loathing himself, he continued to his room to shower.

* * * *

Nolan finished his final entry in Lila's chart and closed it. Filing it in the drawer that sat under the counter at the back of the infirmary, he thought of her. She had handled the news of her injury well, but he felt that she hadn't properly taken time to mourn. He feared that her grief would haunt her down the road. Hoping she would reach out to him, he closed the file drawer.

"I'm heading back to Uteria," Sadie said, entering the infirmary behind him. "Lila's settled at Lynia, and Miranda's morning sickness has abated a bit. Not enough to stop Sathan from worrying, but enough that I feel she's okay."

Nolan leaned back on the counter, nodding. Sadie was a puzzle to him, and he really enjoyed puzzles. Placing the jagged pieces together to form a beautiful picture had always enthralled him. She was a phenomenal doctor, although her burned hand prevented her from doing meticulous surgeries as he did. He couldn't remember meeting a person more kind—except Lila perhaps—but the Slayer was also a bystander. The woman seemed content to heal others and help them live happy lives, but she didn't seem to want anything for herself. It was as if she'd given up on having her own hopes and dreams and was content to live vicariously through her patients.

He assumed it was because of her burns. Although they were severe, he was a clinician and saw them for what they were: scarred tissue. Whereas others might have thought her less attractive, he always saw her unburnt side as her true self, barely even noticing the scars. She used them as a wall, separating herself from having a full life.

As a human stuck in an immortal world, he too had a wall. Unfortunately, his was unbreakable. Three centuries ago, he'd come upon Sathan as he entered the ether, leaving the human world. The Vampyre king had come to inspect some of the flintlock guns that humans used in their wars and had been accidentally shot when one of the guns exploded into his chest. Observing him hold his hand over his gaping wound, Nolan wanted to treat him. Not realizing he had self-healing abilities, or even knowing what Vampyres were, he had curiously followed him through the ether, intent on helping him. That fateful decision had led to his discovery of the immortal world and to a choice he'd always regretted.

The goddess Etherya had offered him death or immortality in the Vampyre kingdom, unable to rejoin the humans. In the stupidity of his youth, he'd chosen immortality. Now, he was locked in a world where he would forever be alone, never one of them, always living on the outside.

In that way, he and Sadie were similar. Both of them lived amongst the immortals but were outliers. Although he cared for the royal family immensely and was thankful they had taken him in, he missed the human world. He couldn't understand why Sadie held herself back from her people. If he had the choice, he would burn his entire body to rejoin the humans.

"I'm worried for Lila," he said, crossing his arms over his chest. "I don't think the gravity of her injury has truly hit her."

"Me too," Sadie said, coming to stand in front of him. "I guess all that we can do is be here for her if she needs us."

"I guess so. I hope she'll reach out to one of us." He studied her eyes, the unburnt one perfectly almond-shaped under her red ball cap with long, brown lashes. The burnt one had no lashes, the surrounding skin jagged and puffy. "You have central heterochromia," he said.

She smiled. "Yup. Multicolored eyes. I've always just said they were hazel because they have brown, green and a bit of yellow."

"They're pretty."

Those eyes widened, and she looked uncomfortable. "Thanks," she said rubbing the back of her neck with her unburnt hand.

"I appreciate you coming in to speak to Lila. I felt it best that she discussed her prognosis with a female physician."

"Of course. She deserves to move on from this and find happiness. There are so many ways to be a mother. So many kids out there need families."

"And what of you? Any plans to have kids or adopt? You're so kind, I'm sure you'd make an excellent mother."

"Oh, no. That's not my path. I'm content to help heal mothers and children. That's my purpose in life."

"It seems a waste, for someone as nurturing as you."

Something flashed across her face. Maybe anger, maybe longing.

"Well, I'm not really a fan of exposing any kid to having a mother that looks like me. They'd be ridiculed for sure." Grabbing her hooded sweatshirt from the hook on the wall, she placed it over her slim arms, zipped it closed and lifted the hood over her head, concealing her burns. "Call me at Uteria if you need anything."

The soles of her sneakers were soft on the floor as she exited through the doorway to the dungeon that led to the main house.

Grabbing the apple that sat on the counter, Nolan took a large bite. Chewing thoughtfully, he decided he was intrigued. She was one puzzle he was going to piece together, no matter how long it took him. He'd locked himself in a prison of eternity; he might as well have something to occupy his time.

Chapter 17

The night to fight Crimeous had come. Latimus looked up at the full moon, his heart just as full with hatred for the bastard who had hurt his Lila. The son of a bitch was going to get his ass kicked before Darkrip struck him dead. Clenching his fists at his sides, he marched ahead of the troops.

As before, they were attacking from two sides. Latimus would lead the soldiers into the mouth of the cave and to the lair where Darkrip was convinced his father would be. Kenden would blow an entrance through the ground and enter from above with his men. Once they had located Crimeous, Darkrip would materialize and strike him dead with the Blade.

That didn't mean that Latimus couldn't spend several minutes beating the shit out of the bastard first.

Lifting the sword from his back, he yelled, "Charge!"

Although he preferred modern weapons such as rifles and TECs, nothing had ever replaced the feeling of plunging a sword into his greatest enemy. He carried one tonight for that sole purpose.

Soldiers ran with him as he charged into the dimly lit lair of the cave. The gritty walls were lined with torches that emitted a sinister glow. Crimeous stood on a large rock, several feet tall, raping a woman on a slab as her hands were bound to two posts. By the goddess, he was an evil creature.

Hearing the soldiers' screams, the Dark Lord ejaculated in the woman and lifted a knife, plunging it into her heart. She died instantly, and Latimus realized she must've been one of his Deamon harem women. Pain coursed through him at the thought of another life lost to this hateful being.

Crimeous turned, facing the approaching troops, and tilted his head back to laugh mercilessly. His shaved teeth formed sharp points, and his long, naked body was covered with gray skin. Furious that he'd ever touched one inch of Lila's flawless frame, Latimus charged until he was fighting the Deamon warriors on the ground of the cave, protecting their leader on the rock above.

Each Deamon he sliced and gutted thrilled him. It was this part of his nature that he questioned. Did it make him evil that he reveled in the deaths of his enemies? Could someone as kind as Lila even begin to understand or accept that part of him? The thought terrified him, so he pushed it from his mind and kept fighting, crushing two of the Deamons' heads together and slamming them to the floor.

Seeing a clear pathway to the top of the rock, he climbed up. He ran to the Deamon woman, placing two fingers on her neck, thinking he could possibly save her. Hope died when he didn't feel a resounding pulse.

"She died honorably, being fucked by the most powerful immortal on Etherya's Earth," Crimeous said behind him. "Don't mourn her."

Gritting his teeth, Latimus turned, lifting his sword to strike the Deamon. A sword materialized in the creature's hands, and he arched one of his razor-thin eyebrows.

"A sword fight. Fun. I haven't done this in centuries," Crimeous said, lifting his weapon.

They proceeded to brawl, adrenaline coursing through Latimus' body as they clashed. As the Vampyre commander, he was the largest man ever born of his species. Even Sathan, hulking and strong in his own right, was an inch shorter and twenty pounds lighter. If anyone could physically outmatch Crimeous, it would be him.

But the bastard was wily and possessed several powers that Latimus didn't. Brute strength didn't compare to the ability to manifest weapons in one's hand or dematerialize. Still, the creature fought him. Latimus knew he was probably toying with him, but it felt so good to fight, to avenge Lila's honor, that he plowed on.

After several moments, both of them mightily swinging and connecting, Darkrip appeared. Pulling the Blade of Pestilence from his back, he swung it at his father. Crimeous' thin arm swung up to block the weapon.

"Go for the back of the neck!" Latimus yelled.

Darkrip started to rotate and then froze. Dropping the Blade, he clutched his throat. The Dark Lord was choking him with his mind. Throwing down his sword, Latimus drew his AR-15 from his back and began to unload the magazine into Crimeous' thin body. The Deamon convulsed each time a bullet impacted, and Darkrip reached for the Blade on the ground. Lifting it, he moved to strike.

Suddenly, the Deamon Lord dematerialized, leaving Latimus shooting into thin air.

"No!" Latimus said, dropping the gun to his side. "How did he dematerialize? You said he couldn't do that when he was being impacted by bullets."

"Fuck," Darkrip said, lifting his fingers to his forehead. "Let me see if I can track him." He closed his eyes, his pupils darting back and forth under his closed lids. Finally, he opened them. "I can't get through his shield. Damn it." Frustrated, he threw the Blade to the ground.

Latimus cursed, realizing that their enemy had grown stronger than he could've ever imagined. The time for seeing Deamons as a nuisance was over. Their leader had surpassed any barriers to his power. He and Kenden were going to have to strategize and revamp their entire plan of attack. Continuing the soldiers' battles in the caves would just lead to more death and loss.

Furious, he yelled, "Retreat!" Kenden nodded to him, still on the floor of the cave.

"Goddamnit!" Latimus said, his deep voice echoing in the chamber. Knowing he needed to rejoin his troops, he jumped from the rock as Darkrip dematerialized with the Blade. Marching from the cave, he began to think. He wouldn't let that asshole get the better of them. That was a fucking promise, and Latimus never broke his promises.

* * * *

Lila had only been at Lynia for a few days, but for the first time in ages, she felt like she was home. She didn't know how to explain it; sometimes, things just fit. For whatever reason, her high-born, aristocratic nature felt settled here—more than she ever had at Astaria. The walls there were so cold, the air filled with a pretentiousness that was stifling. Lynians were so kind and welcoming, and she had yet to meet a stranger. Every single person was quick to tell her their story and ask for hers. For a woman with no blooded family left, it was a blessing.

On her second day, she finally met Jack's uncle. He walked over, knocked on her door and offered her a chicken pot pie that he'd made.

Smiling, she invited him in, but he declined.

"Thank you kindly, ma'am, but I don't want to invade the privacy of your cabin. I hope you like the dish. I've been cooking a lot more lately, trying to find something that Jack would like. He seems to like food, and this is one of his favorites."

"Let me set that in the kitchen," she said, taking the dish from him. "Don't go away." After placing it on one of the tiny oven burners, she walked outside and sat on the stairs that led to her cabin.

"I'm Lila," she said, extending her hand down to him, as he sat on the bottom wooden step.

"Samwise," he said, shaking her hand. "Pleasure to meet you. Everyone calls me Sam."

"Well, thank you, Sam. I can't tell you how grateful I am to you. Not only for the pie, but for defending me when the Deamons attacked. I've rarely met someone so brave."

She thought she saw his cheeks redden a bit, and it made her heart swell. He was a handsome man, with a cap of blondish-reddish hair and kind brown eyes.

"I wish I helped you more. I saw what that bastard did to you. I can't even imagine how much it must've hurt." Lifting the stub of his severed arm, he sighed.

"I was bludgeoned in the Awakening, so many centuries ago, but it still hurts sometimes. Phantom arm, the fancy human doctor y'all have at Astaria calls it."

She rubbed his upper back, wanting to soothe him. "How scared you must have been as a young soldier during that time. I was only a child. Thank goodness we had strong soldiers such as you to help our people."

"So many died that day. It was a damn tragedy. Our king and queen are on the right path to restoring peace. I never thought I'd see the day. It's about time."

"Absolutely," she said, smiling down at him. "I didn't know Jack liked food. Although we don't need it, I love food too. And wine, if I'm being honest. Although, one glass, and I'm a tipsy idiot."

He breathed a laugh. "Well, we all have our vices." His mouth relaxed, forming into a slight frown. "Jack's mom was killed when the Deamons attacked. He's living with me now."

A wave of sadness overtook Lila. Her precious boy had now lost both his parents. Knowing how hard that was, she hurt for him. "Oh, Sam, I'm so sorry. I didn't know she'd passed."

"The bastards invaded her cabin. Jack was inside, hiding in one of the kitchen cabinets. He don't talk much about it but says they jumped on top of her before they murdered her. I think they raped her before they killed her." Sighing, he rubbed his hand over his face. "I can't imagine how he must've felt. He said that he counted to a hundred after the Deamons left and then ran to her and yelled at her to wake up."

"Oh, my god," Lila said, covering her mouth with her hands. Wetness filled her eyes, and she couldn't stop the tears. Wiping one away, she squeezed his shoulder. "I'm so sorry. That's terrible. I hate that we live in a world with so much pain. Jack is such a sweet boy and deserves to be surrounded with kindness. My heart is broken for him."

Sam nodded. "My sister never recovered after her husband was killed. She'd been withdrawn and quiet for the past year. I was living at Valeria before he passed, doing private security, but when her husband died, I moved here to help her with Jack. I'd like to hope that she's found some sense of peace, reuniting with Ralkin in the Passage."

Lila nodded. "Me too. We'll choose to believe that. In the meantime, I'd be happy to help you with Jack. I love children. Please don't hesitate to ask—I mean it."

He smiled. "Okay, Lila, will do. I don't know anything about being a parent, so I might need to call on you a lot. All I've ever been is a soldier and a bodyguard."

"I don't either," she said, chuckling, "but I've spent lots of time with kids and always wanted to have many of my own one day." Lowering her eyes, she studied the wooden step, mourning the children she'd never bear.

Sam stood and lifted her chin with his thick fingers. "Don't let that bastard decide one damn thing in your life. If you want to have kids, have a hundred. There are plenty of kids like Jack who need mothers, and they'd all be lucky to have you."

Heartened by his kind words, she stood and gave him a hug. "Thank you, Sam." Pulling back, she said, "Don't be a stranger, please. I'm so happy to be your neighbor."

"Same here," he said, smiling. "Jack will be home from school in a bit. I'll send him over to say hi."

"I'd like that."

Returning to her cabin, she sat down to work on her most recent painting. It was of the beautiful lavender flowers that grew on the riverbanks of the River Thayne. They'd always been her favorite. As she painted, she thought of Jack. How awful must it be to see one's mother raped and murdered before their very eyes? Determined to help him in any way she could, she painted, wanting to finish the piece before turning in at dawn.

An hour later, she called Arderin, who answered on the second ring.

"Please, tell me you're calling with a one-way ticket to the human world."

Lila laughed, always charmed by how funny her friend was. "Unfortunately not. Is it that bad?"

Arderin spent the next five minutes telling her all the ways she was sure to die from boredom at Astaria. After venting, she said, "Enough about my poor excuse for a life. How's yours going? Tell me everything."

They caught up, and Lila told her about Jack's mother.

"Oh, that poor little boy. He's lost both parents. That's terrible."

"It is. He's such a sweet little man. I can't wait for you to meet him."

"Latimus will avenge him and all the others Crimeous has hurt, including you. He attacked him tonight, although I don't think it went well."

Lila's heart began to pound, as it always did when she thought of Latimus in battle. "What happened?"

"I don't know exactly, but I heard him telling Sathan that he needs to stop the attacks for a while so that he and Kenden can strategize. I think Crimeous is becoming more powerful, and they're struggling to defeat him."

A shiver ran down her spine at the mention of the Deamon's powers. She had seen them first-hand. "There's no one better to defeat him than Latimus. If he sets his mind to it, he'll murder him."

"Said like someone who's in love with my favorite brother," Arderin said, her tone mischievous.

Lila rolled her eyes. "Your favorite brother told me I was a pathetic aristocrat who looks down at everyone from my ivory tower. I'm all set, thanks."

"He's an ass. We all know that. Now that he's taking a break from the monthly attacks on Crimeous, maybe he'll court you."

"I'd hold my breath but I like living, thank you very much."

Arderin chuckled. "How are you doing, Lila? Are you okay? I worry that you seem so...*together* after your injury. I would be a sopping mess."

Lila bit her bottom lip as she lifted her hand to rub her abdomen, right above her scar. "I know I should be screaming at the world, and I want to sometimes. But I haven't felt as angry as I have empty. Like it's all a nightmare and it will go away if I don't think about it. Is that weird?"

"It's not, sweetie. It's called denial. I've read about it in all the human psychology books that Sadie lent me. It's a good defense mechanism, but eventually, you're going to have to let your anger and grief surface. I think that's the only way you can let them go."

Lila inhaled a deep breath, processing her friend's words. "Well, when that time comes, I'll do what I can. In the meantime, I'm enjoying my life here. The people are so amazing. I can't wait to introduce you to them."

"I can't wait to visit," Arderin said. "Miranda swears that she's going to bring me before she gets too big. I'm excited to put faces to all the names you've told me about."

"Yes, I owe her a call so that we can set the date. By the way, when you come, can you bring me my brushes and palette? I forgot to pack them. I think they're in one of the drawers by my armoire, or maybe in my closet. You'll find them if you rummage around."

"Sure thing. I'm so glad you're painting again. You're so good. I don't have any talents."

"Stop that. You're an excellent clinician. Nolan and Sadie both told me that you were fantastic at treating our wounded soldiers after Miranda's battle with Crimeous. Plus, I think you're an expert at driving Sathan insane."

Arderin laughed. "That, I am. Okay, I'll let you go. I miss you so much."

"Miss you too. See you soon."

Lila plugged her phone in to charge and donned her silky pajamas. Closing the cabin's blackout blinds, she fell into a deep sleep.

Chapter 18

Latimus found his sister in the infirmary, her head stuck in a medical book.

"Hey," he said, jarring her from her study. "I have a favor to ask you."

Arderin lifted her head and removed her spectacles. She looked so cute in the damn things, and he felt himself smile.

"Someone's in a good mood," she said.

"Can't a guy just smile at his favorite sister?"

She scowled. "I'm your only sister."

Grinning, he leaned his hip on the counter and crossed his arms. "I need your help."

She lifted a raven-colored brow. "I'm listening. This must be good."

"I want to do something nice for Lila. Our idiot brother has convinced me I should try courting her. I have absolutely no idea how to even begin but figured you could maybe give me some ideas."

Excitement flashed through her ice-blue eyes, and she jumped up to hug him. "Oh, my god! Finally!" She squeezed him so hard that he struggled to breathe.

"Okay, okay, calm down. I'm not granting world peace here. By the goddess, you're strong. I should make you a soldier."

Black curls bobbed up and down as she jumped, her thin hands clapping together in front of her face. "She's gonna die."

He gave her a droll look. "Let's not get ahead of ourselves. She hates my guts. I said terrible things to her when she left for Lynia."

"Oh, whatever," she said, waving a hand. "She told me. You thought she was going to go bond with Camron. What an asshole. Thank the goddess she got rid of him."

"Did something happen between them?"

Fury swam in her eyes. "He refused to court her or bond with her because she's barren. Something about being the last of his line. A line of spineless pussies if you ask me. She deserves so much better."

Anger coursed through him, knowing how much his rejection must've hurt his proud Lila. What a bastard. Latimus wanted to rip every blue-blooded vein from his body and strangle him with them.

"Relax," his sister said, grabbing his forearm. "Let's not pound in the counter. She told him to fuck off. She's stronger than you think. Lila won't take shit like that from anyone."

"I know," he said, sighing. "She's taken it from me for ten centuries without even being phased. She's a fucking rock."

Arderin smiled. "She is. Okay, let me think." Tapping her forehead with her slim fingers, she muttered to herself. "You've been a complete and utter ass to her forever, so we're going to have to be smart about this."

He rolled his eyes. "Don't sugarcoat it."

"Well, you have. Okay, come with me." Grabbing his hand, she led him out of the infirmary. "We have a lot of work to do if we're gonna get this right."

Grinning, he followed her through the dungeon and up the stairs, determined to listen to his impertinent little sister.

* * * *

Lila observed Antonio inspect the three paintings she'd brought with her. Nervousness coursed through her as she waited, his gray head perusing them as they sat upon the table in his booth. Finally, he lifted his head and gave her a huge smile.

"My darling, these are fantastic. I had no idea you could paint this way. Why have you been hiding this from the world?"

Exhaling a breath of relief, she laughed. "You're exaggerating, but thank you, Antonio. I'm so glad you like them. It's been so long since I painted, and it feels so good to accomplish something again."

"My dear, you're going to make me a millionaire." He lifted his finger in the air, shaking it at her. "Please, let me sell them at my booth. I will only take a twenty percent cut for the cost of showing them."

"I'll only do it for a fifty-fifty split," she said. She wanted to give him one-hundred percent of any proceeds from her paintings, since she didn't need the money, but knew that pride would only let him acquiesce to that amount. She planned to use her half to purchase supplies for the literacy group as needed. "That's my one and only offer."

"Bella, that is too much—"

"Fifty-fifty or nothing," she said, interrupting him and holding up a hand. "I insist."

Giving her a warm smile, he grabbed her hands. "Okay, my dear. I agree. You bless me with your paintings."

Chuckling, she shook her head. "You define overstatement, my friend. Let me know how they sell. I'm off to my first literacy group meeting."

"Wonderful," he said, his eyes sparkling in the moonlight. "You are truly an angel, my dear."

Reveling in his compliments, she set off to the compound's main house, about a five-minute walk from the town square. Once inside, Lora greeted her and showed her to the house's large banquet room. She set up several chairs and waited for people to arrive. She had sent out several missives on the official royal radio channel, informing the kingdom of the group, and she hoped people would show.

Slowly, they began to wander in, timid and shy. A few had taken the train from Naria, a few were Lynians. There were eight women and three men. A good start.

She spent the first meeting just getting to know everyone. They went around in a circle, introducing themselves and explaining why they wanted to learn to read. Some were laborers, some were single mothers, some were servants. She was excited to give them tools that would help them to thrive in their sometimes treacherous world.

After going over the course itinerary, Lila instructed them that they would have a standing weekly meeting every Sunday evening. In between, they would have different assignments and things to practice. After the meeting, many of the members came up and hugged her, although it was Lila who was grateful to them for coming. Helping others had always been a great passion of hers, her father instilling that in her when she was very young.

On the walk home, Jack fell into step beside her. He'd come over the day she'd spoken to his uncle on her front stoop, and she'd held him to her breast, trying to absorb his hurt. All those centuries ago, when she'd lost her parents, it had left a hole that she still struggled to fill. Loneliness had always tried its best to consume her, and she'd always fought to stay strong. Determined to help Jack, she made a vow to carve out as much time in her life for him as possible. She knew he missed his mom, but her little man was handling the loss like a trooper. Chatting away as they walked, he mindlessly swung his toy sword through the air.

Once home, she made sure Jack entered Sam's cabin safely. Walking up the stairs that led to her cabin, a Vampyre soldier approached her and handed her a box, about the size of his beefy chest.

"Commander Latimus sent this for you, ma'am. He said that you're to open it tonight, and I'm not to leave until I see you walk inside with it."

"Okay," she said, awkwardly taking the package from him. "Thank you..."

"Draylok, ma'am."

"Thank you, Draylok. You can tell your commander that I've accepted the delivery."

With a nod, the Vampyre pivoted and stalked away.

Entering her cabin, she made sure to lock all the bolts behind her. Carrying the box to her bed, she opened it. Inside were the painting materials that she had asked Arderin to send her as well as a plethora of new, expensive brushes and paints. Lifting the white piece of paper that sat on top, she unfolded it:

Lila,

Arderin told me that you left your painting supplies behind, and I wanted you to have them. I bought you a few new ones too. Hope you can use them. I figured you'd be pissed that I invaded the privacy of your room to find your supplies, but since you hate my guts anyway, I took my chances.

Latimus

Smiling, she held the note to her nose. It held just the tiniest bit of his scent, musky and spicy. Whatever in the world had possessed him to do something nice for her? She had absolutely no idea. Perhaps he'd been hit on the head in his last battle, causing him some sort of temporary insanity. Shaking her head, she removed the supplies, excited to use them.

After organizing them with her other materials, she sat down on her bed and jotted him a note. Opening her door, she called for Draylok. After a moment, he appeared, as if he'd been waiting.

"Can you get this note to Commander Latimus for me?"

"Absolutely, ma'am," the man said. With a nod, he walked away.

Lila painted for a bit, loving her new provisions. Sending Latimus a silent thank-you in her mind, she set about preparing for bed.

* * * *

Latimus sat with Kenden, Darkrip, Miranda and Sathan around the conference room table, discussing Crimeous.

"He isn't even that harmed by a TEC," Latimus said. "Although it means sudden death for any other Deamon, it maims him, but he survives. I'm struggling to see how we can get the upper hand here."

Sathan stood, running his hand through his thick black hair as he did when he was frustrated. "We fucked up, letting him get so strong. None of us but Darkrip has anything near his abilities. Our physicality can't match his capability to dematerialize and manipulate things with his mind. I'll summon Etherya tonight and ask her council. Maybe she can enlighten me on something we're missing."

"There is one other who shares his powers," Kenden said.

"She's as evil as he is. I'd tread lightly." Darkrip said.

"I know that what you say is true," Miranda said, covering her brother's hand with his, "but perhaps you and I can earn her sympathy toward our cause. We share her blood. Doesn't that count for something?"

"Crimeous shares her blood too. Evie will never suppress her dark side as I have. She thrives on it."

Miranda pursed her lips, her nostrils flaring. "We have to try. Having both of you combine your powers against him could possibly render him unable to dematerialize. Then, you could strike him down. Or Evie, if she's the one the prophecy speaks of."

"It will never happen. She's lost to this world."

Miranda stood and began to pace. "I saw our grandfather in the Passage when I was injured. He mentioned her and said that I needed to help her find her way." Stopping, she looked down at Darkrip. "What is that, if not a divine message? I feel that I need to try."

Darkrip shook his head. "I know that telling you not to do anything will make you want to do it more, so I'll stop trying."

Everyone in the room nodded and muttered in agreement, causing Miranda to scowl at them.

"But you all are missing a bigger point here," Darkrip continued. "Now that you're pregnant, it's possible that your babe could also be the descendant of Valktor that kills my father. We have to consider that as well."

Miranda placed her hand over her abdomen, lifting her gaze to Sathan's. "We know. It's terrifying for us. We hope to have you or Evie attack him with the Blade before the baby is born, so that we spare him that burden."

Kenden smiled. "Do you know that it's a boy then?" he asked.

She shook her head. "We don't know yet, but I feel that it is. He's a strong little man like his dad."

Sathan walked over to her and placed his arm around her shoulders, drawing her into his side. "We need to do everything we can to kill Crimeous before the babe is born. I will summon the goddess. For now, everything else is on hold. I need you all to strategize as we work through this."

Kenden stood, nodding. "I'll be staying at Uteria for the next few weeks. Latimus will continue to train the troops, and I'll be coming in to relieve him every few nights. If you need me, I can come back anytime."

"Ken misses his shed," Miranda teased, her love for her cousin swimming in her eyes. "It's his favorite place."

He laughed. "It is."

Latimus stood, sensing the meeting was over. "Okay, then. Let's stay the course. Sathan, let me know when you meet with Etherya."

Adjourning, they began to disperse, and Latimus decided to head to his cabin for the day. Miranda called to him as he strode toward the conference room door.

"Yeah?" he said, stopping a few feet from the door.

Walking up to him, she threw her arms around his waist. Pulling him close, she rested her head on his chest. "I miss you. That's all. I just needed to hug you."

Extremely uncomfortable, Latimus looked at Sathan where he stood at the head of the conference room table. "Your bonded seems to be attached to me. Help."

"Stop it," she said, swatting his chest. "You've been so mean to me. It's awful."

"Well, you've been a pretty big asshole, Miranda. And your husband too," he said, watching his brother scowl. "You all keep meddling in my life. It's fucking annoying."

"Please, don't be mad at me. I'm pregnant. You'll hurt me and the baby."

With an incredulous laugh, he pulled her away from him by her upper arms. "Good grief. That's low, even for you." Although his words were harsh, love for her laced his tone.

"You know nothing's beneath me if it helps the ones I love. And I love you so much, Latimus. Please, don't hate me."

"I don't hate you. Now, you're just being an idiot. I'm allowed to be pissed at you guys. You keep doing really asinine shit that hurts my feelings."

"See?" she said, turning to her husband. "He has feelings. I told you!"

Rolling his eyes, Latimus chuckled and pulled her to him again. Sathan walked over and gave him several affectionate pats on the shoulder. "Be nice to my wife. She's a bear now that hormones are coursing through her. I can't have anyone else making her upset."

"You two are the worst," she said, reaching out an arm to her husband and pulling both of them toward her.

Latimus squeezed her and then stepped back. "I know you guys were trying to help. But it was extremely fucked-up that you kept Lila's relocation from me. I should've vetted her new living quarters."

"I did it myself," Sathan said, looking guilty. "I feel terrible, brother. I'm sorry. You know I would never keep something from you unless absolutely necessary. Considering that you kept Miranda's meetings with Darkrip from me, I know you understand that concept."

Latimus sighed. "Fine. Being pissed at you guys takes up too much energy. Next time, just have some faith in me, okay? I was actually getting up the nerve to ask her to bond with me, and you two sent her away. So, great fucking job."

"Really?" Miranda squeaked, her mouth falling open. "Oh, my god, that's fantastic!"

"Relax. She's three compounds away and detests me. Who knows what's going to happen?"

"She loves you," Miranda said, clutching his forearm. "Oh, Sathan," she said, looking at her bonded, "we're going to have another wedding!"

"Women," Latimus muttered. "Enough. Don't say anything," he said, pointing back and forth between both of them. "I need to do this on my own, without you two interfering in my life. Got it?"

"Got it," she said, nodding furiously. "I promise. Yay!"

Shaking his head at her, he bid them good day and started the trek to his cabin. Draylok was waiting for him in the barracks.

"Sir, Lila asked that I deliver this to you." He handed him a slip of folded paper.

"Thanks," Latimus said, sticking it in his pocket. Afraid to read it, he stalked through the meadow to his cabin. What if she'd written him and told him to fuck off?

After stepping inside and removing his shoes and the weapons on his belt, he pulled the note from the pocket of his black combat pants.

Latimus,

Thank you so much for getting the supplies to me. They're wonderful. Of course, I don't hate you, but I'll make sure not to tell anyone of your thoughtful gesture. I wouldn't want to ruin your reputation of being a hardened, unfeeling war commander.

Lila

Smiling, he placed the note on his bedside table. After he prepared for bed, he placed it under his pillow. He liked the idea of sleeping near something that she'd touched with her pretty, slim fingers.

Chapter 19

As the weeks wore on, Lila found herself loving her life at Lynia. The literacy group was going very well, and Antonio had sold all three of her paintings. She couldn't believe that anyone would buy her work but was thrilled all the same.

She also started a group for family members of the victims of the Deamon attack. They had lost twenty-three Vampyres when Crimeous attacked Lynia, and Lila wanted to make sure they had the proper support they needed. She met with them weekly, under the beautiful oak trees in the park near the town square. As they processed their grief, she felt herself healing along with them. Knowing that others had lost so much comforted her in a strange way. Loss was a great connector.

A week after Latimus sent the first note, Draylok showed up on her doorstep with a large white envelope. Inside, she found a note that read:

Lila,
As I'm sure you've heard, my annoying little sister adopted a dog. His name is Mongrel and his favorite pastime is pissing on my leg. It's extremely infuriating. I have visions of leaving him outside the wall but know that it will crush her, so I just let the damn thing torture me. Enclosed are a few pictures. I thought he might be a good subject for one of your paintings.
Latimus

Reaching inside, she pulled out several pictures of a small, fluffy dog with scraggly brown and white hair. Arderin was hugging him in some of the pictures, joy evident on her pretty face. Lila laughed when she thought of Latimus scowling as the dog relieved himself on his leg. It was a pretty funny mental image.

Grabbing her stationery, she jotted him a note:

Latimus,
Thank you so much for the pictures. Mongrel is adorable. I know you pretend to hate him, but I'm sure you treasure the joy he brings Arderin. You've always loved her so. I hope you'll come and see my painting of him once I'm finished.
Lila

A week later, Draylok showed up with another package. Lila's heart leapt as she opened it up on her bed. Reaching inside, she noticed it was a belt of some sort. A note sat at the bottom of the box.

Lila,

Arderin told me about Jack. I'm so sorry to hear that his parents have passed. I'd like to know his father's name, as I'm sure I knew him if he died in the cave during last year's battle. I can honor him with a medal of valor.

Enclosed is one of my old weaponry holders. It's meant to be worn around the waist, although it's too big for Jack now. I used it before the eight-shooter was invented, and it's probably pretty valuable. You'd know better than me, being that you're an aristocrat, and I never wanted any part of the stuffy world of auctions and expensive things.

Please, give it to Jack and let him know I'm looking forward to meeting him when I come to visit you at Lynia. I hope you'll invite me soon. I never realized how calming your presence was when you were here. With you gone, it's unbearable. Of course, you probably had to leave so I wouldn't keep being an intolerable jerk to you. I'd apologize, but it would never be enough.

Latimus

Lila's hands trembled as she read the letter over and over, not believing that the man who had been so nasty to her for so long had written the kind words. Placing the letter under her pillow, she went to find Jack.

He leaped out of his uncle's cabin, sword in hand.

"Hi, Lila," he called, and her heart swelled as it always did around him.

"Hi. I have something for you." Lifting the belt, she pointed to it with her free hand.

"What is it?"

"It's a weaponry belt, from Commander Latimus. He wanted you to have it." The boy's eyes grew wide as saucers as she placed it gently in his hands. "He used it before the eight-shooter was invented. He thinks you're going to be a great soldier one day and wishes for you to use it as you train."

"Wow," the boy breathed, running his fingers over the material. "This is so cool."

"Yeah," she said, giggling as she mussed his red hair. "Pretty cool."

"Can you put it on me?"

Nodding, she wrapped it around his waist twice, tying it so that it would stay up. Turning him toward her, she said, "You look like a proper warrior. So regal and brave."

"I'll show those Deamons," he said, slicing his toy sword through the air. Lifting her gaze, she saw Sam leaning on the open doorframe, smiling down at them. She winked at him.

"They don't stand a chance against you." She played with him for a while, feigning abduction so that he could save her. Afterward, Sam invited her in, and they all drank Slayer blood around the small fireplace as Jack chatted away.

Once home and ready for bed, she pulled the note out from under her pillow. What the heck was Latimus after? Was he trying to court her? How strange. She had no idea what to make of his unusual behavior. Deciding to let herself enjoy it, she pulled out her stationery and wrote to him:

Lattie,

I can't begin to thank you. You made a little boy who's lost so much smile with joy. You really are such a good man. I wish you would let yourself believe it. You're welcome to visit me anytime. After all, you are the Commander. I'm pretty sure you have free reign of the kingdom. I'm in the cabin with the yellow flowers outside. One day soon, I'm going to plant some violets, but I haven't gotten around to that yet.

I confess, I'm not sure why you've decided to be nice to me, but it's truly wonderful. I imagine you're scowling, since I used the nickname that you hate, but I've always loved it. It reminds me of when we were children. You never minded when I used it all those centuries ago. We were best friends then, and I hope we can find our way to being friends again.

Lila

Folding the note, she stuck it in the envelope and wrote *Lattie* on the outside. Calling for Draylok, he appeared outside her door, and she asked him to deliver it. After preparing for bed, she read his note again, emotion pulsing through her at his words. Smiling, she fell to sleep with the note under her pillow.

* * * *

Lila awoke at dusk with a feeling of excited joy. Arderin and Miranda were coming to visit her. Prepping for the night, she readied herself and then headed into town. She held Jack's hand as he chatted beside her. She'd offered to walk him to school so that he could meet her friends first.

They arrived on the train, and she ran to them, hugging each one tightly.

"You made it."

"Thank the goddess I'm off that compound," Arderin said. "You have to show me everything."

Miranda rolled her eyes. "You'd think she lived in the Deamon caves, for god's sake."

Laughing, Lila led them to the top of the stairs, where Jack stood waiting.

"Jack, these are my friends, Arderin and Miranda. Ladies, this is Jack."

The little boy bowed to Miranda.

"It's a pleasure to meet you, my queen and my princess."

Miranda laughed. "So formal. You must meet my husband. He'd love you." Crouching down, she pulled him into a hug. "Can you just call me Miranda?"

Giving her a huge smile, the boy nodded.

Arderin also crouched down to give him a hug, and then, they were on their way.

"I told everyone at school that the queen was bringing me today. It's Wednesday, so we get fifteen minutes of extra recess. I'm gonna wear the belt that Commander Latimus gave me."

"How magnificent," Lila said, holding his hand as they walked. "It will help you to hold all your mighty weapons."

Miranda and Arderin shot her sly smiles as they walked him to school, unable to get a word in as he chatted endlessly. After dropping him off, she led them into the town square.

"Bella, you've brought me more beautiful women to paint," Antonio said, hugging her. "How am I to breathe with such beauty surrounding me?"

"Well, aren't you a charmer?" Miranda asked, one raven eyebrow arched.

"You don't know the half of it," he said, eyes sparkling. "It is a pleasure to meet you, my queen." Placing his arm across his waist, he gave her a regal bow.

"No way, Antonio. We're not doing that formal stuff. How about you give me a hug so that I can thank you for taking such good care of our Lila?" Smiling, she embraced him.

Arderin extended her hand, and he pulled her in for a hug as well. After chatting for a while, she led them around the square, introducing them to all the vendors she knew. They bought some ice cream and headed to sit in the park.

"Wow, Lila, this place is great," Miranda said in between bites of her rocky road. "You've really acclimated, and everyone seems to love you."

"Everyone's been so welcoming," she said. "I can't believe it. I've never met people more kind."

"Whatever, Lila. You're, like, the nicest person ever. Of course, everyone loves you." Arderin licked the vanilla scoop on top of her cone.

"That's very sweet."

"And how's my brother treating you?" she asked, waggling her eyebrows. "He says he's trying hard to win you over."

Lila breathed a laugh as she took a bite of her chocolate sundae. "It's so strange. He's being so nice to me. I have no idea how to interpret it."

Miranda shot her a droll look. "Um, you invite him here, let him woo you and bone his brains out. It's pretty simple, Lila."

Feeling herself blush, she shook her head. "I don't know the first thing about any of that. I'm so afraid he'll think I'm frigid or something."

"That's absurd," Miranda said. "Let me tell you something about men. If you're naked, they're slobbering idiots. You'll have all the control, trust me."

"I don't know," Lila said. "Just thinking of being with him that way makes me so nervous."

"I can't wait to have magnificent sex," Arderin said, leaning back on her slim arm and gazing at the blackened sky. "I'll rock his freaking world. Whoever *he* is. I haven't figured that part out yet."

Lila laughed at her friend, who'd always had a flair for the dramatic. "I envy your confidence. I've always been shy and tried so hard to overcome it. One can't be a good diplomat if they're burdened with shyness."

"You're an amazing diplomat, Lila," Miranda said, standing to throw her empty container in the nearby trash can. "We'll be ready to roll out the trains to Uteria and Restia soon, and I can't wait for you to lead point. You did a great job with the trains for the Vampyre compounds. The ridership is increasing week by week."

"Thanks," Lila said, standing. "I'm excited for it. Are you all ready to see my place? I warn you, it's really small."

"Let's do it," Arderin said, bouncing up and depositing her napkin in the trash can.

They walked the ten minutes to her cabin and entered. Both of her friends marveled at the various pieces she was working on as they set upon the easels beside her bed.

"My god, Lila, I had no idea you were this talented," Miranda said, staring at one of her paintings of Lynia's town square. "We have a gallery at the marketplace at Uteria. I'd love to have you place some pieces there."

"Really?" Lila said, biting her lip. "That would be great."

"Definitely. I'll speak to Aron. He's friends with the owner. We'll set it up."

"Thank you."

"Mongrel looks so adorable in this picture," Arderin said, pointing to the piece. "He's such a cute puppy. He pees on Latimus all the time. It's the funniest thing I've ever seen." She broke into a fit of giggles.

The three of them sat on her bed in the tiny space and caught up for several more hours. Finally, the faint light of dawn began to streak the horizon outside the window, and they left for the train station. Lila walked them there, hugging them both firmly before they headed down the stairs to the platform. She felt blessed to have such wonderful friends. Happy and tired, she trekked home in the pale glow of pre-dawn.

Chapter 20

Latimus read Lila's note, a chuckle escaping his upturned lips at the nickname she used. She'd called him that when they were small, and he'd always liked it. After they drifted apart, she'd let it slip from time to time. He would always scold her and tell her he hated it. Of course, what he really hated was being reminded of how much he'd loved her, even as a child, when she was promised to his brother.

All these centuries later, he longed to have her use it again. To have her look into his eyes and whisper it as he made love to her, deeply and slowly. By the goddess, he wanted so badly to hold her and kiss away all the pain he'd ever caused.

When dusk arrived, he headed to the main house to find the gardener. He had cultivated the pretty flowers that surrounded the castle for centuries. Finding him, he detailed the man on what he needed. The gardener, a nice man by the name of Elon, knew Lila. Smiling, he told stories of how she'd helped plant some of the flowers over the ages, although she swore him to secrecy because aristocrats weren't supposed to perform the tasks of laborers. According to him, she had a green thumb and was always willing to roll up her sleeves and teach newly-trained landscapers the best way to cultivate the plants so they would thrive.

Latimus smiled as he listened to the man, humbled by her genuineness. He wondered if there was anyone else as selfless on the planet as she. After she ended her betrothal with Sathan, and he'd realized her feelings for him, he'd contemplated how someone like her could care for a black-hearted bastard like him. It was just one more example of pure compassion on her part, caring for him as she did. He was one lucky son of a bitch.

Paying the gardener and obtaining his sworn secrecy, he headed back to his cabin. Kenden was training the troops, but Latimus felt a nervous energy and needed an outlet. Throwing on his training gear, he headed to the field to spar with them.

*****

Lila had a busy night in town. She dropped off two more paintings for Antonio to sell and then spent three hours with her literacy group. After that, she met Sam and Jack and treated them to a lovely dinner of Slayer blood, pasta and warm bread. Sam seemed uncomfortable with letting her pay, but she insisted, and he finally relented. They shared a bottle of wine and laughed as Jack smacked his mouth while eating the food, which he deemed "amazeballs."

Approaching her cabin under the moonlight, she lifted her hands to her cheeks and gasped. Lavender and violet flowers surrounded the wooden cottage in a large circle of vibrant and soft purple. They were beautiful as they swayed in the gentle breeze of the warm night.

"Those are real pretty," Sam said. "I have a feeling your commander had a hand in that." His brown eyes twinkled in the starlight.

She gave him a huge smile. "I think so too. By the goddess, they're magnificent."

"Well, we'll let you get on with thanking him. Say good night, Jack," he said, pulling his nephew to his side.

"Good night, Jack," the boy said and then broke down into giggles.

"Oh, you're so funny," Lila said, bending down and lifting him up to twirl him around. "Our own little jokester. You have to meet Heden. You two can have a joking contest."

"I'll beat him," Jack said as she sat him down on the plushy grass. "Because I'm the joke master."

Laughing, she tousled his hair. "That, you are. Good night, Jack. Good night, Sam."

"Good night, Jack!" the little boy said again, and they all laughed as they entered their cottages.

Pulling out her phone, Lila exhaled a huge breath, her heart pounding. With slightly shaking fingers, she found Latimus' name in her contacts. Pressing the button, she lifted the phone to her ear.

"Please, tell me you like purple flowers and not red ones." His deep voice reverberated through her body, making it throb. "I was intimidated by the insane number of flowers we have on this planet."

"They're my favorite," she said, sitting on the bed and mentally scolding the organ furiously beating in her chest. "I can't believe you did this. How? It's a huge undertaking to plant so many flowers in such a short time."

"You would know. Elon told me that you've been planting flowers with the servants for centuries. Imagine if I told your Aunt Ananda. She'd shrivel up and die, the old bag."

Lila laughed, imagining her rigid aunt doing just that. "You're terrible." Sighing, she cursed herself an idiot since she'd lost the ability to do anything but smile into the phone. "So, you had Elon plant them."

"Along with some of his workers, yes. I would've tried myself, but you'd have a pile of dirt instead of flowers, so I figured I'd leave it to the professionals. I made sure they came on a night when you were busy, so they'd have time. I think they only finished about half an hour ago."

Elation at his thoughtfulness coursed through her. "They're so beautiful. I don't know what to say. I was intending to plant some violets when I had the time. I feel so at home here, and that was going to be my last step."

"Well, I hope you're not upset that I had it done. I always seem to fuck up around you. I wanted to save you the trouble of doing it. And I wanted to do something nice for you."

"I'm not upset at all. I'm so thankful. It's such an amazing gift. Thank you, Latimus."

"You're welcome."

Silence stretched, and she yearned to say so much to him, but she was so nervous. Fear of sounding like a moron kept her quiet.

He sighed, sad and soft, through the phone, and her fangs toyed with her lip as she waited.

"God, Lila. I don't even know where to start," he said. "I have so many things I want to say to you. So many apologies I want to make. But they all sound so lame when I think about them. The way I've treated you is unforgivable. I don't even know how to start making it up to you. But I want to try. If you'll let me."

"Lattie," she said, expelling a soft breath into the phone. "We've both made mistakes. So many, for so long. I hate that our history is filled with so much anger and hurt. I meant what I said about being friends. I want that so badly for us."

He was quiet for a moment. "I don't just want to be your friend, Lila. I mean, of course, I want that. But I want more. It took me a long time to get to the place where I accept that. I need to know if you're at that place too."

Blood pounded in her veins at his words. The man whom she had loved with her whole heart her entire life was finally saying the words she'd always longed to hear. It was terrifying for some reason. Deciding that the moment deserved nothing but genuine honesty, she said, "I think I've always been in that place. I was waiting for you."

His responding puff of air, as if he'd been holding his breath, seemed to travel over the phone, and she rubbed the bumps that rose on her forearms.

"I'd really like to visit you at Lynia," he said. "Kenden's spending more time at Uteria now, so this week is busy for me, but maybe I can come next Monday? He's going to train the troops that night, and I'm free."

Lila contemplated, scared at what his visit would mean. Would he want to sleep with her? Was she ready for that? She was terrified that he'd find her cold and lacking in bed. Chewing her bottom lip, she struggled to say yes.

"Please?" he said, the slight whine in his voice making her smile. "I'd just spend the whole night thinking about you anyway. And I promise that this is just so that I can spend time with you. I'm not looking for anything else. We've got all the time in the world. I just want to be with you. I'll even let you call me by that stupid fucking nickname the entire time."

Lila laughed, so charmed by him. "Okay. Should I meet you at the train platform?"

"Sure," he said. "I'll arrive around dusk, and we can walk into the main square. Arderin said the vendors are really nice, and I'd like to meet Antonio. I need to tell him to stop flirting with my woman."

Chuckling, she nodded. "Okay, see you then. I'm excited for you to visit."

"Me too. Good day. I can't wait to see you."

"Good day. Thank you so much for the flowers. I love them."

"You're welcome. See ya soon."

Lila groaned and threw herself upon her bed, smiling wider than she ever had. The impossible had finally happened. Latimus had decided to let himself care for her. Excitement and nervousness ran through her, warring with each other. Unable to calm herself, she poured a glass of wine and sat on her stairs under the stars, beside the gorgeous flowers.

Chapter 21

A week later, Lila spent a sleepless day in anticipation of his arrival. Frustrated at her inability to sleep, she got up two hours before dusk and readied herself for the night. Spending extra time on her hair and makeup, she applied the finishing touches as she looked at herself in the mirror, deciding she didn't look half bad. Her hair was full, and she'd used extra eyeliner so that the violet in her eyes seemed to glow.

Wearing jeans, a silky, thin-strapped tank top and flirty sandals, she locked up her cabin and headed into town. Nervous anxiety filled her every pore. Arriving at the top of the platform, she waited, telling her treacherous heart to calm down.

Several people exited the train, and she saw Latimus trudging up the stairs. He was wearing a light blue, buttoned and collared shirt, jeans and black loafers that matched his black belt. She'd rarely seen him dressed in anything but tactical gear, and he looked so handsome. She noticed the gun and knife holstered on his belt and figured he was trained to always be armed. His black hair was pulled into a leather strap, leaving his ice-blue eyes to roam over her.

"Hey," she said, her head tilting back as he approached. At six-foot, three-inches, she was tall for a Vampyre female, but he was massive.

"Hey," he said, smiling down at her. "You look so pretty."

"Oh, this?" she asked, fluffing her hair. "I just rolled out of bed this way."

The whiteness of his teeth and fangs surrounded by his full red lips made little pangs of desire burn in her stomach. "Can't wait to see that one day." Embarrassed, she felt her whole body flush.

"Ready to walk me into town?" he asked.

"Ready."

His beefy hand seized her smaller one, and he laced his fingers through hers. "Let's do it."

Walking leisurely, they caught up on Arderin, Miranda and everyone else back home. She laughed at his stories of Arderin torturing Sathan and Heden DJ'ing at the last royal party.

"I was sad to miss the last party but had a survivor's support group meeting that night. Was it fun?"

"Loads," he said, rolling his eyes.

She laughed and squeezed his hand in hers. "You always hated those parties. Why did you come anyway?"

"Arderin always made me promise. And I knew you'd be there. It was always fun to watch you dance and see you happy. The parties were one of the rare times I had an excuse to be near you."

Biting her lip, she decided to let that one go, not wanting to bring all the hurt and pain of their past into the evening.

Antonio called her name as they neared his tented booth.

"So, you have brought the commander to scare me away from you," he said, his eyes glowing with mischief. "It won't work, my friend. She is mine, and I will battle you to the death for her."

Latimus smiled down at him. "Death is a worthy outcome in a battle for our Lila." Sliding his sky-blue gaze, he winked at her.

"No doubt," Antonio said, nodding furiously. "I am pleased to meet you, Commander. Thank you for protecting our people. Your work is noble."

Latimus shook his outstretched hand. "Of course. I strive each night to protect our people so they can lead full lives."

Lila's heart swelled as she observed them speak. Latimus had fought valiantly for ten centuries for their people's freedom and security. Extreme pride in his selflessness and bravery coursed through her.

They chatted for another few minutes, and then, Lila led him through the town, introducing him to the people she knew. They stopped at a wine bar and ordered her favorite bottle of red. Sitting at the long table by the window, they drank Slayer blood and wine, savoring each other.

Finally, several hours had passed, and there were only two hours until dawn.

"I'd really like to see your cabin, if you're comfortable taking me there. I'd love to see your artwork and the flowers. And if Jack's home from school, I'd like to meet him and see Sam."

Lila chewed her bottom lip, studying his handsome features. Deciding that she couldn't deny Jack the opportunity to meet his hero, she acquiesced.

Holding hands, they strolled to her cabin. Latimus scolded her that she should have a soldier escort her each time she took the ten-minute walk to town. Knowing that he wished to protect her, she informed him that she felt safe on the compound. Thankfully, he let it go.

When they arrived at her cabin, they stood at the base of the wooden steps that led inside. "Let me go get Jack," she said, thrilled at how happy her little man was going to be.

Knocking on Sam's door, she waited as she heard pounding footsteps.

"Lila!" the boy said, opening the door. He was always so excited to see her, and it warmed her heart.

"I have a surprise for you."

"What is it? Another belt?"

"Better."

Extending her hand, she gave a tip of her head to Sam, who waved at her from inside. The boy grabbed her hand, and she pulled him toward her cabin. As they approached, she heard him whisper, "No way."

"Jack, this is Latimus. He's very excited to meet you."

The boy's red head tipped so far back she thought his neck might snap. His brown eyes grew wide as his mouth formed an "O" shape.

"Hi, Jack," Latimus said, extending his hand down to the boy. "Lila's told me so much about you. It's a pleasure to finally meet you."

Jack's tiny arm lifted as if in slow-motion, and he shook Latimus' hand. Lila struggled not to laugh as he stood enthralled while the hulking Vampyre commander loomed over him.

"You seem to have rendered him speechless," she said to Latimus. "I've never seen him do anything but chatter. It's amazing."

Latimus smiled at her and then sat on the grass, crossing his bulky legs.

"Are you taking good care of my belt? I wore that centuries ago and wanted to make sure I passed it on to a worthy warrior."

The boy nodded furiously, and Latimus chuckled.

"Good. I hear your father was a great soldier. And your uncle as well. Hopefully, I'll be lucky enough to have you in my army one day."

"I'm really good at fighting," the boy said. "Let me show you. One minute."

In a flash, he was gone, barreling into the house and then returning with his toy sword. Furiously, he swung it through the air, fighting imaginary Deamons. Latimus watched, grinning.

"You're already a fine soldier, Jack," he said, motioning with his hand for him to approach. When he did, he took his small hand and rearranged it around the handle of the toy, giving the boy a firmer grip. "Hold it this way. It will make it less likely that your opponent can knock it out of your hand."

"Okay," the boy said and resumed flinging the sword through the air.

They stayed there for a while, Latimus sitting on the ground while the boy played. Lila had never seen him interact with children, but he was a natural. She thought of the child that Miranda and Sathan were going to have, and a mental image formed of Latimus holding the babe. If she still had a uterus, it would most likely be filled with yearning. Not wanting to dwell on the sadness of her injury, she watched her two men, emotion swamping her.

Sam eventually came outside and shook hands with him. Latimus thanked him for protecting Lila, and he nodded, telling Latimus that he considered her family. He was such a sweet man.

Finally, Sam pulled Jack inside, and they were left alone again.

"Want to show me some of your paintings?" Latimus asked, extending his hand to her.

"Yes," she said, grabbing on for dear life, determined not to let her shyness and nervousness dictate the end of their evening. Pulling him behind her, she walked up the stairs to her cottage.

* * * *

Latimus entered Lila's tiny cabin, thoroughly enjoying their evening. When he'd seen her standing on the train platform, he'd told himself to calm down. She'd looked so gorgeous, dressed in her tight jeans and dark green blouse, her hair full. Visions of pulling that hair to expose her neck to his fangs had threatened to overtake him, and he'd had to squelch them.

Although Vampyres required Slayer blood for sustenance, they were known to drink from each other while mating. Drinking from another Vampyre wouldn't allow for a transfer of thoughts and memories, as drinking from a Slayer would. Instead, it created a union that was only shared by two bonded mates. The act exemplified a deep intimacy, and Latimus longed to connect with Lila that way.

But this evening was about her. He wanted to court her, to make her comfortable around him. He didn't know a lot about romance but he knew it didn't start with him being a horny jerk.

So, he'd pushed those images from his mind and concentrated on being with her. Loving every minute of the evening, he still felt the glow from meeting Jack. The kid was special, and he could see why Lila loved him so.

Releasing her hand, he removed the Glock and knife from his belt, placing them on the little wooden table that sat by the door. Glancing around, he was impressed with what she'd been able to do with the sparse space. Pictures and paintings lined the wooden walls, and her king-sized bed had a pretty royal blue comforter. Little pillows dotted the headboard, and he smiled, recalling how Miranda always chided her for having a thousand pillows on her bed. Light shone from a lamp that sat on a chest beside her bed, and she had a small desk with a wooden chair in the corner. Several canvases with various subjects sat on easels in the middle of the room. She'd painted sunsets and flowers, people and landscapes. They were all quite remarkable.

"Wow, Lila, these are awesome," he said, walking into the room to study her paintings. "I'm definitely not an art expert, but you don't have to be to see how talented you are." Tilting his head to look into her violet eyes, he smiled. "I knew you painted but I just had no idea. You're amazing."

Her pink lips lifted into a grin as twin splotches of red appeared on her cheeks. She was embarrassed at his compliment. It was adorable.

"I'm working on one of you," she said, walking over and pulling the white sheet off a canvas. Underneath was his image, painted in black and gray. It showed the upper half of his body, broad shoulders and wide chest. His expression was thoughtful as he stared in the distance. The only colors on the canvas were his ice-blue eyes. Small streaks of dirt marred his face, and his hair was pulled back, showcasing his widow's peak. It was the painting of a warrior, strong and noble, and his heart swelled to think that she saw him that way, considering he'd been less than noble to her for centuries.

Swallowing deeply, he turned to her. "That's really good. How did you do that from memory? Unless you have some unauthorized pictures of me I should know about?" He lifted an eyebrow, teasing her.

She shrugged. "Your face is the most handsome I've ever seen. I think I have it memorized."

His eight-chambered heart slammed in his chest at her beautiful words. Lost to emotion, he searched her eyes, unable to keep from touching her. Bending down, he slid his hands over her hips, reveling in her gasp. Never moving his eyes from hers, he placed his palms underneath the globes of her gorgeous ass and lifted her. Long, slender arms surrounded his neck, and her ankles crossed at his back. Striding across the room, he gently placed her back against the wall. Lavender irises gazed into his.

Lowering her, he grew instantly hard as she slid down his body. Her arms remained around his neck as he lifted his hands to cup her face.

"It humbles me that you can see me that way after how terribly I've treated you." He rested his forehead on hers and shook his head. "I don't deserve you."

"It's not about what we deserve. It's about how we feel," she said, hugging him into her with her arms, the soft skin of her forehead rubbing his.

Exhaling, he lifted his head slightly to look at her. Into her. "If I'd known there was a chance you wouldn't bond with Sathan, I would've lived my life so differently. I should've fought for you. It's unforgivable."

She smiled, her white teeth so pretty as they glowed in the light of her bedside lamp. "We can't change the past. I've worked hard to come to a place where I've stopped trying. All we can do is make better choices in the present, so that we can have the future we want."

Admiration of her strength surged through him as the pads of his thumbs stroked the smooth skin of her cheeks. "I was so horrible to you. I can't believe you still care for me."

Blond hair fanned the wall at her shoulders as she shook her head. "I never had a choice. I think I was born loving you."

A shudder ran though him at her words, his massive frame shaken by her genuineness. By the goddess, she deserved to be loved and cherished for a thousand eternities. He was terrified to let her down.

"I fought my feelings for you for so long. As a soldier, all I ever learned to do was fight. It served me well in every area of my life except for when it came to you." Sinking down, he palmed her butt and lifted her again. When she wrapped her ankles around his waist, his hand came up to finger through her soft hair. Grasping the strands ever so gently, he tilted her head back. "I'm so tired of fighting and scared as hell that I'll never be worthy of you." Lowering his face, he rubbed her nose with his. "But I just can't fight anymore. I surrender. My feelings for you are the greatest foe I've ever faced." Softly, he brushed his lips against hers, shivering when she huffed a warm breath over his face.

Pressing his thick lips to hers, he groaned when she opened them slightly, giving him access. Thrusting his tongue inside, it roamed and mated with hers. Her taste assaulted him, filled with spring and lavender and a hint of metal, most likely from the Slayer blood they'd recently consumed at the wine bar. Breathy pants filled him as he finally kissed the woman he'd loved for a thousand lonely years.

The shy swipes of her tongue and small movements of her lips against his drove him wild. "Kiss me back," he said, feeling her tremble at his voice.

"I am," she said, gently nipping his lower lip. His erection jerked as it rested in the juncture of her thighs, longing to be inside her deepest place.

"I want you to taste me," he said, jutting his tongue into her mouth and sweeping up every drop of her. "Give me your tongue."

Slowly, she extended her tongue into his mouth, and he moaned. Closing down on it, he sucked, drawing a sexy mewl from her. The smell of her arousal threatened to choke him, and he knew she was dripping for him in her tight jeans. Opening his mouth again, she darted inside, licking him, and he almost came in his pants. God, the woman might just kill him.

He plundered her, grasping her hair, his hips moving in tiny juts against her. Not wanting to rush her, he pulled back, nibbling on her lip before looking into her eyes. They stared back at him, filled with passion and desire, and he knew he was lost. Now that he'd touched her, his life would never be the same. Determined to do right by her, he struggled to calm his breathing.

"Good god. If I get this worked up by kissing you, I can't imagine how it will feel to be inside you."

A rush of red filled her entire face, and he almost chuckled at her shyness. Not wanting to inadvertently hurt her feelings, he nuzzled his nose against hers. "I'd ask you how you got so good at kissing, but I don't want to go to prison for murdering any of the bastards who touched you."

Fangs squished her bottom lip as it turned into a grin. "There's only ever been you."

"Really?" he asked, humbled that he was the only man to touch her this way. He made a mental note to thank Etherya a million times in his prayers for that gift. A bastard such as he certainly didn't deserve it, but he was honored nonetheless.

"Really," she said, nodding. "You kissed me by the river when we were kids, and that was it for me. I never wanted anyone else."

"I think that *you* kissed *me* by the river that day," he said, teasing her.

"I most certainly did not."

"You totally did. I was an innocent boy. You corrupted me."

She slapped him playfully on the shoulder, and he chuckled. "Liar," she said, her smile so brilliant, illuminating her magnificent face. "Besides, I'm sure you don't remember anyway. That was centuries ago. So much has happened since then."

"I remember. Trust me, that day haunted me every time I tried to sleep for ten centuries. It was the last time I remember being happy."

"Oh, Lattie," she said, cupping his face. "I'm so sorry." Regret swam in her exquisite eyes. "I should've told you ages ago that I never loved Sathan. I just didn't think you'd care."

He sighed, lowering his forehead to hers. "It's all my fault. I'm such a coward. I was so afraid that he was the better man and could give you everything I couldn't. I never even dreamed you would care for a black-hearted, war-torn asshole like me. You're the most beautiful woman I've ever seen. I just couldn't fathom that you'd want me."

"I was worried that you wouldn't want me either," she said, rubbing his cheek with the pad of her thumb. "I'm not experienced at all. I'm so afraid I won't be able to please you."

Lifting his head, he looked into her eyes. "Are you serious right now?" he asked.

Her shoulders lifted into a shrug, her smile heartbreaking. "What if I can't satisfy you? You know, physically? I'm still a virgin. It's embarrassing."

Unable to control himself, he breathed a laugh. "That's the most ridiculous thing I've ever heard."

"Don't laugh at me," she said, her pink lips forming a frown. "I'm serious. What if you realize I suck and get tired of me?"

Shaking his head, he laughed again. "By the goddess, woman, you're some kind of fool if you think I'd ever get tired of fucking you." He pushed his erection into the juncture of her thighs, eliciting a gasp from her. "When you're ready, I'm going to kiss every inch of your gorgeous body and fuck you until you can't even remember your name."

The features of her face scrunched together. "Don't be vile."

Chuckling, he stole a kiss from her still-swollen lips. "My proper little blue-blood, always putting me in my place. Wait until I whisper dirty words in your ear. You're gonna come so hard."

"Stop," she said, swatting his chest. "You're a heathen."

"You love that I'm a heathen." He nipped her lower lip. "You love that I say vile things and think dirty thoughts of you. I can smell your arousal. It's so fucking hot. I can't wait to lick every drop from between your pretty legs."

Another wave of her arousal burst through the room, and he had to struggle to control himself. Closing his eyes, he exhaled a deep breath. Lowering her down his body, he set her on the floor and stole one last chaste kiss from her.

"I have to train the troops on Tuesday and Wednesday, but Kenden can train them on Thursday and Friday. Can you meet me at my cabin at dusk on Thursday?"

"Why?"

"It's a surprise. Can you meet me there at dusk?"

White fangs played with her bottom lip, and he had to adjust his swollen shaft inside his pants. The habit was indescribably hot. "I'm going to Uteria to show some of my paintings to a gallery owner on Saturday. I was thinking of maybe heading there a few days early to see Miranda."

"Miranda's great, but I'm better," he said, feeling the corners of his lips turn up into a mischievous smile. "Bring your paintings with you on Thursday, and you can stay with me. I'll drive you to Uteria on Saturday morning."

Her eyes darted back and forth between his, contemplating. He could tell that the thought of spending two full days in his cabin was unsettling to her, knowing he only had one bed, and she'd be in it. Fuck yes. He was determined to make that happen.

"Please?" he asked, giving her his best puppy-dog look.

"You're hopeless," she said, rolling her eyes. "Okay. I'll be there at dusk on Thursday."

"Can't wait." Anticipation coursed through him. He was finally going to have her in his bed. His cock jerked in his pants, and he cleared his throat.

Pulling her to him, he gave her one last kiss. Cupping her cheek, he ran his thumb over her lips. "See you then."

"See you then," she said against his thumb.

Turning, he walked to the door and reattached the weapons to his belt. Gazing up at her, he winked, loving the resulting blush that covered her body. Hating to leave her, but ready to get on with it so that Thursday would come faster, he exited her cabin.

As he walked under the stars to the train platform, he thanked Etherya repeatedly in his mind. He'd finally had the courage to claim his Lila. Knowing that he was now on a path where she was his first and most important priority, he resolved to be worthy of her. She was so rare and precious, and he would do everything in his power to love her properly. Reaffirming the commitment to himself and to Etherya, he boarded the train back to Astaria.

Chapter 22

On Thursday, Lila packed a bag with enough clothes and toiletries to last a few days. Nervousness pulsed in her belly as she grabbed the three paintings she wanted to showcase at Uteria. She would be staying with Latimus until Saturday morning, and then staying one night with Miranda at Uteria before returning home at dusk on Sunday night.

She knew that there was very little chance she'd leave his cabin a virgin, and it terrified her. Not that she was scared to make love to him. She'd dreamed of that for centuries. But he was much more experienced, and she felt so inadequate. Reminding herself of Miranda's advice, that women held the power as long as they were naked, she gave a nervous chuckle and exited her cabin.

Draylok had been tasked with transporting her to the train station, riding with her to Astaria, and then escorting her to Latimus' cabin. When they had spoken on the phone yesterday, he'd been immovable in his decision, and she gave up trying to attempt any of the journey on her own. Such was the way with her stubborn soldier. She figured that as their relationship grew, she'd learn how to pick—and win—her battles with him.

Draylok helped her load the paintings into the four-wheeler, and they were off. The train ride was quick, and a soldier met them at the Astaria platform with a four-wheeler too. Hopping in with Draylok, she forced herself to relax as they neared the cottage.

Night had fallen, the sky near the horizon still emitting a faint glow. Jumping out of the vehicle, she grabbed her bag, headed up the three wooden stairs and knocked on the door.

Latimus' bulky frame filled the opening as he pulled open the door, white teeth glowing from his huge smile.

"Hey," he said.

"Hey," she said, smiling up at him. He led her in and instructed Draylok to place her paintings against the wall by the door. Once the task was complete, the soldier saluted Latimus and exited the cabin, softly closing the door behind him.

"He's a very nice man," Lila said.

Latimus nodded, coming to stand in front of her. "He's one of my best soldiers. Smart and loyal." Lifting his hands, he rubbed her upper arms over the thin material of her sweater. "You look amazing."

As she always did when she knew she'd be near him, she'd spent extra time on her hair and makeup. "Thank you," she said, hating the blush she felt creeping over her pale skin.

"I think I need to kiss you, so that we get it out of the way. What do you think?"

He was teasing her, trying to abate her bashfulness. It was very sweet.

"I think I'd like that."

Red, full lips curved into a sexy smile, and he cupped the back of her head in his large hands. Tilting her face to his, he gave her a searing kiss.

"Mmmm..." he said against her lips. "You taste so good." After thoroughly consuming her again, he pulled back. "Okay, that's enough. Otherwise, I'm going to get sidetracked."

Taking her hand, he led her to the door of his bedroom. "The bathroom is through there. Make yourself at home. I want you to feel comfortable here."

She observed the tiny, one-bedroom cabin. It was sparse but functional. The front door opened onto a small den that led to his bedroom, which housed a separate bathroom. A tiny kitchen sat just off the den. A black comforter covered his king-sized bed.

"I don't have as many pillows as you do, sorry," he said.

Lifting the back of her hand to her forehead, she sighed dramatically. "How will I survive? I don't think I can stay."

Laughing, he pulled her toward the den.

"So, what's on the agenda?" she asked.

"We're going to head outside. Do you need to go to the bathroom or anything?"

She went, giving her reflection a silent lecture in the bathroom mirror. Telling herself to stay calm and enjoy the evening, she walked to meet him by the front door. Taking her hand, he led her to the back of the cabin, where a blanket sat upon the grass. Beyond the blanket, there was an open field and a view of the far-off mountains, under the half moon. She found it quite peaceful and serene. Upon the blanket, there was a picnic basket and a bottle of red wine.

"Oh, a picnic," she said, smiling up at him. "How lovely."

He kicked off his loafers and urged her to do the same with her sandals. Leading her, he sat her on the blanket and then sat across from her.

"I figured we'd start with wine," he said, pouring them each a glass from the bottle. "Since it makes you so tipsy. That way, you'll be less nervous."

Biting her lip, she took the glass. "Is it that obvious? I feel like a moron."

He chuckled. "It so cute. But I need you relaxed, so that we can enjoy each other."

Lifting his glass, he clinked it with hers. "To the most beautiful woman I've ever seen. I'm so honored to be here with you right now." Heart pounding at his words, she sipped her wine, her gaze locked on his.

They chatted as he unpacked the picnic basket. As they sipped the wine, they nibbled on the tiny cubed cheese and sliced meats he'd packed.

"Try this one," he said, lifting one of the cheese cubes toward her mouth. "It's a comté. It's pairs really well with this wine."

She let him feed her, her lips grazing his fingertips. He gave her a suggestive smile. "So hot. I need to feed you more. Damn, woman."

Smiling, Lila leaned on her straightened arm at her side as she chewed. Holding his gaze, she sipped her wine. She was feeling a bit tipsy, and it emboldened her.

"Did you try this one?" she asked, holding a yellowish cube to his mouth. "I think it's a kefalotyri."

He grasped her wrist and consumed the cheese, holding her hand hostage as he licked each one of her fingers. "That's really good," he said, sucking her index finger into his mouth. She felt a rush of wetness at her core and shivered.

"You're incorrigible," she said, pulling her hand from him to rest on it again. Sipping from her glass, she licked a drop of wine from her bottom lip and swore she heard him emit a soft growl.

"Are you buzzed yet? Because I have something awesome planned."

Grinning, she realized she was mildly, pleasantly drunk. "Yup," she said and then felt herself giggle.

His resulting smile was adorable. Setting his empty wine glass on the grass, he said, "Okay, I have a horrible secret to tell you."

"What?"

Reaching behind to his back pocket, he pulled out an iPod. Lifting it, he shook it. "I had Heden help me make a playlist. Although I'm ashamed to admit it, I like human music. Seventies folk rock. It's my greatest vice."

Throwing back her head, she laughed. "Oh no. That's a terrible affliction. How do you live with yourself?"

Chuckling, he flipped through the iPod, connecting it to the little Bluetooth speaker that was sitting by the picnic basket. "It's tough. It makes me doubt every decision I've ever made."

Thoroughly enjoying their banter, she watched him as he fiddled with the device. Lifting his gaze, he took her hand, forcing her to sit cross-legged. "I have a lot of regrets in my life," he said, the blue of his irises seeming to glow under the stars. "But one of the biggest is that I said no to you."

"When?" she asked, feeling her eyebrows draw together.

"When you asked me to dance, at Heden's birthday party, right before we left on the train mission."

"Oh," she said, squeezing his hand. "Yeah, I felt like such an idiot for asking you."

"I wanted so badly to dance with you. Not because I like to dance—because I definitely don't—but because I would've gotten to hold you."

She smiled sadly. "That would've been nice."

"Well, I think the time to make it up to you has come." Standing, he tapped the screen of the iPod, and a song began playing over the speaker.

"This is called 'Dancing in the Moonlight,' Latimus said, his smile almost shy. "Perfect for a nighttime Vampyre picnic."

As the catchy tune played, her hulking commander began snapping his fingers and moving to the music. She couldn't stop her laughter as he tried and failed miserably to keep up.

"You're terrible," she said over the music. "Haven't you ever danced before?"

"Nope," he said, extending a hand to her. "How about you get up here and show me how it's done?"

Joy ran through her as she grabbed his hand and let him pull her up. Unable to control her snickering, she began dancing. Setting her empty wine glass on the grass, she clutched his wrists and tried to move him along with the music, but it was no use. Her man was great at a lot of things, but he was a dreadful dancer.

Unfazed by his lack of rhythm, she moved to the music. Grabbing her arm, he twirled her around, and she tried to remember ever feeling such happiness.

The song was filled with the clunky notes of the seventies-style electric keyboard, and Lila could imagine the bell-bottomed lead singer slapping the tambourine against his hip.

Giggling as they had all those centuries ago when they were children, they danced with each other as the song wound down. After a moment of silence, a slower song began to play.

Latimus pulled her toward him, aligning his body with hers. Unabashed, she circled his neck with her arms and lay her cheek on his chest against the soft fabric of his polo shirt. One of his thick arms encircled her, his palm resting on her lower back; the other lifted so that his hand could soothe her hair as they moved. Swaying, she clutched him to her, feeling his heart pound under her cheek. When the chorus came, he sang softly into her ear, his deep baritone making her tremble.

With words so reverent, he crooned along to "Crazy Love", his soft lips brushing against the shell of her ear, causing her to shudder.

They rocked slowly, under the twinkling stars, until the song ended. As another began to play, she felt him inhale a deep breath. Gently grasping her hair with his thick fingers, he tilted her head back, locking his gaze on hers.

"You look so beautiful right now." Lowering his head, he brushed a kiss across her lips. She felt his erection pulsing against her stomach through his jeans, and a resulting flush of moisture surged between her thighs.

"I don't want to rush you, Lila," he said, the quiet tone of his voice mesmerizing. "But I want so badly to carry you inside and make love to you. I've waited a thousand years to have you. I'll wait a thousand more if that's what you want. But I'm hoping you want me too. It's up to you. I won't force you into doing anything you're not ready for."

Smiling, she cupped his cheek, running the pad of her thumb over his clean-shaven skin. "Of course, I want you. I've dreamed of you holding me like this forever."

Lowering his head, he brushed a kiss across her lips.

"Are you sure?" he asked, nuzzling the tip of his nose against hers.

"I'm sure," she said. "Please, just be patient with me. I'm so afraid I won't know what to do."

"You're fucking crazy, woman," he said, kissing her deeply. Lowering down, he placed his arm under the backs of her knees and lifted her. She clutched her hands behind his neck as he carried her up the stairs to the cabin, closing the door with his foot and locking it behind them. Entering the bedroom, he slid her down his body beside the bed.

"We have all night, so we're going to take our time," he said, palming her cheek when she stood before him. "I need you to be honest with me. If I do something you don't like, tell me. Okay?"

She nodded.

"Have you ever had an orgasm?"

Mortified, she felt her entire body flush with embarrassment. Unable to speak, she shook her head.

"We're going to fix that tonight," he said, giving her a sexy smile. "And I'm going to teach you how to make yourself come, so that you can think of me and do it when we're not together."

Lila breathed a laugh at his arrogance. Of course, he would demand that she only pleasure herself when thinking of him. He'd always been cocky and domineering. Whereas others might have found it off-putting, she'd always been attracted to his dominant overconfidence. She knew he rarely doubted himself, and it made her feel secure with him somehow.

"Lift your arms," he said.

Complying, the muscles of her stomach quivered as he brushed them when he grabbed the hem of her sweater. Lifting it, he pulled off the thin garment, tossing it on the floor. She'd worn her prettiest bra—deep, silky purple, with little black butterflies as a pattern. It barely contained her large breasts, and her skin prickled as he sucked in a breath, his gaze trained on the straining globes bursting from the material.

"Did you wear that to drive me crazy?"

Pulling her bottom lip through her fangs, she smiled up at him. "Maybe."

Chuckling, he shook his head. "My own little temptress. Your fucking breasts are gorgeous." Lifting his hands, he palmed each of her breasts, squeezing gently.

"Lattie," she whispered.

Pulling back, he yanked off his shirt, throwing it on the floor. "I need to feel you against me." Reaching behind her, he unclasped her bra. The mounds of her breasts spilled forward as he threw the silky garment on the ground.

Lifting her by her butt, he pressed her into his chest, skin to skin. Her legs crossed at his waist as he devoured her mouth. Gently laying her on the bed, he lifted his head and loomed over her, stroking her hair as it fanned out behind her head.

Running that hand down her face, he caressed her collarbone and then palmed one of her breasts in his large hand. The pad of his thumb darted back and forth across her nipple, and it stood to attention.

"So fucking beautiful," he said and then lowered his head to take the tiny nub into his mouth.

Her hips shot off the bed, lost in the pleasure of his warm mouth. His thick tongue licked her, sending jolts of desire to her core, and then, he gently bit the tip. Unable to control her tiny mewl, he lathered her again, soothing away the small prick of pain.

Murmuring something unintelligible, he kissed a path to her other breast, lavishing it as he did the first one. She squirmed under him, feeling something build inside her, wanting to let it go somehow.

After pampering her other breast, he lifted, bringing his hands to push the globes together. Desire coursed through her as he slid his mouth back and forth, licking both of her nipples with his velvet tongue.

"Lattie," she breathed, asking him for something that she couldn't name.

Releasing her breasts, he palmed the back of her head and kissed her deeply. "We're just getting started, honey. Don't rush me." He nibbled at her lips, his ice-blue eyes drilling into hers.

"I want to please you too," she said, lifting her hand to caress his cheek.

"I'm so fucking pleased right now, you have no idea. Let me love you. That's what will give me the most pleasure."

"Okay," she said, running her thumb over his thick lips.

Grinning, he nipped at her thumb and then lowered to kiss her collarbone again. Trailing kisses between her breasts, he continued down her stomach, making the muscles quiver. He stood and unbuttoned and unzipped her jeans. Pulling them off her body and throwing them to the ground, his face contorted with anguish. Gently, he ran his fingertips over her scar, hip to hip, above the hem of her thong underwear.

"It doesn't hurt," she said, wanting to ease his pain.

His gaze shot to hers, sorrow swimming in his irises. "I should've saved you from him. It's my greatest failure. I let him maim you." Slowly, he rubbed her scar. "I'll never forgive myself."

"Stop it," she said, shaking her head on the bed as he looked at her, his expression so broken. "Don't let him in here. I'm determined not to let him dictate anything in my life. I sure as hell won't let him ruin this for us."

He gave her a shattered smile. "You cursed again. Now, I know you mean business."

Feeling her lips curve, she bit the lower one. "Please, don't give him any power here. I need it to just be you and me."

"Okay," he said, still tracing her scar. Lowering to his knees, he pulled her to the edge of the bed and placed her legs over his shoulders. Ever so gently, he touched his lips to her wound, kissing the length of it several times over. Tears filled her eyes as she watched her colossal Vampyre commander exhibit such gentle loving.

Lifting his head, he closed his lids, inhaling deeply, and she figured he was smelling her arousal. The silky wetness at her core seemed to be flowing out of her as it always did around him. With his index finger, he fondled the lacy top of her purple thong.

"These are hot."

Smiling down at him, she let him remove the garment, shivering as he returned to his spot between her legs. It was so intimate, her long legs surrounding his head, and she almost giggled. For someone as shy as she, it was a strange place to be.

"Are you laughing at me?" he teased, grinning up at her. "I must look like a fool, staring at you. I've just never seen anything as gorgeous as your pretty pussy." A shudder ran through her body at his dirty words. He nuzzled her triangle of blond hair with his nose and kissed the top of her core softly. "Fuck, I'm going to drown in you."

With his hands, he spread her folds open and began kissing her deepest place. Open-mouthed and thorough, he lapped at her wetness. Throwing her head back on the bed, she clutched the comforter, unable to control the gyration of her hips as he devoured her.

Moving his mouth, he sucked the nub at the juncture of her thighs and then flicked it several times with the tip of his tongue. As he focused on her clit, he eased two fingers inside her, jutting them back and forth.

She cried out, not even understanding how something could feel so good and so torturous at the same time. Every nerve ending in her body was on fire, and she felt she might explode.

"Let it go," he said, his words vibrating against her deepest place. "You can do it, honey."

Moaning in frustration, she tried to release, wanting so badly to please him. Her body was shaking so violently that she thought her heart might burst. His tongue flicked her relentlessly as he fingered her wet channel.

For whatever reason, she just couldn't let go. Wanting to sob, she felt him climb over her. He lay beside her, positioning his hand on her center and rubbing her clit with the pads of his fingers.

Looking down at her, he placed his head on his other hand, his elbow resting on the bed beside her hair. His gaze never left hers as he alternated, rubbing her nub for several seconds and then spearing his fingers into her. Over and over, he continued the maddening caresses.

"I'm not stopping until you come for me," he said, his blue eyes glowing as he stared into her. "You're always so proper and restrained, but I'm not letting that shit fly when I'm fucking you."

Her body convulsed at his words, spoken in the deep timbre of his voice, as his fingers plundered her.

"I think you like it when I talk dirty to you."

She moaned, unable to speak as she gazed into his irises.

"Let go, Lila. I want you to spray my fingers with every drop of come from your wet pussy so that I can fuck you." The words unlocked something in her, and she felt so close to falling off the precipice she was on. "I can't wait to stick my cock so far inside you and pound you so hard you taste me." Lowering his head, he sucked her nipple into his mouth.

Something snapped, shattering inside her, and she began convulsing, crying out as she came. A ringing sounded in her ears as she floated toward the bright light behind the darkness of her closed eyelids. Groaning and panting, she let the feeling wash over her. Through her haze, she heard him say, "Good girl. Fuck, you're so hot."

After several moments, she felt her mind float back into her body. Tremors shook her as she opened her eyes to look at him.

The corner of his mouth was turned up into a sated, slightly cocky smile as his head rested on his hand.

"How do you feel?"

She exhaled, knowing she should be embarrassed but lacking the energy. Shaking her head on the comforter, she stared at him, transfixed.

"Oh, my god."

His deep chuckle reverberated through her shattered body. "You were so beautiful when you came. Fuck, Lila. I can't wait to spend eternity making you come like that. It's the most amazing thing I've ever seen."

She blinked up at him, unable to move any other part of her body.

"Thank you. That felt so good. Sorry, I'm having trouble putting words together right now."

Laughing, he lowered to place a gentle kiss on her lips. "Good. Lord knows, I've made you feel like shit about a million times in your life. At least I finally made you feel good."

Smiling up at him, she lifted a weak arm, cupping his face. "I want to make you feel good. How do I do that?"

He nudged the tip of her nose with his. "You make me feel good just by being near me." Kissing her again softly, he murmured, "Anything else is just a bonus."

"When did you become so romantic?" she asked, lost in the emotion pulsing in his sky-blue eyes.

"When I stopped deluding myself that I could ever let another man touch you. After that, I was a goner. I knew I'd have to win you over."

The corners of her lips turned up as she caressed his cheek. "You did a pretty good job. All the gifts and the letters. They were so sweet. Who knew our fearless commander was a softie?"

Chuckling, he nipped at her bottom lip. "Don't tell anyone. I need them all to be scared shitless of me."

"Your secret's safe with me."

Languidly, they gazed into each other's eyes, lost to their desire.

Finally, she said, "I want you to make love to me."

His grin was so cute that it almost broke her heart.

"It's about time, woman. I think I've almost died a hundred times over the past year from the blue balls I get when I see your ass in those tight jeans."

"You haven't been with anyone else?"

He shook his head. "Not since you broke the betrothal. How could I? I think I was waiting for tonight, even if I didn't know it."

Lowering his head, he plunged his tongue into her mouth, drawing her tongue out so that they mated. Desire began to curl in her stomach again. Reaching up, she pulled the leather strap from his hair, freeing it over his face. As he smiled down at her, she ran her fingers through his hair. He looked absolutely gorgeous as the raven strands fell over his forehead.

"I need it down," she said. "You look so handsome."

With a smile, he rubbed his finger over her cheek. "I don't want to bring up your injury, but I don't want to assume anything. I'll wear a condom if you want me to. It's totally up to you."

Since Vampyres had self-healing abilities, any diseases spread through intercourse were always cured within minutes. However, protection was still used to prevent pregnancy.

"No," she said, shaking her head on the comforter. His concern showed his respect for her, and it made her feel so cherished. "I want to feel all of you inside me. Sadie said everything is normal for me sexually."

The emotion in his eyes was consuming. "I'm so sorry, Lila. I wish I could go back and save you—"

She placed two fingers over his lips, unwilling to allow him to bring the evil creature into their beautiful loving. "Make love to me," she whispered.

Growling, he gave her a sweet kiss, murmuring how special she was, and then lifted from the bed. After removing his jeans and boxer-briefs, he stood before her, in between her legs, which were bent at the knees, the soles of her feet resting on the bed.

Wetness shot to her core as he palmed his large shaft and began slowly jutting his hand back and forth, his eyes never leaving hers. It was the sexiest thing she'd ever seen.

"Do you like watching me do this?" he asked, his tone silky.

"Yes," she whispered, placing her bent arm underneath her head so she could see him better.

"Damn straight," he said, his breath becoming more labored.

Anticipation filled her as he lowered his body over hers. Unable to control her smile, she reached for him, grabbing on for dear life.

* * * *

Latimus stretched over her, encompassed in the most amazing and sensual moment of his life. Lying pale and naked before him, Lila was his every fantasy in the flesh. Humbled by her trust in him as he loved her, he cemented his lips to hers and then stuck his tongue inside her wet mouth to lavish her.

Smelling her burst of arousal, he felt she was ready for him. Palming his shaft, he guided it to her wetness, shivering as the head slid threw her dewy moisture. Locking his gaze with hers, he nudged forward, entering her bit by bit, so that she could adjust to him.

Her nails dug into his scalp as she clutched his hair, causing little pinpoints of pleasure-pain. Groaning, he pushed further into her. The plushy, warm walls of her snug channel squeezed him, and he thought he might die of pleasure. About halfway in, he met her barrier. Jutting into her, he tried to shove through, unable to move forward.

"Shit," he said, rubbing her cheek with his fingers. "I'm going to have to push harder."

"It's okay," she said, her lavender irises so vivid in the light of his bedside lamp.

"I don't want to hurt you."

"Do it."

Gritting his teeth, he cupped the tops of her shoulders and thrust into her, moaning as he felt himself encompassed fully by her tight folds. She gasped, her body tensing under him.

Hating that he'd hurt her, he palmed her cheek. "Honey, look at me. Are you okay?"

She opened her lids, and he felt a resounding slam in his solar plexus. Never had he seen such beauty as her looking up at him, the pools of her eyes filled with emotion.

Nodding, she moved her hips under him, causing him to growl. Baring his fangs, he began pumping himself into her, slow and measured. Her drenched folds clutched every inch of his cock, milking him, and he closed his eyes, lost to the pleasure.

Below him, she moaned, and he increased the pace, lifting his lids to gaze down at her. Her pink lips formed an "O" as her eyes seemed to roll back in her head. Realizing he was hitting the right spot, he began pounding her with the head of his shaft.

A breathy mewl exited her throat as her large breasts bobbled up and down while he fucked her. Lost to passion, he anchored himself on his outstretched arms, palms on the bed beside her head, unable to form a single thought. Mindlessly, he battered her pussy with his straining cock.

"Come," he growled, knowing he wasn't going to last much longer. She felt too damn good around him.

She chortled, her eyes closing as her body moved on the bed, limp as he pummeled her.

"Look at me," he commanded, needing to look into her stunning eyes while he came.

Lifting her lids, she locked onto him, causing his heart to slam in his chest.

"Lattie," she said brokenly, and he knew she was close.

Unable to control his treacherous shaft, he clenched his teeth, feeling his orgasm start in his balls. Her use of that nickname along with the vibrancy of her eyes was too much for him. Throwing back his head, he screamed, the sound so loud he was sure the walls of the cabin shook.

Jetting his seed into her, she convulsed around him, and he felt a jolt of elation that she was coming with him. Needing to feel every inch of her soft skin, he surrounded her with his arms, holding her close as he climaxed. High-pitched little mewls escaped her lips as she fell apart underneath him. Clutching her to him, his massive body jerked as he finished inside her.

Shaking as he never had before, he collapsed fully onto her. Her breathing was labored as she clasped him to her. Thin fingers slid up and down his upper back as they floated back to Earth.

Finally, after what must've been an eternity, he lifted his head, unable to believe he was trembling so badly.

"Lila?" With his thumb, he caressed her reddened cheek. "Are you okay?"

She groaned, her lips forming a smile as her eyes remained closed. "Can't talk. Sorry."

Laughing, he lowered his forehead to hers. "Holy shit. I think we almost fucked each other to death."

The waves of her laughter surrounded him, and he began giggling along with her, their bodies shaking as they clung to each other.

"*Ohmygod,*" she breathed, the words coming out in a rush. "That was amazing."

He sighed, thanking the goddess that she was sated. Although she was worried about pleasing him, he'd been slightly terrified that he'd blow his load before he could satisfy her. After all, he'd dreamed of fucking her for ten centuries. He considered his willpower a small miracle.

They lay there for a while, her rubbing his back, him toying with her hair as it spread across the comforter. Finally, he lifted his head and placed a kiss on her mouth.

"I'm crushing you," he said, nuzzling his nose into hers.

"Don't care." Although her eyes remained closed, her swollen lips turned up in a satisfied smile.

Chuckling, he kissed her again and then began to pull out of her.

"No," she whined, clutching him to her.

"Okay, little temptress. I have to pull out if I'm going to fuck you again later."

"No," she said, her lips forming a pout. "Stay."

Laughing, he shook his head. "I've created a monster. Don't move. I'll be right back."

He popped himself out of her, already missing her wet warmth around him. Striding to the bathroom, he dampened a cloth. Coming to stand between her legs, he wiped his seed from her.

She watched him, lifting her arms over her head as she gazed seductively at him. "You little cock tease," he said, loving how relaxed and sexy she was.

"Let's do it again." Her tongue darted out to bathe her lips.

"Fucking A. You're insatiable. I hope I can keep up."

Winking at her, he deposited the cloth in the hamper in the bathroom and then returned to the bed. Lifting her under her knees, she placed her arms around his neck. While he held her, he pulled back the covers. Laying her down gently, his heart skipped a beat as she looked up at him. Blond hair fanned the pillow under her head, and her pale skin seemed to glow. His eyes darted over the darkened skin of her areola and nipples, her small waist and curved hips and the plushy hair at the juncture of her thighs.

Swallowing thickly, he said, "By the goddess, Lila. You're so fucking breathtaking. I'm so lucky to be with you like this."

Smiling, she extended her arms, beckoning him to her, and he slid into bed, pulling her to sprawl on top of him.

"You're pretty handsome yourself," she said, placing a chaste kiss on his lips.

Reveling in her, he stroked her hair as she lay on top of him. Lost to their lovemaking, her chin resting on her crossed hands upon his chest, they silently communicated all the things they couldn't over the past thousand years. After a while, he noticed her eyelids getting heavy. Pushing her head down so that her cheek rest upon his pecs, he ran his fingers through her silky waves as she cuddled into him.

Sated in the aftermath of their lovemaking, they fell into slumber.

Chapter 23

Restless, Darkrip stepped from his cabin. The light of the moon seemed to beckon him. Returning to his cottage, he threw on a t-shirt and sweatpants, needing to roam a bit. After tying his Koio sneakers, he set out on the plushy grass.

Latimus' cabin sat about a hundred yards from his, and he noticed a blanket and picnic basket. Picking up the half-empty bottle of wine, he sniffed and read the label. Louis Jadot Pommard 2015. Not bad. He was impressed that the arrogant and brooding Vampyre commander had a taste for good wine. He'd thought him only capable of fighting and stomping around the compound like an uncivilized brute.

Lifting one of the empty glasses from the ground, Darkrip poured himself a hefty amount as music emanated from a small speaker beside the basket. Saluting the half-lit moon, he drank, comfortable in his solace. Sniffing around the cheese and meat, he decided it probably had been sitting out too long, so he languidly sipped the wine and stared at the mountains off in the distance.

A loud, deep wail echoed from the Vampyre's cabin, and he realized Latimus must've finally gotten around to fucking Lila. About time. Those two had done the same tired dance since he met them. He didn't like a lot of people on this godforsaken planet, but it was hard not to like the quiet diplomat. She always looked upon him with kindness and seemed to genuinely want to get to know him. Uncomfortable with that, he'd usually managed to avoid her unless being in her presence was absolutely necessary. A creature such as he wasn't really looking to make friends. What a strange concept.

In his world, the goal was existence and survival. As the son of the Dark Lord, raised in his caves for a thousand years, he'd learned that any type of care or concern for others meant sure death. Although he didn't much like this planet, he appreciated his life enough that he wanted to continue living it.

Finishing the wine, he dropped the glass on the soft grass. Still restless, he decided to transport himself to the bank of the River Thayne, by the Wall of Astaria. He always felt a small sense of peace there for some reason. Closing his eyes, he dematerialized.

As he materialized, he silently cursed. Her scent swamped him, and he wanted nothing more than to return to his cabin. Mortified that someone as powerful as he would even contemplate changing course because of *her*, he opened his lids.

Arderin squatted twenty feet away, by the riverbank, talking to something in her hand. Slowly approaching, he noticed it was a wounded bird.

"There, there," she said, pulling on the creature's wing as she held its body in her other hand. "Once we straighten this out, you can fly again."

"The wing is too badly broken," he said, noting her body tense. "It won't regain the ability to fly."

She pierced him with her ice-blue gaze. "And how do you know?"

"I can sense it. My father's blood gives me a certain sense for looming death. The creature's spirit is broken, and it's in pain. It's best if you let it die."

Her exquisite features formed a deep scowl. "I haven't trained in medicine for centuries to let things die. I can fix him." She fiddled with the bird's wing, speaking soft words of encouragement to it.

Darkrip came to stand over her. The bird was in immense pain—he could feel it coursing through his body. Pain was something he was acutely aware of, whether his own or others'.

"You're exacerbating its suffering. I know you mean well, but you're doing more harm than good."

She looked up at him from her crouch, and he struggled not to imagine her kneeling before him with his cock in her pretty mouth. "Leave me alone."

He sat on the grass beside her, observing her efforts to heal the wounded animal. Unable to take the suffering that was emanating from the creature, he pulled it from her hands and snapped its neck.

"No!" she screamed, standing to look down at him. "Why did you do that? I was helping him."

Shaking his head, he lay the bird on the ground. "You were prolonging his pain." Tears filled her eyes as she stared down at him, her expression broken.

"You're a monster."

Rolling his eyes at her always dramatic flair, he stood. Her head tilted back, and her pink lips seemed to glisten in the moonlight. "I've never claimed not to be. Now, go give it a proper burial. It will help you get some closure."

Anger flashed in her icy irises. "How *dare* you even *think* you can begin to tell me what to do. You're an abomination."

"Your self-righteousness is unbecoming, princess. Go bury your wounded bird. I came here for some peace and I mean to get it."

Arderin's tiny nostrils flared as her eyes narrowed. "I can't believe Miranda is related to you. One day, she'll see how evil you are and banish you from this compound. When that day comes, I'll escort you back to the Deamon caves myself. You're despicable."

Unable to stop himself, he laughed. "God, you're such a passionate little brat. One day, you're going to push me too far, and I'm going to stuff my cock in your mouth to shut it."

Her mouth dropped open, and he had to check himself so that he didn't break into a fit of laughter. Her stunned surprise was priceless. The chances were slim that anyone spoke to the spoiled Vampyre princess this way. It was about time someone put her in her place.

"How dare you?" she said, her tone low and filled with rage.

"Go on. Now you're just annoying me—"

"My brothers will kill you!"

"Yes, yes, you've threatened my demise at the hands of your brothers since I met you. I'm terrified." Amusement coursed through him, and he realized he was actually enjoying sparring with her.

"You underestimate me and talk down to me as if I'm an idiot. One day, you'll pay for it."

Darkrip studied her flawless face. "Actually, I think you're very intelligent and let your brothers have too much dominion over your life. You could probably rule the damn planet if you put your mind to it." He'd seen the number of medical books she'd read, courtesy of the Slayer physician. She always blazed through them quickly and retained every word. Her mind was curious and quick. For whatever reason, she chose to stay on the compound. If she wanted to leave, who were her brothers to stop her, really?

Her expression turned sullen, discerning if he was attempting to trick her with his comments. Shuttered blue eyes roamed over his face.

"Go," he said, softening his tone. Not because he cared to be nice to her, but because he was craving the solitude he'd come here to find. Of course, that was the reason. "It will be dawn soon."

Huffing out a breath, she lifted the bird and bounced up the hill leading to the meadow that connected with the castle. He watched her the entire way, black curls bobbing, as his dick throbbed in his pants. Cursing himself for wanting her, he waited until she disappeared from his view. Turning, he sat on the soft grass of the riverbank, craving peace.

* * * *

Latimus awoke with the strange sensation of someone wrapped around the entire left side of his body. Looking down, he noticed Lila sleeping, her lips curved in a sweet smile as her cheek lay upon his chest. She had contorted her body around him, so that he couldn't tell where he ended, and she began. Damn, she was a cuddler. How fucking cute.

Long blond lashes stretched from her closed lids, and he studied her cosmetic-free face. They'd woken up several hours ago, and she'd washed her face and prepped for bed while he cleaned up the remnants of their picnic.

They'd made love again and fallen asleep to the remainder of his playlist, which had emanated softly from the Bluetooth speaker that now sat on his dresser.

Looking down at her as she slept peacefully, he struggled to remember ever feeling so happy. A smile formed as he thought of telling Heden. His brother would probably call him "dude" and gloat that he'd been right about Latimus wanting happiness. Fuck it. He'd let his idiot brother have this one. It just felt so damn good.

Sighing, she rubbed her soft skin against him in her sleep, and his dick rose to attention. Gently, he turned to his side, pulling the front of her body against his. Languidly, her eyes opened as her head rested on the pillow beside him.

"Hey," she whispered.

"Hey," he said, grabbing one of the round globes of her ass and pulling her into him. Aligning the head of his shaft with her core, she gasped.

Looking into her, he silently asked her permission. She slid her silky leg over his hip, opening herself to him. Exhaling a breath, he pushed into her.

Pressing his forehead against hers, he slowly jutted his hips back and forth, coating his cock with her wetness. Her hand slid up his neck, over his face, and she clutched his hair. Locked onto each other, they rode the wave of their desire, unhurried and intimate.

They stayed that way for several minutes, moving with each other as their bodies awoke. Needing more, he rolled her onto her back and increased the pace. Grabbing her hands, one on each side of her head on the pillow, he laced his fingers with hers as he fucked her.

Finally, he felt her walls begin to quiver, and her body grew taut under his. Giving the sexy little mewl that he'd figured out meant she was about to come, he made sure to pound the same spot with the sensitive head of his shaft. With a groan, she snapped, her body convulsing underneath him, and he let himself come. Wave upon wave of pleasure jerked his body as he emptied himself into her. Not wanting to crush her, he rolled them back on their sides, his cock still firmly inside her. Panting, they stared at each other as their breathing began to slow.

"That's such a nice way to wake up," she said, a flush crossing her face.

"Mm-hmm," he said, running his fingers through the hair at her temple.

Smiling, she snuggled closer to him, causing his softened shaft to send resounding tremors through his large body.

As he stroked her hair, he said, "I want to wake up like this with you every night. For eternity. Till death do us part." His heart pounded as he struggled with his fear of being so vulnerable with her. "If you'll let me."

"Oh, Lattie," she said, bringing her hand up to cup his cheek.

"Shit, that doesn't sound like a 'yes.'"

She gave him a warbled smile, and worry began to course through him. Had he misread her feelings?

"Don't tense up," she said, soothing him as she stroked his cheek. "Of course, I want those things with you."

A puff of air escaped his lips as he released the breath he hadn't realized he'd been holding.

"But my life has changed so much in such a short time. I need to take control and make my own choices. I've depended on others to make decisions for me for centuries. It's time I claim my life and establish some independence. It's a commitment I made to myself after my injury, and I hope you can care for me enough to let me keep it."

Disappointment and intense love for her warred within him. Although he understood her need to establish independence and supported her fully, his need to protect her clawed at him. He wanted to be the one she built a life with. He wanted to bond with her and give her everything her heart desired.

Realizing that doing that for her was exactly what she didn't want, he felt sad. Angry at himself, he wished he hadn't been such a damn fool and had claimed her sooner. Now, he'd created a situation where she would impose space and distance between them. Hating to be separated from her for one moment, now that he'd finally accepted his love for her, he gritted his teeth in frustration.

"Hey," she said, "you look like you're going to punch me. Do I need to be worried?"

Breathing a laugh, he shook his head upon the pillow. "Sorry. I'm just so pissed at myself because I fucked up so badly. I should've fought for you and claimed you as my bonded centuries ago. Now, you're going to build a life where you don't need me. I'm a fucking idiot."

"Whoa, I didn't say that," she said, her blond eyebrows drawing together. "I still want you to court me, and I still want to bond with you when the time comes. I just need some time on my own too. Please, understand that this is not about you. It's about me and what I need to be happy. I want so badly to be a good bonded to you, and I think I'll be even better at it once I figure myself out. Does that make sense?"

"Yeah," he said, unable to stop his mouth from forming a pout.

She chuckled, and he scowled at her. "You look so cute right now. Like a scolded puppy. Please, don't be mad at me. I need you to support me in this. I love you, Latimus. With all my heart. I always have."

All eight chambers of his heart shattered at her words. He'd longed to hear them from her for so long. Tears threatened to well in his eyes, and he told himself not to be a fucking pansy.

"I love you too," he said, bringing his hand up to cup her face. "By the goddess, Lila, I love you so much. I'm so sorry I messed everything up. I wish I could change the past. All I want is for you to let me love you."

"I know," she said. Her magnificent lavender eyes filled with wetness, and he stroked away the lone tear that slid down her cheek.

"Don't cry, honey," he said, pressing his forehead to hers. "I understand. I won't push you. But I do plan to spend every single night that I'm not training the troops with you. There's only so much a man can take."

She laughed and nodded against his head. "I'd like that. You can come and visit me at Lynia, and I'll come and see you here. We'll make it work, I promise."

"How long are we talking here?" he asked, pulling back to scowl at her. "Because I need to know what I'm dealing with."

"I was thinking at least a year. That should give me enough time on my own to figure some things out."

"A fucking year," he muttered. "Okay, then, we'll bond exactly one year from today."

She laughed and bit her lip. "It doesn't have to be that stringent. Let's just play it by ear. I think I'll know when I'm ready."

"Fine," he said, already hating how hard the next year would be. But he'd do anything for her, so he resigned himself to his fate. "I'm going to court you so hard, woman. You won't be able to resist me. I'm determined to shave several months off this timeframe. Consider yourself warned."

White teeth seemed to sparkle at him as her mouth contorted into a blazing smile. "Challenge accepted."

Stroking her cheek, he realized she was struggling to say something.

"What is it?" he asked.

Her violet irises darted between his. "I also need you to really contemplate what it will mean to bond with me now that I'm barren. The son of Markdor carries the most important bloodline of all. I really want you to think about what you'd be giving up to be with me."

"I don't give a damn about that, Lila—"

Placing her fingers over his lips, she stilled his words. "That's easy to say now, in the aftermath of making love. But it's a huge decision. I want you to really think about it."

"Good grief, woman," he said, playfully biting at her fingers. "If you think I'd choose having blooded children with another woman over being with you, I need to check you into Nolan's infirmary to be diagnosed with delusion." When she opened her mouth to argue, he placed his hand over it. "But since you're determined to fight me on this, I'll just say that I'll think about it for whatever length of time you need until you realize I'm never letting you go."

When she nipped at his hand, he removed it from her mouth. Loving her gorgeous smile, he reveled in the blood pulsing through his body as he held her.

Overcome with feeling for her, he kissed her brazenly, showing her with his tongue how much he loved her. Afterward, he carried her to the shower, and they slid soapy cloths over each other's skin. He told her to put on something comfortable, and they prepared to head out into the night. He had a special place in mind that he wanted to take her to and hoped she would like it. Determined to love her enough to give her what she asked of him, he grabbed her hand and led her from the cabin, underneath the canopy of stars.

* * * *

Lila smiled as her hair flew in the wind while Latimus drove them away from the cabin. He had taken her declaration that she needed some time well, and relief washed over her. Not so long ago, she would've just agreed to bond with him and let him create their life. Although she knew he would do everything in his power to make her happy, she wasn't that same woman anymore. She'd tasted independence and needed to see it through.

Love coursed through her as she watched his profile, his beefy arm on the wheel as his other hand sat on the long stick shift that rose from the floor of the vehicle. Looking over at her, he winked and gave her one of his sexy smiles. God, he was gorgeous.

Making love with him was amazing, and she felt ridiculous that she had been so nervous. Their bodies fit as if they were made for each other. In her heart, she'd always believed they had been. Although she'd been taught to save her virginity for bonding, she knew it had been right to give herself to him. She'd grown so tired of living by decrees and tradition and felt pride that she'd dictated the terms of her first sexual encounter.

When he'd told her that he loved her, the words had unlocked any trace of fear or doubt about her future. She hadn't been able to stop the tears from forming in her eyes as he'd gazed upon her and spoken so reverently. Never imagining that he would ever utter the words to her, she'd thought her heart might burst from her chest.

Slowing, he brought the vehicle to a stop about twenty yards from the River Thayne. Gasping, she realized it was the exact spot where they used to play as children. It sat down the hill and couldn't be observed from the main house, making it perfect to create unseen mischief.

Stepping from the four-wheeler, he came around and lifted her out, setting her firmly on her feet. Obviously, she could've exited the vehicle herself, but she secretly liked the dominant way he manhandled her.

Grabbing her hand, he led her to the grassy riverbank, sitting down on the plushy grass and pulling her to sit in between his legs. Bending one knee, he maneuvered her back against his upturned leg, hugging her into his chest. Sighing, he placed a kiss on the top of her head.

"It's the spot where we used to play," she said, looking up into his glowing eyes. "I can't believe you remember."

"Of course, I remember," he said, his lips forming a smile. "This is where you kissed me and ruined me for all other women."

Chuckling, she swatted his chest. "You were so cute, all those centuries ago. You would always get mad at me because I couldn't run as fast, but you still waited and let me catch up."

"You always caught bigger toads than me. It pissed me off."

"You always caught more fireflies. But you'd share yours with me and put them in my jar. Even then, you were so sweet."

"I think you know better than anyone that I'm not sweet," he said, his tone acerbic.

"Yes, you are. You try so hard to hide it, but it's always been there."

Squeezing her, he placed a kiss on her hair.

"My aunt was so terrible to you," she said, shaking her head. "I'm so sorry. I always felt awful about that. She was a very mean and troubled lady."

"Did she pass away?" he asked, concern clouding his eyes. His compassion made her heart swell.

Lila nodded. "She and I had been estranged for quite some time. I came upon her one night, centuries ago, yelling at her handmaiden. She slapped her, and I jumped in to help. Then, she slapped me, and I lost it. I went to Sathan, and he was furious. He banned her from Astaria and sent her to live at Valeria. I heard she passed away in some sort of accident about a century ago. I hadn't spoken to her since she was banished from the compound."

"Wow," he said, "I didn't realize. Sathan mentioned to me that she moved to Valeria, but I didn't know the details. I'm glad you went to him. He won't tolerate that shit." Leaning back on his arms, he contemplated her. "I'm sorry for you that she passed though. I know you don't have any blooded family left. That must be hard."

"It has been, over the centuries. When I lost my parents, I clung even harder to the betrothal. It seemed to be my only purpose in the world. I felt that if I messed that up, I'd have no one left. Arderin and Heden were my closest friends, but they're yours and Sathan's family, not mine."

"Believe me, I think Sathan and Heden would rather have you as family more than me any day. That's one contest I'd surely lose."

She rolled her eyes at him, realizing he was half-joking.

"They love you."

"Idiots. They hate me because I'm the smartest and best-looking brother."

Throwing back her head, she laughed. "I would have to agree. But don't tell Heden I said that. It will break his heart."

"I don't want you thinking about my little brother's heart, woman. Got it?" His eyes glowed with laughter as he nipped her lips.

"Yes, sir," she said, giving him a mock salute.

Lifting his arm, he grabbed her hand. "How did your parents pass away?" he asked, concern lacing his tone. "All I ever heard was that they were on a diplomacy mission and never returned."

"My father was a great man who wanted equality for all Vampyres. He felt that our society was too rigid in its classism and tradition. He liked to study the humans and democratic countries like America and the ones in Europe. He felt that they exhibited some good examples of striving toward equality. My parents would visit the human world every few decades or so to gather ideas. Time flows differently there, so they could enter different time periods. A few centuries ago, they left for twentieth century America, to study their civil rights movement, and never returned."

"I'm so sorry," he said, bringing her hand to his face and kissing her palm. "That must've been so hard for you."

She nodded. "It was. But Sathan and Heden and Arderin were so sweet and welcomed me into their family. I don't think I would've survived without them."

"And I was being a dick to you, as usual. Fuck. I should've been there for you too."

"You were so busy with the troops. The Slayer raids were constant, and the Deamons were attacking us more. I think I just realized you were too busy to focus on anything else."

"Thanks for letting me off the hook, but I was a complete ass to you," he said, shooting her a deadpan look. "I was so in love with you and thought you were in love with Sathan. God, I'm such an idiot."

"Well, at least we figured out who I really love," she said, smiling up at him. "It only took us a thousand years."

Laughing, he shook his head. "A thousand years too long. I'd beat the shit out of myself, but now that you've decided to let me fuck you, I need my strength. You're ravenous. I might need to check you in to a sex addicts' group."

She punched him, laughing at his teasing. "I didn't see you complaining."

"Fuck no," he said, hugging her. "My dick might fall off, but it'll be worth it."

"Oh, stop it," she said, swatting his chest.

She leaned into his body as they sat under the stars, enjoying each other, listening to the river gurgle by.

"You should've never listened to her," Lila said after a few moments. "My Aunt Ananda. She told you that you weren't as good as Sathan, and you believed her. That always made me so sad."

Latimus sighed, kicking the toe of his loafer into the grass. "She wasn't the only one. It was pretty much ingrained in me by everyone after the Awakening."

Her eyebrows drew together. "How so?"

"Etherya declared our parents to have two heirs. The first was to be king, and the second was to be commander if anything were to ever happen to them. Loyal to her, they complied. Arderin and Heden came a few years afterward. I was only eight when they were murdered, but I remember how much they loved each other. If they had lived, they probably would've had more kids. They couldn't keep their hands off each other."

"How romantic," she said, smiling up at him.

"Yeah. Sathan reminds me of Father in so many ways, but especially in the way he looks at Miranda. It's so similar to how Father used to gaze at Mother. I'm so happy for him." Scowling at her, he said, "But don't tell him that. He'll tell Heden, and they'll make fun of me for a damn century."

Chuckling, she nodded her head.

Absently, he rubbed the skin on the back of her hand with the pad of his thumb. "Since Sathan was first heir, I was always pushed to the side, an afterthought. Not by my parents—they were amazing—but by everyone else. Sathan always got the purest Slayer blood, the best tutors, the attention of our caretakers. After a while, I stopped expecting it."

She squeezed his hand. "And yet, you never resented him."

He shook his head. "No. He was my big brother. I looked up to him. He was very protective of me and would always share everything with me that others wouldn't give me."

"That's so sweet."

His lips curved. "Yeah, he's okay." She breathed a laugh, and he continued.

"When I took over the army at thirteen, I was coached by a team of ten Vampyre soldiers, trained by my father before the Awakening. They were extremely rigid and wanted me to focus solely on my training. While other teenagers were going to etiquette school and learning how to function in society, I was learning how to torture, maim and kill."

Lila shivered, hating what he'd been forced to endure.

"I was always told that as commander, I wouldn't ever need to know anything other than how to mercilessly defeat our enemies. That I didn't need or deserve nice things, or dance lessons, or the opportunity to attend parties. One of my coaches used to say, '*If you have time to have fun, then you should be training. Soldiers are born to fight, not enjoy themselves.*' He was an asshole, by the way."

Lila's heart swelled with compassion as he recounted the horrible memory.

"I'm so sorry, Lattie," she said, rubbing her fingers over his cheek. "You deserved so much better. I wish I had known. I would've rescued you somehow."

Smiling down at her with love in his eyes, he said, "Only you would offer to rescue the powerful Vampyre commander. I think it's in your nature to save everyone. It's amazing."

"Of course, I would've saved you," she said, feeling exasperated. "I love you. I'd fight to the death for you."

"Well, don't let me stop you. You can join my army tomorrow, and then I'll have to see you every day. It's a perfect way to circumvent this year of living apart that you're forcing on me." His blue eyes twinkled with laughter as he teased her.

"I mean it. I'm so sorry I wasn't there for you. We've both let each other down terribly. My heart hurts for what you went through. You've protected our people your whole life, always putting them first. I hope you understand that in my eyes, you're the most amazing man on the planet."

Lowering his forehead to hers, he sighed. "When you say shit like that to me, I almost believe it."

"Believe it," she said, her eyes pleading with his. "I mean, I couldn't love a jerk anyway. I'm too nice." Biting her lip, she grinned.

"That, you are," he said.

They sat like that, foreheads touching, until he spoke. "I think it happened like this."

"What?" she whispered.

"Our first kiss. You looked at me with those fucking eyes, and I was lost."

Pulsing with all the love she felt for him, she lifted her lips to his. Groaning, he kissed her back, his tongue warring with hers.

"Wait," she said, pulling back slightly. "I think I did kiss you first."

Throwing back his head, he laughed, the veins in his thick neck straining under the moonlight. "Told you. You were so sure you were right. That aristocratic blue blood makes you so haughty."

Giving him an exasperated scowl, she said, "Since you're the son of Markdor and Calla, your blood is actually purer than mine. You do know that, right?"

"Doesn't matter. You're a blue-blood through and through. My regal little temptress. It makes it that much hotter when I whisper dirty words in your ear."

She felt her entire body flush and shivered at his resulting chuckle. "You suck."

"Don't I know it," he said, waggling his eyebrows at her.

Searching his eyes, she decided she was ready to hear those dirty words again. Stroking his cheek, she said, "Make love to me here, in the spot where we first kissed. I want to add to the memory."

His eyes grew serious as he studied her. "Damn, woman, you can't wait an hour, can you? I think we have a problem."

Rolling her eyes, she pulled his mouth to hers. "Shut up," she said against his lips.

Shrieking, she laughed as he flipped her over and covered her with his large body. Under the twinkling stars and the dimming moonlight, he granted her request.

Chapter 24

Two hours before dawn, Latimus loaded up the Hummer with Lila's paintings. He'd asked Draylok to drive it to his cabin and had him return the four-wheeler to the barracks. The windows of the Hummer were darkly tinted, meaning he'd be able to drive back from Uteria without being burned to death by the rising sun.

"Ready?" he asked. She looked so beautiful in her jeans, red V-neck sweater and ankle boots. He was loath to let her go but knew he had no choice. They'd made love once more after returning to his cabin, and then, she had showered, using the flowery shampoo on her hair that made him throb with longing. After a quick shower, he'd thrown on some black pants, a t-shirt and his army boots.

"Ready." Grabbing his hand, she pulled him to her and threw her arms around him. "Thank you for these past two nights. They've been so wonderful."

"We're just getting started," he said, kissing the top of her head. "Remember what I said about courting you."

"Can't wait," she said, squeezing him and reaching down to grab her bag.

The drive to Uteria took about forty minutes. They chatted as James Taylor played in the background from an old CD in the Hummer's stereo system. Upon arriving, he drove into the main square and pulled up in front of the address that she'd given him. Helping her with her paintings, he followed her inside.

"Hey, guys," Miranda said, giving them both a hug. "I'm so excited about this. We need new blood in this stuffy gallery. Aron and Preston should be here in a minute. They're eager to see your work, Lila. I told them how fantastic it is."

Latimus smiled as splotches of red appeared on her cheeks. He loved how embarrassed she became when complimented.

"I'm so thankful that they agreed to come in before dawn. That's terribly kind of them."

"Well, I don't think your business relationship would start on the right foot if they let you burn to death in the sun while bringing in the paintings. You, on the other hand," Miranda said, looking up at Latimus, "we're not as concerned about. I told them I'd decide if we should let you live or shove you into the sun once we see what kind of mood you're in."

"Ha ha," he said, scowling at her. "You're a real Joan Rivers, Miranda. I can't control my laughter."

"He's just mad because I made him carry everything," Lila said, smiling up at him. "But he's such a gentleman that he couldn't refuse."

"Yeah, he's a real charmer."

"Why are you attacking me, woman? I've been so nice to you since we made up."

"What were you guys fighting about?" Lila asked, concern filling her expression.

"Nothing. Miranda just likes to stick her nose in other people's business."

Miranda scrunched her face at him, and he chuckled.

"I'm only staying for a bit anyway," Latimus said. "I told Heden I'd help him test the security system for the trains to Uteria and Restia."

"Awesome, thanks," Miranda said. Grabbing Lila's hand, she pulled her to the far wall to show her the spots where her art would be showcased.

"Latimus?" a soft voice called.

Turning, he broke into a smile. "Moira? Hey. How are you?"

"Oh, my god," she said, throwing her arms around his waist and placing her head on his chest. "It's so good to see you."

Latimus swallowed, awkwardly placing his arms around her. Glancing toward Lila, he saw her watching them from across the room, an intense curiosity on her face. *Crap.*

He'd met Moira centuries ago during one of the Slayer raids. She was rounded up with ten Slayer soldiers, and he'd discovered her in one of the armored carriages they'd used to transport Slayers from Uteria to Astaria. Sathan had always forbidden abduction of women or children, so he'd pulled her from the carriage and tried to send her home. Her deep blue eyes had been filled with terror, and she'd begged him to take her to Astaria, promising to do slave labor if needed.

Understanding that she was running from something, he'd acquiesced, taking her as one of his Slayer whores. Women who chose to live on the outskirts of Astaria in exchange for their blood and sex. Sathan had outlawed the practice, but Latimus was so in love with Lila, believing he could never have her, that he kept several Slayer whores in the cabins surrounding his and went to them when his longing for Lila became too much to bear.

Moira had always been his favorite. Partly because she favored Lila, with her blond hair and pale skin, and partly because they had just clicked. He genuinely liked her. He'd never felt any sort of love for her—that was always saved for Lila—but he'd cared for her. When Sathan and Lila ended their betrothal, he'd released all his Slayer whores, sending them home to Uteria and Restia.

"It's good to see you too. Are you well? I was worried that you might not be safe at Uteria."

She nodded. "My husband is dead."

They'd never gotten personal, but he now understood that he must've been the one she was running from.

"I'm sorry," he said.

"Don't be. Good riddance. I feel like I finally have a second chance at life." Lifting her hands, she palmed his cheeks. "You look great. Happy. What the hell happened?"

He pulled her hands from his face. "Don't look. She's behind you. I finally got up the nerve to claim her."

Realization shot through her blue eyes, and she stepped back from him a few inches. "Shit," she whispered, "I'm sorry." She threw a surreptitious glance Lila's way. "She's absolutely gorgeous. No wonder you couldn't get her out of your head. I hope I didn't mess anything up for you. I was just so happy to see you."

He glanced at Lila, whose frame had regained all of the stiffness she'd let go over the past two days. Damn it.

He sighed. "It's fine. I'll fix it. She's used to me fucking up. I seem to do it with her all the time." Feeling his eyebrows draw together, he asked, "What are you doing here anyway?"

She gave him a huge smile. "You're looking at the top salesperson at the Uteria Art Gallery. I got the job about six months ago and love it. The owner's kind of an ass, but his partner is super-sweet. He helped me get the job here."

"That's great. You look happy too. I hope you're safe. I was worried about you returning home but felt it was time we both stopped hiding."

"I'm glad you had the courage to send me home. I promise I'm safe."

Aron chose that moment to appear through the back entrance of the gallery. Latimus had met him when Miranda made him part of their combined Slayer-Vampyre council. He was one of her top advisors and descended from a very old line of Slayer aristocrats. Latimus didn't know him very well but appreciated his thoughtful input on the council.

"Latimus, hi," he said, extending his hand. "So good to see you on our compound. I hope your trek was okay." They shook hands.

Turning to Moira, he said, "I think there's a painting that needs to be boxed in back before we open at nine. Do you mind doing it? I can help if you like."

Latimus saw the vein on Moira's neck throbbing under her pale skin as she gazed up at the Slayer. He'd been with her enough times to know that meant her heart was pounding. She was attracted to Aron. Interesting. The man smiled at her kindly, not seeming to understand that she desired him. Slayers couldn't smell arousal like Vampyres could.

"No prob," she said, smiling up at him. "Great to see you, Latimus." Giving him a nod, she pivoted and headed into the back.

"I'm a silent partner in the gallery, so I help Preston make sure things run smoothly. We're so happy to showcase Lila's paintings. I'm sure they'll sell in no time."

"I know she's thrilled to show them. Thanks for the hospitality."

"Anytime," Aron said with a smile. "Let me show you around."

He followed the Slayer around the gallery, glancing at Lila while she spoke with Miranda. A man entered the room and hugged Miranda. Latimus figured he was the owner. He proceeded to help Lila hang the paintings.

As dawn approached, he knew he needed to get back to Astaria. Hating to leave Lila, he grabbed her wrist and pulled her to the front corner of the gallery. Miranda had ensured that black out blinds lined all the windows, so Lila could stay in the gallery during the day.

"I need to head back to Astaria," he said, searching her violet eyes. They swam with emotion, and he wanted to strangle himself for ever touching another woman. "Can we talk later? I'll call you after I'm finished with the troops."

"How do you know the Slayer? It seems you two know each other well." The blank expression that lined her face made his heart slam with worry.

Deciding it would be worse to lie to her, he forged ahead. "She was abducted in one of the raids centuries ago. She didn't want to return to Uteria, so I gave her a cabin near mine."

An intense expression of hurt crossed her face. "I see."

"Lila," he pleaded, bringing her palm to rest over his heart. "It's not what you think."

As her hand lay over his chest, those eyes searched his. "It's okay. It's just hard to see you with someone else that you've been...*intimate* with." He started to speak, but she shook her head. "Not here. Call me tonight."

"Okay." Feeling like a piece of absolute shit, he pulled her to him and gave her a soft peck on the lips. Moving his mouth to her ear, he whispered, "I love you."

She shivered in his arms and pulled away. "Talk to you later."

Walking across the room, she rejoined Miranda and Preston beside her paintings as they adjusted them on the wall. Cursing himself an idiot, he jumped in the Hummer and headed back to Astaria.

Once there, he found his brother in the tech room.

"Hey," he said.

"Hey," Heden said, standing from his plethora of computer screens and stretching. "Did you get Lila to Uteria okay?"

"Yeah."

"Whoa, dude. What's wrong? I thought you'd be so happy since you finally knocked boots with the woman of your dreams for two straight nights."

"Moira works at the gallery where Lila's showcasing her paintings at Uteria."

"Awwwwwwwkward," his brother said.

"Yeah. Fuck. Didn't expect to see her there."

"No shit." Walking over, Heden patted him on the shoulder. "Yet again, you fucked up royally. You really have a gift, brother."

Latimus shot him a glare. "Not helpful."

Heden chuckled and motioned for him to sit at the large table in the middle of the tech room. Pulling out a tablet, he began clicking around, ready to go over the security system for the Slayer trains.

Latimus sat down and sighed, resolved to finish the task so that he could get some sleep before training the troops at dusk.

"Besides you fucking up yet again, how were the last two days?"

Unable to stop himself, Latimus smiled. "Fucking amazing. Holy shit. She's unbelievable."

"Yeah? Our proper little Lila? Who knew?" Mischief swam in his brother's ice-blue eyes.

"She's insatiable. I had no idea. It's so different with her. God, I feel like a teenager."

Heden smiled, his lips encased by the goatee that he'd grown several centuries ago. "I'm so happy for you, bro. It's about time you two decided to let yourselves love each other."

"Thanks," Latimus said, cupping his brother's massive shoulder and rocking him back and forth. "I appreciate all your advice. You're pretty okay when you're not turning everything into a joke."

"See? She's already making you nicer. I think that's the first time you've ever thanked me for anything."

Rolling his eyes, Latimus pulled the tablet from his hands. "That's the last time I try to be genuine with you. I should've known. Now, show me these plans, because I'm beat."

They sat with their raven-colored heads pushed together over the tablet for a while, and then, Latimus headed to his cabin for some much-needed rest. Lying down, he inhaled Lila's scent from the pillow and anticipated the next time he'd get to hold her.

* * * *

Lila was thankful that the day was busy. It kept her from thinking about the familiar way the pretty Slayer had hugged Latimus. Realizing their connection had caused her a moment of such intense pain that she had to spear her fingernails into her palms to keep from crying. Of course, that made her feel like an idiot, so she'd been cold to him when he left.

Sighing, she looked down at her phone, wanting to text him and apologize. She hated texting—it felt so informal—but knew that he was probably beating himself up as he analyzed her reaction. She'd always known of the Slayer women he kept in the cabins beside his. Sometimes, over the centuries, she would stand at her window and watch him walk through the meadow, under the moonlight, knowing he would end up in their arms. It had always hurt so terribly.

But she wasn't an innocent party. She had carried on her betrothal with Sathan for ten centuries, letting Latimus believe that she loved him. Since he was so awful to her, she never even fathomed he would care to know her true feelings. Cursing herself, she now realized she should've told him ages ago how she felt. Theirs was a story of complicated misunderstandings and omissions. She hoped to change that for their future.

A nice-looking Slayer male approached, asking about one of her paintings, and she walked over to show it. Several other people came into the gallery, and before she knew it, the day was over.

Then, the pretty Slayer approached her.

"Sorry I haven't gotten to really talk to you today. We've been so busy," Moira said. "But you'll be happy to know that the gentleman you showed your town square piece to just called and purchased it."

Pride swelled in Lila's chest, thrilled that someone would buy her work. He had been a serious art collector. It was very rewarding.

"Thank you," Lila said. "That's great news."

"I'll get the other two sold for you. Don't worry. Your work is incredible."

Lila studied the Slayer, more than half a foot shorter than her, with deep blue eyes and blond hair. She had an open, friendly demeanor. Although Lila hated that she'd ever lain with Latimus, she couldn't blame the woman for what was in the past.

"Look," Moira said, appearing slightly uncomfortable. "I don't know how to broach this with you, but it was never a love match with me and Latimus."

Wanting to avoid this conversation at all costs, Lila shook her head. "I don't wish to discuss this with you."

"Wait," the woman said, holding up her hand. "I know this is super awkward, but I need to say this to you."

"Okay," Lila said, her heart pounding at what the Slayer could possibly want to say to her.

"He was always in love with you. Like, from the second I met him. He told me about you and how he could only be with me because you were promised to someone else. I think it comforted him that I had blond hair, like yours."

Feeling extremely uncomfortable, Lila shook her head. "Moira—"

"He imagined I was you when we were together," she interrupted. "He would call me by your name. I didn't care. We were two broken people who used each other for comfort." Lifting her hair, she pointed to a long red scar that ran down the hairline on her neck.

Lila gasped, wondering how a Slayer, who didn't possess self-healing abilities, could survive a blow that created such a scar.

"He saved me from so much," she said, lowering her hair. "In return, I let him pretend I was you. It was a small price to pay for my life. Please, don't hold his past against him. He's a good man and has always wanted to build a life with you. I hope you'll let him."

Lila studied the woman. In a way, she found her words arrogant. How dare she have the gall to implore Lila to do anything where Latimus was concerned? On the other hand, she understood that the woman was trying to comfort her in her own awkward way. Although it was off-putting, she appreciated the gesture.

"Thank you, Moira. I hope you won't be offended if I ask you to never speak of this again. I just find it too uncomfortable."

She breathed a laugh. "Believe me, so do I. I just needed to take this one time to say it. Now, if you'll excuse me, I'm going to wrap up your painting."

Miranda approached as she walked away. "Um, hi... Is there something going on here that I need to know about?"

Lila smiled at Miranda, who was always a bit nosy. "It's fine. I sold a painting."

"Yay!" she said, white teeth glowing in a brilliant smile. "Let's go have dinner. I have an amazing bottle of red ready to decant. Sadie says that I can have a small glass once a week, and I'm dying for it."

A few minutes later, they closed and locked the gallery. Lila thanked Preston and Aron and then walked with Miranda to the main castle, now that the sun had set. Sadie joined them for dinner, and the three of them had a wonderful time, laughing and drinking the expensive wine.

As the night wore down, Sadie excused herself, leaving her to sit with Miranda at the large dining room table.

"So, now that we're alone, I need to hear everything," Miranda said, sipping the last of her sole glass of wine and waggling her eyebrows. "Spill. How was our amazing commander in bed?"

Unable to control her smile, Lila gnawed her bottom lip. "Unbelievable. I had no idea it could be so amazing. I wish I'd gone to him centuries ago. I can't believe what I've been missing."

"Fuck yes," Miranda said, sighing. "Incredible sex with the man you love is so awesome. Sathan is insatiable in bed. God, I love him."

Lila laughed, watching her friend place the heels of her feet on the table, crossing them at the ankles. Sipping her wine, she said, "And what happened this morning? Don't say 'nothing.' I saw the chill you gave Latimus. What gives?"

Lila swirled the wine in her glass as she contemplated. "Moira is one of the Slayer women he kept for centuries, out by his cabin."

"Ohhhhhhhh," Miranda said, lowering her legs and sitting up in her chair. "Crap, Lila, I didn't know. I would've made sure she wasn't there."

Lila shrugged. "We all have a past. Although I hate that he ever touched her, or anyone else, I have to accept my responsibility too. I could've told him how I felt." Rubbing the pad of her index finger over the rim of her glass, she said, "It just hurts so badly. Knowing that he was with her in the same way he was with me. I've never touched anyone but him. It makes me feel inadequate somehow."

"That's ridiculous. He loves you so much, Lila. Being with you is probably his entire life's dream."

"What if she pleased him in ways that I can't? By the goddess, I feel like an absolute moron. He seemed satisfied with me, but I let him do everything. I want to please him, but I'm so shy and don't really know how to start."

"Okay, let's get down to business," Miranda said, setting her glass on the table. "All you need are a few key things. One," she said, lifting her index finger, "sexy lingerie. Do you have any?"

Lila felt her eyebrows draw together. "I sleep in silky pajamas but I'm not sure if that counts."

"I've seen your PJs. They're a good start, but no. Before you leave tomorrow, we'll go visit Madame Claude's. It's a lingerie store in the main square and they have awesome stuff."

"I'd like that," Lila said.

"Two," her friend continued, holding up two fingers. "You have to give him an epic blow job. Like, suck him dry until his balls are about to explode."

Lila felt a flush cover her entire body, always a bit taken aback by how blunt her friend was. "I don't know how to do that. What if I do it wrong?"

Miranda rolled her eyes. "You open your mouth and let him stick it in. It's pretty basic, Lila."

Lila palmed her face, feeling her cheeks burn. "I'm so embarrassed right now."

Miranda laughed. "Three," she said, holding up three fingers. "You have to let go of this shyness, sweetie. You are one hundred percent, hands down, the most amazingly beautiful woman I've ever met. It's not even a question. He's so fucking lucky to be with you, and you need to let yourself have the confidence to believe that."

"You've always been so confident, and I admire you for that." Shaking her head as she held her cheeks, she said, "I was always taught that confidence was distasteful. That a well-mannered lady exhibits humility and timidity."

"Gross," Miranda said, scowling. "Whoever taught you that should be shot. You're a kick-ass woman who's the head diplomat of our kingdom. You paint like da Vinci and look like Kate Upton and Gigi Hadid had a baby."

"Who?"

"Forget it," Miranda said, waving her hand. "You're *hot*, Lila. Next time you're together, you need to take control. He's dominant, like Sathan, so he'll probably end up taking over at some point, but make him work for it. Control the situation, and he'll never think about another woman again. Not that he ever has, in my opinion."

Lila inhaled a deep breath. "Okay. I'll try."

"Awesome. Now, if you'll excuse me, I have to go lie down." She rubbed her abdomen, showing quite a bit of a curve since she was just shy of seven months. "My husband implanted a Vampyre in my belly, and I'm fucking exhausted all the time."

Compassion for her friend shot through her. "Can I help at all?"

Smiling, Miranda rose. "No, but you're sweet. Let me show you to your room."

Once settled, Lila donned her silky pajamas and looked at her phone. Latimus would be training the troops for several more hours, so she allowed herself to drift to sleep.

Hours later, the phone jolted her awake.

"Hey," she said, pulling the covers tight over her body as she lay on her side. "How did the training go?"

"Fine," Latimus said. "How are you? Did you sell any paintings?"

"Yep," she said, feeling herself smile. "One. It's so nice that people like my work."

"You're so talented, honey." She felt her core grow wet at the deep timbre of his voice. "I'm so proud of you."

Silence stretched as they contemplated what to say.

"I'm sorry about Moira," he said finally. "I didn't realize she'd be there."

"I know," she said, rubbing the soft fabric of the comforter with her fingertips, wishing it was his skin.

"I wish I could change my past, Lila. If I could go back, I'd never touch anyone but you. I know you probably don't believe me, but it's true."

"I believe you," she said as she traced her fingers over the bed. "It just hurts, knowing you touched her in all the ways and all the places you touched me. Does that make it less special between us?"

"No," he said. "Never. You have to understand that I didn't ever see a future where I could be with you. If I had, I would've done things so differently. All I can do is tell you the truth. She looked like you and gave me comfort after every time I saw you with Sathan. I thought you two were lovers. I had no idea that he never touched you until we went to retrieve the Blade with Miranda."

Sighing, she chewed her lip. "I wish I had told you about my feelings. We wasted so much time."

"Regret is a futile pastime, Lila. I regret so many mistakes I've made with you, but we have to move on. I need you to love me enough to forgive me. I want so badly to make you happy."

"I forgive you, Lattie. I'll take solace in the fact that I was the first woman you ever kissed, all those centuries ago, by the river."

His low-toned chuckle reverberated through the phone. "You were. Even then, you were so damn adorable."

Silence stretched as they breathed into the phone. She longed to hold him.

"When can I see you again?" he asked.

"I'll be home at dusk tomorrow, and then I have my literacy group meeting. Monday, I'm free though."

"I have to train the troops on Monday. But I can come over on Tuesday. Does that work? I can be there at dusk."

"Okay," she said, anticipation at seeing him again coursing through her. "I miss you."

"God, honey, I miss you so much. All I can think about is having your silky pussy wrapped around me. It's driving me crazy."

Wetness burst through her core, and she exhaled a tiny pant into the phone.

"Fuck, you're wet. I can tell. You pant like that when you're ready for me to fuck you." He growled, causing bumps to form on her skin. "I want you so badly."

"Tuesday," she said, remembering her discussion with Miranda. She was going to seduce her Vampyre.

"Tuesday. I'll meet you at your cabin. Can't wait."

They disconnected, and she rolled over, groaning in frustration. Although she knew that she was on the right course, charting her independence, she hated that it created distance between them. Closing her eyes, she told herself to sleep, excited for Tuesday.

Chapter 25

Kenden drove Lila back to Lynia early Sunday evening. After spending the day with Miranda, who'd made her buy a sexy black corset with garters to hold up silky black hose, she was ready to get home. She missed Jack and was excited to see the members of her literacy group.

She and Kenden chatted on the two-hour drive, and she thanked him repeatedly for driving her.

"It's no problem, Lila, seriously." She thought him so handsome, with his mop of chestnut hair, kind brown eyes and perfect white teeth. She found herself wondering if there was someone special in his life.

Smiling at her from behind the wheel, he said, "So I hear you've tamed our powerful Vampyre commander. How exciting. I should've come to you centuries ago to figure out how to negotiate with him."

Lila laughed. "We weren't in that great of a place, centuries ago, so you'd have been wasting your time."

"Well, I'm happy you're there now. I've come to think of Latimus as a friend and admire him immensely. He's tireless when it comes to training the troops, and I'm happy he can share some time away from them with you."

"Me too," She grabbed his hand, which sat on the seat between them, and squeezed. "And what of you? You're so handsome. Surely, you have a lady who pines for you at Uteria?"

"Not yet, but I do hope to find someone someday, after we defeat Crimeous. Seeing Miranda so happy has made me realize that I want that too."

"How wonderful," she said, clutching his hand. "I know it will happen for you. You're such a kind man. Whoever she is will be truly lucky."

"Thanks," he said, giving her a smile, showcasing those flawless teeth.

He dropped her off at the main house at Lynia, and after giving him a strong hug, she entered to start her literacy meeting. The group had grown to fifteen now, and she felt a connection with each and every person. She spent several hours with them, making sure each member got one-on-one time. After the meeting, as she was putting away the chairs, Breken entered the large ballroom.

"Hey, Lila. How was your trip? Everyone missed you here."

"It was great, but I'm happy to be home."

He clasped her hands as he stood in front of her. "So, you consider our little compound home now?" Hope sparkled in his blue eyes.

"I do," she said, giving him a big smile. "I love it here."

"The feeling's mutual, believe me. Speaking of, we have an open seat on the council. One of our members is retiring to live with his daughter and her new baby at Naria. As the governor, I appoint the members to the council, and I'd like to appoint you to replace him."

"Really? I'm honored. What do the duties entail?"

"The five council members help me run the compound. Basically, public hearings, community outreach, all the things that go into running our little home. There's been talk of starting a homeless shelter, and I thought you'd be perfect to lead the roll-out. We have several wounded soldiers who can't fight anymore and out-of-work servants who live under the trees by the wall. I want to ensure they have shelter and Slayer blood when they need it."

Elation ran through her at the prospect of helping Lynians on an even broader scale. "I would love to. How often do we meet?"

"Every other week on Wednesdays and public hearings once a month on Fridays."

"Perfect. Count me in. I'm so honored that you would think of me." She hugged him, causing him to chuckle.

"We're so grateful to have you, Lila. You have no idea. You've brought an energy and generosity to this place that was sorely needed."

"Thank you," she said, embarrassed but humbled by his words.

"Do you want me to have one of our soldiers drive you home?"

"No," she said, placing her bag on her shoulder. "My bag's not heavy, and I need the fresh air. Have a good night."

"Good night, dear," he called as she walked out of the door, into the waning moonlight.

Elated, she sauntered home. Jack appeared shortly after she'd started her trek.

"Lila," he said, hugging her waist. "Where did you go? I didn't have anyone to play with at the cabins."

Laughing, she grabbed his tiny hand in hers, pulling him beside her as they strolled home. "I'll have to make sure I play with you extra hard tomorrow night."

"Seriously," he said, squeezing her hand. The gesture almost made her heart burst.

"Did Commander Latimus say anything else about me? I tried to show him how good I was at fighting."

"He was so happy to meet you. He said he'd rarely seen a young fighter with so much potential."

"Wow," the boy breathed. "I'm going to be his best soldier one day."

"I have no doubt about it," she said, grinning down at her dear boy. He truly was so precious.

She made sure he entered Sam's cabin and then entered her own. Inhaling deeply, a sense of calm and purpose washed over her. She'd created a really nice life for herself, and it continued to flourish. Allowing herself to feel pride, she set about unpacking.

* * * *

After returning home from Monday's training, Latimus showered and packed a small bag to take to Lila's. Anticipation at seeing her swamped him, and he forced himself not to count the minutes until he could board the train to Lynia.

Sitting at the small table in his den, he went over the extensive maps of the Deamon caves. Etherya had finally appeared to Sathan, although she'd spoken in maddening riddles as always. His brother had informed him that she'd spoken of the "blinding light of darkness" and the need to "strike as swiftly as the rising sun." Whatever the hell that meant.

Searching the maps, he looked for clues. Unable to find any, he folded up the papers, frustrated with his inability to rid the Earth of the cruel Deamon. All he wanted was a world where there was peace and happiness for his people.

Finally, it was time for him to go meet Lila. Arderin met him on the platform and gave him a smothering hug, telling him to make sure he told Lila he loved her more than all the grains of sand upon the beaches of the planet, or some such nonsense. His sister had always been overly dramatic, and he told her to go bother someone else. She gave him the impertinent-as-hell scowl that he loved so much and bounded back toward the castle.

Sitting on the train, he realized he was in a mood. He missed Lila terribly and was still frustrated from the situation with Moira at the gallery. He hoped that she would relax with him tonight and let herself enjoy their time together. She was so beautiful when the tension left her gorgeous body.

He trudged along the path to her cabin, passing Jack.

"Commander Latimus!" he yelled, causing him to break into a huge smile. The kid was just adorable. There was no way around it.

"Hey, buddy," he said, stopping to crouch down in front of him. "You off to school?"

"Yeah," he said, nodding. "We have field day tonight. I get to be captain and pick my own team."

"Super cool," he said, ruffling the boy's red hair. "Remember that the best teammates aren't always the strongest. Smart teammates are also great warriors."

"Okay," he said, pulling at the straps on his backpack. "There's a girl I was thinking about picking, but she runs so slow. She's smart though. She always gets A's on every test. It's annoying," he said, rolling his eyes.

Latimus chuckled. "Well, it sounds like she could be a great strategic asset to your team. I'd probably pick her."

"Then, I'll pick her too," the boy said, nodding furiously. "She's always looking at me weird, but I think she likes me. Her face gets all red when she talks to me."

"That reminds me of Lila when we were kids. She was so shy, but we had so much fun playing. I was in love with her all the way back then."

"Really?" he asked.

"Yup."

"She's so pretty. I can see why you love her."

"That, she is, my friend. Good luck with your field day. I know you'll do great."

"Thanks, Latimus. I'll see you soon."

He watched the boy run off and lifted a hand to rub it over his heart. Man, the kid just did something to him.

After a few minutes, he reached Lila's cabin and knocked on her door. She opened it, wearing the silky white robe she'd been wearing when he'd left the weapons for her the last night of their train mission. That morning seemed like a lifetime ago.

Smiling, she let him in. He removed the armaments at his waist, placing them on the table by the door. Setting his bag down, he looked at her as she stood at the foot of her large bed.

"Why are you so far away?" he asked. There was a tension between them that he couldn't read, and it made him uneasy.

He began to walk toward her, and she held up her hand. Stiffening, he straightened. "Lila?"

"Can you take off your boots?"

Feeling his eyebrows come together, he complied, throwing them and his socks on the floor. Standing between the door and the bed, he watched her, frozen.

Her blond hair was full as it fell slightly past the tops of her shoulders. She'd used some sort of darker lipstick than usual, and her lips looked full and sexy. Inside his black pants, he felt himself grow hard.

"Saturday was tough for me," she said, holding up her hand again when he tried to speak. "Not because I blame you for your past. I don't. I'm as much responsible as you are for how terribly we miscommunicated."

"It's my fault, Lila. I never should've been with anyone but you."

"No," she said, shaking her head. "I don't want to go there. I want to leave the past behind, for both our sakes. But I need to show you that I can please you. It's something that's been bothering me, and I don't feel I can move on until I satisfy you so that you can't even think of another woman."

He breathed out a laugh. "I never think of any other woman but you. Believe me."

"I do. But I need to do this. You're extremely bossy, and I need you to let me have control."

He gave her a smile, loving her newfound confidence. "Then take control, honey. I'm here."

With that lavender gaze locked on his, she untied the belt of her robe at her waist. When she pulled off the garment and tossed it to the floor, he sucked in a breath.

Standing before him was the most amazing image he'd ever seen. Her blond hair flowed to her bare shoulders. A black corset with what seemed like a thousand laces pulled in her tiny waist. The large mounds of her breasts threatened to spill from the top of the garment. The silky fabric formed a V, covering the tuft of hair that sat at the juncture of her legs. Garters attached to thigh-high black pantyhose, lace trimming the top. The paleness of her thighs, between the hose and the corset, seemed to glow at him.

Unable to stop himself, he approached her. Coming to stand in front of her, he cursed.

"I think I've died and gone to the Passage. Damn, woman. I can't speak."

The corner of her mouth turned up into a silky smile.

"Take off your clothes," she said.

Feeling himself growl, he divested his shirt, pants and underwear. Powerless to do anything but stare at her, he waited.

Taking his hand, she led him to the side of the bed, where a lamp shone atop her bedside table. Sitting on the bed, she slid until her back rested on the large mound of pillows at the headboard.

"Sit down," she said.

Complying, he sat on the middle of the bed, cross-legged.

Her eyes never leaving his, she opened her legs, causing him to groan. Sliding her hands up the silky fabric of the corset, from hip to breast, she pulled her large breasts from the material. Watching him, she grabbed her nipples, twirling them in between her fingers.

"Fuck," he whispered, palming his cock and stroking it while he watched her.

Moving one of her hands down her body while the other stayed to play with her nipple, she inserted her fingers underneath the lacy black thong she was wearing. He felt a sensation rock his core as she slid two fingers inside her wetness and then brought them to her mouth, licking them.

"God, Lila, I need to touch you."

"No," she said, moving her hand back down to her plushy folds. "I'll tell you when you can touch me. For now, I want you to take this thong off me."

"Who's bossy?" he muttered, scooting closer toward her and ripping her flimsy panties to circumvent them around the garters, tossing them on the floor. Unable to stop himself, he reached a hand toward her dripping center.

"No," she said, grabbing his wrist. "I want you to watch me."

Releasing his hand, she touched her fingers to her clit. Beginning to rub herself, she licked her red lips. Latimus thought his cock might explode. Just fucking burgeon and blow itself to bits. He'd never seen anything even remotely as sexy as his proper Lila rubbing her pink slit while her other hand pinched her taut nipple. Stroking himself, he gritted his teeth.

"Do you like watching me play with myself?" she asked.

"God, yes, woman. I've never seen anything as hot. Let me fuck you."

She shook her head against the pillows, giving him a shy, sexy smile. "I have something else in mind. Come here."

Feeling like an excited puppy, he rose and kneeled in between her open legs. Moving her hand from her breast, she grabbed his enlarged cock.

"Goddamnit, Lila."

She laughed, driving him crazy. Grinning up at him, she jerked his shaft with her pale hand. "I like touching you here," she said.

"I like it too, you little temptress. You're teasing me, and I'm about to flip you over and punish you."

"You love it," she said, sitting up and crossing her legs beneath her. She brought her other hand to his shaft, doubling the madness.

Moving her head toward him, she kissed his abdomen, making the muscles there quiver.

Unable to take it, he fisted her hair in his hand, tilting her head back.

"Let go of my hair so I can suck your cock," she said, her voice throaty.

Ignoring her, he pulled her hands from his shaft and placed the tip on her red lips. She smiled against the sensitive head and then extended her tongue to lather him there.

"Lila," he said, a warning in his voice. "Stop teasing me."

As she looked up at him, so vulnerable and hot, he felt like the luckiest man on the fucking planet. Licking her lips, she opened her mouth wide. Groaning, he stuck himself inside.

Intense pleasure coursed through him as she closed around him, moving her wet mouth back and forth over his sensitive skin. Clenching his teeth together, he released her hair, giving her free reign to suck him. Little purrs came from her closed lips as she lathered him. She was inexperienced at the act, but he didn't give a damn. Being between her lips felt amazing.

"Use your tongue," he said, moaning when she complied, intensifying his pleasure. Needing more, he gently pushed her back, urging her to rest against the pillows. Leaning his palms on the wall above her head, he began pumping into her mouth.

"Do you like that?" he asked, looking down into her wide eyes as she took him deep. She nodded slightly as he jutted into her.

"I want you to rub your clit while I fuck your mouth and make yourself come. Can you do that for me?"

She slid her fingers down to her wetness, and he closed his eyes, overwhelmed with desire. Never in his life had he experienced such passion and intimacy. She was such a gift to him. By the goddess, he felt so privileged to be with her like this.

Opening his eyes, he looked down at her. "You're so hot right now." Increasing the pace, he glided back and forth, noticing her skin redden as she played with herself.

"Tilt your head back and open your throat," he said, his voice sounding like a growl alongside the ringing in his ears. She complied, and he thrust deeper, in and out, his balls clenching as his orgasm began to form.

"I'm going to come," he breathed. "Do you want me to pull out?"

She shook her head around him, and he almost wept with joy. Groaning, he plunged into her, back and forth, unable to think about anything but the intense pleasure.

"Make yourself come with me, honey," he said, so close to exploding. "I'm going to come in your pretty mouth. Oh, god—"

Throwing his head back, he screamed, feeling his cock jerk as he shot his seed down her throat. Large spasms rocked his muscles as he supported himself on the wall above her bed. Unable to control the jerking of his hips, he let go, hoping he didn't pummel her face. It was just too good.

Finally, he felt the spurts of his come dissipate, and he was able to suck a breath into his lungs. Lifting his head, his eyes locked onto hers. Her lips were moving slightly, milking him, and he wanted to die from pleasure. Her throat bobbled up and down as she swallowed his seed, causing him to jerk again in her mouth.

Lowering his hand, he caressed her cheek with his fingertips. "Look at you," he said, reveling in the image she made as his now-sated cock sat inside her red lips. "My god, you kill me, woman."

He popped himself out of her mouth, chuckling when her lips formed a pout. "I'm finished, honey. You did me in. Shit. That was amazing."

She bit her lip, and he moved the pad of his thumb there, rubbing. "One day, you're going to use those fangs to bite me while I'm fucking you instead of always driving me crazy when you use them to bite your lip."

"I hope so," she said, smiling up at him.

Laughing, he shook his head at her. "Did you come?"

"No," she said, shaking her head. "But that's okay. I wanted to please you. I need you to know that I don't expect you to always take charge. I want our loving to go both ways, so that you're satisfied."

"Fucking A, woman," he said, lowering down to give her a blazing kiss. "Have you met me? I'm satisfied just by being in the same room with you." Aligning his body over hers, he nudged her nose with his. "You've really got to stop doubting yourself on this stuff. You're incredibly sexy to me. I need you to believe me. Okay?"

She looked so cute as she nodded up at him. "That was my first experience at oral sex. How did I do?"

He couldn't contain his laugh. "Ten out of fucking ten. You're incredible."

"I still need a lot of practice, I'm sure," she said, waggling her eyebrows.

"Fuck yeah. We'll work on that." He ran his large palm over the satin of the corset. "This is so sexy."

"Miranda helped me find it and told me I should seduce you."

"Remind me to send her an extra Christmas card. The woman's a saint."

Lila laughed as he smiled down at her. They stared at each other for a while, sated with desire.

"I know it's been a fucked-up couple of days, but we need to make sure we communicate," he said, running his fingers through her hair as it splayed across the pillow. "I think you and I have been the poster children for terrible communication over the ages, and I want to fix that."

"Me too," she said, absently picking at the black hairs on his chest. "We both assume too much, and it gets us in trouble. I hate that we were kept apart for so many centuries."

"So do I," he said. "But it's only ever been you in my heart. I need you to know that, Lila." Lowering his mouth, he kissed her.

"We'll do better," she said, when he lifted his head. "We have to, if this is going to work."

"Yes, we do. I promise I'll keep myself from jumping to stupid conclusions, like I always do around you."

"And I promise I'll trust your love for me. It's so beautiful, and I'm so lucky to have it. Thank you, Lattie."

His heart shattered at her words. Didn't she realize that he was the lucky one? Stubborn woman.

"What?" she asked as he smiled down at her.

"Nothing. You're adorable. Now, let me make you come. Open those pretty legs, honey. I'm going to sip up every drop."

Lavender irises twinkled with desire and sexy, innocent mischief as she spread her legs. Groaning, he got to work.

Chapter 26

When they awoke, an hour before dusk, Latimus held her as she told him about her new appointment to the council. Love and pride for her swam in his ice-blue eyes, and she felt so happy that he seemed to feel joy at her successes.

He made love to her under the spray of the shower, and she sent him home, chuckling at his pout. His next night off was Friday, and she was going to go visit him at his cabin. It was perfect timing because she could meet with Arderin while she was there to plan Miranda's baby shower.

They had decided to throw it in the grand ballroom at Astaria. Lila loved parties, and so did Arderin, and they were excited to throw a huge fete. No expense would be spared to celebrate the birth of the first Vampyre-Slayer heir. Lila was extremely excited for Miranda and Sathan and honored to help them celebrate.

If she was honest, she felt a bit of sadness as well. She'd always imagined Arderin throwing a baby shower for her, the whiteness of her bright smile shining as Lila opened gifts for her precious babies. In her fantasy, she had many children, the girls with platinum hair and the boys with Latimus' strong features. The images still blazed so vividly in her mind, and she tamped down the swell of depression that welled in her gut.

As the week wore on, she had a survivor's meeting and attended her first council meeting. As she sat around the table, she realized she was the only female. Happy to represent the women of Lynia, she tried to contribute thoughtfully to the meeting. The men were all respectful of her, and she liked them immensely. Breken brought up the shelter, and they all voted unanimously to fund it. Lila volunteered to help get it off the ground.

Returning home, she discovered a beautiful bouquet of white and red roses in a pretty vase upon the stairs outside her cabin. The attached note read:

Lila,
They could never smell as pretty as you, but they're a good start. I miss you. Please, bond with me. I need to hold you every day.
Love, Your Lattie

Smiling, she placed them by her window. Each night, when she returned home, a fresh bouquet was on her doorstep with a sweet note. Latimus had been serious about courting her. It made her feel so special.

When Friday came, she packed a small bag with toiletries and a change of clothes. Draylok appeared at her cabin, and they began the same journey to Latimus' cottage. When she arrived, Latimus looked so handsome, and she jumped into his arms, giving him a blazing kiss as she wrapped her legs around his waist. He made love to her, passionate and intimate, and they spent the night watching human movies about Roman gladiators on his tablet. She didn't really care for those types of movies, but she found Russell Crowe quite attractive. When she mentioned it to Latimus, he scowled at her and told her she wasn't allowed to think any man other than him attractive. She laughed and assured him he was the most handsome man on Etherya's Earth.

At dusk on Saturday, he headed to train the troops, and she walked to the main house to plan the shower with Arderin. After entering through the door that connected the house to the barracks, she walked down the hallway toward the sitting room by the foyer. She squealed as Heden approached, throwing her arms around him and hugging him for dear life.

"Hey, buttercup," he said, squeezing her tight. "I missed you so much. How are you?"

"I missed you too," Lila said, palming his handsome face. "I feel like I haven't seen you in forever."

"Well, you went and fell in love with my stupid brother, breaking my heart forever. I don't know how I'll go on." He gave her a cute smile as he smacked gum between his white teeth.

"Oh, stop," she said, laughing at him. "You know you'll always be my first love."

He winked at her. "Obviously."

"You have to come visit me at Lynia. There's a little boy who lives next to me. I'm dying for you to meet him. He's adorable and is a jokester like you."

"Yeah, Jack. Latimus told me. Said the kid's a charmer. Coming from Latimus, that's saying something. He's never charmed by anything and would rather clean his rusty old weapons than hang with kids."

"I think you're underestimating him. He was great with Jack."

"Really?" he said, lifting a brow. "Well, if anyone can domesticate my heathen of a brother, it's you. I wouldn't want the job, but you're a saint, so keep it up."

She shook her head at his teasing. "I love him so much, Heden."

"I know, sweetie," he said, placing a soft peck on her forehead. "I'm so happy for you guys. Heard he gave you some sweet lovin' to my awesome playlist. Happy to be of service."

Laughter overwhelmed her. "You're too much."

"How are you feeling, otherwise?" Concern clouded his expression as he clutched her hand. "After your injury."

Lila sighed, feeling the despair wash over her. "I've tried not to think about it. I don't know, it seems to help in some way."

His ice-blue eyes roamed over her face, so similar to Latimus'. "Arderin is worried about you. She says you haven't processed your grief."

Lila felt a flare of anger that her friend would speak about her that way, behind her back. "I don't want to talk about it."

He nodded, dropping her hand. "Well, I'm here for you if you need me. You already know that. Send me some dates that I can come visit you at Lynia."

"I will," she said, giving him a hug. He retreated down the hall, his large frame silhouetted in the soft lighting of the lamps that hung along the walls.

Arderin was waiting for her in the sitting room.

"Hey," she said, rushing to give her a hug. Lila hugged her stiffly, and she pulled back. "Um, are you mad at me?"

"I don't like you telling Heden that I haven't processed my grief. It's my business, and I don't want the fact that I'm barren being discussed by everyone at the compound."

Arderin's eyebrows drew together. "I'm just worried about you. I would never betray your trust."

"Well, you did. Don't do it again. I don't want people pitying me and looking at me like I have some sort of disease."

"That's not fair," Arderin said, ire flashing in her gorgeous blue eyes. She was a passionate person and always became angered quite easily. "No one pities you, Lila. We love you and want to support you."

"I don't want your support," she said, not understanding where her anger was coming from and unable to control it. "I want you to treat me normally."

"You were raised your entire life to have kids. I would think that being rendered unable to have them would hurt. Sorry if I'm worried about you."

Rage filled Lila as she looked at her oldest friend. They had never argued like this, but she couldn't stop herself. "I can't do this with you. I'm not going to sit here and let you tell me how my life has no purpose anymore because that bastard maimed me."

"That's not what I said," Arderin said, groaning in frustration. "Why are you being such a bitch?"

Hurt sliced through Lila. Many had accused her of being frigid and cold in her life, and it always caused her immense pain. "I won't stand here and let you call me names." Lifting her chin, she turned to leave the room, almost plowing down Miranda.

"Whoa," Miranda said, grabbing Lila's upper arms. "What the hell is going on in here?"

"Lila's being a huge A-hole because I'm worried about her since her injury. Sorry I care, okay?"

"Stop it, Arderin," Lila said, her tone icy. "I don't want us to say things that will hurt each other more." Looking at Miranda, she shook her head. "I can't plan the shower now. I'll be in my old room. I have some things there that I want to go through."

Miranda's green eyes were filled with concern. "Okay," she said finally.

Lila exited the room, hearing Arderin whine about how mean she was. Shaken, she headed up the steps of the large spiraled staircase to her old room. When she entered, she closed the door behind her, locking it. Taking several deep breaths, she studied the dim chamber.

Boxes were scattered around, packed by her but left behind when she went to Lynia. She had some things that she'd saved and wanted to give to Miranda. Heading into her large walk-in closet, she located the container she was looking for.

Sitting on the carpeted floor, she opened it and rummaged around. Her fingers touched the soft fabric of the white gown. Pulling it from the box, she ran her face over it.

It was a ritual gown, passed down from her mother. She had worn it the day she'd been baptized as the king's betrothed, all those centuries ago when she was just a baby. Small and white, her mother had passed it to her, hoping she would use it when her own daughter was baptized in the name of Etherya.

Clutching the fabric to her face, tears welled in her eyes, and she began to cry. She'd always imagined having a daughter with long blond hair and lavender eyes. Very few immortals had her eye color. It was a recessive gene that was rarely passed on amongst Vampyre or Slayer. When she was young, many of the children had made fun of her, calling her "Ugly Eyes." Latimus had always defended her honor even then—one of the many reasons her tender heart had loved him so.

Rubbing her hand over her abdomen, she inhaled the scent of the gown. Shaking with her cries, she lay on the floor, curling into a ball. She would never have a daughter with pretty violet eyes. Nor a son with Latimus' strong widow's peak. Crimeous had robbed her of her sweet babies. After all the weeks that had passed since her maiming, she finally let the loss overwhelm her.

* * * *

Latimus was watching the troops from the hill when his phone buzzed. Lifting it to his ear, he said, "What's up, Miranda?"

"Something's wrong with Lila. She got in an argument with Arderin and locked herself in her old room. I can hear her crying."

Worry flashed through him. "I'll be right there."

Lifting his walkie, he commanded Draylok to continue the drills and ran to the main house. When he entered the foyer, his sister's face was laced with tears as Miranda held her while they stood under the large diamond chandelier.

"I'm sorry," Arderin said, her eyes pleading with him. "I brought up her injury and hurt her feelings although I didn't mean to. I swear."

Latimus loved his little sister dearly, and his soft spot for her rarely allowed him to be angry at her. "I believe you. Don't cry, little one." Pulling her out of Miranda's arms and into his, he hugged her. "She's upstairs?"

His sister nodded, still beautiful even though wetness ran from her nose and her eyes.

"I'll take care of her. Go clean yourself up."

"I'm sorry."

"I know." Kissing her forehead, he shot a glance at Miranda. Her olive-green eyes were filled with concern. "Get her cleaned up."

Miranda nodded, and he pounded up the stairs. Coming to Lila's door, he knocked. With his acute Vampyre ear, he could hear her sobbing. Turning the handle, he realized it was locked.

"Lila?" he called, knocking on the door again.

Heart pounding with worry for her, he lifted his foot and kicked in the door with his black army boot. Following her cries, he found her in the closet, his heart shattering with pain.

His beautiful Lila was curled in a ball on the carpeted floor, clutching a white piece of fabric to her chest, wailing as her body convulsed. Removing the Glock and knife at his waist, he set them upon the table by the bed. Stalking toward her, he lowered himself and pulled her into him.

"No," she said, sobbing as she shook her head. "Leave me alone. I don't want you to see me like this."

"Stop it," he said, pulling her back against his front as he spooned her body with his. Clutching her with his massive arms, he let her cry.

"You need to process this, Lila. All of us have been worried about you. It's okay to cry, honey. We love you and support you."

"You all think he beat me. That my life isn't worth anything anymore. I hate that everyone pities me. It hurts so much." Clutching the gown to her face, she wept into it.

"No one pities you. You made that up somewhere along the way, and it's bullshit. All of us are amazed at how you've handled this."

"I can't have babies," she cried, shaking her head on the carpet. "All I wanted were babies with pretty purple eyes, so that I wouldn't feel so alone."

Latimus' heart shattered at her words, understanding how lonely she must've felt for centuries since her parents died.

"You're not alone, Lila. It hurts me to hear you say that. I love you, and so does my family. You belong to us, and we need you."

"My baby girl was supposed to wear this," she said, rubbing the white fabric over her face. "I was supposed to hold her and feed her and love her. Why does Etherya take away everything I love? One day, she'll take you too."

"No," he said, shaking her. "I'm not going anywhere. Get that through your stubborn skull. I love you, and you're stuck with me."

Groaning, she broke into another full round of tears. Latimus was terrified she would make herself sick. "Honey, you have to calm down. This isn't doing anyone any good. We need to find a way for you to process your grief in a healthy way. Sadie would be happy to sit and talk with you. I think you should let her."

"One more person you all talked to behind my back. I'm glad to know you all think I'm so pitiful that you need to discuss me." She wiped her nose with the back of her arm, her tears seeming to abate a bit.

"Now, you're pissing me off. You can pull that haughty ice-queen shit with my sister, but I'm sure as hell not letting you do that with me." Turning her, he loomed over her, looking into her wet eyes. "I won't let you tell me that I'm an asshole because I love you and want to help you. You spend your entire life helping other people. It's about time you let us love you enough to help you back. I mean it, Lila."

She lifted her slim hand, cupping his cheek. "I wanted so badly to have your son. I thought about it all the time. He'd be so handsome. And now, I can't give that to you." Her face contorted with pain, and she began sobbing again.

"Hey," he said, shaking her. "Look at me. I need you to stop crying, honey."

Pulling her up, he sat her in front of him, separating her jean-clad legs so that they draped over his thighs. As she straddled him, he palmed her face, tilting it to him. "I would be lying if I said I haven't imagined you pregnant with my child. We have to be honest about that and what we lost here. But I never really even thought about having kids until I decided to stop being a coward and claim you. Now, I want them with you so much. Mostly because it will make you happy, but also because I think that with you by my side, I might actually be a pretty okay father."

She gave him a broken smile. "You'd be so great."

Grinning, he felt his heart swell in his chest. "I don't care that you're barren. I truly don't. There are plenty of kids who need homes. If you want babies, I want to adopt them with you. As many as you want. As long as you look at me with those gorgeous eyes, I'll agree to adopting quintuplets with you."

Joy speared through him as she gave a soft laugh. "Now, you're just being crazy."

"Maybe a little," he said, "but you have to know I'd do anything for you."

"I know," she said, placing her forehead against his.

"I need you to do something for me though," he said, lifting her chin with his fist to lock onto her eyes. "I need you to sit down and talk with Sadie. Not because I pity you, or whatever bullshit you've concocted in your stubborn brain, but because I love you and need you to process this. Can you please do that for me?"

Inhaling a deep breath, she nodded. "Okay. I just don't want everyone feeling sorry for me. I feel so inadequate that everyone in the entire kingdom knows I'm barren."

"Fuck them. People focus on others' drama because their lives are shit. No one who cares about you feels sorry for you. I promise."

Sighing, she wiped her face with her hands. "I must look terrible."

"You look beautiful," he said, running his hand over her hair.

"It's hard for me to be vulnerable. I rarely cry in front of other people. Sorry you had to see it."

"Why?" he said, stroking her hair. "I want you to come to me when you're sad or angry, or any other time you feel you need to. That's what being bonded is about. I'm honored to be here for you."

She gave him a warbled smile, and love for her bloomed in his chest. "You're such a good man."

"That's what you keep telling me," he said, grinning down at her.

"Thank you." Palming his face, she gave him a sweet kiss.

"Of course," he said, pulling her closer. His shaft rested in the juncture of her thighs, and he told himself not to ruin the moment by being a horny jackass.

"I want to stay with you and head home on Sunday, at dusk. I told Sam I'd have dinner with him and Jack tonight, but I can push it."

"Don't do that. I'll drive you to Lynia when I'm done with the troops, and we'll stay at your place. We'll take the Hummer so we can drive during the day. As long as you don't mind me inviting myself to have dinner with you guys," he said, arching his eyebrows.

Her smile was brilliant. "Jack will be so thrilled. I would love that."

"Great," he said, placing a kiss on her forehead. "I'll be done at dawn. We're doing some new drills that Kenden implemented but it should only take a few more hours."

"Sorry I pulled you away from your troops. Your work is so important. I don't want to distract you."

"You've been distracting me since we were kids, woman. Don't stop now."

Breathing out a laugh, she looked down at the floor. "I was so cold to Arderin. I feel terrible. She was just trying to support me."

Latimus rolled his eyes. "I'm sure my sister's not innocent in this situation. She rarely is. She's a brat."

"You love her so much. It's so nice to see."

"I do." Shifting, he stood and pulled her up.

"I'm going to wash my face and get myself together. I'll meet you at your cabin at dawn."

"Okay, honey." Leaning down, he gave her a kiss on her soft, pink lips. "See you then." With one more gentle caress of her face, he returned to his troops.

* * * *

Lila cleaned herself up in her old bathroom. Feeling like an idiot, she stared at her reflection in the large mirror over her sink. Although she was terribly embarrassed that Latimus had seen her so vulnerable, she felt a bit lighter after her breakdown.

Returning to her closet, she lay the ritual gown on one of the bare shelves. She wanted to give it to Miranda, for her children, but decided that she wasn't quite ready to part with it yet. Heading out of her room and down the stairs, she went in search of Arderin.

She found her in the infirmary, down by the dungeon, her head buried in a medical book. Coming to stand behind her, Lila ran her hand down her soft black curls.

Her friend turned, wetness swimming in her light blue eyes as she stared up at her from the stool she sat upon.

"I'm so sorry, Lila."

"Shhhh," Lila said, leaning down to embrace her. They hugged for several moments, squeezing each other tightly.

"I didn't mean to call you a bitch. I feel terrible. I know how much that hurt you."

"It's okay, sweetie," she said, pulling back and soothing her palm over her hair. "I was very angry and took it out on you. I'm so sorry."

"I love you, Lila. You're my best friend. I'll die if you're mad at me."

Lila smiled at the innocent sincerity swimming in her friend's beautiful face. "I could never be mad at you. You're my little Arderin. And you were right, I haven't processed my grief in the way that I should. I'm going to reach out to Sadie. I think talking to her will help."

"She's so great," Arderin said. "Like, the sweetest person and such a good doctor. She's studied human psychology for centuries. I'm so happy you're going to talk to her."

Lila smiled, thankful for her quick forgiveness. "Me too. I'm so lucky to have people like you and Latimus who care for me so much."

"I've never seen him like this, Lila. He's so happy and smiles more than I've ever seen. Hell, I don't think I even knew he had teeth."

Lila laughed, leaning her hip against the counter. "He's made me very happy too. I love him so much."

"So amazing," her friend said, squeezing her hand. "You and Miranda have tamed my two idiot brothers. I'm so happy for you guys. I wish I was in love. It seems so incredible. Unfortunately, the only person who shows any interest in me is Naran, and he's so lame."

"You'll find your mate one day. You're so special that Etherya probably just needs extra time to find him for you."

"I hope so," Arderin said, her gaze dropping to stare wistfully at the floor. "I'm so tired of being a virgin. I might just find someone and do the deed just to get it over with."

"It's so much better if you wait for someone you love. Trust me," Lila said, squeezing her hand. "I promise that when the time comes, and your man finds you and claims you, you'll be happy you waited. I am."

Arderin smiled, mischief in her eyes. "So, my brother must really be boning your brains out. Gross, but awesome."

Lila giggled, loving her sense of humor. "Yeah, it's pretty awesome."

Arderin closed her book and stood. "If you're up for it, I'd really like to start planning the shower. I'm so excited for Sathan and Miranda and want to make sure it's perfect."

"Let's do it."

They walked through the dungeon and up to the sitting room. Arderin texted Miranda, and she joined them. Lila gave her an apology, and Miranda waved her off, in her always affable way.

They planned for a few hours, and then, Lila walked through the darkened meadow, back to Latimus' cabin. Using the key he'd given her, she entered, locking the bolts behind her. Walking to stand in front of the thin window in the den, she lifted her phone from the back pocket of her jeans.

"Hey, Lila," the Slayer answered, in her always pleasant tone. "How are you?"

"I'm fine, Sadie. How are you?"

"Great. Everything's calm here for the moment. I'm hoping the Deamons continue to leave us alone. What can I do for you?"

"I need to talk to you," Lila said, fingering the curtains that hung on window. She felt extremely uncomfortable asking for help but she knew this was the path forward. "I had a breakdown tonight. It wasn't pretty. I think I need to set up some time to speak with you so that I can process the grief from my injury."

"I'm so glad you called, Lila. I'm happy to speak with you about your injury and anything else that you need. Although I'm not a licensed psychologist, I've studied the specialty for two hundred years and feel well-versed in it."

"Okay," Lila said, taking a deep breath and struggling to remain open. "How do we do this?"

"Since you're at Lynia and I'm at Uteria, I think the best course would be to start with some one-hour phone sessions, twice a week. I'm flexible. You let me know what works for you."

"How about eleven p.m. on Tuesdays and Thursdays? That way, I'll have started my night, and it will give you time to finish dinner and wind down your evening."

"Perfect. I'm looking forward to it. I'll call you at eleven p.m. on Tuesday."

"Thank you so much, Sadie."

"You're welcome. Talk to you then."

Lila ended the call, staring out the window at the moonlit field. Dawn was just beginning to flirt with the horizon, and her heart longed for Latimus. As if she conjured him from her thoughts, his large frame appeared, plodding toward the cabin in his black army boots. Smiling, she watched him approach, knowing she'd be in his arms soon.

When he entered, he smiled at her, and she ran to him, clutching him to her and giving him a blazing kiss.

"Damn, woman," he said, nibbling at her lips. "I need to come home to you like this every morning."

"Make love to me," she said, pulling him toward the bed.

They loved each other, passionate and thorough. Once finished, they showered, and he packed a bag. Draylok met them with the Hummer, and they climbed inside. Latimus dropped him off at the barracks and then started the hour drive to Lynia.

Once back at her cabin, they loved each other again and waited for dusk to fall. When the night stars finally glistened over the grassy field outside the cabin, they headed to see Sam and Jack. Sam had prepared a lasagna and had bought her favorite bottle of red. As she sat, surrounded by her men, her heart was so full. Crimeous could've done so much worse to her. In the end, she had her commander, her dear little boy and his sweet uncle.

Silently thanking Etherya, she sipped her wine and smiled at her precious men.

Chapter 27

A few nights later, Latimus lay with Lila inside her cabin, absently stroking her hair. It was the first night he'd had off since the dinner with Sam and Jack, and he had missed her terribly. His phone buzzed on the nightstand beside her, and he picked it up to read the text. Cursing, he sat up.

"What's wrong?" she asked, concern clouding her expression.

"Crimeous is attacking Uteria. Fuck. I have to go."

She nodded as he rose. Calling Kenden, he put the phone on speaker as he dressed.

"We're ready to roll out," the calm Slayer's voice said over the phone. "Takel and Larkin are set."

"Send Draylok to come get me in the copter. I'll meet you guys at Uteria."

"Ten-four." The phone's light dimmed as Kenden ended the call.

Lila had thrown on her white robe, and her arms were crossed below her ample breasts. He hated to leave her but had no choice.

"Sorry, honey. I'll make it up to you."

"Don't be sorry," she said, coming to stand in front of him. "I feel terrible that you're so far away. I realize how selfish I've been to pull you away from Astaria. You need to be stationed there with your troops."

"It's fine. We have the copter. It's nice to visit you here. You're so happy when you're here. And it's probably good for me to get away from the troops every once in a while."

Pulling her close, he tilted her face to his. "Now, kiss me before I go."

Lifting her lips, she kissed him softly. As she stared up at him, her eyes were laced with concern and a slight bit of fear.

"I'll be fine," he said, soothing her cheek. "This is what I was trained for. I don't want you to worry about me."

"How can I not worry?" she asked, her eyes becoming glassy. "You're going to fight a war. I'm terrified to lose you."

"You'll never lose me. You're not that lucky." Winking at her, he tried to lighten the mood.

"Stop it," she said, swatting his chest. "I would die if I lost you."

"That's never going to happen," he said, hugging her. "Now, come outside and give me a proper farewell."

The sound of the helicopter roared outside, and it landed on the plushy grass of the meadow, twenty feet from her cabin. He stalked down the stairs of the cabin and turned, giving her one last kiss as she stood on the stair above. "See you soon."

"See you soon," she said, her voice scratchy.

He jumped in the copter and placed the headphones over his ears so that he could communicate with Draylok. Looking down, he saw her, so beautiful as her white robe flitted in the wind from the copter's blades. Determined to protect her and everyone else he loved, he prepared for battle.

When they arrived at Uteria, he hopped out of the copter, approaching Kenden where he'd set up point thirty feet from the wall that surrounded the compound.

"Do we need to go inside?" he asked, turning his head to observe the two hundred Astaria-based troops who awaited their command outside the wall.

"Larkin and Takel and their two hundred men are holding for now. I say we let them continue."

Latimus nodded, knowing that it was imperative the Uteria-based troops learn to fight independently from the Astaria-based troops. The Uterian combined Slayer-Vampyre army consisted of a hundred troops of each species, and they had become a solid team.

The walkie at Kenden's side buzzed, and Takel's voice transmitted through the device. "We're holding the Deamons, but Crimeous is here. He's dematerializing and reappearing everywhere. I think you should send in fifty more soldiers."

Latimus nodded to Kenden. "I'll lead them in."

Raising his hand, he extended his five fingers, holding them high above his head. His troops were trained to understand that he needed fifty men to fall in line. The soldiers formed behind him, and he led them to the thick wooden doors that comprised the entrance of the compound.

Entering, Latimus marched two hundred yards to the open meadow where the battle was occurring. He could see Crimeous, appearing and stabbing a Slayer then disappearing, only to reappear twenty feet away and deploy an eight-shooter at a Vampyre soldier.

Rage for the bastard swamped him, and he charged. Unloading the magazine of his AR-15, he shot several of the Deamons dead. He saw Larkin battling Crimeous, the strong Slayer soldier knocking the rifle from the Dark Lord's hand. Sneering, the Deamon materialized an eight-shooter in his pasty hands.

As if in slow-motion, Latimus watched the next events unfold. Crimeous lifted the eight-shooter, training it on Larkin's chest. Takel appeared, seemingly out of nowhere, and jumped in front of the Slayer to save him. As the bullets of the eight-shooter pierced Takel's massive chest, Latimus screamed.

Preparing a TEC, Latimus ran toward Crimeous, oblivious to all the other fighting around him. When he approached the bastard, he attached the device to his head, deploying it. The Deamon screamed in pain, his beady eyes popping, and he dematerialized.

Dropping to his knees, Latimus cradled Takel into his chest.

"Shit. He jumped in front of me," Larkin said, lowering beside Latimus. "Damn it!"

Latimus clasped the massive Vampyre, watching him gasp for breath. They had been comrades for ten centuries. Both only eight during the Awakening, they had learned the ways of war together, and Latimus considered him a true friend. He had seen enough death to know that he wouldn't survive. Sensing his imminent demise, he spoke, looking into the soldier's blue eyes.

"I will take care of your family," he said, swallowing thickly and struggling with emotion. "You have been a brave warrior and a true friend, Takel. May you find peace in the Passage."

The man's eyes searched his, filled with intense pain and fear.

"You have fought nobly. Greatness awaits you in the Passage. Let it go."

Takel gasped, his eyes growing wide, and then he let out a long exhale, his massive body relaxing as Latimus held him. Unashamed, he rocked his friend, his eyes filling with wetness. Profound agony swept through him as he lay him gently on the ground.

Filled with rage, Latimus stood, grabbing a sword that had fallen on a nearby patch of dirt. Giving a mighty scream, he attacked, mercilessly slaying every Deamon in his path. He reveled in the slaughter of each and every one of the beady-eyed creatures. As he gutted them, he screamed in anguish, avenging his friend in the only way he knew how.

The dark part of himself that he'd always questioned roared inside him as he dragged the steel blade through countless organs of his enemies. Giving in to his base instincts, he relished in the blood that spattered from their bodies as it washed over his face and arms. The beast inside pushed him, fueled by the loss of his friend and a hefty dose of adrenaline.

Lifting his sword, he struck another Deamon down, proceeding to ruthlessly stab him in the heart, over and over, as his body lay dead on the ground.

"Latimus!" he heard Kenden yell behind him.

Ignoring him, he pounded the dead Deamon's chest with the blade of the sword.

"Latimus," the Slayer said, grabbing his shoulder and turning him.

Holding the sword high above his head, as he'd been about to strike again, he glared at Kenden.

"The Deamon is dead, Latimus. Drop the sword."

Latimus felt his nostrils flare and clenched his teeth.

"Drop it," Kenden said in his always-unflappable tone.

Shouting a curse, Latimus threw the sword to the ground.

"Come," Kenden said. "All the Deamons are dead. We need to start the clean-up."

Rubbing his forehead with his fingers, he nodded. "I need a minute."

"Take Takel's body back to Astaria. I'll run point here and work with Larkin to organize the clean-up."

"I just need a minute," Latimus said, waving his hand.

"Take the Hummer and go home, Latimus," Kenden said, clutching his shoulder. "Even you are fallible sometimes. It's best if you go process this."

Sighing, Latimus nodded. "Okay. Thanks, Ken."

"He was an excellent soldier. I'm sorry for your loss."

"He was one of the few people I considered a friend," Latimus said, shaking his head. "That motherfucker is really pissing me off. We have to kill him. I'm tired of this shit."

"We will," Kenden said, shaking Latimus by the shoulder. "We'll slaughter that bastard. Now, go."

Giving the Slayer commander a nod, he stalked off the field, through the compound's wooden doors and entered the Hummer that held his friend's body.

Transporting him home, he allowed the grief to overtake him. Swiping his arm under his runny nose as he drove, he fought off tears. Fucking A. It was a huge loss.

When he got to the barracks, he instructed two of his soldiers to prepare Takel's body. Locating the phonebook, he found the number for Takel's mother, who lived at Valeria. In the darkness of the barracks, he called the woman, hating to tell her the terrible news. She cried miserably, and he did his best to soothe her over the phone.

Promising her that he would prepare her son's body for a proper entry to the Passage, he ended the call. Cradling his head in his hands, Latimus rocked back and forth in the chair he'd fallen into, unable to comprehend the loss. Finally, he inhaled a deep breath and stood. He was covered in Deamon blood and needed to shower.

Beginning the trek to his cabin, he seethed in his hurt and anger, feeling his rage intensify with every step under the slitted moon. Thanking the goddess that Lila was at Lynia, he let his anger simmer. He never wanted her to see this dark, hidden part of him that reveled in the death of his enemies. Knowing she would see him as a monster, he was terrified for her to see his hidden truth. Trudging forward, he wallowed in his fury.

* * * *

Lila worried for Latimus, knowing he was fighting the Deamons at Uteria. Unable to calm down in her cabin, so far away, she dressed and headed to the train. Wanting to be there for him when he arrived home, she exited the train at Astaria and walked to his cabin. Using the key that he'd given her, she entered.

Turning on the light of his bedside table, she waited for him, rubbing her damp palms on her jeans as she sat upon his black comforter. The thought of him getting maimed or injured, or even dying, caused her throat to close up in terror. Reminding herself that he was the strongest soldier who had ever lived on Etherya's Earth, she waited.

After what seemed like an eternity, the handle of the door turned, and he stepped through. Anger swam in his ice-blue eyes as she lifted from her perch on the bed to walk into the den.

"What are you doing here?" he asked, and her heart began to pound at his tone.

"I wanted to be here for you," she said, starting to approach him slowly.

"No," he said, his voice harsh as he held up a hand. "Don't. I'm covered in Deamon blood. I don't want you to touch me like this."

Concern jolted through her. "I don't care. I want to hold you."

"No!" he said, his breathing labored. "I don't want you to see me like this, Lila."

"Like the man who fights mercilessly for our people? There is no one nobler in my eyes."

He gave an angry laugh and rubbed his forehead with his fingers. "I wish you hadn't come. Tonight was fucked-up, and I'm not in the right head space to be with you right now."

Hurt coursed through her. "I won't let you push me away. I want to support you. You're so strong and supportive of me. Let me comfort you."

She timidly began approaching him again.

"Stop," he said, shaking his head. "I can't do this right now. I need to wash this blood off. Go back to Lynia. I'll call you tomorrow." Stalking to the bathroom, he shut the door.

Lila huffed out a breath, understanding that he was struggling with something heavy. The battle must've gone poorly, and she ached to soothe him. Hearing the water of the shower begin to spray, she sat on the bed, absently gnawing her lip.

After several minutes, she heard him turn off the shower. Heart pounding, she walked to the bathroom door. Turning the knob, she slowly opened it.

He stood in front of the mirror, his arms supporting his weight as he leaned over the sink. Since the mirror was fogged, she only saw the back of his head and the muscles of his wide back. A white towel was tied around his waist. Gingerly walking in, she placed her palms on his lower back, needing to touch him.

He growled, and she saw a muscle clench in his jaw as she stood behind him.

"Lila," he said, a warning in his tone. His fists clenched on the bathroom counter, the knuckles white.

"Let me comfort you," she said, her voice sounding so small in the tiny bathroom.

"I'm not myself right now," he said, his breathing coming in short pants. "I don't want to hurt you."

"You won't," she said, sliding her palms over the smooth skin of his back.

He scoffed. "There's a part of me that you'll never understand. It's dark and awful, and I don't want you exposed to it."

"That's not fair," she said, continuing to slowly rub him. "I want to know every part of you, even the bad parts."

"No," he said, turning to face her and grabbing her wrists. "Not this part. I won't have you looking at me like a monster."

She felt her eyebrows draw together. "I could never—"

"No, Lila!" he yelled, and she jolted, unable to believe he was shouting at her. "I'm on a razor-thin line of control here. I'm afraid I'm going to hurt you. I need you to go back to Lynia."

"Lose control, then," she said, lifting her chin. "Scream at me or make love to me or whatever you need but don't push me away. I won't let you hide a part of yourself from me. That's not what I want from my bonded."

Grabbing her sweater at the hem, she pulled it over her head. His breathing became even more labored as she removed her bra. "Take me. Let me hold you and comfort you."

His nostrils flared as his eyes roved over her bared breasts. "I don't have the ability to be gentle with you right now."

"So, don't be gentle," she said, pulling his hands and placing them over her breasts. "Fuck me as hard as you need to. I won't break." She'd never said the curse word in her life but felt that she needed to harshen her tone to match his.

Staring into her, he tentatively squeezed her breasts. "Lila," he breathed, and she could see his struggle.

"Fuck me," she said, sliding her arms around his neck.

Groaning, he lifted her by her butt, slamming his mouth into hers while she wrapped her legs around his waist. Tossing her on the bed, he removed her jeans and thong. Throwing his towel on the ground, he grabbed her ankles, pulling them high in the air, one on each side of his head.

Gritting his teeth, he plunged into her, pistoning his hips back and forth, slapping his balls against her. Lost in the pleasure of seeing him so raw, she let him take her, moaning from the bed.

Pulling out of her, he flipped her over to lie on her stomach. Grabbing her hips, he brought her to her knees, positioned his cock at her wet slit and shot into her from behind. Lying on her elbows, she rested her forehead on the bed as he battered her relentlessly.

Gasping, she felt him clench a large chunk of her hair in his fist. Pleasure-pain shot through her as he pulled the tresses, turning her head so that her cheek lay on the soft comforter. Lowering over her, still fucking her, he plunged his fangs into the juncture where her neck met her shoulder.

Stiffening in shock, she tried to relax, opening her body to him in all the ways that he needed. While he sucked her, his cock moving in and out of her tight channel, he palmed one of the cheeks of her ass. With his thumb, he touched the sensitive entrance of her anus. Shivering, she felt him circle the puckered entrance with the pad of his thumb. The sensation was surprisingly pleasurable, and she mewled below him.

Lifting his fangs from her, he groaned in her ear. "Goddamnit, Lila. You deserve better than this." Turning her head, he plunged his fangs into the other side of her neck, causing her to moan. He pulled her blood into him, growling as he moved in and out of her, clutching her ass cheek with his large hand.

"It feels so good," she said, her voice strained from his ceaseless pounding.

Popping his teeth from her, he rested his forehead on her upper back. Cupping her shoulders, as he lay on top of her back, he pushed himself into her, over and over. She'd never felt him so deep.

Grunting, he began to tense up, and she knew he was close to coming. Fisting her hair in his hand, he pulled her head back, placing his lips on her ear.

"You'd better come for me, you little cock tease," he commanded, making her body shudder. "You forced me to fuck you like this, and you'd better spray me with your come. Do you hear me?"

Feeling her eyes roll back in her head, she let him pound the sensitive spot deep inside her, giving in to the pleasure. The orgasm built as she felt her entire body flush with heat.

"God, I love your wet pussy. Damn it, Lila, you'd better come for me." Lifting his head, he screamed, cursing as his seed began to jet into her. Feeling something snap, her orgasm overtook her, and her body began convulsing in wave upon wave of pleasure.

Giving in to their passion, their bodies shuddered and shook. With long, labored breaths, they collapsed in a heap upon the bed.

* * * *

Latimus opened his eyes, shame washing over him at how he had treated his precious Lila. Removing himself from her, he rolled her over, his hand shaking as he touched her shoulder. Her eyes were shuttered as she stared up at him, and his heart slammed in his chest.

Long trails of blood ran down both sides of her pale neck and shoulders from where he had pierced her so thoughtlessly. He hadn't even licked her soft skin first to lather it with his self-healing saliva, protecting her from the pain. No, he'd just bitten her, like a selfish bastard, and he wanted to retch.

"Hey," she said, cupping his cheek. "I'm okay."

Self-revulsion ran through him. "Let me close your wounds." Lowering his head, he licked one of the puncture sites closed and then moved to lick the other. She shivered as his tongue darted on her skin.

Lifting his head again, he stared down at her.

"I'm sorry," he said, shaking his head as he stroked her cheek.

"Why?" she asked, genuine concern in her eyes.

"I was so careless with you. You deserve so much better. I told you I wasn't myself. I tried to warn you that I wouldn't be gentle."

Her pink lips curved into a breathtaking smile. "That was amazing. What in the hell are you talking about?"

He felt his shattered heart slowly start to beat again. Even though he'd been so reckless with her, she'd seemed to enjoy it.

"I'm tough, Lattie," she said, rubbing his cheek with her thin fingers. "You don't have to coddle me. If you need to be rough with me, I can handle it. I love how dominant and aggressive you are. It's extremely attractive to me."

Lowering his head, he gave her a thorough kiss. "You're so fucking special, Lila. I want to treat you that way. I don't want to be careless with you."

"Stop it. Now, you're making me mad. That was incredible. It felt so good to see you let go."

"I don't deserve you," he said, sadness swamping him. "You should belong to someone who isn't plagued by war and death. I wish I could be a better man for you."

Her blond eyebrows drew together, and her magnificent eyes clouded with emotion. "Are we back to that? Please, don't go back there. I need you to understand that I love you, even the parts of you that are trained to maim and kill. I don't see them as evil. I see them as necessary. You've protected our people your whole life. I need you to be able to trust me enough to show that side to me. I want to spend eternity with you and comfort you after your battles. If you can't let me do that, then it won't be real. And I need it to be real, Lattie. All of it."

He lowered his forehead to hers. "That part of me is so vile. I hate it."

"I love it," she said, caressing his face. "I love each and every part of you. That's what real love is. You need to let me give it to you."

Shaking his head, he gazed into her violet irises.

"What?" she asked, grinning up at him.

"I'm just wondering how in the hell I got so lucky. I was a bastard to you for a thousand years, and yet here you are, staring up at me, loving me. It's humbling."

Smiling, she shifted underneath him. Wanting to cuddle with her, he lifted her and placed her under the covers, crawling in beside her and drawing her to his chest.

"What happened tonight?" she asked, resting her chin on her hand, the palm lying flat on his chest.

He told her about Takel, struggling to keep the emotion from his voice.

"Oh, Lattie," she said, sliding her silky skin over him as she maneuvered on top of him and kissed his lips. "That's terrible. He sounds like such a good man and a dear friend."

"He was," he said, twirling a strand of her hair around his finger. "It's a devastating loss."

"Will there be a sendoff to the Passage at Valeria? I'll go with you."

Smiling at her kindness, he nodded. "I'd like that."

"I'm so sorry," she said, placing a tender kiss on his chest. "I wish you didn't have to hurt like this."

Remaining silent, he stroked her hair, lost in her lavender eyes.

"I need to set some ground rules for us after my battles. I've always dealt with the aftermath alone but I'm honored that you want to support me."

"Of course, I do. What do you need from me?"

Inhaling a deep breath, he threaded his fingers through her silken tresses. "I don't want one drop of Deamon blood ever touching your skin. I couldn't live with myself. We need to have a rule that you won't touch me after my battles until I've showered. Otherwise, I can't reconcile letting you comfort me afterward."

"Okay," she said, nodding. "You have my word. What else?"

The corners of his lips lifted. "You have to look at me like you are now every time I come home. You're so fucking gorgeous." He ran the pad of his thumb over her plushy lips.

"Done," she said, nipping at his thumb. Smiling, they gazed into each other.

"Thank you for being here for me," he said finally, needing her to understand how much he appreciated her. "I'm sorry I was an ass to you tonight. I'm terrified for you to see who I really am. You're so convinced I'm a good person."

"You *are* a good person," she said, hugging him tight. "One day, you'll believe it. For now, I'll just believe it for both of us."

"Okay, little temptress," he said, reveling in the softness of her hair as he caressed it with his fingers. "I can't believe you liked the way I fucked you tonight. You shivered when I touched you here." Lowering his other hand, he rubbed his finger over her puckered little hole, causing her to quiver against him.

"It felt good," she whispered.

"Goddamnit, woman. You're going to kill me. I can't wait to explore that down the road."

She bit her lip, her face flaming with embarrassment, and he placed his arms around her, hugging her tight. Thanking Etherya for his magnificent woman, he fell into an exhausted slumber, her body wrapped around his.

Chapter 28

Lila held Latimus' hand as they rode the train to Valeria for Takel's send-off to the Passage. Quiet and pensive, he sat beside her, staring out the darkened window. Wanting to support him, she laced her fingers through his and squeezed. He looked down at her, his ice-blue eyes filled with love, and squeezed her back.

When they arrived, they headed to the Dome of Etherya that sat a hundred yards from the main house. As they entered, a woman came up to hug Latimus.

Embracing her, her murmured in her ear, comforting her.

The brown-haired woman pulled back, cupping Latimus' cheeks.

"Thank you for preparing my son's body for the Passage. He looks so handsome. He was such a good boy." Lowering her face to her hands, she began to cry. Latimus pulled her to him, stroking her hair as he comforted her. Lila's heart almost broke into a thousand pieces as she watched her hulking Vampyre comfort his friend's mother.

Holding the woman's hand, he escorted her to the front of the Dome, and she sat in one of the front pews. Latimus sat behind her, and Lila lowered in beside him.

The ceremony was beautiful. Takel's casket lay open, and many stood to speak of his bravery and skill as a soldier. When Latimus spoke, she couldn't control the tears that streamed down her cheeks. His words were reverent, and every person in attendance watched him with respectful admiration. Although he never wanted the accolades of a royal, as Sathan always procured, he was a born leader, held in high esteem by their people. As the son of Markdor and the protector of their species, she was intensely proud of the way the people revered him. She felt so lucky to be his future bonded mate.

Afterward, they headed to the main house at Valeria where the reception was being held. Small cups of Slayer blood were passed around, and Lila stood in the corner of the large room as Latimus spoke to some of Takel's cousins, in the front of the banquet hall by his casket.

"Lila," a man's voice said behind her. Gritting her teeth, she forced a smile and turned to look up at him.

"Hi, Camron. How are you?"

His brown eyes were filled with pity, causing anger to course through her veins.

"You look beautiful," he said, guilt flashing through his irises.

"Thank you. I'm very happy and have made a good life for myself at Lynia."

"I heard. Breken told me he appointed you to the council. How wonderful. I never even thought of appointing a female to the council, but with your condition, you probably needed something to occupy your time since you can't have little ones. I'm happy you found something to fill your void."

What a sexist, misogynistic ass. Lila clutched the glass of blood she was holding, imagining throwing the entire contents in his face. How could she ever have contemplated letting him court her? Fury surged through her as she gave him her sweetest smile.

"Yes, thank the goddess I have something to do with my nights."

"Lila," a female voice called, fake and high-pitched. "How wonderful to see you. Did you hear the news? We're betrothed." Melania appeared, holding her hand up to Lila's face and showing off the large diamond ring on her third finger.

"Congratulations," she said, lifting her glass in a salute. "I wish you both happiness."

"And what of you?" the woman said, her expression filled with mock concern. "Now that you're barren, how will you find a mate? I just feel so awful for you."

"She's found a mate," Latimus' deep voice said from behind her, and she wanted to weep with joy that he'd come to save her from these awful people. Placing his arm around her, he pulled her into his side. "I am honored to be her mate, and we will be bonding within the next year. The son of Markdor can only bond with a female that Etherya deems worthy. You wouldn't understand that, as you never would be. I am proud to have Etherya's blessing to bond with her and bring her into the royal family, where she can cement her place as a leader in our people's history."

Lila looked up at him, her heart threatening to burst from his amazing words and his firm protection of her. Loving him more than she ever had, she sank into his side, as he pulled her toward him with his thick arm.

"Well, I never," Melania said, huffing out an angry breath. Although she was pretty, with her black hair, blue eyes and pert features, her face contorted into something rather ugly. "I am the daughter of Falkon and Marika. My bloodline has existed since long before the Awakening, and I have never been insulted as unworthy."

"I don't care if you're the daughter of a garbage collector or Etherya herself. You'll never be fit to touch Lila's shoes. I hope you two enjoy spawning more selfish, classist brats. Now, if you'll excuse me, I need my mate."

Latimus led her away as the woman sputtered, Camron consoling her as he scowled.

"Oh, my god," Lila said, smiling up at him. "You just insulted two of the most esteemed aristocrats in our kingdom."

"I don't give a shit," he said, his mouth curved in that sexy grin. "They were hurting your feelings. I won't let anyone do that."

Pulling him to her, she wrapped her arm around his neck and gave him a passionate kiss. The old Lila would've drawn him into a darkened corner, knowing that a public display of affection wasn't proper. But she didn't care. She needed him to know how thankful she was for him.

Chuckling, he spoke against her lips. "Although I like pissing off aristocrats, you need to stop kissing me. I don't think it would be proper if I ripped your clothes off here."

Smiling up at him, she shook her head. "You're incorrigible. I love you."

Placing a kiss on her lips, he led her to a group of soldiers, introducing her to each of them as his mate. Watching him from the corner of her eye, she realized that she was ready to bond with him. Although she'd originally said she needed a year, she loved him mindlessly and wanted to start a life with him. Deciding she'd tell him soon, she clutched his hand in hers as he chatted with his men.

An hour later, Latimus hugged Takel's mom again and handed her an envelope. She clutched him to her, begging him to visit her. He promised he would.

As they sat on the train home, she looked up at him.

"What was in the envelope that you gave Takel's mother?"

"A check for a million mira."

Mira was the currency of the Vampyre kingdom.

Lila's mouth dropped open. "That's a small fortune."

Shrugging, he smiled down at her as she looked up at him. "I don't need it. We have more money in that castle than we know what to do with. I promised Takel I would take care of his family, and I don't want his mother to struggle."

"Oh, Lattie," she said, shaking her head at him. "You're too good."

Lifting her hand, he kissed the back of it. "You make me good. Watching you do nice things for people makes me want to do them too."

Tears burned her eyes, and she snuggled her head into his shoulder. Placing his arm around her, he held her as they approached Astaria.

Chapter 29

Several nights later, Lila sat outside, pruning the pretty flowers that Latimus had planted around her cabin. He was set to arrive within the hour, and she was excited to tell him that she was ready to bond with him. Imagining his handsome face as he smiled down at her with love, she hummed as she trimmed the flowers in the moonlight.

Her ears perked as she heard screaming by the wall. Snapping her head around, she saw soldiers rushing to the far wall. Heart pounding, she pulled her phone from her back pocket and called Latimus.

"Hey, honey, I'm on my way—"

"The Deamons are attacking," she interrupted.

He cursed into the phone. "I was about to board the train. I'll have Darkrip transport me there. I need you to round up everyone in the cabins. I'm going to radio some of the soldiers to pick you up in their four-wheelers and take you to the main house. It's safer there. Got it?"

"Yes," she said, standing, her hand covering the organ in her throbbing chest.

"You can do this, Lila. Now, go. I'll see you soon."

Placing her phone in her back pocket, she ran to Sam's cabin. Opening the door, he looked off in the distance and cursed.

Four soldiers pulled up in four-wheelers.

"Take Jack to the main house," he said. "I'll round everyone else up and get them in the remaining four-wheelers. You two are the most vulnerable, and we need you to get to safety."

Nodding, she looked down into Jack's wide brown eyes, filled with fear.

"Don't be afraid," she said, extending her hand to him. "I won't let anybody hurt you."

He grabbed her hand with his, so tiny and small. Pulling him behind her, she climbed into the vehicle, placing Jack on her lap and holding him tight. The hulking Vampyre soldier behind the wheel gave her a nod and put the car into gear.

Halfway down the dirt path to the main house, Crimeous appeared. Materializing in the path of their oncoming four-wheeler, the Vampyre gritted his teeth.

"Hold on," the soldier said in a deep baritone.

Pushing his foot on the pedal, he accelerated. The Deamon wailed as he hit him with the vehicle. Lila clutched Jack, gripping the rail that ran across the dash with white knuckles.

"You'll pay for that," Crimeous said, and the four-wheeler suddenly lost power. Clicking and sputtering, it came to a stop. The soldier leapt from the vehicle, drawing a rifle and spraying the Deamon with bullets. Throwing back his head, Crimeous gave a mighty scream, absorbing the bullets as if they were cotton balls.

When the rifle's magazine was empty, Crimeous approached the soldier, an eight-shooter materializing in his hands. Holding it to the massive Vampyre's chest, he deployed, and the soldier crumpled to the ground.

Heart surging with terror, Lila ran from the four-wheeler, clasping Jack in her arms. She sprinted as fast as her legs would take her, but she was no match for Crimeous' powers. Gasping in pain, she felt him seize a chunk of her hair.

He threw her to the ground, and she made sure to hold Jack tight as they fell onto the dirt path. When they landed, she whispered to him, his eyes so full of fear.

"Once he starts hurting me, I want you to run as fast as you can. Okay?"

Jack nodded, and she squeezed him. "As fast as you can, Jack. I love you."

Turning, she stood and felt his tiny arms wrap around her thigh as he hid behind her.

"Hello, Lila. How nice to see you again. I've come to rape you, as I promised I would. But we'll wait until Latimus gets here, so that he can watch. How does that sound?"

Straightening her spine, she summoned every ounce of courage in her shaking body.

"I'll never let you touch me again, you son of a bitch. Latimus will slaughter you."

Throwing back his head, he gave an evil laugh, his pointed teeth seeming to glow in the moonlight. "Latimus is a fool, weakened by his love for you. It's disgusting."

Lila heard shouts behind her and saw the battle advancing toward them. Vampyre fought Deamon under the stars. She'd never seen so many Deamon soldiers. There was one Vampyre for every five Deamon soldiers.

"I've figured out a way to grow my soldiers faster. A cloning technique that I borrowed from the human world. Aren't they magnificent?" He lifted his hands, palms facing the sky.

Jack was gripping her thigh for dear life, and she reached behind, rubbing his hair, urging him to stay calm. The Deamon approached her, and her heart throbbed with terror.

Suddenly, she felt a burst of air, and Darkrip appeared with Latimus.

"Go to Uteria and get Kenden and materialize back here with him," Latimus commanded to Darkrip.

The Slayer-Deamon nodded and disappeared.

Latimus pulled out a TEC and approached Crimeous, attaching it to his head and deploying it. The cruel creature laughed and flicked it from his head. "I was getting tired of your silly weapon, so I studied it. It no longer has the ability to maim me. But good try."

Reaching out his thin arm, he latched his hand around Latimus' thick neck. Lila brought her fingers to her mouth as she watched him struggle, trying to dislodge the Deamon's grip with his bulging arms. His efforts were futile, and she started to lurch forward to help him. Stretching out his arm, Latimus' palm faced her as Crimeous held him, several feet away, silently instructing her to stay as the creature choked him.

Complying, she clutched Jack behind her legs, feeling helpless.

Another rush of air floated by her, and Darkrip materialized with Kenden. The Slayer hurried toward them and stuck a Glock to the side of Crimeous' face. Clenching his teeth, he pulled the trigger.

The Dark Lord wailed in pain, releasing Latimus. Sucking air into his lungs, he backed away from the Deamon.

Darkrip pulled the Blade from the sheath on his back and raised it to strike his father. Lila gasped when the creature looked directly into her. Lifting his hand, he pulled her to him with his mind.

Feeling herself being dragged across the ground, the evil creature yanked her hair, clutching her to his legs. Darkrip stood above them, the sword held high, his expression unsure. She knew he was afraid he would accidentally hit her with the Blade if he struck.

Gasping, Lila felt the Deamon align his front with her back, making her want to vomit. Using one of the techniques that Latimus had taught her in their training sessions, she kicked his knee with her heel and elbowed him in the stomach. Expelling, his grip softened, and she began to run.

A sinister cackle preceded the invisible tug, and she was being hauled toward him once more.

"So, the commander taught you how to defend yourself?" he sneered against her ear. Struggling to elbow him again, she suddenly lost all control of her muscles. "Let's see you move now that I've frozen you with my mind, you little bitch!"

Pulling her back against him, he taunted Darkrip.

"Strike me, son," the Dark Lord said, as she tried to struggle against him, the action futile. "You'll kill this woman, but who is she to you? You have the chance to murder me. Take it."

Indecision swam across Darkrip's face. Lila understood his dilemma. Sacrificing her to kill the Dark Lord was probably worth it in his mind. Certain of her death, she began to cry.

"No, Darkrip!" Latimus pleaded. "Please, don't hurt her. There's another way."

"We have to rid this world of his evil!" Darkrip screamed. His green eyes, so much like Miranda's, blazed into hers, filled with sorrow.

"It's okay," she said to him, tears streaking down her cheeks. "I understand. Strike the Blade through both of us. If it kills him, it's worth it."

"No!" Latimus screamed, his voice sounding so far away.

"Do it!" she yelled at Darkrip.

His face contorted with pain as he swung the Blade even further behind his head and lowered his arms to strike.

She heard Jack scream her name in his sweet voice and she felt intense sadness that he would have to watch her die this way. He'd experienced so much pain, and she wanted so badly to shield him from more.

Closing her eyes, she braced for impact.

Suddenly, a bright light formed beneath her eyelids. Crimeous wailed behind her and released her. She fell backward, Jack falling on top of her. Her precious boy must've tried to save her. How brave.

Unable to understand why the light was so bright, she lifted her lids. Above her, the sun shone brightly in the sky, almost blinding her. Unable to see, she squinted, her eyes watering uncontrollably. Touching her forearm, she realized her skin wasn't burning.

"He burns in the sunlight!" Kenden screamed. "Help me hold him down."

Latimus rushed to Crimeous' convulsing body as the sun shone bright overhead. They held him down as Darkrip rushed over with the Blade. In one sure thrust, he plunged it into the Dark Lord's chest.

The creature gasped and pulled at his burning skin as it melted off him. Lifting the Blade again, Darkrip chopped off the Deamon's head.

Standing back, Darkrip stared down at him. As had happened when Miranda struck Crimeous, his head slowly reconnected to his body. Tissue and blood vessels recongealed around his neck, and his beady eyes opened. Thin, pasty lips widened to pull in a deep breath. Sputtering and seizing as his skin burned, he dematerialized.

Darkrip cursed, throwing the Blade to the ground. "I'm not the descendant to kill him. Fuck!"

"No time for that now," Latimus said, clutching his shoulder. He ran over to Lila, running his hands over her body to assess damage.

"I'm fine," she said. Crawling toward Jack, who lay on the ground, she turned him over. Crying out, she saw the large wound that ran from his neck to his pelvis.

"No!" she wailed, grabbing him to her and holding him in her lap. "Please, no. No, no, no, no..."

"I must've hit him when I swung the Blade. I tried to stop the blow, but he jumped in front of you," she heard Darkrip say behind her, his voice so quiet due to the ringing in her ears.

"Let me see," Latimus said, assessing the boy in her lap. As he examined Jack, his expression was lined with severe sadness and resignation, and she realized that the child was dead.

"Lattie," she said, rocking back and forth with him in her arms. The sun shone so brightly that she had to focus through slitted eyes. "Please, save him."

Latimus pulled her to him, enclosing her and the boy in between his massive legs and arms. Holding them, he consoled her as she swayed.

"Jack," she said, turning his head so that she could see his face. "Please, come back to us. We love you. Please." Lowering her forehead to his, she sobbed, unable to believe that her precious boy was gone.

Powerless to control her tears, she let them flow, praying to Etherya to let her trade her life for his. Unimaginable pain coursed through her as she struggled to inhale breath into her spasming lungs.

She heard Sam's voice from above. "Is he dead?"

Latimus nodded as he held her.

"My sweet boy," she heard the man say. "I let him down. I'll never forgive myself."

Kenden walked to Sam and put his arm around him, consoling him.

"Lila," Latimus said gently, "you have to let him go, honey."

"No!" she screamed, clutching him tighter to her breast. "He's not dead. He's not. Wake up, Jack." She slapped his face several times with her hand. "Please, wake up." Lowering her head, she collapsed even further as she wept.

Feeling a rush of wind, she shivered. From above, a voice screeched.

"Lila, daughter of Theinos, I have heard your cries and feel your agony. Why do you summon me?"

Looking up into the blinding sun, she saw Etherya, her hair blazing as she floated above her.

"Why do you take everything from me?" she screamed, loathing the goddess who would let her feel such pain. "I have done nothing but serve you, and all you do is take everyone I love. I hate you!"

Latimus squeezed her, and she knew he was scared that she was screaming at the all-powerful goddess, but she didn't care. She'd lost too much to care.

"You are too familiar, daughter of Theinos. I would tread carefully."

"She is your faithful servant, Etherya," Latimus said. "She is obviously fraught with grief."

"And do you love this woman, son of Markdor?"

"Yes. With all my heart."

"I was angered when she broke her betrothal to your brother. It showed a willfulness that I do not wish to tolerate. But she also has such kindness. She has done much to help her people."

Lila wiped the tears from her face. "Let me help Jack. Take my life for his."

"No!" Latimus said behind her. "I won't let you do that."

"I have to," she said, looking into his ice-blue eyes. "I have to, Lattie."

"Take my life, Etherya," Latimus said, his gaze never leaving hers. "In exchange for the boy's."

"No," Lila cried.

"Enough," the goddess shrieked. "Your pleading is futile and is starting to anger me." Floating over, she lifted Lila's chin with her cloudy hand. "In exchange for your kindness, I will offer you a choice. Save the boy, or reclaim your ability to have your own children. It is an offer I am only making because of your selflessness. What do you choose?"

Lila contemplated the goddess. Closing her eyes, she inhaled, taking the moment she needed. An image of a girl's face, young and sweet, with violet-colored eyes and soft blond hair flashed through her mind. It was the baby girl she'd always imagined holding and feeding from her breast. Lifting her gaze to Latimus', she imagined his ice-colored eyes in the face of their handsome son.

Looking down at Jack, she smoothed her hand over his soft cheek. In her heart, there was never truly a debate.

"I choose to save Jack," she said, lifting her chin.

"So be it," the goddess said with a nod of her fire-red head. "I have chosen to let the Vampyres walk in the sun again. Go forth with the knowledge that Crimeous does not have the same ability. Use this to kill him. Valktor's descendant that will cause his demise with the Blade flourishes on the Earth. Find the one of which the prophecy speaks."

With a puff, she vanished.

Lila looked down at Jack, slapping his freckled cheek. Inhaling a huge breath, he began to cough and sputter. "Jack!" she said, clutching him to her breast. "Oh, thank the goddess."

"I tried to save you, Lila," he said, his brown eyes so vibrant as he looked up at her.

"I know, sweetheart. You were so brave. My little soldier."

Running her hand over his chest, she felt for his wound. It was gone. The goddess had saved him. Joy flowed through her as she cried, unable to stop her tears. Latimus still held her, and she pushed her back into him, showing him with her body how thankful she was that he was there.

Finally, Jack started to squirm under her. "Don't cry, Lila," he said, rubbing his tiny fingers over the wetness on her cheek. "Girls always cry. You have to be strong."

Laughing through her tears, she clutched him. "My strong little boy. I love you so much."

"I love you too, Lila. You're my best friend."

Looking up at Latimus, he smiled at her, love swimming in his eyes. As they sat on the ground, with the smoldering rays surrounding them, she rocked her boy to her chest as her Vampyre held her.

Chapter 30

Lila headed to Sam's cabin at the urging of Latimus. He wanted her to stay with him and Jack while he spearheaded the cleanup. Wanting to wash away the evil Deamon, she took a quick shower and headed to their cottage, hugging them both tight when Jack pulled open the door. They sat in Sam's tiny living room, sipping blood, quietly chatting as the gravity of the battle washed over them. Jack fell asleep, his head in her lap, as she stroked his soft scarlet hair.

When her phone buzzed, she pulled it from the back pocket of her jeans.

Latimus: Done with cleanup. Need to take a quick shower at your place. See you soon.

Half an hour later, he knocked on the door. Thanking Sam for his bravery and giving a sleepy-eyed Jack a hug, he led Lila to her cabin. The sun was setting, and she pulled Latimus toward the open field, wanting to experience her first sunset in a thousand years with him. Standing behind her, he drew her back into his body, holding her as they watched the streaks of red and orange finger across the horizon.

The auburn orb of the sun glowed as it put on a magnificent display. Rays of light stretched from the blazing circle toward the white clouds that flitted by. Birds flew in the distance as they cawed, forming a "V" as they aligned across the sky. The earth seemed to hum, singing a one-noted song of renewal and peace.

"It's so beautiful," she said, tears welling in her eyes. "Etherya finally lifted the curse. Thanks to you and Miranda, Sathan and Kenden. All of you are so brave and have united the species. My god, Lattie, it's so breathtaking."

Inhaling beside her ear, he squeezed her. "It's unbelievable. I'd forgotten. All these centuries, we've lived in darkness. I can't wait to make love to you under the sun, by our spot at the river. Your eyes will look so pretty." He kissed her temple, and she slid her hand up his shirt to caress the back of his neck.

Silent, they watched the skyline grab the sun, devouring it until it disappeared below the field. Clutching her hand, he led her inside. Beside the bed, he lifted his large hands and cradled her face.

"I almost lost you. Again. I would die if you were taken from me, Lila. I can't do this without you." His eyes glowed as blue as the daytime sky, which she'd seen today for the first time in a thousand years.

"Shhhhhh..." she said, rubbing her hand in slow circles over his heart. "I'm here. You saved me, like you always do. You're like my own personal soldier."

Red lips turned up into his sexy grin. "I am. It's funny because I was furious at Sathan for ordering me to guard you on the train mission. Now, I'd give everything to guard you every second of every day."

"Were you really that mad?"

"Livid," he said, chuckling. "I knew that spending all that time with you would make it so hard not to touch you. I wanted you so badly."

Smiling, she rubbed the back of his neck with her slim fingers. "You were so mean to me."

"I know. I'm an ass. What else is new?"

Laughing, she pulled his face to hers, and their tongues mated as they drew each other closer.

"Wait," she said, placing a palm on his chest. "Let's call Arderin. I want to speak to our family. They must be so excited. We've waited a thousand years for this."

"Okay," he said, smiling down at her.

Pulling her phone from her back jeans pocket, she opened her video call app and dialed Arderin.

"*Ohmygod*," her friend said, the words spoken as one as her face appeared on the screen. "Lila, it's incredible. I can't believe it!"

"I know," she said, nodding. "It's amazing."

"Hey, Latimus," Arderin said, waving her hand. "Heard that Kenden had to save you. You're getting rusty."

"Quiet, imp. I was going to ask Sathan to send you on the Slayer train mission with us, but if you're mean to me, I'll tell him to lock you in the dungeon."

"Oh, Latimus, really?" she asked, clutching the fabric of her blouse over her heart dramatically. "That would be awesome. I'm dying of boredom over here. Please, please, please!"

Miranda's face came into view as she leaned her head against Arderin's.

"We're torturing her here by giving her everything she ever wants or needs. It's terrible. Please, save her."

They chuckled as Arderin swatted playfully at Miranda.

"Everyone's here," Arderin said, switching the screen so that Heden came into view. He gave a salute, and then Kenden came into view, giving a wave. Darkrip stood with his back against the wall, the bottom of one foot against the wallpaper, scowling. Finally, Sathan's face appeared.

"You did it, brother," Sathan said. Admiration for Latimus emanated from his expression and seemed to pulse from the screen. "You've always vowed that you would end the curse, and it's finally over. I'm so proud of you."

"We all did it," Latimus said, placing his arm around Lila's shoulders and drawing her into his side. "Especially you and Miranda. You guys were able to be the leaders that we needed and align our people. I guess you're pretty okay at this king shit."

Sathan chuckled. "Yeah, I guess so. When you get back to Astaria, let's take a bottle of Macallan to the place where Mother and Father used to take us on picnics before our annoying little siblings were born. We can salute them with a glass under the sun."

"Hey!" Arderin said, turning the screen and holding the phone up so both her and Heden's faces showed. "We want to come too. You guys are the annoying ones. We're both awesome and better-looking."

"Obviously," Heden said, rolling his eyes and giving a wide grin.

Lila couldn't contain her laughter as Latimus smiled. "We'll all go," he said. "Although, Arderin will be drunk off one sip of Macallan."

"I will not!" she said. "I can drink like a fish. Try me."

"By the goddess, I'm sorry I ever mentioned it," Sathan muttered offscreen.

"We love you guys," Miranda said, coming back into view. "Now, go to bed. Thankfully, you heathens can sleep when it's nighttime now. Ken and I were getting tired of you blood-suckers messing up our sleep schedules."

"We love you too," Lila said, waving at the screen. "See you soon." Hitting the red button, she disconnected the call.

Smiling up at her man, she grabbed his hand. "We're so lucky to have all of them."

"We are," he said, squeezing back.

"Now, make love to me," she said, throwing her phone on the nearby table and sliding her arms around his neck.

"Good grief, woman, I'm exhausted. I fought a battle tonight. Can't you wait for one second?" Ice-blue eyes twinkled as he teased her.

"Nope," she said, unable to control her smile. "As you've pointed out, I'm insatiable."

"You sure are. Thank the goddess." Lowering his lips, he gave her a blazing kiss.

Lifting his head, she observed the corner of his mouth lift.

"Tell me to fuck you."

"I just told you to make love to me—"

"No, tell me to fuck you. Don't think I didn't notice you used the word when I was being an ass to you. You think I let you off the hook, but I didn't. Say it."

Feeling her face enflame, she shook her head. "I can't. It goes against everything I was taught. It's not proper."

"Say it, you little temptress," he said, nipping her lips with his.

"I can't," she said, hearing the tiny whine in her voice. "I only said it that night because you were being so dreadful to me. That was the first time I've ever said that word in a thousand years."

Chuckling, he shook his head. "My little blue-blooded aristocrat. I'll get you to say it." Lifting her by her butt, he cemented his lips to hers and carried her to the bed. "I've never lost a challenge when I set my mind to it."

He proceeded to love her, thorough and intimate, until she was throbbing underneath him. Finally, when her body was tense, and he was moving in and out of her deepest place, he spoke in his velvet baritone.

"Do you need me to fuck you harder?" he asked, moving with sure thrusts above her.

"Yes," she said, her voice breathless.

"Tell me," he said, giving her that sexy, cocky smile.

"You suck," she said, smiling up at him as her body drowned in pleasure.

"Tell me, you little cock tease. You can do it."

Lifting her hand, she cupped his cheek. "Fuck me harder, Lattie."

Groaning, he complied. Together, they reached their peak. Afterward, they collapsed in a heap on the bed. Gathering her in his arms, he drew back the covers and placed her head on the pillows. Climbing in, he pulled her front to his. Looking into her eyes as their heads shared a pillow, he stroked her hair.

"Will it ever go away?" she asked. "The way we make each other feel? It's the most amazing thing I've ever experienced."

"Never," he said, caressing her blond tresses. "We have a thousand years to make up for. That's a lot of fucking."

Laughing, she swatted his chest. "You're hopeless."

Chuckling, he stole a kiss from her.

Lips curved, they stared into each other.

Several moments later, she said, "I had to save him, Lattie."

"I know," he said, his blue eyes so understanding. "You're so selfless. Many others would've made a different choice. I'm so humbled by you."

Lifting her hand, she stroked his cheek.

"The son of Markdor should have blooded heirs. I'm so sorry that I robbed you of that. I wanted so badly to give you children."

"You will, honey," he said, rubbing his thumb over her lips. "I told you, we'll adopt as many as you want."

"But I took your heirs from you. Anyone else of your station would reject me in favor of someone who could continue their bloodline."

His nostrils flared, and anger flashed in his eyes. "Like Camron? What a fucking asshole. Screw him. I don't care about that, Lila. Sathan and Miranda will have blooded heirs, and Arderin and Heden too, when they bond. All I've ever wanted was you. And I know that you want lots of babies, so we'll adopt as many as you want. You have to be patient with me though, because I have no idea how to be a father. I'll try my best. I hope I can do a good job. I think I can, with you by my side."

Unable to control herself, she began to cry.

"Honey," he said, cupping her cheeks. "What did I say? Please, stop crying."

"You're just so good," she said, hating that she couldn't control her tears. "I don't know what I did to deserve you."

"Good grief, woman," he said, pulling her head to his chest and embracing her with his beefy arms. "I'm the one who doesn't deserve you. I'm a war-torn, uncivilized asshole. I'm so lucky to be with you."

Lifting her head, she stared into his eyes. "We're lucky to have each other. Thank the goddess that we finally stopped fighting it. I never knew it could be like this."

"Me neither," he said, placing a kiss on her lips. "We know the consequences of wasted time. I think we've both learned our lesson on that. It's a mistake that we'll never make again."

"Never," she said.

There, in the soft bed, they fell asleep holding each other, knowing that they would gaze upon the sun when they awoke.

Chapter 31

It turned out that prepping a kingdom for living in the sun when they had lived in the darkness for so long was no easy task. The next morning, Latimus headed to Astaria to help Sathan and Miranda implement the transition.

Sathan addressed his subjects from the desk at his study, Miranda sitting by his side. Together, they transmitted their message over the royal TV channel, detailing how the rollout would proceed. Since fifty Slayers already lived at Astaria, they would help transition that compound to living in daylight. The other three Vampyre compounds would follow suit, slowly progressing from living by the light of the moon to thriving under the rays of the sun.

Lila traveled to each compound as the kingdom's head diplomat, setting up makeshift booths at each town square, where the governors and council members could hold sessions to answer questions. Upon arriving at Valeria, Camron greeted her at the train platform, asking if they could start fresh. Lila agreed, in her always amicable way, thankful to start a new chapter with her old friend.

Thanks to Miranda, the Slayers donated a plethora of sunscreen, and Lila made sure each compound was stocked so that the Vampyres' skin didn't burn. Although their self-healing properties would heal the sunburns quickly, they felt it best to prevent any burns if possible.

Latimus outfitted his troops with special sunglasses that allowed them to train during the day. The tint on the lenses could be lessened as time wore on, ensuring that eventually, the soldiers could fight in the daytime without them. He also decided to continue holding night trainings twice a week so the men were competent in every environment.

Eventually, the Vampyres would learn to live in the sun again. Thankful to Etherya for the gift of the bright orb's rays, they flocked to the Domes at each compound, anxious to bestow worship upon her. Even the Slayers, who had disowned Etherya after the Awakening, were slowly accepting her back into their hearts again. The Earth was gradually piecing itself back together.

Two weeks after the elusive sun had returned, Latimus watched the female he loved with his whole heart drag her massive suitcase down the stairs of the train platform at Lynia.

"Seriously, woman?" he asked, shaking his head at her.

"Oh, stop it," Lila said, releasing the bag and tossing her golden hair back from her forehead. "Please, help me. It's so heavy."

He'd taken the train from Astaria to meet her. Once they connected, their plan was to travel back through Astaria and then on to Uteria. The underground tunnels were complete, and trains now connected all six of the compounds of the immortals.

As with the rollout to the Vampyre compounds, Lila was tasked with introducing the Slayer compounds of Uteria and Restia to the trains. Unlike the previous trip, Latimus had whole-heartedly volunteered to be her bodyguard on this mission.

"What can you possibly be wearing that takes up that much space? We're literally traveling for four days."

They were scheduled for two days at Uteria, and two at Restia. As before, Lila would be responsible for doing press, appearing at social functions and answering any questions that the Slayers had about the new transit system. Miranda had assured her that Slayers were much more progressive than "stuffy Vampyres," so she felt the mission would be relatively easy and uneventful.

"It's all the shoes. They weigh a ton."

Approaching her as she stood on the stairs, he grabbed the suitcase. "I charge one kiss for every pound."

"Worth it," she said, giving him a dazzling smile.

He loaded her luggage onto the train, and they sat down for the hour-long trip. Unlike last time, he held her to him with his thick arm across her shoulders, plugging away on his tablet during the Astaria-Uteria part of the journey.

Miranda greeted them at the Uteria platform, Sathan by her side. Together, they walked in the sun to the main castle.

"Isn't it great?" Miranda asked, extending her arms as she sauntered in front of them. "The sun is so bright today. I'm thrilled that you guys can see it."

Sathan pulled her to him by one of her outstretched arms. "Careful, sweetheart. This path isn't paved yet. I don't want you to fall."

Throwing her arm around her husband's waist, she rubbed her extended abdomen. "He's annoyingly protective of me right now," she said, looking up at Lila. "I might come stay with you at Lynia just to have a few moments of peace."

"Quiet, minx," Sathan said, drawing her close as they walked.

Latimus smiled, pleased that his brother had found a mate who made him so happy. Claiming Lila had changed his entire world, and he felt that he and Sathan were so lucky to have their amazing women.

They had dinner together, the four of them sitting at the head of the large dining room table, laughing as Miranda slowly drank her one glass of wine.

"You guys don't even know the half of it," she said, shaking her head as she swirled the tiny bit of red left in her glass. "He stuffs a baby in me, and then, I'm not allowed to drink except once a week. It's torture. I'll never forgive him."

Sathan scowled and scrunched his features at her. "I'll never touch you again. That will alleviate any future issues for you."

"Whoa, whoa," she said, setting down her glass and holding up her hands. "Let's not get crazy."

Sathan winked at her, and they all chuckled. Afterward, Miranda walked them to their room, situated upstairs in the large castle.

Two days later, Arderin joined them at Restia. Latimus had asked Sathan to let her accompany them on that leg of the trip, and his brother was excited that Arderin was taking her royal duties more seriously. Arderin had been quite helpful in the sunlight transition so far, ensuring that the younger subjects reached out over social media if they had questions. She seemed elated to get a break from Astaria, and they finished their mission uneventfully.

Lila stayed with Latimus at his cabin for a night before returning to Lynia. As the first light of dawn began to caress the sky, he watched her dress.

"You have your literacy group meeting tonight, right?"

"Yes," she said, nodding. "I missed it last week. I'll be happy to get home and see them."

Walking toward her, he drew her to him and kissed her. "I'm happy you consider Lynia home. I really like it there too."

Her brilliant smile almost made his knees buckle. "I'm so glad. I don't want to pull you from your troops here, but I love it there."

"I know. I can't believe I won't see you for two days. How are you going to survive without me fucking you? You're a machine."

She whacked his chest, her cheeks turning red. "I'll be just fine, thank you. But I will miss you." Lifting to her toes, she gave him a peck. "Will you miss me?"

"Always," he said, kissing her pink lips.

He watched her leave, his heart breaking a little as it did each time his cabin door closed behind her. Making sure he waited long enough, he walked to the platform and rode the train to Lynia. Sam met him there, and they walked into town, finding a coffee shop near the main square where they could sit.

"Thanks so much for the reference, Latimus," Sam said, sipping coffee from the brown paper cup. "That along with the referral from my last family helped move things along."

"Happy to help," Latimus said with a nod. "But are you sure, Sam? This is a big step. I want to make sure you really understand what's at stake here."

The man seemed to glow as he smiled. "I've never been more certain of anything."

"Okay, then. I'm so happy to hear it. Looks like you and I will be seeing a lot of each other."

They chatted, finishing their coffee, and Latimus' heart swelled as they discussed their plans.

Afterward, he headed to the spot by the creek that he was now so familiar with. Handing the last check to the contractor, he surveyed the work, knowing she would be pleased. Feeling excited and a bit anxious, he headed back to Astaria and dreamed of Lila during the night, before he trained the troops.

* * * *

Lila played with Jack under the late afternoon sun as she waited for Latimus. He was now training the troops primarily in the daytime, and she expected him to arrive shortly. Lying in the plushy grass, she feigned death as Jack rushed to save her. Wielding his tiny sword, he fought off imaginary Deamons.

"Latimus!" he yelled, dropping the sword and running to him. Sitting up on the grass, her heart threatened to burst as she saw him pick up the boy and hug him. Smiling, he ruffled his hair while Jack chattered.

"Hey," Latimus said, looking down at her. "Look at you rolling around in the grass. That's not proper at all. What would your etiquette school teachers say?" His ice-blue eyes swam with laughter.

Chuckling, she stood, wiping her hands on her jeans. "My days of being proper ended when I fell in love with you, you heathen," she said, lifting to give him a kiss.

"Ew, gross," Jack said, still encompassed in Latimus' beefy arms. "You guys are kissing. I'm gonna puke."

Latimus set him on the ground. "You'll change your mind one day, believe me. You'll find a pretty girl you want to kiss as much as I like to kiss Lila."

"No way," he said, his mop of hair shaking as he shook his head back and forth vigorously.

"We'll see."

He took her hand and squeezed it, winking at her in that sexy way of his. She'd wanted to tell him she was ready to bond with him the night Crimeous attacked, but walking in the sun again had derailed everything, and life had gotten in the way. In the weeks since, she'd hesitated telling him for some reason. Knowing she needed to get on with it and start building their life together, she decided to tell him tonight. Excited anticipation coursed through her.

"Hey, Latimus," Sam said, trailing down the steps that led from his cabin. "How are you?"

"Good." They shook hands. "I'm ready if you are."

Lila felt her brows draw together in confusion.

"Okay," he said with a nod. "Jack, it's time for you to go do your homework. I'll be inside in a bit."

"But I want to play more," he whined.

"I made spaghetti, but we can't have it until you finish your homework."

"Okaaaaaaaay," the boy said, as he rolled his eyes. "Bye Lila. Bye Latimus. See you tomorrow!" Full of energy, he shuffled up the cabin stairs.

The men exchanged a look, and Lila's heart began to pound.

"What's going on with you guys?" she asked. "I feel like I'm missing something."

Latimus gave a nod to Sam, and he trained his deep brown eyes on her.

"I've been offered a position as Head of Security for one of the aristocrats at Valeria. It's a great opportunity, and I've decided to take it."

"Oh, Sam, that's wonderful," Lila said. Personal bodyguards for aristocrats were highly regarded and did very well financially. "I'm so happy for you."

Sadness rushed through her as she realized that meant she wouldn't see Jack every day. Not wanting to ruin the mood, she smiled and grabbed his hand, squeezing hard.

"The life I'm going to lead there isn't conducive to raising kids. I'll be working a lot and won't have time to properly take care of Jack." Clutching her hand, he gave her a kind smile. "I'd be honored if you'd take him in, Lila. You're so great with him, and he loves you so much. If you're open to it, I'd like to have you adopt him and raise him. With the caveat being that I can still come and see him when I have time off."

Tears burned her eyes, and she struggled to keep them from falling. "That's such a kind offer, Sam, but I don't want to take him from you. You're his family, and he loves you."

"I know," he said, nodding, "but I want to do what's best for him, and that's letting you raise him. I feel it in my heart. My sister was a good mother to him, and you'll be a great one as well. I hope you'll do this for us. I want him to have a good life and I truly feel this is what he needs."

Unable to control her tears, she threw her arms around him and clutched him tight. "Are you sure? I'd be so honored to raise him. I love him so much."

"I know, darlin'," Sam said, stroking her hair. "You're his family as much as I am."

Pulling back, she wiped the wetness from her face with both hands. Looking at Latimus, she asked, "Did you know about this?"

Smiling, he pulled some folded papers from his back pocket. "These are the adoption papers. I had Sathan draw them up. I put both of us as the adoptive parents. I hope that's okay."

"Of course, it's okay!" she squealed, jumping into his arms and hugging him tightly.

"All right, honey, you don't have to cut off my circulation. I'm trying to do something nice for you."

Playfully swatting him, she stepped back. Looking back and forth between them, she grabbed each of their hands. "Thank you both so much. I'm so honored to raise him and do the best I can to be a good mother to him. Sam, you'll have to come and visit as often as you can, and we'll bring him to Valeria to see you too."

"I'd like that."

"When should we tell him?" she asked, excitement coursing through her.

"I guess now's as good a time as any," Sam said. Turning, he walked to the cabin door and yelled for Jack to come outside. He bounded down the stairs, looking up at all of them.

Sam crouched down and gently grasped his upper arm. "I have something to tell you."

"Okay," Jack said.

"I got a new job at Valeria. It means I'm going to have to work a lot and won't be able to take care of you as much. I don't want you to have to leave your home and your friends here at Lynia, so Lila has offered to adopt you and let you live with her here while I go work. How do you feel about that?"

"Really?" the boy said, gazing up at Lila.

"Really," she said, crouching down beside Sam. "I love you so much, Jack, and I'd be so happy to adopt you and have you live with me while Sam goes to work at his new job. Only if you want to, though."

Scrunching the features of his face, he contemplated. "Will you still come and see me?" he asked Sam.

"Of course. Every chance I get."

Jack looked at Lila. "Do you know how to make pasta? Because Uncle Sam makes it really good."

Lila laughed. "I won't lie, I don't know how to make pasta. But I can certainly learn. Maybe we can learn together."

Jack smiled, showing his tiny white fangs, and she swore her heart burst inside her chest. "Okay, I'll come live with you, Lila. You're so fun to play with, and we can play even more now."

"We sure can." Needing to hold him, she pulled him close. "I'm so happy that you're going to live with me. We'll have so much fun."

Jack nodded furiously, his red hair swishing around his forehead.

She hugged him once more, and he retreated inside to resume his homework. Sam would be departing for his new job in a week, so they had a few days to work out the logistics. Thanking him again with a thorough hug, Latimus tugged her back to her cabin.

Noticing the four-wheeler that sat outside, she asked, "Are we going somewhere?"

He nodded. "Hop in. It's a surprise." Opening the door for her, she complied.

The wind whipped her hair as he drove out toward the wall and then along a tiny creek. Slowing the vehicle, they approached a house that looked to be newly built.

Two stories tall, it had a wraparound porch with several white rocking chairs, and purple flowers grew from the ground surrounding the foundation. Her heart began to pound in her chest.

Stepping from the vehicle, he came around and lifted her out. Setting her on her feet, he grabbed her hand and pulled her toward the house.

"Latimus?" she said, her tone questioning.

"Yes?" he responded, his blue irises sparkling with mischief.

"Did you build me a house?" she asked, looking up at him with wonder.

Nodding, he said, "Yep. I built you a house. Where else are we going to put all the quintuplets we adopt?"

Laughing with joy and surprise, she held her hands to her cheeks. "Oh, my god, Lattie. How did you...? When did you...? I had no idea," she said, shaking her head.

"I hired the contractor after the first night I stayed with you at Lynia. I knew I needed to do something big to win you over. Plus, you gave me a fucking awesome blow job, and I needed to ensure I'd continue to get that sweet lovin' from you."

Giggling, she felt her face turn ten shades of red. "Stop being vile," she said, swiping at his chest. "I can't believe you."

"Let's go see it." Pulling her up the stairs to the porch, they entered. The house was beautiful, with a large living room, den, dining room and kitchen. The upstairs had five bedrooms, the master being exceptionally large. The master bathroom had a shower and a separate whirlpool bath.

"I figured we could get into some trouble together in that bathtub," he said, waggling his eyebrows at her.

Laughing, she bit her lip. "Oh, yes, I think we can."

Pulling her down the stairs and back outside, he stared at her in the setting sun.

"There's a little creek that runs behind here. Not as big as the river where you seduced me when we were kids," he said, grabbing her wrist and nipping her hand when she lightheartedly slapped his pecs, "but it's a good place to make some new memories. If you're ready for that."

"I'm so ready," she said, wondering if she'd ever even dreamed she could feel this happy.

"Good."

Pulling a small, felt-covered box from his pocket, he dropped to one knee. Lila lifted her fingers to her lips, her eyes clouding with moisture as she gazed down at him.

"My mother had four rings that she wore on each of the fingers of her left hand. One was meant to go to each of us when we turned eighteen. When she was killed, we all got to choose which one we wanted."

Opening the case, she saw a silver ring topped with a large, square-cut amethyst. "I chose this one because it reminded me of my best friend's eyes."

Lila let out a sob at his reverent words.

"I know you said you needed a year, and I won't push you, but I'm so ready to bond with you, Lila. Now that we have Jack, I want to start our life together. I'll live here with you and take the train to be with the troops five days a week. I don't need to live at Astaria now that we have the trains. I hate sleeping in that tiny cabin without you. Please, put me out of my misery and bond with me."

Lila observed his handsome face through her tears, realizing that this was why she hadn't told him yet that she was ready to bond. Somewhere in the back of her mind, she wanted the formal proposal. And, boy, had he delivered. Elation swam through her body as she tried to control her tears.

"Lila?" he asked, shaking the ring box. "Are you going to answer me?" he teased.

"Yes!" she said, lowering down to her knees and throwing her arms around his neck. Placing multiple kisses on his red lips, she felt him chuckle.

Grabbing her hand, he slid the ring onto her third finger.

"It looks so pretty on you," he said.

"Oh, Lattie. Thank you. For the ring and the proposal and the house and for Jack. You've done so much for me. I feel like I don't do enough for you. You make me so happy."

"It's not a contest, woman," he said, pulling her to stand. "You make me happy too. Remember the blow job thing? Yeah, that's pretty much worth ten houses."

Throwing back her head, she laughed. "You're insufferable."

"You love it," he said, nipping her lips.

They drove back to the cabin in the dim light of dusk. Once there, they made love, and she thanked him again for everything. Her heart was so full that she was going to build her life with him and Jack in the house he'd built for her. As she lay with him, his front spooning her back, she thought of the loneliness she'd felt over the centuries. During those times, she couldn't have even fathomed that she would end up where she was today. She had lived with her secret love for Latimus for ten centuries, believing it unrequited. Thankfulness swamped her as she fell asleep in the arms of the man who she truly felt was her destiny.

Chapter 32

One month later...

Latimus stood under the wooden altar lined with white and purple flowers. Inhaling a deep breath, he waited for Lila to walk down the aisle.

"Nervous?" Sathan asked softly behind him.

"He looks like he's going to puke," Heden said, standing next to Sathan.

"Will you two idiots shut up?" Latimus murmured. "I hate public displays like this, but I'm bonding with the woman of my dreams, so I'm trying to muddle through it. You're not helping," he said, throwing a glare at Heden.

"Shhhh!" Miranda scolded, standing across from him. Arderin snickered behind her. He thought they both looked so pretty in their formal dresses, Miranda's a deep green over her nine-and-a-half-month distended abdomen, and Arderin's a deep blue.

Latimus scowled at Miranda and looked down the felt-covered aisle, waiting.

Thirty people sat in the chairs that surrounded the carpeted aisle. His eyes roamed over Breken and Lora, Sadie and Nolan and Takel's mom who was sitting beside an animated Antonio, eyes twinkling as he flirted with her. Sam, Darkrip, Glarys and Kenden sat in the front row. The Slayer commander smiled, and Latimus gave him a nod.

Finally, Lila appeared, and he struggled to breathe. Her blond hair was in some fancy updo that looked gorgeous. Her flawless face glowed under the sun, the lavender of her irises seeming to pulse. The long white gown she wore hugged every curve of her voluptuous body, and he imagined slowly dragging it off her silky skin after the ceremony.

Holding Jack's hand, they walked down the aisle toward him. His heart swelled in his chest as she came to stand before him.

"You've never looked more beautiful," he said softly.

She gave him a brilliant smile, causing him to feel a throbbing pang in his solar plexus. By the goddess, she was magnificent.

Holding one of each other's hands, and each holding one of Jack's hands as he looked up at them, they each recited the bonding vows. They promised to love and cherish each other for eternity, through sickness and health, darkness and despair. At the end, he pulled her into his embrace and gave her a blazing kiss. Fuck everybody else. If he had to do this formal shit in front of everyone, he was at least going to get a good kiss from his woman.

Afterward, they headed to the ballroom. Decorated in purple and white, a band played at in the corner. Leading her to the large table that spanned the front of the room, they sat down to watch everyone dance.

"Should I ask you to dance with me, or will I be rejected?" she asked, a teasing light in her eyes.

"I'll dance a slow one with you," he said, squeezing her hand. "Later though. I need some blood. And some whiskey. Lots of whiskey, if I'm going to contemplate dancing."

Laughing, she shook her head at him. Arderin bounced over and dragged her away. His heart swelled as he watched the two women he loved most in the world dance together. Jack ran up and joined them, and the three of them giggled as they shimmied to the human pop song.

He was surprised to see Darkrip sit down next to him, in Lila's vacant seat.

"I was hoping to have a word with you."

"Sure," he said with a nod.

The Slayer-Deamon's gaze was firm. "It's hard for me to feel any sort of emotion about death and destruction. Being that I was raised in the Deamon caves and that bastard's blood runs through me, I struggle with the feelings that you all exhibit. I figured you could probably understand that better than anyone else. I've seen you kill on the battlefield."

Latimus studied his olive-green eyes. "I can. It's a part of me I wrestle with, especially now that I'm with Lila. She doesn't seem to care, but I hate it."

Darkrip's expression was contemplative. "The evil that courses through me is so much darker than yours, but I've tried to control it. It's extremely difficult."

Latimus nodded, feeling a strange sense of empathy and comradery toward him.

"I guess I'm telling you this because I wanted to apologize for even considering striking Lila when we last fought my father. I've been taught to take down the enemy no matter the cost, and that compassion is weakness. I should've tried harder. She's been extremely kind to me, and I like her immensely. I hope you both understand that it wasn't personal. I just hate my wretch of a father and want to rid him from this world."

"I understand," Latimus said. He'd never really spent a lot of time with Miranda's brother, but he was starting to see a bit of what he struggled with on a daily basis. It must be so hard to tamp down a part of yourself that was so evil. He admired his restraint and control. "I want to kill that bastard too."

Darkrip gave a short sigh. "We're going to have to find Evie. It's the next logical step. It won't be easy. I'll need your help. She's extremely evil, and I'm worried to bring her into our world."

"I'll help in any way I can. We must sway her to our cause. I'm willing to find a way."

"Thank you," Darkrip said. Standing, he extended his hand. "I know I like to chide you for being an arrogant brute, but I do admire what you've done with your army. I'm honored to be your ally."

Latimus stood and shook his hand. "Thank you. We're also honored to have you on our team."

With one last firm shake, the Slayer-Deamon gave a nod and walked away. Latimus thought it an interesting conversation. A peace offering of sorts. They would have to work together to find his evil sister and convince her to kill Crimeous with the Blade of Pestilence. The road would be long and winding, but they had no choice. They had to rid the planet of the Dark Lord's malevolence.

Deciding not to waste this beautiful day thinking of Crimeous, he walked onto the dance floor and pulled Lila to him. A slow song was playing, and he wrapped his arms around her as they swayed to the music. Looking over at Arderin, he observed her wide eyes and her mouth, which had fallen open in shock. She'd been trying to get him to dance for a thousand years, the little bugger. Sticking his tongue out at her, he chuckled at her responding scowl. Slowly, he rocked Lila and closed his eyes, loving the feel of her body against his.

Later, they decided to stay at his cabin. Miranda and Sathan had offered to watch Jack. Miranda was calling it her "mommy boot camp." As they entered the bedroom of his tiny cottage, Lila looked at the packed boxes.

"Will you miss this place?" she asked, shrugging off her white cardigan.

"No," he said. "I was lonely and miserable in this cabin. I spent every day longing for you as you slept in the castle. I'm ready to move on and build happy memories with you at Lynia."

Compassion swam in her beautiful eyes. "I'm so glad those days are over."

"Me too, honey," he said.

Approaching her, he drew her into an embrace. "You look amazing in that dress, but I can't wait to pull it off of you."

Wrapping her arms around his neck, she asked, "So, what are you waiting for?"

Chuckling, he rotated her and touched her hair.

"Take it down," he commanded.

"Okay, bossy," she said, turning her head to look at him.

Lifting her arms, she pulled the pins from her head, throwing them on the nearby dresser. Golden strands fell to her shoulders, and she fluffed her fingers through the thickness.

Latimus stuck his nose in the soft strands, inhaling the fragrant scent. "Your hair always smells so good."

She nuzzled her back into his front. "I thought you were going to get me out of this dress."

Laughing, he tugged on her hair. "Who's bossy?

It had become one of their favorite ways to tease each other, and she grinned as she tilted her head to gaze at him. With her hand, she pulled her hair aside, allowing him access to the zipper.

Thick fingers grabbed the tiny zipper at the back of her neck. Slowly lowering it, he kissed the exposed skin that was left in its wake. Once it was to her lower back, he slipped his hands under the dress, around the skin of her stomach and pulled her back into the front of his body.

"You're not wearing a bra," he growled, lifting his hands to clutch her large breasts.

"Nope," she said, looking up at him. "It wouldn't work with this dress."

"Fuck," he whispered, grabbing her nipples and twirling them between his fingers.

Her eyes closed as she leaned her head back on his shoulder and whispered his name. He played with her breasts for a bit and then pushed the dress from her arms. Skimming down her body, he slid it off her soft skin until it puddled on the floor. Turning her as he lowered to his knees, he bit at the top of her white thong.

"Let's get this off so I can suck your pretty pussy." Grabbing the sides, he pulled the underwear down her curvy hips, tossing it to the floor, unable to comprehend how beautiful her body was.

Drawing her to him, he lifted one of her legs over his shoulder. As she gasped, he placed his mouth on her core, stroking her wetness with his tongue.

"How do you always taste so good?" he murmured into her.

Clutching his hair, she pushed further into him, exciting him more. His tongue flicked her little nub, and then, he sucked it in between his lips. Pulling on it, over and over, he felt her body tense, tight as a bow. She reached out and grabbed the nearby bedpost, giving her balance as her other hand continued its death grip on his hair. Holding her to him, she came all over his mouth and chin, her thin fingers threatening to pull every strand of the raven tresses from his head. He didn't care. He loved making her come and rubbed his face into her wetness, consumed by her.

Placing her leg back on the floor, he lifted her up to carry her to the bed. Gently, he lay her across the black comforter. He removed his clothes, his gaze never leaving hers. Lifting her arms over her head, she beckoned to him, biting her lip as he undressed. Large, gorgeous breasts...pink, soft lips...the plushy blond triangle of hair between her sexy thighs...they all called to him, and his stiff shaft seemed to reach for her as he threw his boxer briefs on the floor.

Lowering over her, he began nudging into her, loving the desire that pulsed in her eyes. Moving his face toward hers, he kissed her lips, forcing his tongue inside.

"I can taste myself on you," she said.

"Fuck yes," he whispered, licking her tongue. "You drenched me, honey. I love that you get so wet for me."

Ending the kiss, Latimus gazed into her irises as his hips gyrated back and forth into hers. Fisting her hair in his hand, he lifted her head, aligning the vein on his neck with her mouth.

"Drink from me."

Her sexy tongue began to lick his neck, preparing him for her invasion. Dying with anticipation, he clutched her hair as he moved in and out of her. He felt the points of her fangs on his skin, and then, they pierced him, as he gasped.

"Oh, god..." he moaned, clenching her hair tighter. "Fuck, Lila. I've dreamed of this for so long."

She purred, squeezing his shoulders as he fucked her. His thick cock was being choked by her flowing pussy as her lips pulled blood from his neck. The sensation was overwhelming, and he felt his climax on the horizon.

"It feels so good. Shit, I'm going to come. I'm sorry, honey..."

"Don't be sorry," her sweet voice said in his ear. "Just do it harder. I'm close too."

Threading his hands under her shoulders, he hammered into her as she resumed sucking him. Drowning in her, he found himself wishing he was a soothsayer, if only to tell her how amazing she felt and how magnificent it was to be with her like this. His balls began to tighten as he focused on pounding her with his shaft.

"I'm coming," Lila cried, her head falling away from his neck as she threw it back on the bed. "Oh, god, Lattie, yes..."

Clenching onto her ever so tightly, he gritted his teeth and let himself explode inside her. Their bodies spasmed together as they held each other. He let himself relax on top of her, knowing that she loved feeling his weight over her but being careful not to crush her. His beautiful bonded mate lifted her lips to his neck, placing a soft kiss on the two bite marks and then licking them closed. His massive body trembled as her tongue darted over his skin. Eventually, the wound healed, and he lowered his forehead to hers as he panted.

"You sexy little temptress. It was about time you drank from me. It felt so good."

Opening her eyes, she smiled. "I loved it. You taste good."

"Not as good as you. Every inch of your body tastes amazing."

Her swollen lips curved into a shy, sated grin as she ran her fingers through his hair. "Maybe next time, we can do it at the same time."

"Mmmm...yes, let's do that," he said, waggling his eyebrows, causing her to laugh. They stayed that way for a few minutes, gazing into each other. Then, he lifted her up and stuffed her under the sheets.

Afterward, lying on their sides, ice-blue irises stared into violet ones. They stroked each other softly, as they so often did after they loved each other.

"We're bonded," she said with a smile. "How exciting. Are you happy?"

"So fucking happy, woman," he said, lifting her hand to kiss it.

"You finally kept your promise to me," she said, her lavender eyes twinkling.

He felt his eyebrows draw together. "What promise?"

"You promised me all those centuries ago that you would rescue me and save me from a forced bonding."

"Did I?" he asked, pulling her closer to him. "It took me too damn long. I can't believe I was such a coward with you."

"It was the course we needed to take," she said, caressing his cheek. "Maybe that's why it's so good now. We just needed to fight for it."

"I'll never stop fighting for you, Lila. I love you more than you'll ever know."

"I love you too" she whispered.

Lying on the soft sheets, they gazed at each other, willing their eyes to stay open but unable to after such a long day. As the moon hung overhead, they drifted off to sleep, her body entwined with his, where it had always belonged.

Epilogue
One Year Later...

Lila rode the train to Uteria, absently chewing her lip as the car chugged along. Sadie had called her and told her she needed some help in the infirmary at Uteria. She'd been quite vague but she'd explained that she was looking for volunteers, and Lila was always happy to volunteer her time to help others.

In the year since she'd been bonded to Latimus, she'd opened the shelter at Lynia and helped Yarik open one at Naria as well. It was important to her that no one in their kingdom suffered and that everyone was allowed an equal opportunity to succeed and flourish.

Arriving at Uteria's platform, she departed the train and strolled to the main castle where Sadie's infirmary was housed. Heading inside, she nodded to some of the staff members and proceeded down to the bottom floor. Entering the infirmary, she saw the Slayer physician, pink baseball cap upon her head, writing in a chart.

"Hey, Sadie," Lila said.

"Hi," the Slayer said, her smile showcasing her white teeth. "You made it okay."

"Yep. The ride is really easy. The trains are great."

"Good. And how are you feeling otherwise?"

They had lessened the frequency of their sessions so that they only spoke once a month now. Lila found it very helpful to speak to the kind woman, and she also liked her immensely.

"I feel great. You've been so amazing, Sadie. Thank you."

"Of course. Talking to you has also been cathartic for me. So, thank you for that."

Lila felt the corners of her lips curve. "So, what did you need me to do here? I couldn't quite figure it out."

The Slayer arched her tawny eyebrow, her multicolored eyes twinkling. "I have to confess, I lured you here under false pretenses."

"Oh?"

"There's a teenage girl who lives at Restia. She got pregnant and has decided to give up the baby for adoption. She wishes to remain anonymous and feels that the baby could have a better life with a mother who is fully ready and able to support her."

"Okay," Lila said, unsure as to why her heart was pounding.

"Come with me."

Lila followed her through a doorway, into a room with a crib. Lila looked down at the baby, swaddled in a white blanket. She had a tuft of raven-black hair and slept peacefully upon the alabaster sheets.

"They say don't wake a sleeping baby, but you have to see this." Lowering her hand, Sadie softly tapped her finger on the girl's cheek. "Wake up, little one. Open those eyes for me."

Lila's heart constricted as the tiny creature scrunched her features together and then opened her eyes to stare at them. Bright, violet-colored eyes. Lila gasped.

"She has purple irises."

"Yep," Sadie said, nodding. "She's one of the few immortals who got the recessive gene that you have. It's so pretty and extremely rare. I thought you might want take her home and see if you click. If so, you could possibly think about adopting her."

Lila's heart burst into a thousand happy pieces in her chest. "Oh, Sadie," she said, hugging the Slayer. "This is so amazing. She's so beautiful." Lowering her hand, she rubbed the baby's soft cheek with her finger. The tiny child squirmed inside her swaddle, and Lila was sure she was already in love.

"I'm not sure if Latimus is ready to adopt another child. We've been so busy with Jack."

"I think he'd do anything you ask him to do, Lila," she said with a grin. "But it's up to you. If you want to take her home, I can prepare some formula, a carrier and all the other stuff you'll need to take care of her for a few days."

Lila inhaled deeply, contemplating. As she stared at the precious baby, she knew she'd already decided.

"Okay, I'll take her home for two nights. Let's see how Latimus feels about that and then assess afterward."

"Great," Sadie said. "Give me a few minutes."

While the Slayer prepared the provisions, Lila picked up the baby and held her in her arms, rocking and cooing softly to her.

"What's her name?" she asked, when Sadie returned with some travel bags and a carrier.

"She doesn't have one yet. The birth mother decided to let her adoptive parents name her."

"Okay," Lila said, rubbing the girl's soft hair. "Oh, Sadie, she's so precious."

"She really is. I have a feeling she's never coming back here," she said with a laugh. "Okay, you're all set. Have fun."

Lila placed the baby in the carrier and then gave Sadie a firm hug.

"You're such a kind person, Sadie. I'm so thankful that we're friends."

"Me too, Lila. You're awesome."

They embraced once more, and Lila threw the bags over her shoulder, lifted the carrier and headed to the train.

Once she was set on the train, she texted Latimus.

Lila: I have a surprise for you when you get home. Don't want to tell you over text and I know you're busy with the troops. I hope you won't be mad at me. I'm worried you might be.

She laughed at his responding text.

Latimus: You know I could never be mad at you, woman. And if I am, just give me one of your amazing BJs. See you in a few hours.

When she got to Lynia, she asked one of the soldiers to drive her home. Latimus had given her strict instructions that as his bonded, she should ask the soldiers for help anytime she needed something. It made her feel so warm and protected.

Once home, the baby started crying, and Lila fed her, falling more in love with her each time her tiny lips sucked a swipe from the bottle. She heard Jack hurdle through the front door and turned to smile at him.

"How was school?"

"Good," he said, coming to stand in front of her. "Where'd the baby come from?"

"Her mother couldn't take care of her, so I'm going to watch her for a few days. Isn't she sweet?" Lowering the baby as she sucked from the bottle, Lila waited for his reaction.

"I guess," he said, his brown eyes wide. "She's so small."

"Yep," she said. "The Slayer doctor said she was only born a week ago."

"She's a Slayer?"

Lila nodded.

"Cool. Can I have a popsicle?"

She laughed at his short attention span, realizing he was done with the infant. "Sure, but only one. And then homework, okay? Once Latimus gets home, we can play."

"Okay." Skipping to the freezer, he pulled out an orange popsicle and ran upstairs to his room.

Lila placed the baby in the carrier and waited for her bonded to come home, little pangs of nervousness flitting in her stomach.

Finally, she heard his boot steps on the front porch. Jack vaulted down the stairs and into his arms as he entered the front door.

"Lila brought home a baby!" he said, squirming as Latimus picked him up playfully.

"Really?" he asked, training his ice-blue gaze on her as she stood in the living room beside the couch, where the baby lay sleeping in the carrier.

Biting her lip, she stared at him, feeling anxious and hopeful. "Surprise," she said and held up her hands.

From the carrier, the little girl started to wail. Soothing her, Lila picked her up and started to feed her, rocking her in her arms.

* * * *

Latimus watched his woman holding the baby, already understanding that she was halfway in love with the little creature. She looked so beautiful as she rocked the tiny girl, and he knew there was no turning back.

"I think she wants to adopt her like you guys adopted me," Jack said beside him.

"Yeah, I think so, buddy," he said, rubbing boy's hair. "How do you feel about that?"

He shrugged. "It's okay, I guess. She's a Slayer and a girl, so she's going to be really weak. We'll have to protect her."

Latimus smiled at the boy, who he now considered his son deep in his heart. "We sure will. I'll need your help with that."

"Okay," he said, his brown eyes swimming with innocent sincerity as he looked up at him. "I'm getting really strong now, so I'll help you."

"Good." Lila smiled at them, and he knew she was hearing every word of their conversation.

They ate a dinner of Slayer blood and mac and cheese that Lila made for Jack. After catching fireflies with Jack in the yard under the setting sun, Latimus helped him get ready for bed. Once tucked in, Latimus headed into their bedroom, where Lila had placed the sleeping baby in the carrier.

"I guess I'm going to need to get a crib on my way home from training tomorrow."

She gnawed her lip, looking so nervous, and he chuckled. Walking over to him, she placed her palms on his chest.

"Are you mad?" she asked, her violet eyes glowing.

"No. But you can still give me a BJ anyway."

Shaking her head, she laughed. "I'm serious. I know I should've called and asked you first, but I didn't want to bother you."

"She has your lavender eyes. I've never seen them on anyone else."

"Sadie said that it's an extremely rare recessive gene. I can't believe I've found someone else who has it. It makes me feel like she's destined to be ours. Am I crazy?"

"No," he said, placing a kiss on her forehead. "She probably is meant to be ours. What's her name?"

"She doesn't have one yet. Her adoptive parents will choose the name."

"Well, let's get on with it, so I can have Sathan draw up the papers tomorrow."

His knees almost buckled at her brilliant smile. Sliding her hands around his neck, she asked, "Really? Are you sure?"

Giving her a peck on her pink lips, he nodded. "As long as you smile at me like that, I'll adopt every damn baby on the planet."

"Oh, Lattie, thank you. I think I'm already in love with her."

He felt his lips turn up. "I know. She's precious."

"She is." Giving in to his need to hold his woman, he pulled her close.

* * * *

Two weeks later, Lila awoke to the sound of Adelyn's cries. They had decided on the name together, and Lila thought it so pretty. Throwing off the covers, she started to rise.

"Let me feed her," Latimus said, urging her back on the bed. "You had a long day with the council meeting and the shelter. I've got it, honey."

Love for her amazing man washed over her. "Okay. Thanks."

She watched the muscles of his broad back as he grabbed some sweat pants from the drawer and threw them on. Lifting Adelyn from the bassinet, he took her downstairs to feed her. Unable to sleep, Lila threw on her robe and headed downstairs.

Arriving at the bottom of the stairs, she almost burst into a fit of joyful tears. Her massive Vampyre was rocking their tiny daughter in his arms, singing softly to her as he fed her a bottle. She'd never in her life seen anything more precious.

"I sang this song to your mom on our second date," he said softly to the baby. "And then, she screwed my brains out so hard I almost lost my favorite appendage."

Opening her mouth, she gave him a laugh laced with mock mortification. "Latimus, don't talk to our daughter that way."

"Oh, were you there?" he asked, laughter twinkling in his eyes. "I didn't see you."

Coming to stand beside him, she nipped playfully at his shoulder. "Liar."

He rocked Adelyn as her small, red lips pulled on the nipple of the bottle.

"She's so sweet," Lila whispered.

"Like her momma," he said.

Smiling, she placed her arm over his shoulders. "We have a family. It's so amazing. I was alone for so long. I love you all so much."

"We love you. We're all so lucky to have each other. You've domesticated the shit out of me, Lila. I never hear the end of it from my brothers. It's awful."

Chuckling, she laid her cheek on his arm. "It's wonderful. You're so good with her and with Jack. I'm so proud of you."

"Thanks, honey," he said, placing a kiss on the top of her head.

"Jack is so amazing with her too. Although, I shouldn't be surprised, after seeing him with Tordor," she said, referring to Miranda and Sathan's son.

"He's such a caring kid with a huge heart," Latimus said. "I'm determined to do right by him. By all of you. I never imagined anything like this. It's unbelievable."

"You deserve it," she said, kissing his upper arm. "We all do. After a thousand years, it's time for us to be happy."

"Damn straight," he said, his full lips curving into that always-sexy smile.

There, under the pale light of the kitchen chandelier, they held their daughter. Lila's heart swelled with gratitude at everything her strong, loyal man had given her. Lost in happiness, she swayed with them, more hopeful for the future than she'd ever been. With her warrior by her side, she would continue to fight for goodness and equality in their kingdom. She knew that one day soon, her powerful commander would defeat Crimeous.

With the light of the sun above, and the strength of her bonded at her side, she felt an indomitable fortitude. This was only a chapter for everyone she loved upon Etherya's Earth, and she was ready to embrace the future for her family and her people.

If you liked this book then *please* leave a review on Amazon, Goodreads and/or BookBub. Your friendly neighborhood author thanks you from the bottom of her heart!

Acknowledgments

When I informed my family and friends that I was leaving my twelve-year career as a respected and high earning medical device sales rep to become a fantasy romance novelist, I expected their jaws to hit the floor. Most did, but I was also surrounded with such love and support, for which I am truly grateful.

Since this is the second book in the series, I have a few special people I'd like to highlight who have been extra supportive!

Thanks to Shelby, for being the Don Juan to my Kandi Burruss. You were the first to ever purchase The End of Hatred and your support has been amazing. Hey, maybe you'll even read it one day? ☺ I think you'll like the steamy scenes, but we'll see!

Thanks to Lina for being my unofficial PR manager. We're gonna get these books into every crevice of Edgewater no matter what! I truly appreciate your support!

Thanks to Brooke, Susan, Melanie and Jaime for being the first to review The End of Hatred on Amazon. Reviews are so crucial to a new author and I truly appreciate you all reading the book and taking the time to review. Here's hoping you like The Elusive Sun as well!

Thanks to Dorothy and Grace at Ambience, the amazing clothing boutique in Edgewater, NJ, where I held my first book signing/promotion. I'm so proud to partner with other amazing women to get the word about all of our kick-ass offerings out there!

Thanks to Megan McKeever for the great editing, once again. I love seeing this series through your eyes!

Thanks to Susan Olinsky for the super-hot cover and map of Etherya's Earth.

And from the bottom of my heart, thanks to ALL of you who purchased a copy of The End of Hatred. It warmed my heart to get your texts showing the book sitting on your coffee table or on your Kindle. I'm so lucky to be surrounded by such amazing people and am so honored and thankful for your support!

Keep on following your dreams people! They're ready to be seized when you are! Peace and love! Xoxo

About the Author

Rebecca Hefner grew up in Western NC and now calls the Hudson River of NYC home. In her youth, she would sneak into her mother's bedroom and raid the bookshelf, falling in love with the stories of Judith McNaught, Sandra Brown and Nora Roberts. Years later, that love of a good romance, with lots of great characters and conflicts, has extended to her other favorite authors such as JR Ward and Lisa Kleypas. Also a huge Game of Thrones and Star Wars fan, she loves an epic fantasy and a surprise twist (Luke, he IS your father).

Rebecca published her first book in November of 2018. Before that, she had an extensive twelve-year medical device sales career, where she fought to shatter the glass ceiling in a Corporate America world dominated by men. After saving up for years, she left her established career to follow the long, winding and scary path of becoming a full-time author. Due to her experience, you'll find her books filled with strong, smart heroines on a personal journey to find inner fortitude and peace while combating sexism and misogyny. She would be thrilled to hear from you anytime at rebecca@rebeccahefner.com.

FOR MORE ON THIS AUTHOR:

www.rebeccahefner.com

Facebook: https://www.facebook.com/rebeccahefnerauthor/

Twitter: https://twitter.com/RebHefnerAuthor

Instagram: https://www.instagram.com/rebeccahefner/

Amazon: http://author.to/RebeccaHefner

Goodreads: https://www.goodreads.com/author/show/18637390.Rebecca_Hefner

BookBub: https://www.bookbub.com/authors/rebecca-hefner

Don't forget to purchase Darkrip and Arderin's story, Book 3 in the Etherya's Earth Series entitled **The Darkness Within**.

eBook available at your favorite online book retailer

Or

In paperback

Or

Coming soon in Audio format

Or

You can also ask your library to order these books

Thanks for your support!

Made in the
USA
Middletown, DE